Notorious

Center Point
Large Print

Also by Allison Brennan and available from
Center Point Large Print:

The Lucy Kincaid Series
  Stolen
  Cold Snap

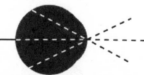

**This Large Print Book carries the
Seal of Approval of N.A.V.H.**

Notorious

ALLISON BRENNAN

CENTER POINT LARGE PRINT
THORNDIKE, MAINE

This Center Point Large Print edition
is published in the year 2014 by arrangement with
St. Martin's Press.

The text of this Large Print edition is unabridged.
In other aspects, this book may vary
from the original edition.
Printed in the United States of America
on permanent paper.
Set in 16-point Times New Roman type.

ISBN: 978-1-62899-097-3

Library of Congress Cataloging-in-Publication Data

Brennan, Allison.
Notorious / Allison Brennan. — Center Point Large Print edition.
pages ; cm
Summary: "Maxine Revere, an investigative reporter, solves cold cases.
But the one unsolved murder that still haunts her was that of her best
friend in high school. Thirteen years later, Max feels compelled to
investigate that death as well as the apparent suicide of the friend
accused of murder and another cold case murder at her old high
school"—Provided by publisher.
ISBN 978-1-62899-097-3 (library binding : alk. paper)
1. Women journalists—Fiction. 2. Murder—Investigation—Fiction.
  3. Large type books. I. Title.
PS3602.R4495N68 2014b
813'.6—dc23
                                                    2014007834

Some people say that it takes a village;
for me, it takes a family.

My kids, Katie, Kelly, Luke, Mary, and Mark;
my mom, Claudia;
and my husband, Dan.
I love you.

Acknowledgments

After twenty books, I'm lucky and blessed to have a core group of experts who consistently help me get the details right. If there are any inaccuracies, they are my fault alone.

I was born and raised in the San Francisco Bay Area, in a small town called San Carlos. Much of what I have included is based on my memories, both from my childhood and my repeated trips home to visit friends and family. But this is fiction, so please forgive any liberties I may have taken—or faulty memory.

A special thanks to FBI Special Agent Steve Dupre, who has always made himself available to answer even the most arcane questions I have. I particularly need to thank Steve and SWAT Senior Team Leader SA Brian Jones for allowing me to participate in numerous training scenarios with access to a broad group of law enforcement.

Dr. D. P. Lyle, fellow author, who has the patience of a saint and the devious mind of . . . well, let's just say he's one of my favorite people to consult for forensic details.

My good friend, author Toni McGee Causey, is one of the few people I trust with my very rough drafts. Her sound, practical advice on the earliest chapters of this book helped make Max a stronger character.

My editor, Kelley Ragland, and the entire Minotaur team have been amazing to work with, and I feel truly blessed to be part of their family. Kelley's editorial guidance was spot on, and her assistant Elizabeth Lacks juggles many balls with good humor and patience. Thanks also to Andy Martin and Matthew Shear who brought me into the fold and have been consistently supportive and enthusiastic.

I especially want to thank my agent, Dan Conaway. Three years ago I pitched this story to him when all I had was a basic premise involving an investigative crime reporter named Max Revere. He said, "I love the idea. But what if Max was a girl?" Everything then came into focus, and *Notorious* was born.

Notorious

Prologue

Hester has returned.

Lindy Ames double-underlined the sentence, the ballpoint pen leaving a deep gouge in the paper. She slammed the diary shut and slid it back onto the bookshelf, the spine blending in with all the other books that no one would read. Decoration. Stately books in a handsome room.

It had been luck—or maybe some cruel god rubbing her face in her own failings—that she'd seen the slut at the clinic and put two and two together. The timing was right. Why should Lindy be upset? It wasn't like she and William had an exclusive relationship—they were both sneaking around behind the backs of their friends and significant others.

But sitting down, talking to the girl, finding out the truth . . . it was eye-opening. Lindy saw her future and it sucked.

She was just as bad as William. Worse, there was no one she could talk to about it because they'd agreed to keep their relationship secret. Friends with benefits, she'd told him.

Lindy ran up to her bedroom; her bed still smelled of sex even though William had left fifteen minutes ago. Why had she even slept with him?

11

Because you wanted to.

Their fight had been the worst yet, but at the same time she finally felt free. She didn't want to be his girlfriend. She never had. She'd wanted William because others coveted him—he was gorgeous and smart and richly arrogant. And he was a Revere—who wouldn't want to marry into that family? But she'd lost so much playing this game with him, and after Kevin broke up with her, she realized that she needed to get her life in order before she left for college, or she'd continue to make the same, stupid mistakes.

William didn't understand—for the first time, he said, they were both free, they could go public with their relationship. But all the secrets and lies and sneaking around for the last year had caught up with her. She couldn't even pretend with him anymore, not even for the summer.

Determined to forget William, she gathered up her sheets and put them in the washing machine. "There."

The low hum of the washer reminded Lindy that she was alone. The mansion was empty—her mother had joined her dad on his business trip to New York. She considered calling Kevin, but he wasn't talking to her. Their breakup had been bad, and when she tried to talk to him yesterday, they'd argued all over again. She couldn't blame him. He'd found out she was sleeping with another guy and wanted to know who; she hadn't told him.

How could she? They were all friends. If Kevin found out she'd screwed William a half-dozen times while she purported to be Kevin's girlfriend, he wouldn't have been able to keep his mouth shut. And then *everyone* would be mad at her. She thought of calling Maxine, but even her best friend had been acting aloof. Or was Max just preoccupied with preparing for college? Or so wrapped up in her own boyfriend problems that she didn't have time anymore? Or maybe—maybe it was Lindy's fault. Max had this uncanny way of knowing when Lindy was lying.

Max was blunt and smart and didn't put up with anyone's bullshit. Lindy missed her and had screwed up their friendship, just like everything else.

It was time to break away, she told herself. Clean slate. She was going to college in three months, she'd put William and Kevin and even Max behind her. If her best friend was going to be so damn judgmental, she didn't need her.

Lindy left the house and walked across the lawn to her clubhouse, built into a grove of trees in the back corner of her property. As soon as she entered, she felt at peace. More than a mere clubhouse, it was a three-story guesthouse with a full kitchen and pool table (from when her brother was still at home) and television and huge collection of movies. It might seem odd to forsake a nine-thousand-square-foot mansion for a thousand-square-foot bungalow, but it had been her sanctuary ever since she was little.

They'd had a club, she and Caitlin and Olivia primarily, and others through the years, and when Max moved to Atherton, she hung out with them, too. They had sleepovers and parties and on occasion got drunk or stoned. And more recently, since Kevin left and all the weirdness with William, it had become Lindy's private haven, where she could disappear.

Sometimes, she wished she could get away from herself. To be someone else. Sometimes, she wondered what would happen if she just came clean with everyone, spilled all the secrets she knew, and let the shit fly. It might be fun.

But it would hurt everyone she cared about. Which is why she didn't tell William the real reason she was calling it off. He'd find out soon enough, anyway.

Lindy opened her clubhouse refrigerator and took out a beer. If her parents knew she kept a stock of drinks in here, they'd never said anything. Probably thought it was better for her to drink at home than risk driving drunk to parties all over town.

She sensed the door opening more than she heard it. She turned around and stared at her visitor, surprised. The last thing she needed was more drama in her life.

"Go away." She turned her back to the door, determined to postpone any confrontation. "I'm not in the mood for you to bitch at me again."

Maybe this was how it was supposed to be. Get rid of all her baggage, once and for all.

The door closed and she heard a cry. Not like someone was hurt, but like someone was in pain. A guttural cry, like a trapped animal.

Something isn't right.

Heart racing, she started to spin around again, instinctively bringing her arms up, though she wondered why on earth she'd have to defend herself. A sharp pain on the back of her head brought Lindy to her knees before she could face her attacker.

"Wh-what are—you—" She felt sick, like she was going to puke, and struggled to get up onto all fours. Her vision blurred, and for one brief second she thought it had been an accident.

Hands grabbed her neck from behind and pushed her down. Her attacker sat on her back, held her down, and squeezed her neck.

She tried to talk, tried to scream, but she couldn't draw in any air. Her arms flailed, trying to hit the person behind her, but she had no control over her limbs. She couldn't breathe.

Stop!

She couldn't speak, the scream was trapped in her lungs.

Why are you hurting me? I've known you forever . . .

Her vision went from blurry to black to nothing.

Chapter One

Going home was a bitch.

Maxine Revere had flirted with the idea of flying in solely for Kevin's funeral so her perfect and dysfunctional family wouldn't hear about her visit until she was already on a plane back to New York City. Three things stopped her.

Foremost, Max did not run away from uncomfortable situations. She recognized that she wasn't the same nineteen-year-old who'd defied her family.

She'd also get a kick from walking into the family mansion unannounced and watching a reboot of *Dallas*, set in California. The Sterling-Revere family could take on the Ewings and win without breaking a nail or going to jail. Being the blackest sheep in the herd was more fun than taking two cross-country flights in one day.

But the primary reason she was staying for the weekend was for Kevin's sister, Jodi O'Neal. Kevin had been Max's former best friend and confidante. He'd killed himself and Jodi had questions. She had no answers for the college coed, but she understood why Jodi sought truth where there had only been lies. Max had survived grief, she'd been a close acquaintance to death, and maybe she could give Jodi a modicum of peace.

Traveling first class had advantages, including prompt disembarking. Max strode off the plane at San Francisco International Airport, her long legs putting distance between her and the other passengers. Her two-inch heels made her an even six feet, but her confident stride and stunning looks caused heads to turn. She ignored the attention. Her cell phone vibrated and she ignored that, too.

Her full-time assistant and as-needed bodyguard, former Army Ranger David Kane, easily kept up with her. He turned heads as well, mostly from fear. When he wasn't smiling, he looked like he'd kill you with no remorse or pleasure. He didn't smile often. But as Max had learned, looks were a form of lying. David's steel core protected him as much as her pursuit of truth protected Max.

"I don't need you," she told him. "We settled this yesterday, or were you placating me?"

"All I suggested was that I drive you to Atherton before I head to Marin."

"It's foolish for you to drive an hour out of your way. I'm not incapable of driving myself." She ignored David's subtle smirk. "And I need a car. This isn't New York where I can walk everywhere or grab a taxi. *Go.* Emma is waiting."

"If you're sure."

She glared at him. "She's your daughter."

"She comes with her mother."

"I'm not the one who screwed Brittany in a failed attempt to prove I wasn't gay," Max said, "and I will not let you use me as an excuse to avoid the selfish bitch." Tough love. David adored his twelve-year-old daughter, but her mother made their relationship difficult. Brittany wouldn't let David spend a minute more with Emma than the court mandated, and the flight delay had already cost him two hours.

They wove through the crowd at baggage claim without slowing down, and stopped at the carousel where their luggage would be delivered.

"Emma wants to see you," David said.

"The funeral is tomorrow. You'll be on a plane to Hawaii Sunday morning. Enjoy your vacation—when you get back, if I'm still here, we can meet up in the city for lunch and I'll take Emma shopping."

David grunted. "She doesn't need more clothes."

"A girl can never have too many shoes." Max doubted she'd have kids of her own, and she enjoyed playing aunt to David's daughter when Emma visited him in New York.

Max parked herself near the carousel opening because she didn't want to be here any longer than she had to. Airports were part of her life, but she grew tired of the waiting part. Before leaving Miami, she'd shipped one of her suitcases back home to New York; the second, smaller bag of essentials she'd brought with her to California. She didn't plan to stay in town long.

"Ms. Revere?" an elderly voice behind her asked.

Max turned and looked down at an older couple. The man, at least eighty and maybe five foot four in lifts, stood with his wife, who barely topped five feet. They both had white hair and blue eyes and would have looked like cherubs if their faces weren't so deeply wrinkled.

Max smiled politely. "Yes, I'm Maxine Revere." She expected them to ask for autographs or question what investigation brought her to California. The true crime show she hosted every month on cable television had been moving up in the ratings. When she only wrote newspaper articles and books, few people outside of the business knew what she looked like. Now that she was on camera, people approached her regularly.

There were pros and cons to being recognized. She was on a tight time schedule today, but the couple looked sweet.

"I told you, Henry," the woman said to her husband. "I'm Penny Hoffman." Mrs. Hoffman extended her hand nervously. It was cold, dry, and fragile, like the woman in front of her. "This is my husband, Henry. I knew it was you." She gripped her purse tightly with both hands, the straps worn and frayed. "Do you believe in divine providence?"

Touchy subject. Max answered, "Sometimes."

David was standing to the side, watching the

19

situation. He was always on alert, even when it was wholly unnecessary. Ever since the incident in Chicago last year when Max had been attacked in a parking garage by someone who hadn't wanted to hear the truth on her show, David was suspicious of everyone.

Even little old ladies.

"We just flew in from Phoenix," Henry said.

"For our granddaughter's wedding," Penny added. "Last year, we were here for a funeral."

"My condolences," Max said.

Penny blinked back a sheen of tears and smiled awkwardly. "Our other grandchild. Jessica's brother, Jason."

"Penny," Henry said, taking his wife's hand, "Ms. Revere doesn't want to hear about this now."

Penny continued. "The police say they have no leads."

The way she said "no leads" had Max's instincts twitching. The police may have no leads they shared with the family, but there was always a lead—and it was obvious by her tone that Penny had her own theories.

In Max's experience, murder was almost always personal. There were stranger murders and serial killers, but they were few and far between. Most victims were killed by those they trusted most. A friend. A spouse. A parent. A child.

David cleared his throat. He grabbed Max's red

case from the conveyor belt. He'd already retrieved his smaller khaki bag. He wouldn't have checked it at all, except he'd packed a gun.

"They need to go," Henry told Penny. "It was very nice to meet you, Ms. Revere. Very nice. You're even prettier in person."

"Thank you," Max said. "If you'd like to write me a letter about your grandson's case, here's my office address and e-mail." She pulled a card from her pocket.

She received hundreds of letters and e-mails a week from families wanting her to do any number of things, from proving a loved one innocent to a killer guilty. Most dealt with cold cases and contained few leads. She didn't have time to investigate all the unsolved murders she heard about, and she couldn't always solve the ones she investigated.

But she always gave the families whatever truth she found. For better or worse.

She took a pen out of her pocket and wrote on the back. "Here's my personal e-mail."

Henry took the card but Penny looked upset. "I have written. Twice."

By the sound of her voice, she hadn't received a response. A sliver of anger ran up Max's spine. Her newest assistant was going to have some explaining to do if she wanted to keep her job. All e-mails and letters must be responded to within a week. Max had drafted four form letters that fit most situations, and what didn't fit she was supposed to review.

Henry said, "We thought you might be interested in the case since Jason was killed at Atherton Prep."

Max was speechless—a rarity. She'd graduated from Atherton College Prep thirteen years ago, but no one told her about this murder. The second in the history of the campus.

"When?" she managed to ask.

"The Saturday after Thanksgiving."

Nearly five months ago.

"I'll be in town all weekend," Max said. "I'd like to hear your story. I can't promise I'll investigate, but I will listen."

They both smiled and tears moistened Penny's eyes. Max didn't want to see tears. Especially genuine tears, like Penny's. "Thank you. We'll be here for two weeks. You don't know what this means to us."

Max had Kevin's funeral tomorrow, she was meeting with Jodi in an hour—she was going to be late—and then there was her own family she had to deal with. That she could put off.

"Where are you staying?"

"The Embassy Suites in Redwood Shores," Henry said. "Our son said we could stay with them, but they have so many last-minute things to do for the wedding, we didn't want to be a bother."

Max smiled. "I'm sure you wouldn't have been any trouble. I can meet you at your hotel tomorrow morning. Is eight too early?"

Penny said, "We always rise at dawn."

David was giving Max his version of the evil eye. For him, it was a sterner frown than he normally wore.

Max attached her laptop case to the top of her suitcase and said good-bye to the Hoffmans. She and David stepped out of the terminal and into the spring morning, a cold wind rolling off the Bay that made her shiver. It had been seventy degrees and clear when she left Miami Airport at 6:00 A.M.

They walked down the wide sidewalk toward the rental car shuttle stop.

"Why?" David said.

She didn't answer his question. "Call Ginger. Tell her to find the letters the Hoffmans mentioned and get them to me, verbatim, before she leaves the office today. I want to know why I didn't see them in the first place."

"Maybe she thought you had enough on your plate. Or maybe she didn't see them at all. They could have come in when Ashley was still in the office. Or Josh."

Max didn't want to think about Ashley. What a train wreck. And Josh? Every time she thought about him, she wished she could fire him all over again.

Max didn't have a great track record with office managers. David had been with her for eighteen months—in that time, she'd gone through six office managers. So far, Ginger had been with her for three months. Two more weeks and she'd win the prize for longest assistant.

They stopped under the shuttle sign. David handed Max his cell phone. "It's Marco."

"He's calling you, not me."

"Because you haven't been answering your phone. This is the third time he's called me."

Max didn't take the phone, so David answered. Max tried to ignore the conversation as she looked for any sign that the shuttle was near. It was nowhere in sight.

"She's right here," David said. "No, she didn't lose her phone."

Max swore under her breath and took David's phone from his hand. "I didn't answer my phone because I didn't want to talk to you."

"You have to talk to me sometime, sweetheart." FBI Special Agent Marco Lopez spoke low and clear, working double-time to control his Cuban temper.

"Not today."

"You intentionally left before I saw the news."

"I told you yesterday I had a funeral in California."

"You didn't tell me that you filed your article, and you had plenty of time to record a three-

24

minute spot for the local news. You exposed my informant and jeopardized my case!" His voice rose in volume as he spoke.

Max had a lot of experience remaining calm while talking to Marco. "Your informant put one of his hookers in the hospital for a week and thwarted the investigation into Candace Arunda's murder."

"He was my only link to the Garbena cartel!" Though Marco was born and raised in Miami, his parents had both come from Cuba, and when he got angry and spoke fast, he adopted a hybrid Americanized Cuban accent.

"I'm not rehashing this with you," she said. "I told you why I was in Miami when you asked last week."

"You should have warned me."

"Last time I gave you an early copy of an article, your boss attempted to have it scuttled."

"That was nine years ago!"

"Fool me once," she said.

"Dammit, Max! You avoided me because you *know* you overstepped this time." She pictured Marco pacing his office, his free hand opening and closing.

"Overstepped?" Max took a deep breath. Marco, more than anyone, could raise her blood pressure. "Is that what you call exposing the truth about the brutal murder of an underage prosti-tute? Is an 'in' with the cartel more important than justice for a seventeen-year-old girl?"

"Don't twist what I said! You know I care. You should have given me twenty-four hours to clean up this mess. Ramirez would have been in prison either way."

"Your team screwed up, another girl was in jeopardy, and I'm supposed to give you time to fix it because we're having sex? Garbena is costing you your soul, Marco."

David cleared his throat. Maxine didn't care about attracting an audience as much as her assistant, but she stepped farther away from the other travelers waiting for the shuttle.

"You're the most frustrating woman I've ever known!"

"I've never lied to you, Marco. I wish you could say the same to me." She hung up and returned David's phone.

Her stomach was twisted in knots. She wished she could have left things differently with Marco.

"You should have told him before you left," David said.

"He knew why I was in Miami, and he lied to me."

"He couldn't tell you—"

Max rarely interrupted, but she didn't let David finish. "He *lied.* He didn't say, 'Max, I can't talk to you about this case,' which he's done in the past and I accept. This time, he deliberately gave me false information to protect his criminal informant, and then he expected me to put it in print. You know as well as I do that Marco and his team want the big fish, and if innocent guppies get eaten in the process, it's collateral damage."

"You still should have told him. He shouldn't have read it in the morning paper." He glanced at her, understanding narrowing his eyes. "You intentionally sabotaged your relationship. Why?"

She didn't answer right away because the shuttle pulled up. There were five of them, and Max sat in the back row of the twelve-passenger van. David sat next to her. Maybe because of David's appearance, or her previous phone conversation, the other passengers crammed into the front.

David was perceptive. She may not have consciously wanted to end her mostly off relationship with Special Agent Marco Lopez, but it was primarily physical. They had a long history. But she couldn't allow her libido to control her career. She never had in the past, and just because she had feelings for Marco didn't mean she'd allow it to happen now.

"In the nine years I've known Marco I've never lied to him," Max said after the van started moving. "I've never told him I was someone I'm not. He thinks he can change me, and every time I see him we screw like rabbits and he tries to get me to bury my story. When I don't, he accuses me of not caring who I hurt. I'm tired of explaining myself to him, and I'm not going to change just to please him."

"I give you six months."

"For what?"

"To find a story to cover in Miami so you have an excuse to go back."

Max laughed, a deep throaty genuine laugh. "That's why I love you, David. You remind me that I am flawed."

He smiled, which made the two-inch jagged scar across his left temple almost charming. "It's the least I can do."

The shuttle van pulled up in front of the rental car kiosks. David had previously taken care of the arrangements and handed her the paperwork. While the other passengers disembarked, Max said, "Marco needs to find a sweet Cuban girl who likes his macho bullshit and does what he says when he says it. I'm done."

She thought saying it out loud would make her feel better, but all it did was remind her how rigid she could be. No matter how much she cared about someone, she couldn't—she *wouldn't*—compromise her core values for them. She had no doubt Marco felt the same way, which left them at an impasse.

A dark sense of melancholy overcame her. It was, truly, over.

Chapter Two

Not much had changed in the small, wealthy town of Atherton since Max's mother left her to live with her grandparents twenty-one years ago. The same beautiful landscape hid the same dark secrets. Lies streamed from subdued mansions set back from the meandering, tree-lined streets. There were few nouveau riche monstrosities because the town council wouldn't stand for it, but the few that existed were beacons to longtime residents, signaling the crassness of money in the wrong hands.

The truly wealthy, those with old money and old secrets, didn't flaunt their riches. They often lived frugally, within strict though ample budgets, spending primarily to grow their wealth. They kept their ostentatious afflictions hidden behind closed doors.

Max quickly drove through Atherton, surprised at conflicting feelings of nostalgia and regret. Even though she'd been nine when she moved here, Atherton was the only place she truly considered home. Yet she'd never live here again.

She'd deal with her past later. The travel delays put Max behind schedule, so she hurried through Atherton to the adjoining city of Menlo Park. Kevin's sister Jodi worked part time at an independent bookstore. Max had spent many hours in Kepler's as a teenager, a reprieve from her family. As a young adult, Max never considered that one day she would write a book that graced the shelves of her favorite bookstore. She'd planned on being a travel writer, photographing hidden treasures around the globe, writing stories about interesting cultures and people and events. Interviewing locals and tourists to find out what made each destination so special. Searching, perhaps, for a place she wanted to adopt because her current home never fit the meaning behind the label.

But life has plans, her mother told her three months before she walked out on Max. As if life itself was capable of independent thought.

Life has plans, Maxine. Sometimes they're not what we want, but we don't always have control.

Max never believed her mother until her best friend disappeared during their last spring break of college and Max spent a year of her life searching for answers. Though she consciously made the decision to change her career path, she wondered if her vivacious, irresponsible mother was wiser than she'd given her credit for.

Max entered the bookstore and breathed in the wonderful aroma of new books. Though she had an e-reader, she used it primarily when traveling. Her Manhattan apartment was filled with books she'd be hard-pressed to part with.

She passed a display of books written by local authors, amused to find her own four true crime titles displayed in the middle row. But even more bemusing were the stacks of an investment book that filled the top row—written by Andrew S. Talbot, IV.

Andy certainly didn't need to write a book to supplement his wealth, but he knew more about money and investing than anyone she knew. Considering her grandfather had owned a bank and her uncle had founded one of the top dot-com companies and sold it at the height of the dot-com boom, she knew many smart money people.

She picked up the book and read the inside cover.

"Max?"

She looked up and saw Jodi O'Neal, Kevin's sister. She only recognized her from a photo on the Internet; the last time she'd seen Jodi, the girl had been six. Now she was nineteen—the same age Max had been when she left Atherton. What Max hadn't seen in the photo was that Jodi had Kevin's big brown eyes, the kind of eyes that shout honesty.

"Hello, Jodi. I'm sorry I'm late. My flight was delayed."

Tears brimmed in Jodi's eyes. The girl took Max's hand and squeezed. "Thank you so much. I wasn't positive you'd come, I know you and Kevin had problems."

"I haven't spoken to Kevin in twelve years. I came because you asked."

Jodi bit her lip. "I waited to take my break until you got here. Do you have time for the café? Coffee?"

"I have as much time as you need."

They walked next door and took a table outside. Atherton was thirty minutes south of San Francisco, and it was always warmer here than in the city. Max took off her blazer and hung it over the back of her chair. A well-established oak tree in the middle of the courtyard provided filtered light on their table. It looked exactly the same the last time Max had been here, when her cousin Thea married Duncan Talbot the second, Andy's cousin, two years ago. She'd flown in the day before the wedding, and was on a plane back to New York the morning after.

Jodi chatted aimlessly about working at the bookstore while going to college at the California College of the Arts. She took the train to the city three days a week for classes.

Max hadn't come home just because Jodi asked. It was the way she'd asked her. As much what she'd said as what she didn't say.

She'd said she didn't believe that Kevin committed suicide, but she didn't tell Max why she didn't believe the police report.

After the waitress brought them coffee and cake, Max said, "I read everything you sent me. There's nothing in the newspaper or initial police report that indicated Kevin was murdered."

Jodi cringed at the word, or maybe it was Max's blunt statement. She needed a lighter touch. She'd just come off an investigation where being direct was expected and, in fact, necessary to find answers. Jodi was a survivor, one of the walking wounded in a family that was facing the unexpected death of a loved one.

Jodi said, "I know what Kevin's death looks like, I know what everyone thinks. But I swear, Maxine, he was finally getting his life together. He hasn't used in years. I mean, he might have drank a bit, but he wasn't using drugs."

The files hadn't indicated anything of the sort. Kevin was a heavy drinker and had been arrested three times on drug possession. Marijuana twice, heroin once. He'd done six months in prison for the last bust. During the death investigation, two ounces of marijuana had been found in his apartment, along with empty whiskey and beer bottles. The only constant in his life seemed to have been a part-time job in a coffee place. Enough to pay his rent, buy his alcohol, and not much more.

Max didn't tell Jodi any of this, because Jodi must have known the life Kevin lived. She watched the girl twist her long brown hair into knots. Max had many questions, but she didn't want to lead Jodi down a specific path. When it was clear Jodi was too nervous to talk without prompting, Max asked, "Why did you ask me to come to Kevin's funeral?"

"You were friends." Her voice squeaked.

Max leaned back and pulled a bite-size piece off her carrot cake. She gauged Jodi's state of mind. "I haven't spoken to Kevin since I left twelve years ago. If he told you something different, he wasn't telling you the truth."

Jodi swallowed and leaned forward. "Ever since I can remember, Kevin has been trying to find out what happened the night Lindy Ames was killed."

Four months ago, right before Christmas, Kevin had left a message asking her, in her capacity as an investigative journalist, to follow a lead he had on Lindy's murder. A murder that occurred when they were high school seniors, a murder for which he'd been arrested, stood trial for, and walked away a man in limbo: the hung jury split evenly, six to acquit, six to convict.

Worse, she'd been friends with both Kevin and Lindy; in fact, growing up, she and Lindy had been inseparable. Only during their senior year had they drifted apart, and Max was unclear why that had happened. Lindy had become moody and secretive. Lindy, of all people, knew how Max hated deception, so when Max caught her in a series of little white lies, Max had overreacted. Max could forgive it now, but then her best friend's dishonesty—especially about such trivial things like where she was going—had hurt and offended her. Would anything have been different had Max been more tolerant of Lindy's behavior?

She'd asked David to call Kevin back and say she wasn't interested in hearing from him. David wouldn't have been swayed by Kevin's pleas as she might have been.

A twinge of guilt crept in. When she heard his message, the time slipped away and she was the nineteen-year-old friend of a boy on trial for murder who'd lied to her to ensure her loyalty. Had she said no to his olive branch out of spite? As payback for making her feel gullible?

"Did you know Kevin called me before Christmas asking for my help in Lindy's cold case?"

Jodi nodded. "He said he understood why you didn't want to, but—" She bit her thumb. "What happened after the trial? Why did you stand by Kevin, then turn your back on him?"

"Do you really want to know?" Max wasn't sure she wanted to say anything, because after twelve years her reasons for walking away seemed petty. But she'd never forget how she felt when Kevin told her he'd lied about his alibi. It was as if she'd been gutted—not because she thought he was guilty, but because he'd been able to lie so smoothly and she hadn't known.

Jodi straightened her spine. "Yes."

"Kevin lied about his alibi."

"I don't understand. He had no alibi—he said he was home. The prosecutor said he could have easily snuck out of the house."

"He did sneak out of the house."

She looked stricken. "You—you think he's guilty."

"No. But, he made me doubt him because I didn't understand then why he lied, and I understand less now." She sipped her coffee to calm her nerves, because remembering how inadequate and helpless she'd felt back then made her queasy. "After the trial, Kevin told me that he wasn't home, that he was with Olivia Langstrom."

Jodi looked perplexed. "Why didn't he tell the police that?" she asked.

"I asked him the same thing. He didn't think he'd be arrested for a crime he didn't commit. And then, when he was, he said they couldn't have evidence against him because he was innocent. And yet, the circumstantial evidence was strong enough for six of the jurors to think he was guilty."

"That doesn't make any sense."

"No, it doesn't. According to Kevin, Olivia was physically and emotionally abused by her father. She was going through a hard time, and thinking of running away, but Kevin thought she was going to hurt herself. They talked half the night at Fake Lake and he took her home between three and four in the morning." The man-made lake had been a favorite party spot for Atherton teens.

"She could have told the judge that. Or the police or someone!"

"She could have—she *should* have—but she didn't, and Kevin thought if he changed his story after the arrest no one would believe him. And he'd promised Olivia he wouldn't say anything. She was afraid of repercussions."

"So he went through hell to protect her reputation?"

Jodi was having the same questions and doubts that Max did.

"You wanted to know what happened. That's what happened. I didn't trust him anymore. I didn't understand why he lied in the first place, or why he felt the need to tell me about Olivia after trial. I felt manipulated and used because I'd defended him. I defied my family and lost friends because I stood by Kevin. And the lies he told seemed so . . ." How could she put it? It *still* didn't make sense to her. "So *unnecessary*. I didn't want anything more to do with him. He could have saved himself—and me—and you and your parents so much pain if he'd told the truth from the beginning. And that's what I had a hard time coming to terms with."

Jodi didn't say anything for several minutes. She stared into her coffee cup and Max gave her the time to process the new information. Unless he was retried, Kevin hadn't planned to tell anyone.

Except it *was* important. Had he told the truth from the beginning, the police could have followed other leads. They might have found out who really killed Lindy, and brought him to justice. And that, frankly, was what Max couldn't forgive. And because Kevin had told her about Olivia, it made her feel culpable. And though Kevin told her never to tell anyone, she'd gone to the police. At least, she tried to. The detective in charge of the investigation nearly threw her out of the police department and threatened to arrest her for giving a false statement.

If that happened now, after all the cold cases and hot trials she'd worked on as a reporter, she would never have left without finding the truth. Now she feared the truth was unattainable. And Lindy would never see justice done.

Finally, she asked Jodi, "Did Kevin share any information or theories about Lindy's murder?"

Jodi shook her head. "Nothing specific. He didn't want to talk to me about it. My parents— they had a real hard time during the trial. We moved to Los Gatos, but they were never the same. Kevin moved to San Francisco. I barely saw him while I was growing up. We just reconnected a few years ago."

It pained Max how cruel families could be. Not only had Kevin lost friends, he'd been disowned by his family.

"Though he wouldn't talk to me much about

what he was doing," Jodi continued, "I know he was researching a lot."

"What kind of research?"

"I don't really know. He had a lot of legal documents, but he put them away whenever I came over."

"Where's his research now?"

"I went to his apartment on Wednesday, once the police said I could go in, but his laptop was gone. It was the only thing he cared about, he didn't even own a TV. He had a file cabinet but—I didn't look in there."

"Did you get a copy of the final police report?"

She shook her head. "I haven't seen it."

Max suspected she wouldn't look at it. Jodi was a young, grieving sister and the police report would be a bright and impartial light on Kevin's last days. She didn't need to see it.

But Max did.

"Where was Kevin living?" Atherton was a small town in the middle of a major metropolitan area. She could be dealing with any number of police departments.

"An apartment on Roble Avenue." Roble was nearby, in Menlo Park.

"On Wednesday," Jodi continued, "before I called you, I got this in the mail."

She reached into her pocket and pulled out a letter, then hesitated.

Though Max was curious about what had

prompted Jodi to call her, she didn't reach for the document. She waited and sipped her latte.

Jodi bit her lip, a nervous habit that was beginning to annoy Max. If it was anyone else, she would have immediately branded them as deceptive or hiding something. Ninety-nine times out of a hundred, Max was right in picking out lies and diversions. But coupled with Jodi's over-all demeanor and the tragic circumstances, Max suspected Jodi was simply confused and didn't know what to do with information she had.

Jodi said, "I need to know that you believe Kevin didn't kill Lindy Ames."

How could Max answer that when she didn't know what she believed? She said, "When Kevin was arrested, I stood by him. I never believed then that he killed Lindy, because he told me he didn't. He was my best friend. I postponed college for a year so I could stay here and support him during the investigation and trial.

"But after the jury came back undecided and the prosecution said that they wouldn't retry unless new evidence surfaced, and I learned that Kevin lied about his alibi, I didn't know why. Why did he lie? Why did he feel the need to tell me? I can't give you what you want. I came to listen, and to say good-bye to Kevin. I can't promise anything more."

In the back of Max's mind, she asked herself: *Where is Kevin's laptop?*

Tears welled in Jodi's eyes. She put the envelope on the table, then pulled out her cell phone.

"On Monday morning, I woke up and had a text message from Kevin. That was before I found out he'd died late Sunday night." Her voice cracked.

She pressed a couple of buttons and handed Max the phone.

The message from Kevin was brief: Call Max. I love you, J.

Jodi pocketed her phone. "I have to go back to work," she whispered. "The funeral is at St. Bede's tomorrow at noon. I don't think anybody's going to come."

Max took Jodi's hand. "I'll be there."

Jodi handed Max a key on a Minnie Mouse key chain. "Kevin's apartment. If you need it."

"You're going to be okay, Jodi. It takes time." Being okay was one thing; forgetting was impossible. You never forgot the people you lost.

She watched Jodi leave, her head down. When she was out of sight, Max picked up the envelope.

It had been mailed on Saturday from Menlo Park, addressed to Jodi in care of the bookstore where she worked. There was no return address, but the initials in the corner were K.L.O.

Why would Kevin send his sister a letter at her place of employment?

Max hadn't asked where Jodi lived, whether with one of her parents or in an apartment or if she had a roommate. Because she hadn't been investigating Kevin's death.

Now she had two questions.

She removed the single sheet of paper and unfolded it.

It was an uncertified copy of Lindy Ames's death certificate. Cause of death: asphyxiation by manual strangulation.

Max turned over the paper and read the note Kevin had written: *Lindy drowned.*

Chapter Three

The Stanford Park Hotel was among the nicest hotels in the area, though it didn't look elegant from the outside. Set back from the busy El Camino Real, it looked more like condominiums than a luxury hotel. Max had traveled extensively for both business and pleasure, and the Stanford Park, though small, ranked close to the Biltmore Arizona, the Broadmoor in Colorado Springs, and the Villa in Miami, which is why on the rare occasions she came home, she stayed there. If the clerk recognized her name, he didn't let on. By now her family would know she was in town. Though nestled at the north end of the bustling, sprawling Silicon Valley, Atherton was a small, close-knit community of seven thousand. She'd met Jodi in a public place; inevitably someone who knew *someone* in her family would have reported in by now.

She needed to decompress before facing the family firing squad. They didn't need bullets to inflict a mortal wound.

Max sat at the desk in her suite, put her cell phone on the charger, and booted up her laptop. She tried to put Lindy's death certificate out of her head, at least for the time being.

She dealt with her e-mails swiftly. She preferred to use her phone for most communication, but if she had to type more than a short paragraph, she waited until she had her computer up and running.

A message from her current assistant Ginger popped up: You're impossible to work for. I quit.

It was simple and to the point. If Max wasn't so angry that Ginger had quit while she was on the road, she'd have admired the brevity of the statement. If she'd been that succinct while on her personal calls, Max might have tolerated more.

Max almost called David, but Ginger had cc'd him in the message and he'd know soon enough. She didn't want to interrupt his limited time with his daughter. He gave her 24/7 anytime she asked, she could give him a week off.

She opened a browser and ran a quick search on the murder of Jason Hoffman, and clicked on the initial newspaper article dated Monday, December 2.

CONSTRUCTION WORKER SHOT AT ELITE COLLEGE PREP SCHOOL

ATHERTON, CA—Late Saturday night, a construction worker was shot and killed at Atherton College Preparatory Academy off El Camino Real in Atherton.

Jason Hoffman, 23, was found early Sunday morning by school maintenance staff. Atherton Police Department Chief of Police Ronald Clarkson gave a brief statement that the Menlo Park Police Department's Homicide Squad was taking the lead in the investigation, but Atherton PD would remain closely involved. As of now, the police have no leads.

"It's still extremely early in the investigation," media representative, Officer Donna Corbett, said. "Our department is fully invested in solving this brutal murder and will devote all necessary resources and staff. Atherton Police Chief Clarkson has graciously offered his department's resources as well."

Atherton, a small, wealthy, residential community with no commercial business within its borders, maintains a large and impressive police force, but defers capital crimes to Menlo Park in a MOI that was recently renewed for three years. Atherton boasts one of the lowest crime rates in California. Hoffman is the first homicide within the town limits in thirteen years. The last murder, the strangulation of high school senior Lindy Ames, also occurred on the ACP campus.

Hoffman, a lifelong resident of San Carlos, had recently graduated from Virginia Tech with a degree in architecture. He began working full time for Evergreen Construction, a family business owned by his mother, Sara Robeaux Hoffman, and her brother, Brian Robeaux.

Evergreen is contracted to build the new 80,000-square-foot sports complex, partnering with Cho Architectural Design where Hoffman had interned for three consecutive summers. Because the project was only recently green-lighted, security was not in place that might have prevented or recorded Hoffman's murder.

Hoffman was shot twice and according to the medical examiner's office, he died instantly. A full report will be released by MPPD when available.

The police had made no public comment regarding the murder other than the usual non-statement. After skimming the press coverage for the subsequent weeks she determined that the police believed it was a robbery and Hoffman an unfortunate victim. There were no follow-ups by the press, other than a funeral notice. That was often the case with suburban media. Menlo Park didn't often rate the dailies from San Jose or San Francisco unless it was a major investigation or event; a homicide, though tragic, wouldn't get play unless it was high profile—or someone like Max came in and pushed.

This was the point where she wished she had a competent assistant who could pull together the preliminary information about the homicide investigation, Evergreen Construction, the family, Jason Hoffman, and any connection they had with Atherton Prep, including scouring social media for possible angles. Ginger had been the queen of social media—if she wasn't gossiping on the phone, she was posting pictures on Instagram or pithy comments on Twitter. Max had often wondered how she could condense her incessant chatter into 140 characters or less.

Ginger's ability to pull useful data from the Internet was diminished by her social life. But at least she knew how to type and answer the phone. Ashley burst into tears anytime Max looked at her. And Josh? He had been the bane of her existence the three weeks he was in the office.

Max pushed the whiny, sycophantic, incompetent jackass far from her mind because she couldn't deny the shimmer of excitement in her stomach, and she wasn't going to let the loss of yet another assistant keep her from this case. Hoffman's murder was exactly the type of case she liked to investigate. Almost five months cold. Not so long ago that there couldn't still be evidence and information to unearth, but long enough that she could move around the investigation without initially irritating law enforcement.

She had one burning question that hadn't been answered in any of the press reports: *Why was Jason Hoffman at the construction site late on a Saturday night?*

She glanced down at her hands and realized that while she'd been reading the articles about Jason Hoffman, she'd scraped the polish off her left thumb. Dammit, she'd just had a manicure in Miami. She pulled out her nail repair kit, but then David's name popped up on her cell phone.

"Did you get the message from Ginger?" David asked when she answered.

"I might start to like her."

David laughed.

"You talked to her? I thought you were supposed to be the nice one," Max said.

"I was. She didn't like an assignment that might require her working through the weekend."

Max had found that to be a problem with many of her assistants. Intellectually, she understood that most people didn't intend to give up their social life when they took an office management

47

job, but Max didn't work nine to five. She tried to do her part to give grieving families justice after the horrific loss of their loved ones. The cops sometimes can't—or won't—search for answers because they're too overwhelmed or uninterested. Some cases fall through the cracks—like Jason Hoffman—and someone like her can dig it out and shine light on the evidence once again. Is it too much to ask that an assistant actually work when needed instead of traipsing off for a skinny latte every hour on the hour? Max had made it clear when she hired each of her assistants that the hours would be difficult, but she'd make up for it with generous paid vacations and flexibility.

She told David, "Call Ben and have him line up interviews for Friday. That'll give him enough time to weed out the idiots, the criers, and the lazies."

"You've already decided to stay and help the Hoffmans."

He hadn't asked a question, so she didn't answer it. She put David on speaker and quickly started working on her nail. She had it down to a science. "Right before Kevin committed suicide, he sent Jodi a copy of Lindy's death certificate. No explanation. I'm going to the clerk's office on Monday to pick up a certified copy. There's something strange about Kevin's actions the week before he died."

Max had been a crime reporter for nine years.

She never assumed that any copy of an official document was real.

"If you need anything before Sunday, let me know."

"I'm not going to stomp on your vacation."

He laughed.

"Okay, *much*. How's Emma?"

"It's not even one, Max. She's in school until three."

She should have realized that.

"When she gets home, put all this aside. Get ready for your trip. I wish I could go."

"You wouldn't be able to relax on the beach, though you need it."

"Like you can?"

"I'll be snorkeling, hang gliding, and hiking. Best way to relax."

Like her, David was a workaholic. But he also had a kid, and she wanted him to enjoy the rare time alone with his daughter. Max never had a dad, even a part-time dad like David. When she was younger, she would have given anything to spend time with her father. To *know* him. Of course, she'd have had to know his real name. Her mother never told her the truth before she walked out, leaving her with grandparents who barely acknowledged her existence before they were confronted with her care and maintenance. Max had to admit, for all their faults, her grandparents had never made her feel like the bastard child she was. To them, warts and all, blood always won out.

"Tell your beautiful daughter I said hi. Don't say anything to Brittany, because what I want to say wouldn't be polite."

"When has that stopped you in the past?"

"You'd be surprised how often I bite my tongue."

She hung up and finished reading her e-mail while the new polish on her thumb dried. One-handed, she dealt with anything that couldn't wait until Monday.

Thirty minutes later, she stood and stretched, then unpacked and stowed her suitcase in the closet. She spent so much time in hotels that she had routines she religiously followed, and that included making the room her home whether she was staying for two days or two weeks.

A shower would refresh her and wash the travel grime from her body. She hung her favorite turquoise-colored sheath in the bathroom so the steam could refresh the cotton and remove faint wrinkles. She stripped and stepped under the hot spray. Through the glass partition she sighed at the oversized bathtub with massage jets. Pampering would have to wait until her familial duty was complete. By that time, she would certainly need a hot bath and glass of wine.

She could count on one hand the number of times she'd been home in the past twelve years, and all of them centered around a wedding or funeral. She wouldn't have come home for any of them, except to honor her great-grandmother's memory.

Genevieve Sterling would have expected Max for every important family event, while understanding Max's need to escape. She'd been a hard but fair woman, loyal to family and friends, generous but not a pushover. Her husband had built his fortune from nothing, with Genie at his side, and when he died young of a heart attack, she ran his business with even greater success, seeing the future clearly and investing in technology before technology was considered a viable investment. Max laughed when people said, "I wish I'd invested in IBM." Genie Sterling had been that kind of visionary.

Ten years gone and Max still missed her.

She recognized that her life was filled with loss—her mother, her great-grandmother, her friends—and while she liked to think that she had dealt with each one as it came, today a cloak of melancholy smothered her. Probably because she'd spent an hour talking to a grieving sister and trying not to remember her own grief when Lindy was murdered and Kevin accused of the crime. That year had torn apart every friendship she'd had growing up. One day, they were a close-knit group of privileged kids, all going to college, all ready to take on the world . . . the next they were divided, angry and grieving and casting blame. They'd been eighteen, hardly ready to take on the world like they thought, and completely unprepared to face the brutal death of one of their own—and the accusations that came after.

She looked down at her flat stomach and touched the tattoo she'd had since her seventeenth birthday.

Max's birthday was on New Year's Eve. Her mother had once told her she planned it that way so Max's birthday would always be cause for worldwide celebration. Max would have preferred cake and ice cream.

But when she turned seventeen, the first birthday that she didn't receive a card from her mother, Lindy had invited her to go with her family to New York. They had an apartment there because her father traveled often for business, and Max had joined them a couple of times, but never for New Year's Eve. Lindy told her she had a surprise, and had her driver take them to a tattoo parlor.

Max had balked at first.

"I'm not getting a tattoo."

Lindy laughed and led her inside. "Of course you are!"

"My grandmother will kill me."

"When has that stopped you from annoying her in the past?"

True, but tattoos were permanent. "Lindy, your mom will kill you."

"They don't have to know. We'll get them on our ass."

"I'm not getting a tattoo on my ass."

Lindy pouted, but it was exaggerated. Max and Lindy had talked about getting tattoos together for years. It was forbidden and exciting. They'd looked at pictures and picked out favorites. Max didn't know if she'd go through with it, but it was fun to imagine what she'd get.

"I had one specially designed for you, for your birthday," Lindy said.

Lindy was used to getting her way, no matter what it cost, so their age and lack of parental consent was glossed over. She asked the owner— whose muscular arms were canvases for his art— to show the girls his sketches.

Max had been expecting something wild and fun like Lindy. What she saw left her speechless.

Lindy sounded worried when she said, "You don't like it?"

It was a small dandelion with wisps flying away and turning into birds. It was tasteful, both delicate and bold at the same time. There was a sense of movement as well, because the birds were in different stages of flight.

"I love it." Sometimes, Max wondered if Lindy listened. Now she realized that Lindy knew her better than anyone. "Are you getting the same thing?"

Lindy laughed. "Oh, no. I'm getting something far more dangerous."

The tattoo guy showed Max another sketch. It

was of an angel, a beautiful angel, with both a halo and a devil's tail.

Lindy said, "I was going to get an angel on one shoulder and a devil on the other, but this seems more like me, don't you think?"

"It's definitely you."

Max stood under the shower far longer than she needed, washing and rewashing her body until she could face the rest of the day without the cloud of bittersweet memories. Water rejuvenated her as well as cleansed her.

As soon as the water was off, she heard a knock at the door. She slid into the hotel's white terry robe and tied the sash. She looked through the peephole.

William.

She wasn't surprised that the family had chosen William to confront her; she was surprised that he acted so quickly.

She opened the door. "Five hours since my flight landed. This must be a new record."

William walked in and closed the door behind him. "Why didn't you call?" he said.

"Good to see you, too, cousin." William hadn't changed since high school, other than filling out in the shoulders and a few hairline wrinkles around the eyes. He was impeccably dressed in a custom-tailored navy chalk-stripe Huntsman suit: only the best for the son of Brooks Revere. Max wondered how many of the pricey British suits her cousin owned. She'd never seen him wear anything else, because his father never wore anything else. But William fit the suit, in style and substance. He was smart, a sharp corporate lawyer, and attractive.

But she'd never forget the teenager who so desperately wanted to have fun, even though he rarely found time for it. On those few occasions he relaxed, Max adored her cousin above all others.

She smiled. "Seriously, it *is* good to see you."

She hugged William, and he said, "You're wet!" But he accepted her embrace and kissed her on the cheek. "It's really good to have you home, Maxine."

"You caught me getting out of the shower." She crossed the room and sat on one of the two oversized chairs in her suite. She motioned for William to sit on the love seat across from her. He sat and leaned forward, his arms on his knees.

"You didn't just come here to say hello," she said.

"Are you here for Kevin O'Neal's funeral?"

She sighed. So much for catching up and enjoying William's company. What did she expect? The memories of Lindy and her child-hood had clouded her judgment. She should have known why her cousin had come. "Someone told you I had coffee with his sister."

"It's not like no one in town knows you."

He didn't tell her who'd leaked her arrival.

She and William had been close growing up. Partly because they were the same age and went to the same schools, partly because she'd lived with his parents, Uncle Brooks and Aunt Joanne, when her grandmother was angry with her, which was often, and partly because Max had dated his best friend, Andy Talbot, most of high school. They hung out with the same people. Did the same things.

But they didn't always see eye-to-eye on family matters, and he'd been the first to jump on the "Kevin O'Neal is guilty" bandwagon after Lindy's murder.

"Yes, I'm going to Kevin's funeral tomorrow."

"But he killed Lindy! I don't get how you can forgive him so easily."

"He wasn't convicted." William knew that, but it bore repeating.

"Dammit, Maxine! The jury was deadlocked. There wasn't enough evidence, but we all know he did it."

Max tilted her chin up and stared William in the eye. "I never believed Kevin killed Lindy."

"Lindy's murder has been hanging over the town like the plague," William said.

"That's a bit dramatic, don't you think?"

"Maybe now, with Kevin no longer stirring the pot, we can finally move on."

"Are you upset that I'm here for the funeral, or that you think I'm investigating Lindy's murder?"

"Are you?" he asked pointedly.

"I didn't come here to investigate," Max said. "I promised Jodi I would look at the evidence in Kevin's suicide. The girl needs peace, William. Kevin was a recovering drug addict. He had a drinking problem. She believed he was sober, but she'll accept the truth if I can give it to her." Max paused. "I can't turn my back on his sister." Maybe, she thought, because she'd turned her back on Kevin.

"Why didn't you call me? I could have run interference for you with Dad and Grandmother."

"Sweetheart," Max said with a lighter voice, "I'm not going to put you on the firing line. You live here, you need to keep the peace. I appreciate your offer, but I've grown up." She didn't like gossip as a rule—most of it was based on lies—but William was pretty good at discerning fact from fiction. "Anything I should know before I surprise Grandmother Dearest?"

He scowled. "It's those kind of comments that get you in trouble with her."

"Eleanor has a far sharper tongue than I do," Max said. She'd received the brunt of her grandmother's verbal lashings many, many times.

"How long are you staying?"

Max had interviewed enough people to know that most questions had a dual purpose. William had come here impulsively, probably had just learned she was in town and checked the Stanford

Park Hotel first because this was where she always stayed. But the way he asked about her stay made her think he was nervous, and nerves made her suspicious.

"I haven't decided."

"Don't you have a career in New York?"

"Really, if you want me to leave, just tell me."

"N-n-no, not that, it's just, it's complicated right now."

"You stutter when you're nervous."

He frowned. "Maxine, I would love to spend time with you, you know that. I guess I'm irritated that you haven't been home to see me or the rest of the family in two years, yet you drop everything for the guy who killed Lindy."

"Kevin is dead, William," she said bluntly. "I came for Jodi." But what he said stung because it had a hint of truth. She added, "Launching the cable show took more time and energy than I thought."

"But you still wouldn't have visited." He sounded more sad than angry because he knew why it was hard for Max to visit. The arguments about the family trust, the lawsuit that the family had waged against her when great-grandmother Genie Sterling's will gave Max her missing mother's share of the estate, the constant friction and disagreements between Max and William's father, her uncle Brooks, that went back years.

William added softly, "Lindy was your friend, too."

"William, don't start. Please." Because Max had sided with Kevin, she'd nearly lost William's friendship. It was only because they were family that William stuck it out. Over time, they'd mended fences—William was the closest person to a brother she had—but Kevin's suicide had reminded both of them about that horrible time.

"Fine. I tried to help—"

"Help? By telling me what I already know? It's always complicated when I come home. It's why I rarely do. I love my job, I love New York, I'll never move back. But for better or worse, I'm a Revere, and you and Brooks and Eleanor and everyone else in our big, messed-up family is stuck with me."

William frowned. "You're not being fair. I've always stood up for you."

She stared at him, almost not believing he could lie so smoothly.

"You've always stood up for me?" She asked it bluntly, and he had the good sense to back down.

"Don't look at me like that, Maxine. I don't always agree with you, but you're family."

She sighed. *Family*. William was the most loyal to family, out of all the Reveres, and he included her in there as well. It was, perhaps, ironic that he always stood up for her when it wasn't a family matter, but as soon as they closed the doors, he slipped comfortably into his role of the good son.

Arguing a subtle point that she wasn't sure he

even understood wasn't going to make her stay easier. "Truce. Okay?"

He nodded, then smiled. "Come to my house for dinner."

She wrinkled her nose. For some reason, Caitlin Talbot—now Caitlin Revere—had always considered Max a rival. Everything was a competition with her. Sports, grades, boyfriends, college acceptances—and Max, who was naturally competitive, had contributed to the rivalry. Lindy had been the mediator, though she, too, was competitive. With everyone *except* Max. But at some point the competition between Caitlin and Max had turned unhealthy and Max had cut ties. Hard to do when the Talbots and Reveres were longtime family friends.

And then William married her. Which wouldn't have been a problem for Max because she lived three thousand miles away—except when she visited, Caitlin scratched at old scabs. She had rewritten history to the point that Max could barely have a civil conversation with her. If Caitlin was to be believed, she'd been Lindy's closest friend and confidante, her best buddy, they never fought. On the contrary, Lindy put up with Caitlin because she was part of their group. Nothing more.

"Caitlin would serve hemlock with my salad."

William laughed, spontaneous and genuine, and Max smiled. "Neutral ground then."

"I don't think tonight—" Max began.

"Grandmother's," William said.

"Hardly neutral."

"She won't poison you."

"True. She's afraid I have secrets about the family that will be revealed on national television when I die." She'd have to go home at some point, but not tonight. Not when she was tired from a full travel day and still had work to do before the close of business. "Tomorrow," she said.

"I'll talk to Grandmother." William stood. "I need to get back to work."

She walked him to the door. "By the way, do you know anything about this construction guy, Jason Hoffman, who was killed at the site of the new ACP gymnasium?"

He shook his head. "I was stunned when I heard. A robbery or something, right? Construction is a loss-intensive business."

"They'd just broken ground. There was nothing to steal."

"I didn't know the guy—but I do know Jasper Pierce."

"That name sounds familiar. Why?"

"He graduated from ACP a decade before us. He's one of the two major donors on the gym—the other is Uncle Archer. They're calling the building the Sterling Pierce Sports Center."

"I really have been out of the family loop."

"Your choice, Maxine."

He was right.

She wasn't quite ready to talk to William about Hoffman's case; she honestly didn't think he knew much about it. "Can I drop your name if I want to talk to Pierce?"

"You hardly need to drop *my* name. Revere will get you in to see him. Why?"

"Nothing specific. Just curiosity. It was good to see you, William."

He looked at her a moment too long, and Max knew he had something else on his mind. But he didn't say anything. Instead, he kissed her on the cheek and left.

William definitely had a secret.

Chapter Four

Max was cognizant of the fact that most cops didn't like her. Much of the time it simply had to do with the fact that she was a reporter. Cops, as a general rule, shunned the media. But some in law enforcement downright hated her, particularly when she shined light on a faulty investigation or blatant incompetence. It didn't seem to matter that she went out of her way to highlight good cops and skilled investigations, they only remembered embarrassments. She always walked in as a professional, but Max could and would play hardball when warranted.

She left the hotel at three impeccably dressed in her turquoise sheath and a short navy jacket. Accessories matched, makeup flawless, new notebook in her shoulder bag. She had an iPad and a laptop, but most of her research she wrote longhand. In her new notepad, she'd already jotted down basic research on the Menlo Park Police Department—clearance rates, political connections, crime statistics—it was best to be prepared.

The police station, hidden behind established trees and a wide expanse of lawn, bordered an older residential neighborhood. It hadn't changed much since the last time she was here, when she tried to convince the police that Kevin had a solid alibi and they should try to find Lindy's real killer. *That* hadn't gone well.

Max walked through the public entrance. A small, clean, empty waiting area with a female desk clerk behind glass. Doors, accessed by a digital passkey, were behind the gatekeeper. Soundproof walls cut most noise from the main office, though a faint hum of machines crept through. Everything seemed smaller now than it had when she was a teenager.

She approached the window and slid her business card through the slot. A screen allowed her to speak to the trim, middle-aged woman on the other side. No uniform, likely a civilian clerk. Her nameplate read D. BELL.

"Maxine Revere. I need to speak with the detective in charge of the Kevin O'Neal death investigation."

All nonattended deaths were investigated, even if it was a cut-and-dried accident or suicide. A suicide would not generally be confirmed as such until after the coroner's report, even if the initial police investigation ascertained there was no evidence of foul play and the crime scene was consistent with suicide.

Bell picked up her card. "Do you have an appointment with the PIO?"

"I'd like to talk to the detective in charge of the investigation," Max said.

"All reporters are required to go through the PIO. I'm sure you're familiar with the process."

Max couldn't assess whether Bell was being particularly difficult or simply following the rules.

"I understand, but this is a personal matter, not professional."

"Officer Corbett will make the decision whether to allow access to our investigators."

Max could play games and kiss up, or threaten when needed, but she didn't enjoy it. She much preferred straightforward communication. Unfortunately, most people, especially law enforcement and lawyers, expected the games.

Max conceded. "Thank you, Ms. Bell."

Pick your battles.

Battling gatekeepers was rarely a wise move.

Virtually every successful cold case she'd investigated, she'd first befriended the frontline staff—those who controlled information and access.

She stepped away from the window but didn't sit—she'd done enough sitting on the airplane. She'd also missed her morning run because she'd left Miami so early, which made her irritable. She took advantage of the waiting time to send an e-mail to her producer Ben, explaining that she hadn't fired Ginger; the girl had quit. She supposed he had a right to think Max had axed her newest assistant—she'd done it to all the others.

You have until Friday to find me someone, Max typed. Or I'll quit.

It wasn't a hollow threat. She was independently wealthy and had never wanted to host a cable news show. But Ben Lawson was a visionary. He had a way of making her see the possibilities. He'd sold her on the idea of highlighting specific cold cases and high-profile trials that could impact the criminal justice system, a cause she'd embraced after her best friend in college disappeared during spring break, ten years ago.

"Think an in-depth 'America's Most Wanted,'" Ben had said, "focusing on the unknown killer and questions. Investigation. What the cops got right and what they got wrong. Cold cases that you solve."

It was still the smaller, quieter crimes that she'd

pursued for the newspaper before the show—like the murder of Jason Hoffman—that drew her in. The survivors, like Penny and Henry Hoffman, who only wanted the truth so they might have peace.

But, if she was going to be honest, Hoffman's murder appealed to her mostly because it had happened on her high school campus—the same campus where Lindy Ames had been killed thirteen years ago.

Ben ran the ship and made sure she never had to deal with newsroom politics. As long as she could do what she wanted—investigative reporting in the field and not at a desk—she'd agreed to tape the monthly show. A competent assistant was critical to the part where she wasn't required to sit at a desk.

Ben hadn't responded to her e-mail before Ms. Bell called to her through the screen. "Officer Corbett will be out momentarily."

"Thank you," she said and pocketed her phone.

Whether Officer Donna Corbett intentionally made her wait, or whether she truly had been delayed, Max didn't know, but it took another fifteen minutes before the PIO came out. "Ms. Revere?" she asked.

Max bit back a sarcastic reply, considering she was the only person in the waiting room. "Yes, Officer Corbett?"

"I have a few minutes." She didn't make any

move to bring Max into the main station, but motioned for them to take two chairs in the waiting room.

If Corbett thought the move would intimidate or demoralize her, the PIO hadn't worked with enough reporters.

Max sat. "Kevin O'Neal is a family friend. The preliminary report indicated he committed suicide, but his sister hasn't had the closure she needs to accept that. I'd like a copy of the file so I can explain to her what happened."

"We don't give out files."

"I'd like the report. If it's not an ongoing criminal investigation, that shouldn't be a problem?"

She didn't tell the PIO that she already had the initial police report from Jodi. Additional information may have been added—including the all-important coroner's report. She'd really wanted to talk to the detective, but that could wait because Corbett wasn't going to make it easy.

"I can do that," Corbett said. "It's twenty-five cents a page."

"Today?"

Corbett glanced at her watch. "It's four thirty— I'll see what I can do."

All she had to do was send the report to the printer. It was all computerized. But Max didn't say anything because Corbett would make her wait until Monday just to spite her.

"I appreciate it," she said politely. "If I have

further questions regarding the report, I should direct them to you?"

Corbett handed Max her card. She said into her radio, "Jill, can you print a copy of the O'Neal report and bring it to the lobby? Thanks."

She turned back to Max. "You came a long way to help a family friend."

The only hint of curiosity. Max didn't say anything, because she didn't like open-ended questions. Instead, she switched gears. "I'd also like the initial report of the Jason Hoffman homicide investigation from November. I'm writing a follow-up article on the murder." That was neither true nor untrue—if there was enough material, she certainly intended to write something about it, even if it was just a couple paragraphs for her show's Web page. "I read in the initial media reports that MPPD handled the case?"

"It's an active investigation," Corbett said.

"Active? You have a suspect?"

Corbett switched gears to full PIO mode. "Currently, the Menlo Park Police Department is in the process of reviewing all cases over three months old to determine if they will remain active or classified inactive pending new evidence. All homicide investigations will remain open until solved, regardless of the status."

"I'd just like information you've already shared with the media."

"And your interest?"

"I'm a reporter."

"You're not local."

"No, I'm not." Max left it at that. Corbett had her card, and Max really hated when cops or anyone tried to weasel information out of her without simply asking her. If they were more forthcoming, she'd be more forthcoming. Let them think the national press corps was interested in their small-town homicide investigation.

"I'll have to get back to you on Monday. As I said, the case is under review and I need to pull together the public information."

"Can I pick it up at nine Monday morning?"

"I'll call you."

Max would be here first thing Monday morning if she couldn't track down the detective on her own. She wasn't going to rely on the PIO to make contact.

A young plainclothes assistant came out and handed Corbett a file.

"What do I owe you?" Max asked, pulling out her wallet.

"Seventy-five cents."

Max fished out three quarters from her wallet and took the papers. As she was thanking Corbett for her time, the door leading from the squad room opened. A squat detective emerged and glared at Max with small, hate-filled eyes.

"I didn't believe you'd actually show up here."

Though Detective Harry Beck had more weight

and less hair than when he'd taken the stand during Kevin's trial, Max recognized him immediately. Then he'd intimidated her with his blunt hatred of Kevin and disdain for her—because she'd taken the stand as a character witness. Today, he didn't have the same effect. She'd met cops like Harry Beck in virtually every jurisdiction she'd investigated a case. However, Beck could be a problem in her getting information from the department.

"Nice to see you again, Detective."

He snorted. "What does she want?" he asked Corbett as if Max had already left.

Corbett was slow on the uptake, watching the exchange. Max answered the question instead. "Kevin O'Neal's death investigation report."

Beck's face darkened. "The fucker killed himself. I wish he'd done it thirteen years ago and saved the state a ton of money, but he should never have walked free to begin with."

Max had many things she wanted to say to the bastard, but she fought her temper and said to the PIO, "Thank you for your time, Officer Corbett."

She wanted to leave before a confrontation, but Beck wouldn't let it go.

"You're not here to dredge up shit? Of course you are," he answered his own question. "That's what you are. A shit disturber. I swear to you, Maxine, if you cause any grief for the Ames family, I'll arrest you. Your privileged ass wouldn't last a night in prison."

Max bit her tongue. She wanted to lash out at the brash detective, but she understood the consequences. In her early career, she hadn't always been so controlled. She'd spent several nights in jail over the years for butting heads with the wrong cop. She survived the ordeals quite well—even wrote an award-winning article about the rights of reporters to protect their sources.

Harry Beck was definitely the wrong cop.

Using all her well-earned—and well-learned—self-control, Max walked out, catching only part of Corbett's comment before the door shut.

"Why are you giving her ammo—"

Max could predict the conversation. Corbett was young; she hadn't been with the Menlo Park Police Department thirteen years ago when they caught the murder investigation of Lindy Ames in neighboring Atherton. Corbett may know who the Revere family was; she may in fact know that Max was an investigative crime journalist. But she likely didn't know that Max had been friends with both the victim and the number one suspect—the *only* suspect—in Lindy's murder.

Beck would be giving her an earful. And she would take it and either be so intimidated by Beck and his threats that she wouldn't lift a finger to help Max, or she'd be ticked off that he yelled at her and go out of her way to help Max.

Max, of course, hoped for the latter.

She sat in her rental car, under a magnolia tree,

and calmed down. She may have walked out without reacting to Beck, but that didn't mean he hadn't affected her.

Harry Beck had been in his late thirties when he was the lead detective on Lindy's murder. He'd interviewed all her peers, her family, and Kevin. He'd been the one who arrested Kevin and had been one hundred percent confident of his guilt.

Years of experience and meeting hundreds of law enforcement officers in jurisdictions big and small taught Max that when a cop was absolutely confident in his assessment, one of two things happened: he either set out to prove that his theory was right by working evidence that would incriminate his key suspect or he set out to disprove his theory by looking at the case as if the lead suspect were innocent.

Cops didn't have to believe people were innocent until proven guilty, and rarely did they. Threatened, spit upon, shot at, and dealing with the worst end of the human spectrum, cops were usually jaded. But even the jaded cops, if they were good, focused on dispelling all other scenarios in order to nail their suspect. They didn't dismiss evidence because it didn't fit their theory.

Max couldn't say what Beck did or didn't do; all she'd seen were his actions toward Kevin. Then after the trial, when she'd told him about Kevin's true alibi, he'd said unspeakable things. And he'd said ultimately that he didn't care if there was any evidence that suggested Kevin might be innocent—in Beck's pea-sized brain, he knew with certainty that Kevin was a killer.

She should pull the transcripts of the trial and—

No.

She wasn't here to investigate Lindy's murder. She was here to satisfy Jodi that her brother had killed himself.

She opened the envelope Officer Corbett had given her and read the incident report.

The first two pages were identical to what Jodi had previously sent. Officers Blankenship and Lake were the first responders to the 911 call from Kevin's apartment manager. His alarm clock was going off and disturbing a neighbor. When the manager, Anita Gonzales, couldn't reach Kevin by phone or knocking, she'd let herself in and found his body in the bathroom.

He was found in shorts, no shirt, in the bathtub. There was no sign of forced entry. Barbiturates and hard alcohol were found nearby. They interviewed neighbors and friends and learned Kevin had a history of drug use, though he also held down a part-time job at a local coffee shop, and worked part time in construction when there was work. Which wasn't much lately.

The third page, which Jodi hadn't had earlier in the week, was the preliminary coroner's report. Kevin had drowned with a contributing cause of overdose. Essentially, he took enough pills to kill himself, passed out, and drowned in the bathtub before the pills finished the job.

Lindy drowned.

Why had Kevin written that on the death certificate? Did it have anything to do with his suicide? Had he planned to drown himself, a difficult way to commit suicide unless there was a contributing cause like unconsciousness from an overdose of drugs. It could have been an accident. He could have been in the bathtub, high, and passed out.

Why get into the bath with his shorts on?

If it was suicide, he wouldn't want to be found naked. It made sense. Or he was so stoned that he didn't know he was wearing clothes.

Max rubbed her forehead. She wished she could be surprised, but Kevin had been going down this path ever since his trial. She could only imagine the stress and humiliation of having a murder charge hanging over his head. She'd told him twelve years ago when the DA declined to retry Kevin until additional evidence surfaced that he should leave the Bay Area, go far away where no one knew who he was. Only then would he find peace.

He opted to stay. He was desperate to clear his name. But thirteen years after Lindy was killed, he had a drug addiction, no college degree, a menial job, and few friends.

The officers hadn't made note of the missing

laptop, and Max wondered if they'd interviewed Jodi before or after she'd gone into the apartment. Jodi's grief had interfered with her logic, which was common in these types of interviews. Jodi wanted to believe Kevin hadn't done it, so she looked for every possible proof that someone had killed him. There could be a logical explanation for the missing laptop. Someone could have stolen it before he died. He could have loaned it to a friend. Left it at work. Sold it. Drug addicts would sell anything of value to get their next fix.

But that didn't explain why Kevin sent Jodi Lindy's death certificate. Why he thought she'd drowned. Or why he'd sent Jodi a text message to call Max.

Call Max. I love you, J.

It was his good-bye note. His suicide note to his sister. Of that, Max was certain. But would Jodi believe it?

Maybe Kevin had reached a dead end in his own private investigation and in frustration and despair, killed himself.

Then why tell Jodi to call Max? In an attempt to make Max feel guilty because she wouldn't help him in his pursuit of Lindy's killer?

It was too late to go to the DA's office and find out what, if anything, was going on with Kevin's trial. If he thought he'd be facing another trial— that new evidence had been uncovered—that might have tipped him over the edge. Instead, she

drove to his apartment. She needed answers—
namely, Kevin's state of mind when he OD'd.

The apartment complex on Roble was tired
but clean with trimmed hedges and blossoming
rosebushes along the front walk. There were
twelve units in Kevin's white, L-shaped building,
six on the top and six on the bottom, an open
staircase leading to the long second-story balcony.
The building next door mirrored Kevin's, connected by a small courtyard with benches framing
an old oak tree.

Jodi had given her a key, but Max decided to
first talk to the apartment manager, Anita
Gonzales.

Ms. Gonzales opened the door quickly, her
smile warm and genuine. The older woman was
short and plump with naturally gray hair in
unnaturally tight curls. Her home smelled like
cinnamon and vanilla. The muted television in the
background showed a game show. Her dark eyes
assessed Max quickly. "I saw you walking up. You
must be Jodi's friend."

"Maxine Revere," she said. "I didn't want to go
up to Kevin's apartment without talking to you
first."

"Please, come in," she said and opened the
door. She straightened her apron and brushed a
loose curl away from her face. "I'm sorry for the
mess."

The apartment was cluttered and hot, but

immaculate. Gonzales had hundreds of small glass animals in a cabinet along one wall, a light above illuminating the menagerie.

"I love your figurines," Max said, eyeing in particular the section of birds.

She beamed. "My husband used to travel for business and would bring me back one every time. After he died, my son started buying them for me for my birthday and Christmas. Sit, please—I just made snickerdoodle cookies. Fresh out of the oven."

Max wasn't hungry, but she accepted the offer. "Thank you."

"Coffee? Milk? Kevin always liked milk with my cookies."

"Water, if that's not a problem."

Max understood people pleasers like Anita Gonzales. By the pictures on the wall, she had only the one son. She'd stayed home and raised her son, took care of the house, enjoyed doing for others. She'd have been the first person to bake a casserole for someone who lost a loved one, and would be the person organizing the prayer group when someone was sick. Max wasn't surprised that after her husband died and her son moved out she found the apartment management job. It gave her the opportunity to take care of others. Max would bet she knew the personal business of everyone who lived here.

Anita brought the water and plate of cookies to

the table. Max took a bite. They were delicious. "I'll bet Kevin ate a lot of your cookies."

"When I could get him to eat," she said, shaking her head. "Poor boy. So lost." Tears welled in her eyes. "It wasn't like him."

"Taking his own life?"

"Being selfish like that. He'd have to have known Jodi or I would be the one to find him. He didn't have a lot of friends, but Jodi, dear girl, came by at least once a week, and he helped me around this place, fixing this and that."

Max didn't know what kind of person Kevin was recently, but he'd always been considerate as a teenager. He was the type of guy who'd mow the lawn for his neighbors if they were sick, or the one who would stand up for a kid who was being picked on. He baby-sat Jodi all the time, as an infant and toddler, without complaint. He was also the type of guy who used his fists. He'd decked her cousin once, in eighth grade, because William had made a crude remark about Jenny Foster's breasts. Max always suspected that's why William never particularly liked Kevin. That, and Kevin was a scholarship kid at Atherton Prep, not really one of them.

"You told the police that his alarm clock was ringing and a neighbor complained."

Ms. Gonzales nodded. "He was usually very thoughtful. Most of my tenants are retired folks. The walls are thin, and his alarm was beeping for over an hour. Mrs. Dempsey was very upset about it."

"What time did the alarm go off?"

"It was set for six thirty. He had to be at the coffee shop by seven thirty on Sundays. I went up at seven thirty thinking he'd made a mistake and reset it or something, and gone off to work."

"How long had he lived here?"

"Three years."

"Do you know where he was before that?"

"San Francisco. I don't know much about it."

"Did he ever talk to you about his past?"

"Do you mean did I know that he was accused of killing that poor girl thirteen years ago? Of course. I've lived in Menlo Park my entire life. Back then, my husband was still alive and we had a small house over off Santa Cruz. We followed the news. I knew who he was when he applied."

"Jodi gave me the apartment key—would you mind if I went up there?"

"Go right ahead. It's been cleaned because of . . ." her voice trailed off. "Rent is paid through the month, and I told Jodi she could have whatever time she needed to pack up Kevin's things." She sighed. "He didn't have much."

Max thanked Mrs. Gonzales for the refreshments, then went upstairs to Kevin's corner unit.

The one-bedroom apartment had been sanitized. The cloying scent of bleach and Lysol irritated her nose. She opened all the windows in the living room and kitchen before she looked around.

Kevin had set up the small dining nook to be his office, and in it there was a desk, printer, filing cabinet, but no computer. She went through his desk and found the usual—pay stubs, tax returns, receipts, mints, pens. The two-drawer filing cabinet had a lock, but it was easy to pick.

Inside were several empty hanging files, stretched and worn as if they'd once held extensive paperwork.

Each folder was labeled: *Investigation, Atherton PD; Investigation, MPPD; DA; Autopsy; Ames; Revere; Talbot; Media; Transcripts.*

Jodi had said that Kevin was obsessed with Lindy Ames's murder and this proved it. Except there were no documents in any of the folders.

The Talbots were a large, extended family in Atherton, as established as the Reveres. Why was Kevin researching the Talbots? Which Talbot? All, or just those who'd been in high school with them, like Andy? When he listed Revere, did he mean her or William? Or any of the others in her family?

Everyone who'd seen Lindy the twenty-four hours before she'd been killed had been interviewed by the police thirteen years ago. Including Max and William and Andy.

Missing computer, missing files.

Could mean absolutely nothing. Could be a logical explanation.

Max walked through the rest of the apartment, looking through the cabinets and drawers. In Kevin's sparse bedroom was a bed, dresser, and a bookshelf filled with mostly fantasy and science fiction, but also a shelf of nonfiction—history, biographies, and two of her true crime books. It felt odd to know that even though she hadn't spoken to him, he still bought her books.

A tinge of regret scratched Max until she had to acknowledge, at least to herself, that she'd lost more than her faith in people when Kevin lied to her. She'd lost her best friend. Kevin made her laugh. He knew everything about her—about never hearing from her mom except through sporadic postcards—which stopped when she turned sixteen—about not knowing who her dad was, about feeling like she was being punished by her grandparents because of her mother's failures and her own drive to find her father against their wishes. They didn't have a problem with Max because she was born out of wedlock, but because she didn't act like a Revere.

Ironically, scandal was part of being one of the privileged in Atherton. It was how one responded and behaved during the disgrace that meant one belonged, and Max never behaved the way she was supposed to. When she learned Uncle Brooks was having an affair, she called him on it. Apparently, that was a big no-no—especially considering she'd been fifteen at the time. But from the minute her mother left her with her grandparents shortly before her tenth birthday, she'd felt the disdain coming from William's father. Now, with maturity and experience on her side, she accepted that it was because of something her mother had done that made Brooks take it out on her; then she'd just felt the animosity and had no idea how to address it, except through disobedience.

She turned her attention from Kevin's books to his closet. It was cluttered, stacked with boxes of papers and clothes, and she realized she would likely need to go through the papers to find out if there was anything important and if the missing files had been boxed up. She would task Jodi with helping.

Max stood at the end of the bed and looked around, suddenly sad. Kevin had once had a future, as bright as any middle-class teenager. Better, really, because he had dreams unencumbered by family legacy or expectations—he'd wanted to work in genetics, the research end of medicine, to find cures for deadly childhood illnesses. His older sister had died of a rare genetic disorder when Kevin was six.

She'd stood by Kevin because the Kevin O'Neal she'd grown up with could not have raped anyone, nor strangled Lindy. In her gut, she knew he hadn't done it. Which made lying about his alibi hard to understand. Though the police were certainly responsible for not pursuing other lines of inquiry, Kevin was just as responsible for not clearing himself immediately.

She looked back at Kevin's bookshelf where her books were displayed on the bottom shelf, with his other nonfiction titles, in alphabetical order. He only had two.

Her eye skirted along the rest of the shelves and she noticed a familiar spine in the middle of Kevin's complete Terry Brooks collection.

It was her first book.

She'd started the book as a journal when her college roommate Karen Richardson had disappeared during spring break, when they'd gone to Miami to have fun. Max had spent a year in Florida trying to find out what happened to Karen. That was when she'd met FBI Agent Marco Lopez, a new recruit eager to make a name for himself. But neither of them had found Karen's killer. Or her body.

Or, rather, they *knew* who the killer was but couldn't prove it. Ten years later, it was considered a cold case, even though it wasn't cold. It was solved—without justice. It still angered Max when she dwelled on it. Writing the book had helped, but it hadn't purged all her pain and rage at the injustice of that year.

She pulled the book from the shelf to put it with the other two, or maybe just to see it again, reminding her of who she'd been and who she was now. Kevin's trial had set her on a path of doubt and distrust. Karen's disappearance had given Max her calling.

An envelope was sticking out a mere quarter-inch, noticeable only now that she'd removed the book. She took it out. It was addressed to her, stamped and dated last December. That was when Kevin had e-mailed her asking for help in solving Lindy's murder.

The seal had been broken. She took out a sheet of lined paper. A key fell to the carpet. She picked it up. It was unremarkable, a standard key, but there was a number on it—110. Another apartment? A storage unit?

She read the note.

Max—

I can only ask for forgiveness once. You rejected it, and I guess I understand. You're still hurt and angry. I get that. And I understand that I should have, from the beginning, told the police I'd been with Olivia. At the time, I thought I was doing the right thing because I didn't kill Lindy and there was no evidence that I did. I was so naïve about the system.

Even when you left, angry, you told me you believed me. For years, I tried to put it all behind me. I moved to San Francisco, but then I got into drugs and drank too much and nearly died. I finally woke up and knew what I had to do: find the truth.

I don't know if I can do it alone. That's why I e-mailed you. Maybe you'll reconsider when you see what I found. Maybe you can find the truth about the night Lindy was killed. Don't do it for me. Do it for Lindy. She loved you, just like I did.

—Kev

Kevin had written a P.S. in a different pen. The writing was sloppier, but it was still his scrawl.

P.S. Tell Jodi I'm sorry, but this is the only way. And Max—I'm really proud of you. I always thought you were amazing, but following your career, you proved it. I hope you're happy.

The comment was passive-aggressive in a way that stabbed at Max's heart. As if her happiness had led her to turn her back on Kevin. Forgiveness was hard for her, but more than that, she didn't want to return to the past. Investigating Lindy's death would be taking her back to a time she wanted to forget.

Behind the single sheet of paper was a copy of a parking ticket. It was dated the night Lindy had been killed, 11:28 P.M. It had been issued to a black Mercedes 320 SL, registered to Brooks

Revere, Max's uncle, two blocks from Lindy's house.

Max remembered the car. William had driven it more than Brooks.

Why had he been at Lindy's house the night she'd been killed?

The sound of a door closing made her jump.

"Mrs. Gonzales?" Max called out.

No answer, but something fell. Max rushed out of the bedroom as the apartment door slammed shut. Mail on the counter fluttered to the floor from the sudden air circulation. Max pursued the intruder.

She ran down the corridor in time to see a man in jeans and a dark windbreaker jump over the railing as he ran down the stairs, and then hightail it across the courtyard.

She kicked off her heels and ran after him, but he was faster and had a head start. She lost him before she got to the street.

Max looked up and down the street for a car, a person, anything that was out of place. But the street was quiet.

Mrs. Gonzales rushed out of her apartment as Max walked back toward Kevin's unit. "What happened? I saw you running down the stairs. Is everything okay?"

"Someone came in Kevin's apartment, but didn't know I was there."

"Are you okay?"

"Yes. He ran when he heard me."

"I'll call the police."

Max didn't stop her, but she knew what the police would do. She had no description beyond fast, white, and male. But she might as well get the intrusion on record. Maybe he'd been there before. Maybe he'd been the one to steal the laptop and the files.

Max reached into her pocket and pulled out the key to locker 110. No facility name, nothing to give Max a clue as to where to go or what she'd find when she was there. But important enough for Kevin to hide.

Or maybe, he was after this.

Chapter Five

The Menlo Grill, attached to the Stanford Park Hotel, had always been one of Max's favorite restaurants. It had a warm, relaxing, semiformal atmosphere without being ostentatious. Since her last visit two years ago they'd remodeled extensively, and she wasn't sure she liked all the changes, but the menu looked good—she'd skipped lunch and was ready for an early dinner.

She asked for a table in the bar, pointing to a dark corner booth. Less likely anyone she knew would spot her there. She didn't care if she was seen, but she was in no temperament for conversation. The cross-country flight had caught up with her, but she despised eating a meal in her hotel room. Along with the need to unpack her suitcases and make her temporary lodging a temporary home, not using room service was a rule she rarely broke.

She ordered the fish of the day, fresh trout, because she planned on making it an early night and didn't want a heavy meal right before bed. She pulled out her iPad and folded the case so it angled toward her, and checked her e-mail while she ate.

She'd avoided Ben's phone calls through the day, so she wasn't surprised that he'd sent her a long message about how difficult it was to find a competent assistant, how difficult she was to work for, excuse after excuse. Then near the end he wrote: However, I agree with you about Ginger.

She laughed out loud, then covered her mouth.

I have an idea that might work, hope to have answers by Monday.

When will you be back in the city? We need to strategize on the Bachman trial, there's a stack of documents up to my ass you need to review, and Gertrude Grant wants to interview you about your Ramirez article. Gert's show has fantastic ratings to promote "Maximum Exposure" within our key demographic, and it'll give you the opportunity to follow up on the case and file another article, plus I think it would make a good two-minute slot.

I can't believe you went to fucking California when we're up to our necks in work. You'll be back on Monday?

Max loved Ben even though he drove her crazy. She supposed that was the role of a television producer, but if she hadn't been friends with Ben since college, if they hadn't grieved together over Karen's death, she'd never have put up with him.

Likewise, she doubted he'd have tolerated her. They were oil and water, and not in the good, sexually combustible way, either.

She responded to his e-mail:

Don't know when I'll be back. We have three weeks before the Bachman trial, more than enough time to prepare.

I don't know how many times I have to turn Gert down before you understand that I'll never go on her show. In case you misunderstood my previous sentence, I will not go on Gert's show. I do not like her. She's a bitch. So am I. It'd be bloody if we're on set together. And Gert ask *me* questions? Never going to happen.

However, I like the idea of a two-minute

slot on Ramirez. I'll write it up and we'll shoot it as soon as I get back. Squeeze it into the May show.

That would irritate Ben. The May show was already cut and promo'd, he'd hate cutting in a two-minute "ministory," but there was a timeliness factor he'd appreciate.

She thought a moment and sent another message:

On second thought, let's do a live cut-in with an up-to-the-minute status on Ramirez, with a ninety-second historical overview. Also, I might have an article for the Web page on a cold case I discovered when I got here.

She sent it off and grinned. The waiter took her plate and brought a second glass of wine. Ben was going to flip, because it would be a lot more work and he couldn't edit her, but it was a good idea. The last time they'd done a live cut-in, it had been featured on multiple news programs that night and the following day.

"Thinking about a friend . . . or a lover?"

She looked up, startled but not surprised to see Andy Talbot standing at her table. She was speechless, a rarity.

"May I? You *are* alone."

"Good deduction."

He sat, though Max hadn't explicitly invited him.

The waiter came over immediately and asked Andy if he'd like a menu. Andy looked at Max, and she shook her head.

"Not dinner, then," Andy said. "Glenlivet, neat."

"Yes, Mr. Talbot." The waiter glanced at Max. "Another pinot grigio, Ms. Revere?"

She shook her head. She still had nearly a full glass in front of her.

The waiter left, and Andy turned to her with a mock frown. "I'm hurt."

"I'm tired. And I'm not big on surprises."

"I should have called." There was no apology in his tone and Max was as irritated by this as she was of the way he trailed his fingers up and down her arm. "You're stunning, as usual."

She put her hand on his and squeezed. "Andy, it's always good to see you, but I truly am tired and I have a lot of work to do."

"You're here on business then."

"You know why I'm here." She lifted his hand off her arm and placed it on the table. Leaning back she sipped her wine. Being near Andy was always problematic. It wasn't simply that he was attractive, like Paul Newman as Butch Cassidy if Butch wore a Caraceni suit. It was their history. The familiarity and chemistry, the love and hate. After Thea's wedding, she'd ended up at Andy's house and in his bed. That had been a mistake, just like the time before when she visited for William's wedding. Andy had been her first boy-friend, her first lover, her first love. Being with him made her feel young and nervous when "nervous" wasn't in her personality. Could she even admit that she still felt insecure with him? For someone like her, anyone who made her apprehensive was someone she tended to avoid.

Two years ago, Andy had sensed the same distance she had. They weren't the same teenage lovers. They weren't the same people. Max respected Andy—she even loved him in a way, since he'd been an important part of her life for so long. But she wasn't in love with him, and had a hard time with forgiveness. Being back for Kevin's funeral reminded her that she and Andy had split because of Kevin: Max believed he was innocent, Andy believed he was guilty. There was no middle ground. But that fundamental disagree-ment was only a symptom of why they wouldn't have worked for the long haul.

The waiter brought Andy's drink. When he left, Andy said, "I'd offer you a penny for your thoughts, except you've always given them away for free."

Max raised an eyebrow. "Why are you here?"

"Why do you think I'm here?"

"I honestly don't know. I'll tell you what I told William when he came by earlier. Jodi O'Neal asked me to come to Kevin's funeral. I had the time, so I came."

He stared at her in that deep way he had, making her think he could read her mind when Max knew he'd never truly known what she was thinking. He said, "Jodi has made it clear to anyone who'd listen that she doesn't think Kevin killed himself. You show up. You investigate crimes."

Max held up her hand. "I'm not here because of my job."

"You didn't answer my question."

"Why do I think you're interrogating me?"

She stared at Andy pointedly. Most people, including William, would glance away at her stern look. Not Andy. She'd never intimidated him, as a teenager or as an adult. She used to be able to read him well, but thirteen years was a long time. And if she were honest with herself, which she always tried to be, the few times she'd seen him since— the few times she'd slept with him—they'd each had a wall up, knowing they couldn't go back to being eighteen.

Andy avoided her question by asking bluntly, "Do you think, like Jodi, that Kevin was murdered?"

"I'm not investigating his death." She'd found his postscript akin to a suicide note. She could tell Andy that she believed it was suicide, but she didn't want to explain why, to Andy or anyone, until she had more information.

"Is that why you were at the police station this afternoon?"

"Who told you that?" But as Max answered with the question, she had a dozen more. Why did he care? What was he hiding? Why did he feel the need to confront her tonight, without warning?

Andy's jaw was tight, and while he leaned back in the booth casually, his neck muscles were also tense. "Kevin's doing it to us again."

"Kevin's dead."

"It's because of him that we broke up in the first place. And it's because of him that we're fighting now."

She sighed, weary and in sore need of eight hours of sleep. "I'm not fighting with you, Andy. I was having a very pleasant working dinner. Alone. I'm in town for Kevin's funeral. I'm gathering information for Jodi so she can move on with her life." She hesitated, then added, "Kevin didn't break us up. We were eighteen-year-old teenagers who had a fundamental difference of opinion. There's no 'agree to disagree' when you have two hotheaded, young, passionate people who both are certain they are right."

"And I guess we'll never know," Andy said.

"I know I was right. I never believed then or now that Kevin killed Lindy."

"You're still so positive. If not Kevin, then who?"

"I don't know."

"But you're here."

"Not to find out who killed Lindy."

"I don't believe you."

Max glared at him. He was essentially calling her a liar, a serious charge. "I'm talking and you're not listening."

"I'm looking at the evidence."

"I'll tell you the truth. I didn't come here to investigate Lindy's death. I didn't come here to write about Kevin or his trial or the fact that the police never seriously looked at any other suspects. I came here for Jodi."

Max stood, her anger building, and she needed to get out of the bar before she lost her temper.

"But," she added, bending over the table, her face inches from Andy's, "if I decide to stir the hornet's nest, it's certainly none of your business."

Chapter Six

Max was by nature an early riser, but when deep in a case she also developed insomnia. There were other triggers—unresolved questions and family being two of the biggest. She had both. So when her mind woke up at 4:00 A.M. after less than five hours of sleep—unable to go to bed earlier because of her confrontation with Andy—she knew sleep time was over. A five-mile run on the treadmill in the hotel's gym, followed by a hot shower and personal pampering, went a long way in hiding her tired eyes.

"You're not old," she said to her reflection. But several late nights in a row definitely made her feel much older than her thirty-one years.

Max believed that if she was to be taken seriously as a crime reporter, she needed to present herself as a professional. She'd learned while a college senior investigating Karen's disappearance in Miami that if she looked like a punk college kid, she'd be treated as such—and not given any information. But if she dressed like a Revere—essentially, someone of means who looked and acted important—she would be taken seriously. When she launched her monthly cable crime show nearly two years ago, she took more care in her appearance. Part of it was vanity, but mostly it was her image and how her appearance helped her gather information. She could change her look in a moment if she needed to dress down or blend in.

Max left her hotel early in order to meet the Hoffmans, who were staying in a hotel fifteen minutes up the freeway. She normally didn't have a problem changing gears while working on simultaneous investigations. In a perfect world, she preferred to focus on one case at a time, but Max was often researching one case while interviewing for another while proofreading an article or preparing her opening remarks for a broadcast related to a completely different crime.

This morning, though, she couldn't get William's parking ticket out of her head. She wanted him to explain why he was at Lindy's house; if it wasn't him, then who borrowed his car and why hadn't William told the police? She debated how to discuss the ticket with her cousin. There was no question that she would.

And then there was Andy's visit to the hotel bar. The visit that had kept her up half the night in knots, even after taking a hot bath and drinking a third glass of wine. He was clearly angry—and Max wasn't positive it was solely directed at her, even though she was certain she was part of his frustration. It was his questions and deflection that had her concerned.

She pushed her suspicions aside; she walked into the hotel's restaurant and asked for coffee, then glanced through her notes and put her head firmly into the Jason Hoffman murder investigation. She'd promised to listen to the Hoffmans and they deserved her undivided attention.

The research she'd gathered yesterday was limited. An online search of newspaper archives identified Detective Nick Santini out of Menlo Park as the lead investigator. That was at least more than she'd gotten from Corbett. She decided to postpone calling him until after she met with the grandparents. She needed more information about Jason Hoffman's murder so she could ask

Santini the important questions. One thing she'd learned early on was that cops would give you the basics anytime you asked, then dismiss the more probing questions. If you already had the basics covered, they were more willing to answer the tough questions. Research was key.

She'd also dug into Santini's past when she couldn't sleep the night before and learned that he'd been in Menlo Park for only two years, coming north after a decade with the Los Angeles Police Department, the last three years there as detective. Prior to his twelve years as a cop, he'd spent six years in the Marines, right out of high school. All that information was posted on a public relations site in L.A.; she could find little on him here in Menlo Park. But that didn't surprise Max. Most people in law enforcement guarded their private lives. Max wished she could do the same, but her career required her to open up more than she was comfortable with.

The only information she had on Jason Hoffman's murder was what was in the newspapers immediately after his death and his obituary. The news never said what had been stolen at the Evergreen construction site, if anything, just that Jason Hoffman had been shot in an "apparent" robbery. There had been no follow-up articles, no public police interviews, and no editorials on the investigation.

Max switched gears and looked at the family.

His sister, Jessica Hoffman, was three years older than Jason, a graduate of UCLA who'd returned home and worked in local government for the Board of Supervisors. It was unclear what she did, but she worked in the government center. Depending on who she knew and what she did, Jessica could be a help or a hindrance in getting information about Evergreen or working with the police.

Her fiancé was a corporate attorney for a dot-com company in Santa Clara—not good. Attorneys as a rule didn't like anyone talking to reporters or cops, even if they didn't practice criminal law. Max would have to work around him if at all possible.

By all appearances, the Hoffmans were an average middle-class family in the San Francisco Bay Area—meaning, if they lived most anyplace else outside of here or New York City, they would be wealthy. But here they were typical of their friends and neighbors. The parents had two kids, raised them in a small house in San Carlos that had more than quadrupled in value since they purchased it twenty years ago, and didn't appear to live above their means. Jason's father, Michael, was an accountant for a major San Francisco firm, but not a partner. The mother, Sara, owned the construction company with her brother and managed the books. They were in their early fifties, they had a small mortgage on their home, and didn't appear to have extensive debt.

Typical, normal, common.

Jason's murder could have been a robbery, but what had thieves been after at a construction site that had no equipment yet? She supposed she couldn't be certain of that—she'd need to talk to Detective Santini or Evergreen. Or it wouldn't be a stretch to think that the thieves had been after something at the school, and Jason's presence surprised them.

His family deserved to know what happened, and the killer deserved to be in prison. Just like whoever killed Lindy should be in prison.

She shifted in her seat as the waitress refilled her coffee. She wasn't here to investigate Lindy's murder, but the more she kept telling herself that the more she realized she couldn't get Lindy and Kevin out of her head. Kevin's messages, aimed at her, were both troublesome and thought-provoking. Memories, the good and bad, crept in. It didn't help that everyone *thought* that's what she was doing in town. Maybe she should just do it. Shake things up because it was expected of her.

Max thought of their first real fight, when she and Lindy were in seventh grade, when they still considered each other best friends and Max spent as much time at Lindy's house as her own. It was the kind of fight that could have destroyed their friendship. It hadn't, but it had changed it.

Like she did nearly every day after school, Max rode her bike over to Lindy's house. She bypassed the grand main house and made her way straight to the tree house.

Tree house was a misnomer—the stately, three-story clubhouse had been built around two old trees. Lindy's father originally had it built for her older brother, Jerry, but Lindy had taken it over when she was eight, marking her territory by painting the inside pink.

The pink had long ago been replaced by a pale green that her mother said spurred creativity. But the house was all Lindy's. It's where they talked, where they played, where they shared. And today, Max had something big to share with Lindy:

She'd gotten a birthday card from her mother.

It was three weeks late and short, but it was from her, signed with her flowery "Mommy" even though Max had stopped calling Martha Revere "Mommy" when she was six.

"Happy birthday, Maxie! Happy big thirteen. I hope you have a wonderful year. I'd hoped to visit, but something came up and I couldn't get away. I love you! Mommy."

She said the same thing every year, and every year Max had a flash of hope—hope that her mother meant it, that she'd truly meant to visit, but knowing in her heart since that Thanksgiving she'd left Max with her grandparents, the month before Max turned ten, that she'd never see her mother again.

Lindy wasn't in the clubhouse, but the door was never locked and Max walked in. She collapsed on the overstuffed couch and reached into a popcorn bowl with day-old popcorn. That's when she saw Lindy's diary.

It was out in the open, right there on the table. Lindy was possessive of her diary. She'd let Max read things in it, because they were best friends, but she didn't let her read everything.

The hardest thing Max had ever done was not pick up that diary. She desperately wanted to, but Lindy trusted her, and trust was important. She stared at it, and Lindy walked in.

Lindy had always been one of the most beautiful girls on campus. They were in seventh grade, but Lindy had never gone through the awkward, gangly stage. She grew from cute, blond, Kewpie doll, when Max had met her in the middle of fourth grade, into young teenage beauty queen. Max had a growth spurt over the summer and went from average to five foot ten practically overnight. She was suddenly the tallest girl in junior high, all arms and legs and no breasts.

"Did you read that?" Lindy snapped and grabbed the diary.

"No."

She glared at her.

"I'm not lying," Max said. "I wanted to, I was sort of willing a breeze to come in and turn the pages."

Lindy laughed. "Okay, I believe you." She opened the diary to the middle, flipped through, and handed Max the book. "Read Monday."

Max did. Her eyes widened. Ms. Blair was cutting herself? The PE teacher? Why? "You have to tell Mr. Horn."

Lindy grabbed the book. "No way, then Mr. Horn and everyone else will know that I was kissing Andy in the locker room."

"You can say you were just getting something you left. Or—"

But Lindy cut her off. "You think this is the only secret I have on the teachers at school? Really? I know everything about everyone in this town—and if I don't know it, I will."

"She needs help."

Lindy wasn't even listening to her. "I know that Mr. Horn's secretary gives him a blow job under his desk, and the janitor, Miles, he jerks off after watching our swim meets."

"That's disgusting."

"People are gross. Take Kimberly. I know she's cheating on my father. I'm going to prove it."

Lindy and her mother were constantly at odds. She called her Kimberly to get under her skin.

"You're spying on all these people?"

"Hardly. I'm just more observant than most people." Lindy stared at her. "So are you. You're the one who told me Miles was a creep."

"I didn't know why."

"Now you do. Be glad you're not on the swim team."

"Still, you have to do something about Ms. Blair. I really like her, and she needs help." Max had read a book about cutting. She couldn't imagine anyone hurting themselves, but she knew it was something serious.

"No."

"How can you be so cold?"

"How can you be such a bleeding heart? I'm sorry I showed you anything. My diary's off-limits to you."

Max walked out and didn't speak to Lindy for two weeks. Instead, she followed Ms. Blair, trying to catch her cutting herself, because then she could go to Mr. Horn and say what she saw, and not bring Lindy into it.

But she never saw anything. And a month later, Ms. Blair took a leave of absence. Lindy—of course Lindy would know—said she checked herself into rehab. In addition to cutting, she was a drug addict, and she'd nearly OD'd. Lindy had heard that from a school board member who was having dinner at her house with her parents.

True to her word, Lindy never let Max look at her diary again. They managed to rebuild their friendship, but conversation about the diary—and Lindy's secrets—were off-limits. But two years later, in the middle of their freshman year, the book would come back to bite Lindy in the ass.

The waitress refilled her coffee cup a third time, startling Max from her memories. Max thanked her then looked back at her notes, needing to get her head out of the past. She noticed she'd scraped the polish off her thumbnail again. Why did she even bother with manicures when she always trashed her nails?

Penny and Henry Hoffman walked into the hotel's dining hall and seemed relieved and nervous that Max was already there. They smiled and sat across from her. Penny said, "I was afraid you'd changed your mind."

Max got right to the point. "I did a little research last night, but have a few questions for you, if you don't mind."

"Please, anything we can do to help."

"Did Jason's parents, or anyone else, hire a private investigator to look into the homicide?"

They glanced at each other and shook their heads. "I don't think so," Henry said. "Mike would have told me."

Possibly, though it depended how close the family was, and whether Jason's parents wanted to spare the older couple.

"Did the police say anything to you or to Jason's

parents about the investigation? If they had a suspect or if there were similar crimes?"

"Maybe you should talk to Mike and Sara," Penny said, her hands clasped on the table in front of her. "They really haven't told us much of anything, though we've asked," she added quickly.

Max feared she'd let her affection for the couple yesterday and her frustration with her assistant cloud her judgment. She should have known better than to be brought into an investigation by grandparents. They usually meant well, but didn't have much information or access to those who did.

"In your original letter, do you remember why you thought Jason's death was something I'd be able to investigate?" Max phrased the question carefully. "Other than the fact that he was murdered at my old high school." She didn't want the Hoffmans to think that she wasn't going to pursue this, but if she had to start from ground zero, she wouldn't have the time, at least not for the next few months. She had several commitments, not the least of which was covering the Bachman trial back in New York City.

Penny brightened and said, "Oh, yes. I have a copy of the original e-mail I sent right here." She reached into her purse and pulled out a slightly crumpled paper.

Max took the paper from Penny and unfolded it. The header showed that it had been sent two months ago to Max's "hot line" e-mail reserved for information about cold cases or upcoming trials, on February twenty-sixth, three months after Jason's murder, and two weeks after Ginger had been hired.

The opening didn't give Max any information she didn't already know, mostly background on Jason and the information that had been revealed in the press. But the second to last paragraph gave Max that sizzling twitch again, that there was something here she could work with.

I'm sure you get many letters like ours, asking for your help to solve a case the police feel is hopeless. I hope that the fact that Jason was killed at Atherton Prep will be enough to interest you into investigating this case. Even just a word from you on your show would give us hope—maybe someone will come forward with information if they see it on the national news.

I wasn't going to write to you except for something my granddaughter said when she and her fiancé came to visit us. The police came to their house and questioned them about Sara, my daughter-in-law. Jessica said the questions were typical, and when I expressed concern Jessica changed the subject. She told Henry later that she hadn't wanted to upset me, that she thought the questions coming so long after Jason's murder was stranger than the questions themselves. And nothing came of it, so the police were probably trying to close off lines of inquiry or resolve something. We were heartened that the police were working again, except we still don't have any news about what really happened to Jason. When we talked to our son, Mike, he said the police had no new leads and he feared they were going to stop looking into Jason's death.

I just want to know why my grandson died.

Max asked the couple, "When was Jessica interviewed?"

Penny shook her head, but Henry answered. "A month before her visit. That's why Jess thought the questions were strange, because they hadn't heard anything from the police in two months, then the detective came to talk to her about her mother."

"Did Jason have any problems with his mother or uncle?"

"No. Sara is a wonderful mother. And Brian, we've adopted him like he was our own son. He's a little gruff and rough around the edges, but he treated Jason like he was his own son. Brian never married."

"Was the construction company having any financial problems?"

"Construction is such a tough business right now, but they were scraping by. The contract with Atherton Prep to build the sports facility came at the right time. They already have offers for work when they're done."

That was the way it often was—land one choice job, the rest of the jobs came easier. And being affiliated with ACP where there were alumni who had money, Evergreen was probably set for life.

Max needed to run a background on Sara, her brother Brian, and Evergreen Construction. There could be secrets, and construction was one of those businesses that could draw in shady investors. She'd like to talk to Jessica first, but the girl was getting married next week. Except, if she waited Jessica would be gone on her honeymoon and Max couldn't stay more than a few days. She'd have to think that through before she made her next move.

She really wanted to know what spurred the police to interview Jessica again two months after Jason's murder. Something must have come up. DNA? Contrary to popular television, DNA testing often took months, particularly if there was no viable suspect. Most other lab results would take a few hours to possibly weeks, depending on the agency and the backlog. Or, it could be a standard follow-up on a case before being put in the inactive file—running through potential witnesses and statements and wrapping things up before the detective felt comfortable putting the case aside.

She said to the Hoffmans, "I can't promise that I'll adopt your grandson's case, but I have a couple of days free and I'll talk to the detective in charge. Whatever I learn, I'll make sure you know. But you need to understand that there might not be any new information. The police may not have any suspects, or if they do but can't prove it, they're not going to share that with me."

Penny nodded, wide-eyed. "Of course. I just really appreciate your time. I know you're very busy."

She dismissed that comment. Everyone was busy, she no more so than anyone else. "Do you have your son and granddaughter's contact information? I may need to talk to them."

"Yes, right here." She pulled her wallet from her purse.

Henry put his hand on Penny's, but looked at Max. "Mike isn't going to appreciate us getting involved. I talked to him after Jess's visit, and he was very angry that Jess had worried us. This is her wedding. I don't want to ruin it."

"Nor do I." Max couldn't tell him that what she learned wouldn't impact Jessica's wedding or divide their family. What she wanted and what usually happened whenever a murder was close to home rarely matched.

Henry seemed to understand. His eyes watered. Penny was a bit more clueless.

"I can walk away," Max said. "Tell me now, and I'll leave the case alone."

Penny looked panicked. "No, please—"

Again, Max focused on Henry.

He let go of Penny's hand. "The truth is better than not knowing," he said quietly.

Max believed it, but few other people did. Most people *said* they wanted the truth, but few appreciated it. Many people hated her for telling them the truth—truths that they asked for.

She thanked the Hoffmans and walked out, melancholy and unsettled. But she wasn't thinking about Jason Hoffman. She was thinking about Lindy.

No one was asking her to look into Lindy's murder. If anything, people wanted her to steer clear of it. Detective Beck. William. Andy. Max was the one who wanted the truth. Could she live with the truth if she uncovered it?

Max had enough time before the funeral to check out Evergreen Construction. The main office was in downtown Redwood City near the county center, but there was no one in the office today. In this economy, a construction project would be working weekends, and since Jason was killed at Atherton Prep that's where she would start.

She considered calling Jasper Pierce, or even

her great-uncle, Archer Sterling, but decided to use that card when she needed it. Gather information first. Besides, Archer was her grandmother's brother—he would tell Eleanor everything Max was doing.

She wanted to get a feeling for the business. Maybe someone would talk—it had happened to her more than a few times. Share what they know. Give her a direction, a lead to pursue.

Nostalgia hit her when she drove through Atherton to her high school campus. It was a beautiful campus, most of the land donated by the Ames family, who'd once owned a large chunk of the town. The Sterling Pierce Sports Center was on the south side of the campus—it had once been grass and trees; most of the trees remained, she was pleased to note—the complex made good use of the open space for the substantial footprint of the building.

She used the construction entrance, not the main school entrance. She was surprised at how quickly the building was being constructed—the sign out front boasted that the gym would be open in December. Right now, they had a basement dug out—according to the plans posted near the entrance, the basement would house the wrestling room, weight room, locker rooms, and practice gym. She felt a little thrill at the excitement of the project—what a remarkable facility. She would love to see it when it was complete.

Construction sites had valuable equipment, not just machinery and tools, but wiring, pipes, heating and AC units. Had something been delivered that weekend? Valuable enough to kill for, Max supposed, but in the construction thefts she'd read about they usually went in and out late at night, at a site that wasn't guarded or had no security cameras, and took what they could haul off in a few hours. The thieves were about low risk/high reward—murder wasn't usually a result.

As soon as she got out of her rental sedan, Max was approached by a burly fifty-year-old in a hard hat. "Can I help you with something, miss?"

She handed him her card. "Maxine Revere. I'm a freelance reporter working on an article about theft on construction sites. I'm also an alum of Atherton Prep. I wanted to talk to the manager about the theft here last year."

"I'm the foreman, I run this project, but you'd probably want to talk to Mr. Robeaux. He won't be back until Monday."

"Actually, I'd rather speak with you."

He didn't like the idea of talking to her. "I'm really busy. We run on reduced labor over the weekend, I have deadlines to meet and—"

"Five minutes. I promise."

He sighed, and said, "You can't quote me, not without Mr. Robeaux's permission."

"Agreed."

"What paper?"

"Freelance."

"So you don't have a job."

Max was amused. "I've had my work published in the *San Francisco Chronicle*, *The New York Times*, the *Los Angeles Times*—most major newspapers, in addition to numerous magazines."

"You mean they still have papers?" He laughed. Max did not. She followed him into one of the trailers. A young woman, not more than twenty, was sitting at a desk typing on an electric typewriter, a stack of triplicate forms next to her. She glanced at them without slowing down.

"So, Ms. Revere, what do you want to know?"

He sat behind a cluttered desk with a partially obscured nameplate. She pushed aside the paper blocking his first name. Roger Lawrence.

She pulled out her notepad. "According to my research, there were a total of twenty-eight construction thefts in San Mateo County last year. This robbery was the only one that resulted in a death."

"Jason." He shook his head. "Loved that kid."

"You knew him well?"

"I've worked for Mr. Robeaux for fifteen years. Jason loved the business. He loved building design, creating structures that blended in with their surroundings. Not really my cuppa, but he had me sold—just the way he talked about it." He jerked his thumb toward the door, but Max had no idea what he was referring to. "That big oak in the courtyard? We were going to remove it. The law says we have to preserve as much as possible, a minimum number of trees and such, but not everything. Jason tweaked the plans so the tree could stay, and honestly, the whole place is going to look better for it. He would have made a terrific architect. Gordon Cho, our architect on the project, was particularly devastated by Jason's death. He'd been Jason's mentor for years."

"I haven't been able to reach the detective in charge of the case, so I don't have a copy of the police report yet. Do you remember what was taken?"

"Nothing—that's the thing, there was nothing to take. We'd surveyed the site, were ready to break ground and do some preliminary work that wasn't dependent on weather. I always thought the thieves were after something in the school, or that they saw Jason lurking around and thought he was a guard or whatever. I don't think we'll ever really know."

"Why was Jason here late on a Saturday night?"

"I have no idea. Honestly, Ms. Revere, I don't know why he was here, other than he loved the project and was excited to start working on it. We'd planned the ground breaking on Monday morning, by the oak tree. He and his uncle had spent most of Saturday here—oh, you know, the trailers had been delivered to the site the Wednesday before. Maybe the thieves thought something was inside."

A lot of maybes and what-ifs.

As Roger spoke, Max noticed that the secretary was typing slower. More deliberate. The girl was eavesdropping. Max wanted to talk to her, but not here, and not in front of Roger.

"What about security? About half the construction sites had some surveillance, the others took their chances with lock and key." Max was making up those statistics—she had no idea whether that was true, but she couldn't quickly think up another way to question Roger about Evergreen security.

"We were putting in a state-of-the-art security system—part of our agreement with the school and financing company. But it wasn't in at that point."

Roger grabbed his ringing phone. "Sorry, but this is a supplier, and he's been calling me for the last three minutes."

"Not a problem. I have another appointment. Thank you for your time." She stood and let Roger answer the phone. She walked over to the girl. There was no nameplate on her desk. "Hello," she said quietly. "Maxine Revere."

"Dru." She glanced at Roger. "I can't talk."

Max slipped Dru her card. From behind her, Roger said, "Dru! Take these contracts to the post office now. They have to be there by Monday." He put an express envelope on her desk. "Excuse us, Ms. Revere, we're really busy right now."

"I understand." She walked out and glanced back at the trailer as she drove off. Dru was getting into a bright yellow VW Bug with the package.

The secretary definitely had something to say. Max was going to find out what.

Max waited for Dru outside the closest FedEx office. What was truly odd about the exchange is that most businesses had a shipping account that picked up packages, even on Saturdays. It certainly wasn't cost-effective to send staff to the storefront for daily shipments. Had Dru not left the construction site, Max may not have gotten suspicious, but it was clear to her that Roger didn't want Max to talk to the secretary, and that made Max twitch. She sent David a message with Dru's license plate number, her employer, and her description, and asked him, when he had time, to dig up what he could on her, as well as Roger the foreman.

David sent back a message: Have any last names for me, or are you trying to make this particularly difficult?

She smiled and responded: Roger Lawrence. Nada on Dru.

Dru walked out of the shipping office and toward her car. Max was parked next to her, but Dru didn't notice her until Max stepped out of her car. The girl jumped, then glanced around.

"Hello, Dru."

"Did you follow me?"

"No." Not technically. She'd made an educated guess as to where she'd go to mail the package. Considering it was already preprepared in a FedEx pouch, it wasn't difficult. "Let's talk."

"I can't."

"Roger isn't here."

"Roger?"

"He didn't seem to want you to talk to me."

She shrugged it off. "He's just protective of Evergreen and Mr. Robeaux. There were a lot of people hanging around after Jason's murder. . . ." Her voice trailed off. "I have to get back."

Max walked around her car and put her hand on Dru's door as she tried to close it. "Dru, don't you want to know what happened to Jason?"

"He's dead. I'm sorry, really—I liked Jason a lot. But I don't want to get in the middle of this."

"You're already in the middle of this. If you know anything, you need to tell me."

"I thought you were a reporter, not a cop."

"Jason's family wants to know who killed him."

Dru stared at her like she was crazy. "I *really* gotta go."

"Dru, please—"

"I can't talk to you!" She was beginning to get scared and her voice increased in pitch. Several people looked over at them.

"You have my card. Call me. I promise you, keeping secrets will tear you up inside."

Dru drove so fast out of the parking lot she ground her gears.

Maybe Max should have a talk with Jessica today and follow up on the conversation that Jason's sister had with Detective Santini.

She looked at the time. Dammit, if she didn't go straight to St. Bede's, she'd be late for Kevin's funeral. Jason's murder was going to have to go on the back burner until tomorrow.

Chapter Seven

Max sat in the pew to the left of the altar during Kevin's funeral service at St. Bede's where she could watch who came to pay their respects. Anita Gonzales sat near the front with several elderly women who were probably Kevin's neighbors. In the back, as if to make a quick getaway, were a hodgepodge of casually dressed young people, who Max suspected were Kevin's coworkers at the coffee shop. A few other people dotted the pews of the large church, including Kevin's mother, Helen, who sat in the back and didn't talk to anyone except Jodi. His father hadn't shown up at all.

Mrs. O'Neal had aged greatly. They'd moved out of Atherton after the trial, and Max didn't think either Helen or Rob had truly recovered from the stigma of having a son on trial for rape and murder. Adding to this was Kevin's subsequent drug and alcohol abuse and now, his suicide. But the least Mrs. O'Neal could have done was to help Jodi deal with the mourners, with the church, with closing up Kevin's apartment. Max considered her selfish in her aloofness, letting a nineteen-year-old handle the pressure of the funeral. Mrs. Gonzales showed more sincere affection for Jodi and her grief than Jodi's own mother. It was clear that Jodi was trying to do everything for her brother, who had few people who cared whether he had a funeral or not.

Jodi had asked her to give a eulogy, but Max declined. What could she say about him? She hadn't spoken to him in more than a decade. And she certainly couldn't talk about his suicide or what she'd found in his apartment. She hadn't even told Jodi yet, waiting for the right time—which was not going to be now. The girl was a bundle of nerves as it was.

After the readings, Jodi walked up to the pulpit to talk about her brother to the church that sat six hundred and fifty, but currently had only thirty people in the cavernous space.

"Kevin was my big brother. He always supported me and encouraged me to pursue my art, even when our dad said I'd never make any money from my drawings." She tried to laugh, but it came out as a half sob. "We both loved books, shared them all the time. Kevin particularly loved science fiction and fantasy, and he used to laugh at my collection of Nora Roberts books. But you know, I always wanted the happy ending."

As Jodi spoke, the rear doors opened and William entered, taking a seat in one of the back rows. Though Saturday, he was dressed in a suit and tie and looked like the lawyer he was.

Before Lindy's murder, William and Kevin had never been best buddies, but they'd gotten along because they all hung out with the same people. In some ways, Lindy had been the glue of their extended group. She knew everyone. She organized every party, every event, served as class president, had been homecoming queen. Max often wondered if Lindy's life was one long checklist of things to do. Swim team, check. Student body president, check. Date the high school quarterback, check. Max wasn't surprised she hadn't maintained any friendships from high school, other than her cousin, because after Lindy was killed, no one in their school would talk to her because she sided with Kevin.

She'd never forget what Caitlin Talbot had said to her the first day of Kevin's trial, after the judge closed the courtroom to everyone except those who needed to be there. Max had been sitting on a bench outside, waiting for information. Caitlin was there—maybe to give testimony, or to show support to Mr. and Mrs. Ames, Max didn't know at the time—and stood in front of Max.

"Lindy always said you were her best friend, but you're showing your true colors now."

"True colors? What do you mean by that?"

"I hope Lindy haunts you for the rest of your life. She always defended you and stood up for you even when you were a total bitch. No one trusts you. You're siding with the enemy. A killer. Kevin raped and strangled her, and it's going to be proven in court. I told her you were white trash, and this proves it."

"Proves it?"

"You shouldn't have the Revere name. Oh, but wait, you don't even know what your real name is, do you?"

Caitlin had always been good at pulling out the most hurtful thing she could say and using it when a person was at their lowest. Max had always prided herself at being able to verbally defend herself, not letting Caitlin or anyone else get under her skin. But that day, it had. That day she'd wondered if she was betraying Lindy in some way. What else could she have done? Kevin looked her in the eye and swore he hadn't killed their friend. Max believed him.

William caught Max staring at him, and he looked away. Max took a deep breath and focused on Jodi talking about how Kevin used to take her to the park every Sunday afternoon, just the two of them, and how she'd never forget him pushing her higher and higher on the swings.

She half wanted Olivia Langstrom to show up at the funeral, but so far she was a no-show. Last night, when she couldn't sleep, Max had dug around and learned that Olivia was living in nearby Palo Alto, married to a college professor who looked at least fifteen years her senior.

For a long time, Max didn't believe Kevin about his odd relationship with Olivia, but she kept coming round to the fact that Kevin didn't have to tell her. She'd believed him when he told her—and the jury—that he'd been home when Lindy had been murdered. There was no reason to confess that he'd really been with Olivia, except that the guilt of his lie had been too much for him to keep to himself. Olivia had been part of their clique, the daughter of a respected and feared town council member; her testimony would have removed any cloud of doubt. In fact, Kevin would never have been charged had Olivia come forward.

The more Max thought about it, the more confused she was about why Kevin lied, why he told her the truth—if it was the truth—and why Olivia never spoke about that night. There was definitely something more to that part of the story, which now only Olivia Langstrom could answer.

What was Max thinking? That she was going to solve Lindy's murder? She would be here for weeks if she was going to do it right, and she wouldn't have any cooperation from the police or prosecution or survivors wanting the peace of knowing who killed their loved one. She never took on an assignment unless someone involved wanted her there. She'd gone against that rule once, and though she learned the truth, it had come with a hefty price.

Was she willing to let her own personal involvement and interest drive this investigation? Did she have a stake in the resolution?

Maybe she did. Maybe Lindy had been haunting her, just like Caitlin had wanted her to.

"And, and—" Jodi couldn't stop the tears when Detective Harry Beck blustered into the back of the room. The sight of the cop froze the college student.

Beck looked around and sneered, then caught Max's eye. Max knew exactly what he was doing—kicking Kevin at his own funeral. To make sure that everyone here knew that the police still thought Kevin was guilty—that he'd gotten away with murder.

And Jodi knew it.

Max couldn't bear to see the girl fall apart. She rose from her pew and walked up to the altar. She put her arm around Jodi to walk her back to her seat.

Jodi looked up at her with damp eyes. "Say something," she whispered. "P-please."

Max wanted to shake her head and leave the pulpit with Jodi, but this was Kevin's little sister. The same little sister he'd adored. Jodi hadn't done anything wrong. And funerals were for the living, not the dead.

What could Max say to make Jodi feel better?

"Sit," Max said and motioned toward the closest pew. Then Max stood behind the simple wood pulpit, adjusted the small mic upward, and looked out at the audience. She caught Helen O'Neal's eye.

"I haven't spoken to Kevin in twelve years," Max began, "but I came here for the same reason most of you came here—because his sister Jodi asked." She looked at William, who couldn't hide his stunned expression that she was speaking for Kevin.

"Kevin moved to Atherton when he was eleven, into the house down the street from my cousin William. I'd only been living here for a year, and I felt a kinship with Kevin. Two outsiders in a small town that didn't care much for outsiders.

"I don't know who Kevin was the day he died. But I know who he was growing up. He had a wonderful, wicked sense of humor. One year, right before the championship basketball game, William, Kevin, Lindy, Andy, and me"—Max didn't realize she'd said Lindy's name out loud

125

until it came from her lips—"broke into the Crystal Glen high school gym, our rivals, and filled it with four thousand helium balloons in blue and silver, our school colors." She smiled at the memory.

"And for Halloween when we were thirteen and too old for trick-or-treating, Kevin converted his garage into a haunted house. I was the Grim Reaper. Lindy did my makeup and it was damn good. Kevin was the killer clown. Andy was the executioner, William lured people in with his Ted Bundy charm, Lindy played a ghost." Suddenly, the humor from that night, five years before Lindy died and Kevin was accused of her murder, disappeared. "We raised money to buy turkeys for Thanksgiving for the food bank in Menlo Park, and Kevin gave his allowance for the month. Kevin never had a lot of money, and that he'd given what he really couldn't part with meant something. And then William, in true fashion, donated his allowance—much more than Kevin's. But it didn't hurt as much."

Max caught William's eye and wondered if he remembered that as well.

"The Kevin I knew would give you the shirt off his back. He helped everyone who asked, and even some who didn't. He never bragged about his accomplishments or that he mowed his next-door neighbor's lawn because her husband lost so much money in the stock market they couldn't afford maintenance. He wanted to fix everyone's problems, and he usually did it with humor. If you were sad or angry, he'd lighten the mood to where the pain was bearable or the anger extinguished."

Max wanted to say more, but there was no need to bring up the trial, or that she'd always believed he was innocent, or why she hadn't spoken to him in twelve years. None of that was relevant to the fact that he'd killed himself because he'd never recovered from the trial that destroyed his life.

"Kevin was a good person and a good friend."

Max left the altar and sat next to Jodi who looked at her with adulation that Max didn't want or deserve.

Had she truly been a friend of Kevin's, she would have forgiven him for lying to her. But lies were the one thing Max had a hard time forgiving. Hard? Impossible. Her mother had lied to her. Kevin lied to her. Marco lied to her. Even Lindy, their senior year, might not have outright lied, but she'd been keeping secrets. There was nothing she wanted more than to say it didn't matter, but it *did* matter, and Max couldn't change the way she felt. She wanted to, sometimes, because the darkness that filled her, a deep despair she never showed— that she could trust no one—tormented her.

Then she hadn't cared as much about *who* killed Lindy as supporting the person who *hadn't*.

Now she wanted to know the truth. About everything.

She wanted the truth for herself, and she was willing to live with whatever secrets she uncovered. She could expect no less from herself than she asked from the people who wanted her to find their truths.

She looked out at the audience again and William was gone. Mrs. O'Neal was silently crying. But Detective Beck glared at her. She stared back. He turned away first.

Max wondered what he knew about Lindy's murder that she didn't. And how she could make him talk to her.

Max pulled Jodi aside after she said good-bye to the few visitors. "Are you joining us at Mrs. Gonzales's?" Her tone was hopeful.

"I can't," Max said. She pulled the key from her purse. "Does this key look familiar?"

Jodi took it, looked at both sides, then returned it to her. "No. Why?"

Max put the key back into the zippered compartment inside her purse. "I found it at Kevin's yesterday."

"Does it mean anything? Maybe he had evidence and the people who killed him couldn't find the key and—"

"Jodi, I'm still looking into it, but Kevin committed suicide."

Jodi's bottom lip trembled. "But—you said—"

"I said I would find the truth." She didn't show

128

her the letter Kevin left. Max was angry at Kevin for doing this to Jodi, to his mother, to the people who cared about him. He was hopeless, maybe, but killing himself hurt his family more than him.

It was a coward's way out.

"Did Kevin rent a storage unit?"

"Not that I know about. I can look—"

"I'll do it." Max didn't know what she'd find inside, but she'd rather locate the facility herself. Especially since someone else was interested in whatever Kevin was doing.

"Go with the others, Jodi. I have some things to do."

"Thank you for everything." Jodi spontaneously hugged her, then walked back into the church.

Max had a long list of things to do, starting with checking out the Evergreen construction company, calling Detective Santini, and visiting Olivia Langstrom Ward.

She wouldn't call Olivia. The woman would no doubt avoid her. Best to show up on her doorstep. Max could more easily tell if someone was lying or obfuscating if she was face-to-face.

Detective Beck was getting into his unmarked sedan, but it was an official car according to the plates and the police lights in the grille. Max strode over to him and said, "I need a minute, Detective."

He closed the door on her, then rolled down his window. "You're a piece of work, Ms. Revere."

"So I've been told." She looked down at him through the open window. "You're on duty but you came to Kevin's funeral. For work?"

"To say good riddance."

"You could have done that at the morgue."

"You talked a good game in there, Maxine, but your friend was a killer. No sugarcoating that."

"He didn't kill Lindy."

"Case is closed."

"Technically, it's not."

"As far as I'm concerned, it is."

"Maybe that's why no one's in prison. You only looked at the evidence you wanted to see. I told you twelve years ago after the trial that Kevin was with Olivia Langstrom the night Lindy died. You never followed up on any other suspects."

Beck pushed the door open and Max stepped back. He pulled his hefty girth from his seat and said, "I don't need a big-shot New York reporter coming in here and fucking with my case. Kevin had no verifiable alibi, he and Lindy fought the night before, and several people testified that Kevin was livid that Lindy was involved with someone else. Classic if-I-can't-have-her-no-one-else-will punk attitude. I've seen it many times. I'm sure you have too."

"Don't you find it odd that no one admitted to being involved with Lindy?"

"Kevin had a key to the pool house where Lindy was killed."

"So did everyone on the varsity swim team." Not to mention these were teenage boys and girls—it would be easy to lose a key, or steal, or borrow . . .

William had been on the swim team. Duncan. Caitlin. Lindy. Lindy's older brother, who'd graduated several years before, had also been on the swim team.

"Stay away from this," Beck said. "You're not getting any cooperation from my office to dig into a closed case. I will not let you drag the Ames family though this shit again."

"Lindy had been my friend, too," Max said. Her voice cracked. She was too emotional. She had to find a way to step back, take herself out of the equation. She took a deep breath. "I don't suppose you have an update on the break-in yesterday in Kevin's apartment."

Beck snorted and got back in his car. "Give it up. Kevin O'Neal killed Lindy Ames. Thirty years of experience tells me I'm right. Besides, I *did* talk to Olivia Langstrom. She said she was home, with her family. Face it—Kevin deceived you. Maybe you're not such a fucking good reporter after all." He drove off.

Jodi approached and said, "What was he talking about? Why did he come?"

"The detective is an ass," Max said. "Don't worry about him." But her heart was racing and she felt hot and dizzy. Why would Beck lie about

131

talking to Olivia? Had he really followed up? Had Olivia lied? Had Kevin?

"Do you think—do you think that the police might open up Kevin's case? Do you think that they don't care if he was murdered because they still think he's guilty?"

Max didn't know how to sugarcoat the truth, so she said, "Jodi, from what I've seen in the police report, the coroner's report, and Kevin's apartment, the evidence shows that Kevin killed himself. The police are right about this."

Her bottom lip wavered. "But what about his laptop?"

"That's not the only item that's missing. I'm not leaving tomorrow, so I'll figure out what happened to his things."

"You think the key leads to his computer."

"Possibly. But—"

"Then why the message? The death certificate?"

She was asking questions Max was only beginning to seek answers for. "I'll find out," she repeated. "Kevin loved you and you were probably the only good thing in his life."

"He was so sad all the time," she said quietly. "Haunted." She took a deep breath. "Thank you for everything. I think—I think maybe I'm okay now."

"Good."

Jodi might be okay, but Max wasn't.

Max said polite good-byes, slipped into her

rental car, hooked her phone up to the Bluetooth, and left the church.

She was going to find out if Beck was telling the truth about Olivia Langstrom. If he was, then maybe—maybe—Max had been wrong. That Kevin was a killer and Max betrayed not only her family, but her best friend. How could she call herself an investigative reporter if she could be so easily deceived?

She'd also forgotten about the pool house and how the rules had been much looser on her small private school campus than on most schools. Max had played volleyball and had a key to the locker room. So did all the other athletes. Did the key Kevin left for her to find—because there was no doubt in Max's mind that Kevin intended her to find that letter and the key—fit the pool house? Were they assigned keys? If so, would that matter? Did the locker room have the same lock as the pool house?

Which meant that anyone, including Lindy, could have unlocked the pool house where she'd been killed and dropped into the Olympic-sized indoor pool.

Lindy drowned.

According to the testimony, Lindy had been raped, strangled, and dropped into the swimming pool after death. The chlorine and chemicals had destroyed any physical evidence that may have been on her body. She'd been clothed, according to the testimony that had been made public. Had the killer dressed her after raping her? Why?

Max had time and experience on her side now. She needed the trial transcripts, and she knew where she might be able to get them over the weekend—if she could reach Kevin's defense lawyer.

She first called the Menlo Park Police Department and asked to speak with Detective Nick Santini. She was a bit surprised when the receptionist said he wasn't on duty and asked if she'd like his voice mail or to speak to another detective. Max happily left a voice mail, pleased she didn't have to identify herself to the receptionist.

She spent the rest of the drive tracking down Kevin's defense attorney.

Gregory Q. Jones was no longer working for the legal defense company he'd started with. Now he was a corporate attorney, who would likely be moving in the same circles as William had he not relocated to Los Angeles.

His new law office refused to do anything but take a message, and Max didn't want to wait until Monday for the information she needed. She hesitated a moment before calling David. She really didn't want to disturb his weekend with his daughter, except he was a miracle worker in getting her the information she needed when she came up against a brick wall. Sometimes she didn't know how he did it. She'd once accused him of being psychic and he'd laughed. A rarity.

"David, I need a phone number. I'm sorry to—"

"Tell me what you need."

"Gregory Q. Jones. He's with Blanchard, Dixon, and Grossman out of Los Angeles, a firm specializing in corporate law. He specializes in criminal law. The weekend receptionist did nothing but take a message, but I'd really like to talk to him before Monday."

"Give me five minutes." He hung up.

David would text her the information, so Max felt comfortable leaving her car when she arrived at Olivia's house, instead of waiting for his call.

She didn't know how connected Olivia was with the people from their hometown, but Max hoped she had the element of surprise on her side.

A long stamped concrete walkway framed by evenly spaced and pruned rosebushes led to the wide stairs and stately Craftsman-style home in an historic neighborhood near Stanford University.

According to the Stanford faculty Web site, Christopher Wallingford Ward was a European history professor specializing in the Georgian and Victorian periods. Originally from Montecito, California, a wealthy community near Santa Barbara, Ward got his B.A. in history from USC, his M.A. at Boston College, and his Ph.D. in Georgian history at Stanford. He had several books published in the field and had been a tenured professor for the last five years. He was forty-seven years of age, but with a full head of salt-and-pepper hair, looked years older. Distinguished, but certainly not anyone Max expected one of her own thirty-something peers would marry.

The veranda was wide and had carefully placed cushioned outdoor furniture and potted plants that practically screamed staged. A little too picture-perfect for Max.

Or maybe she was reading into her recollection of the perfect Olivia Langstrom from the perfect home that Max had learned was less than "perfect."

Max rang the bell. Chimes, not a buzzer, rang through the house. Several moments later, the door opened.

Olivia Langstrom Ward had changed little in thirteen years. Her delicate features seemed more refined; her tall, willowy frame and pale hair suited her porcelain skin and gray, almost drab, conservative attire. But her ice blue eyes spoke the truth—she recognized Max immediately and knew exactly why she was here.

She looked scared. And angry. An interesting combination.

"Hello, Olivia."

"Maxine—wow." She glanced behind Max, toward the street. To escape or to determine if Max was alone?

"May I come in?"

"This isn't a good time."

"It's a nice afternoon. We can sit here on the porch." Max walked over to a chair and sat. Olivia stared at her as if she didn't know whether to follow or bolt the door.

Olivia glanced behind her into the house. Was someone home? Her husband? Staff? A friend? A child? Max didn't know what happened to Olivia after she left Atherton.

Olivia closed the door so quietly that Max barely heard it click shut. The skittish woman sat on the edge of the love seat, her long, slender hands clasped in her lap. "I don't know why you would come here."

"Your behavior is odd to me," Max said. "Considering we used to run around in the same circles."

"That was a long time ago."

"I have just one question for you. Why didn't you tell the police you were with Kevin the night Lindy was killed?"

Olivia stared at Max, frozen. It was clear she hadn't expected *that* question.

Max waited her out. She'd faced reluctant witnesses many times. Reluctant witnesses, scared witnesses, angry witnesses—people who didn't do the "right thing" just because it was the right thing to do. People who needed poking and prodding and confrontation before they gave up the truth.

"I—I think you're mistaken," Olivia said, her

voice barely audible. She looked beyond Max, her cheeks flushed, her right hand turning the narrow platinum and diamond watch on her left wrist around and around until Max wanted to slap her hand to make her stop.

"Kevin told me he was with you at Fake Lake the night Lindy was killed. You could have spared him a trial and the police would have focused on other possible suspects. You alone could have done that. But you remained silent."

"You need to leave."

"What secret is so dangerous that you can't even speak of it thirteen years later?"

"You wouldn't understand."

Max continued to stare at the spineless woman in front of her. "You were Lindy's friend, I know you cared about her. Your statement would have exonerated Kevin. They might have found her killer. So I will ask one more time: why didn't you go to the police?"

Olivia shook her head, twirling the watch slowly around her wrist.

"Did Detective Beck ask you, after Kevin's trial, if you had been with him that night?"

Olivia didn't need to answer the question, the surprise on her face told Max what she needed to know.

"Did you tell the detective that you hadn't been with Kevin? That you were home with your family?"

She nodded.

"Was that the truth? Or were you with Kevin at Fake Lake?"

She didn't make eye contact. "I was going to run away, from home. Kevin talked me out of it, but I didn't want anyone to know that he was with me."

"Does Anita still work for your parents?"

Olivia frowned and looked at Max quizzically. "Yes, why?"

"I'll ask her."

"No!"

So Olivia did have a voice louder than a whisper.

"It would be easier for you to tell me the truth now, but if you don't, I will figure it out. It's what I do, Olivia. And if Anita doesn't know, I'll ask your father."

The fear that crossed Olivia's face was so tangible that Max almost felt it. Everything Kevin had said was true: Olivia was terrified of her father.

The front door opened and Olivia jumped. Christopher Ward stepped onto the porch. "Olivia, I didn't know where you'd run off to."

He assessed Max, quietly curious, but he didn't know who she was.

Olivia rose, pulling herself together immediately. She was good at it—too good. This woman was a seasoned liar, Max would bet her career on it. "Christopher, this is Maxine Revere, a friend from school."

"Revere. I don't know the name."

"She's visiting from New York, just stopped by to say hello."

"It's not like you to neglect to offer refreshments, Olivia."

"She can't stay."

Very interesting conversation. Max wanted to contradict Olivia to make her squirm, but she didn't have time for games.

Max stood. "It was nice to meet you, Professor Ward."

"Will you be in town long?"

"A few days. Maybe a week." She smiled at Olivia. "Why don't you walk me to my car? I'll give you my contact information."

Olivia wanted to decline, but Christopher nodded and said, "I'll meet you back inside, dear. I'm ready for afternoon tea."

Christopher closed the door behind him and Olivia stared at Max. "Please, don't talk to my father."

"Walk me to my car," she repeated. Olivia reluctantly walked down the path with Max. "Ward is a bit old for you." He was certainly old for Max, and she didn't mind dating older guys. Just not *that* much older. "When did you get married?"

"Nine years ago," Olivia said quietly.

To each his own, Max said, though it wasn't lost on her that Christopher was very much like

Olivia's father, Bryant Langstrom. Refined, formal, controlling.

Max gave Olivia her card. "You didn't answer my question."

"It doesn't matter anymore."

Max stared at the woman. Olivia had always been aloof compared to the rest of the group, but she'd been smart, focused, and sweet. Very kind. That she and Lindy were friends had always seemed odd, except that they were both from old money and longtime Atherton families—but Lindy was nicer to Olivia than to anyone else. Maybe she knew about Olivia's home life. Lindy had her moments, when she wasn't completely self-absorbed.

"It matters."

Olivia shook her head. "You know I was with him, why does it matter if anyone else does? If he'd been convicted, I would have come forward."

"Why did you tell Beck that you *weren't* with Kevin?"

"The trial was over. It didn't matter."

"It did. If you told the truth, they might have looked at other evidence, other suspects. They might have found the person who really did kill Lindy."

"My father—he was there."

"When Beck questioned you?"

She nodded. "I wasn't eighteen, my father

insisted. I had no other choice. You don't know my father like I do."

Max didn't understand her reasoning. "Kevin's life was ruined. And then you went off to college while Kevin was ostracized and became a drug addict. You didn't even go to his funeral today."

Tears moistened the prim woman's eyes, and Max didn't know if they were genuine or an act.

"I loved Kevin. But I was more scared of my father."

"And you still are. Does your husband know?"

Olivia shook her head, her face reddening. "Don't come here again."

Max didn't make her any promises.

When Max drove off, she called Gregory Q. Jones's cell phone number. Normally, she'd be amused and a little curious as to how quickly David procured the information she needed; after her conversation with Olivia, she was agitated and not a little bit angry. A testament to growing up was that she hadn't lost her temper, much. It happened on occasion, but the passion of anger would have been lost on that woman.

"Jones," Kevin's defense lawyer answered on the third ring.

"Mr. Jones, this is Maxine Revere. I'm a friend of Kevin O'Neal, who you represented thirteen years ago in a capital case."

Pause. "I know who you are, Maxine. I can't talk about Kevin with you. I don't even represent him anymore, I moved to Los Angeles eight years ago."

"Kevin is dead," Max said. "I was at his funeral today."

"I hadn't heard. I'm sorry."

"I have some questions about his case."

"Are you asking as a reporter or as a friend?"

"Does that matter?"

"I don't know," he responded truthfully.

"A little of both." Max paused, then added, "Did you know that Kevin lied about his alibi?"

"No, I didn't. Do the police have new evidence?"

"Kevin told me after the trial that he was with a girl. Olivia Langstrom."

"The name sounds familiar, but I don't remember why."

"I talked to her today, and she admitted it, but didn't tell me why she never came forward."

"Maybe she was lying."

"Why would Kevin tell me twelve years ago, after the trial was over, that he was with her if he wasn't? I believed him when he said he was home alone."

Jones didn't say anything.

"You didn't," Max said.

"I had doubts."

"You thought he might be guilty?"

"I thought there was more than enough reasonable

doubt," Jones said. "I became a criminal defense lawyer because sometimes, the system is fucked. I don't care if my client is innocent or guilty, but I don't want to know. I want the cops to do their job right and I want the trial to be fair. Too often, they cut corners to get a conviction. Everyone is guilty, from the cops to the lawyers to the media. There was no hard evidence against Kevin. Only circumstantial evidence. If Lindy Ames wasn't the daughter of Gerald Ames who had the clout to move the DA into an indictment, the case would never have gone to trial."

"What did you think of the investigation into Lindy's death?"

"It was bungled from the beginning. Little of this made it into the trial, but the Atherton Police Department didn't call the MPPD for nearly twelve hours *after* the body had been found. The crime scene was completely contaminated. By the time MPPD got there, they could only work with what was left, and most I got tossed."

"Anything that pointed to Kevin?"

"I don't understand."

"Did any of the evidence you had tossed point to Kevin's guilt?"

"No—but it didn't exonerate him, either. It was neither—simply that all the evidence collected by Atherton PD was tainted because it was stored improperly and without a clear chain of custody. The judge agreed with me. The DA never fought it, and I believe it's because the evidence wouldn't have helped their case."

"Detective Beck showed up at Kevin's funeral. I had words with him. I was under the impression Kevin was the only suspect they pursued."

"I think they had another suspect but dismissed it when Kevin was handed to them on a silver platter."

Max's heart skipped a beat. "Who?"

"I have no idea. It was never turned over to me as part of discovery, and my investigator never found anything to support another killer—nor did he find evidence to support Kevin being guilty. It was clear that an anonymous tip to the police hotline told them that Kevin had been spotted in the high school parking lot the night Lindy was killed. Then the police learned about her fight with Kevin the night before, their previous relationship, that he was jealous because she was seeing someone else—"

"Someone the police never named."

"True."

"And you don't know who?"

"I do not. Kevin didn't know who it was, but said that's what they'd been fighting about."

"Mr. Jones, do you have your files on the case?"

"No."

Max's heart sank. She realized she'd just driven past her hotel. She made an illegal U-turn and headed back.

"I'd really like the transcripts."

"You do know that Kevin was obsessed with Lindy's murder."

"I didn't, not until his sister told me after he killed himself."

That information obviously surprised Jones. "He committed suicide?"

"Do you find that odd?"

"I feel bad because I was avoiding his calls for the last couple of months. He'd become so obsessed with the case I couldn't keep talking to him, it was taking too much of my time. Maxine, I gave Kevin my personal files."

"All of them?"

"Last summer. After so many years, I didn't see the harm—I never thought the police were going to uncover new evidence, or the DA was going to retry the case. I thought maybe reading my notes and the information would help him find closure."

"Do you have copies?"

"No. My old law office has the official files, including the transcripts, but my personal notes all went to Kevin. I'll call on Monday if you'd still like a copy of what they have."

"Yes, I would, thank you. And thank you for your time."

She sat in the parking lot of her hotel and stared out the window without seeing anything.

If Kevin had his attorney's files, where were

they now? Max had been through his entire apartment. They weren't there.

And if that revelation wasn't surprising enough, Max had one more surprise: not two minutes after she hung up with Jones, she got a call from Detective Santini, the cop in charge of the Jason Hoffman murder.

"Detective, thank you for returning my call."

"It's not every day I get a message from a national news reporter."

She couldn't read his voice, whether he had an opinion about her or not. "I'd like to talk to you about the Jason Hoffman homicide from last November. Do you have time?"

"Not today."

"Tomorrow?"

He didn't say anything for a minute. "I just put the case in the inactive file this week, so you can maybe understand why I'm curious about your interest."

"If you meet with me, you'll find out."

"I don't talk to reporters."

Max couldn't figure out where he was going with this conversation. "Detective, you returned my call—you didn't send me to Officer Corbett. If you weren't interested, you wouldn't have called. Twenty minutes. I've already done my background on the case. I just need a bit more information."

"I won't say anything on record. If you can't agree to that, this conversation is over."

"I didn't take this case to write an article."

"Oh?" He now sounded surprised—and intrigued. Good.

"I'm in town for a friend's funeral. Jason's grandparents asked me if I could find out the status of the investigation and maybe give them closure. Because I'm an alumni of Atherton Prep, I agreed to help."

"Hard to give closure when the killer hasn't been caught."

Max couldn't disagree. "If I write an article, I promise not to quote you without permission."

"Hmm."

"What does that mean?"

"It means nothing. Your reputation is mixed."

She laughed. "That's kind. Probably very mixed."

"Essentially, you're a bitch, but your word is gold."

"That's accurate."

This time Santini laughed. "I have time tomorrow, late morning. Make it noon."

"I'll buy lunch. Menlo Grill. I have one question first. During the initial investigation did you interview the young, blond secretary? Dru—I don't know her last name."

"Dru Parker. She had nothing to contribute to the investigation."

"I think you might want to talk to her again."

"Why?" His voice went from light to serious in a word.

"I visited the construction site where Jason was killed and talked to Roger Lawrence, the fore-man. When he saw me talking to Dru, he sent her on a needless errand. I tracked her down and she left, panicked."

"Reporters can have that effect on people." His tone was serious. "I have to go."

He hung up before Max could say anything else. She'd planted the information in his head that she wanted, and from the sound of his voice, he was going to follow up.

Chances are, if the cops showed up at Dru's house, she'd call Max in a panic. Wanting to get her story out to cover her bases. It had happened enough times in the past that Max had a good grasp of the people she could manipulate like this.

She was surprised that Nick Santini agreed to meet with her. After her confrontations with Beck and Corbett, she certainly hadn't expected anyone in the Menlo Park Police Department to be forthcoming with information. He'd been calm and even-tempered on the phone, but all business as soon as she brought up the secretary. She expected he would be the same tomorrow during their lunch meeting.

Maybe this weekend would end on a bright note after all.

Chapter Eight

Max stopped by her hotel room to drop off supplies she'd picked up earlier. A couple of trifold project boards, sticky notes, markers, tape. She'd bought enough to create expanded storyboards for each case, both Jason Hoffman and Lindy Ames. She didn't know when, exactly, she'd committed herself to Lindy, whether it was when she saw her death certificate and Kevin's accusation of drowning, Kevin's apartment and his suicide postscript, or at the funeral when she realized that she owed it to Lindy to find out the truth. But she wasn't going to back down.

Still, time wasn't on her side. She had a commitment with her cable station to cover the Bachman trial for them, and though she didn't need to be in New York on Monday like Ben wanted, she couldn't stay in California longer than a week. She feared that spreading herself between two cases was going to mean she solved neither, but she didn't see that she had a choice. She only hoped that Detective Santini cared and would pursue any threads she uncovered, because she didn't think she'd be here long enough to follow them.

She changed into a simple black dress and wrapped a multicolored blue and purple scarf around her shoulders. She didn't have clothes to last a week, which meant hitting both the dry cleaners and the mall—something she enjoyed when she wasn't pressed for time.

As she was getting ready to leave, she sat down at the hotel desk to straighten her notes when she saw the light on, indicating that she had messages. Had it been blinking, she would have noticed it as soon as she walked in, but the subdued orange light didn't attract her attention when her arms had been full of office supplies.

She pressed the message button, and instead of being sent to voice mail, the desk clerk answered.

"Yes, Ms. Revere, this is Assistant Manager Devon Hardy, how may I help you?"

"I have a message light on my phone."

"Yes, thank you, a message was called in. If you can wait one moment." Less than ten seconds later, the clerk came back on. "I have a message that was called in at four forty-five today."

That was ten minutes before she returned to her room.

"The caller didn't want to leave a voice mail, but asked that I take down this message. He said, 'The Ames case is closed. The family doesn't want you or anyone else reopening that can of worms. Go back to New York.'" Devon hesitated, then added, "He refused to give me his name. I'm sorry, Ms. Revere, but I have a standing order to give you all messages, even anonymous."

She always had that policy when she traveled because many people she interviewed felt uncomfortable sharing information, even their name and phone number. Many high-end hotels wouldn't forward an anonymous message.

"Thank you, Devon." She hung up.

The family doesn't want you . . .

Who'd called in the message? Detective Beck? Max didn't think so, even though he'd said almost the same thing to her at the funeral. He'd had no problem getting in her face before, he would have left a belligerent voice mail, or used his name with the threat of tossing her in prison. That it had come in not more than an hour after she left Olivia Langstrom Ward's house made Max wonder who Olivia called after she left. Was she still close to the Ames family? Or had Max been followed?

Or it could have been Andy. He'd been so . . . *odd* . . . last night when he crashed her dinner. He hadn't taken well her threat to stir things up.

Someone was speaking for the Ames family. Generally, Max avoided the immediate family during an investigation unless they had invited her in—until she got to the point of needing to talk to them. This time, however, she would make an exception. Though Gerald and Kimberly Ames would never get over Lindy's death—Max had rarely found a parent who found any true peace after their child was murdered—enough time had passed that Max didn't feel like she'd be intruding.

She wanted to know if the family told someone to send her out of town. If they simply didn't want to be reminded of the tragedy, Max could assuage their concern about what she was going to do—which, right now, was nothing but uncovering the truth. She had no intention of writing an article or a book on Lindy Ames's murder. But if either Gerald or Kimberly Ames was hiding something—information or evidence that pointed to a motive or killer—then Max wanted to make sure they knew she would find out exactly what they didn't want to get out. She might want to talk to them separately. She'd have better luck with Gerald than Kimberly—Kimberly had never particularly liked Max, but she truly hated her after Kevin's arrest. In many ways, Max couldn't blame her for that. If she was a mother, she might have felt the same way.

She left quickly, not wanting to be late to dinner, but needing to make a stop. Since she had decided to review Lindy's case, and everyone thought that's why she was here anyway, why be discreet? She'd find out who had left that message before the night was over.

Max did not take well to threats, subtle or otherwise.

She drove into the town of Atherton, nostalgia taking her by surprise.

Her childhood had not been all bad. And honestly, most people who didn't know her would think she was a fool to even think she had it rough. Certainly, she'd never wanted for necessities, at least from the time she was left with her grandparents. A beautiful home, a high-quality education, never any fear that she wouldn't be able to go to college for lack of money. She'd been given a car on her sixteenth birthday, and had traveled around the world before she was eighteen.

Sometimes, growing up, she'd felt guilty for wanting *more*. For wanting to know why her mother left her. Wanting to know who her father was—and why her mother had lied to her about him. Why the birthday cards stopped after she turned sixteen. Why her uncle Brooks hated her so much he could barely look at her. *Before* she'd exposed his adultery. *Before* she'd been given one-fifth of her great-grandmother's estate. He'd hated her from the minute Martha Revere showed up on Thanksgiving and surprised the family with Max.

She drove past the elementary school she'd attended through eighth grade, a small private school that fed into Atherton Prep. ACP was one of the most expensive but rigorous schools on the West Coast. Two decades before Max started, it had been an all-boys school that included boarding, but that had all changed. It had grown in size to more than five hundred students, but still graduated overachievers who went on to study at Stanford, Harvard, USC, MIT, and more. Lawyers, doctors, businesspeople, inventors, investors, authors, professors.

There were subtle differences between East Coast old money and West Coast old money that Max had never appreciated until she moved to New York City. One key difference was household staff—in the west, particularly the old money of Atherton, families didn't have full-time, live-in help. Max's great-grandmother Genie was the only person she knew who had two live-in household staff, but her stately mansion—where her uncle Brooks now lived with his much-younger second wife and five-year-old daughter—needed full-time maintenance. Max hadn't been there since the family, who controlled the Sterling family trust, voted to allow Brooks to live there. She'd been the sole dissenting vote—and Brooks thought it was because she didn't respect him.

She supposed that was part of it.

Max wouldn't have had to stay at a hotel if Brooks wasn't given Genie's home, even if temporarily. Genie had always wanted the grounds to be for the family—there were twenty-two rooms in the main house, a guesthouse with three bedrooms, an apartment over the garage, and the small two-bedroom caretaker's house. Now

Brooks treated it as if it were his property and Max dreaded seeing what he and his wife had done to it.

She was still trying to find a legal way to remove him from the house.

She couldn't bear to pass the Sterling property, so she drove the long way around until she reached the Ames spread on the far east side of town. There were no sidewalks in Atherton, but horse trails paralleled many of the streets, the yards of the spacious lots kept trim and tidy.

Marriage. Why get married when you lied and screwed around and manipulated? Max had no desire to get married. There was a blind trust involved that made her nervous. Not to mention she liked her freedom, independence, and opinions. Who was she supposed to marry, anyway? Marco? Certainly, the sex was amazing and she loved their heated arguments, but they drove each other crazy and he hated her career. Was she supposed to give up her career for him? For any man?

Or should she consider Andy, her first love, her first lover, whom she could no longer trust? They both knew it was over thirteen years ago, after Lindy was murdered, even if they pretended when they saw each other that the feelings were still there. Or maybe one of her occasional lovers who never seemed to rise to her expectations? Maybe her expectations were high, but why settle when settling would make her miserable? She wasn't unhappy being single.

Max pulled down the long, circular driveway to the front entrance of the Ameses' house. She stopped and got out. The house hadn't changed over the years. It was a two-story contemporary style that looked smaller on the outside than it was inside. Trees blended in with the home to make it almost appear to be a tree house. It was one of the nicest and largest parcels of land in a town that had primarily one- and two-acre lots. As kids, Max and Lindy had enjoyed exploring the grounds, most of which were landscaped with hidden nooks, pathways, and retreats. Lindy's three-story playhouse that had its own heat, air and electricity with a minikitchen and reading nook. Once it had been filled with little girl things, but as a teenager it had been Lindy's refuge.

Max was probably one of the few people who understood Lindy's need to escape her family, even within the bounds of a nine-thousand-square-foot house.

The Ames family had once owned 10 percent of Atherton. They'd sold some land and gifted other plots, including a hundred acres that made up the grounds for Atherton Prep, which adjoined the Ames property on the east.

Max rang the bell and waited for someone to answer.

Kimberly Ames had aged well, Max noted,

when Lindy's mother opened the door. Immediately, Mrs. Ames recognized Max.

"What are you doing here, Maxine?"

Her voice was as cold as her expression. Max wasn't surprised.

"I'd like to speak with Gerald, please."

Thirteen years ago, Max would never have called Mr. Ames "Gerald." She'd always addressed her elders properly unless she deliberately wanted to get under their skin; it was the way her grandmother had raised her—both tactics, of knowing how to be polite and how to manipulate. Eleanor Revere was the queen of manipulation.

"I'm certain he will not see you."

"Please tell him I'm here."

Mrs. Ames hesitated, realizing that she'd already slipped and let on that he was in the house.

"I'll wait," Max said.

Mrs. Ames recovered and held her head up, her haughty chin out. It had a sharp enough point to cause serious damage. "No, you will not. Neither of us want you here. You take pleasure in people's pain and suffering. You nearly ruined my marriage, you turned your back on your best friend, and you defended my daughter's killer. Leave. Now."

Max battled her natural inclination to verbally lash out at the woman who twisted the truth. She probably believed every word she said.

But Max wasn't here to rehash ancient history, she needed to know whether Gerald Ames had called her hotel.

"I received a message at my hotel from someone claiming to be speaking for Gerald. I think he should know about that."

A cloud crossed her face. Had she asked someone to leave the message? Disguised her voice to sound masculine? Maybe Gerald knew nothing about it.

"Just tell him I'm here," Max said, "if he doesn't want to talk to me, I'll simply make a note that he has *no comment.* Maybe you do?"

"You have audacity to show up here after everything, Maxine."

Max couldn't let Lindy's mother get to her. She stood still, kept her mouth closed.

Mrs. Ames closed the door without further comment and Max stood, waiting. Was Kimberly talking to Gerald? Trying to decide what to tell her? Whether to talk to her? Trying to figure out what she wanted?

Several minutes passed and Max grew annoyed. She rang the bell again, but no one came to the door. She became even more irritated when an Atherton police department car turned down the drive and parked behind Max's rental.

Kimberly Ames had called the cops.

Two uniformed officers, one male and one female, exited the patrol car. The male officer started up the stairs. "Ma'am, if you could please come off the porch."

"I'm waiting for Gerald Ames. Kimberly said she would tell him I was here." She hadn't. It was implied.

This comment seemed to surprise the officer, but he still asked her to step off the porch.

Max obliged. This wasn't the time to pick a battle with the police.

The female officer, D. Sherman per her nameplate, said, "We had a complaint of trespassing and harassment."

"Officer Sherman, I can assure you that I was neither trespassing nor harassing anyone."

"You're on the Ames property even though you were asked to leave," Sherman said.

The male officer, G. Grant, said, "Identification, please."

Max pulled her wallet from her purse and flipped it open to show her New York State driver's license as well as her press credentials. She didn't say anything.

"Please remove the license from the wallet."

Max complied, suddenly realizing that the two cops were named Sherman and Grant. She let out a short laugh, but didn't comment.

Grant took her license and walked back to his vehicle. He got on the radio.

Max stared at Sherman. She didn't find the need to make small talk or explain herself. They asked,

Max told them she wasn't trespassing, and that should be the end.

Except this was Atherton, and rules were oddly enforced.

Sherman seemed uncomfortable with the silence, and said, "You're a long way from New York."

No shit.

"Three thousand miles, take or leave."

The cop realized that Max was ridiculing her and she reddened. "Why are you here?"

"In California, or here?" She pointed to the ground.

"You know what I mean."

"You could be more specific." Max was antagonizing the cop, but she almost couldn't help herself. This was a ridiculous situation made more humorous by the fact that she was being interrogated but two cops who were younger than her named Grant and Sherman. Sherman obviously watched too many cop shows. Her hand rested on the butt of her gun, which irritated Max even more.

Grant came out of the car and spoke quietly to Sherman. Whatever he said, Sherman didn't like. She got back in the car.

"Ms. Revere, you're free to go."

"I know."

He frowned. "I need to ask you not to come back to the Ames house. The owners have requested that if you return, we arrest you for trespassing. I'm sure you don't want to embarrass your family by causing a situation."

Max stifled a laugh. "Oh, sweetheart, I live to embarrass my family."

"Ma'am, I think—"

"I understand, Officer Grant. By the way, you might want to help Officer Sherman with her geography."

Max drove away.

Chapter Nine

Eleanor Revere, Max's grandmother, lived only a mile from the Ames family, at the end of a long, meandering cul-de-sac. Eleanor had always liked modern, contemporary architecture, but a sign of the times when she and Max's grandfather designed the house more than forty years ago was the influence of Frank Lloyd Wright—both modern and nostalgic. The smooth, linear style of Wright also appealed to Max. Guests often asked if Wright himself had designed the house, and Eleanor was always pleased. "No," she'd say, "but we asked the architect to adapt Wright's style to our unique landscape and the original frame of the house." She'd also doubled the footprint of the single-story house, though it was impossible tell from the outside how large the home truly was.

Max could practically hear Eleanor lecture: *We don't flaunt our wealth; it's uncouth.*

When Max rang the bell, it was William who answered the door. He looked relieved.

"Did you think I would bail?" She kissed him on the cheek.

"Of course not," he said.

"Then don't look so concerned."

In a low voice, William said, "The chief of police just got off the phone with my dad. Why were you at Gerald Ames's house?"

"The rumor mill is working double-time." Max wasn't surprised that Chief Clarkson called Brooks; she just thought she'd have more than fifteen minutes to figure out what to say to her family.

The large, tiled foyer flowed seamlessly into a lowered gathering room that, weather permitting, opened onto a rose garden surrounding a fountain and a large koi pond. Max had always loved the fountain, the sound of running water was soothing. She'd spent many hours on the bench behind the fountain, where she couldn't be seen from the house. Reading, thinking, crying when her mother forgot her birthday. Again.

The Reveres had lived here for more than fifty years. Her mother had been raised in this house. It was a spacious one-story, not a grand mansion with sweeping staircases, but quietly appointed with lots of glass, pinpoint lighting, polished floors, hand-crafted rugs, and every piece of furniture picked and placed for that exact spot.

Max breathed in and her mouth watered at the authentic Sicilian smells. "I'm so glad Regina is still here."

Regina had been her grandmother's house-keeper for fifteen years. She worked nine-to-five and often prepared meals, especially when James Revere was still alive and Eleanor was more involved with charity work.

Conflicting feelings of nostalgia, regret, and anger—anger Max thought she'd left behind—flitted to the surface. She'd never hated her family, but the expectations and fundamental disagreements had weighed on Max her entire life. Though her grandparents hadn't made her feel inadequate for being born out of wedlock or abandoned by her mother (those subtle attacks were reserved for her uncle Brooks), Max sensed she was expected to be faultless, as if required to repent for her mother's many transgressions.

"Don't avoid me," William growled.

"I hadn't planned on it," she said. She smiled at him, bemused. "Why do they think I was at Gerald's house?"

"Maybe this dinner was a bad idea."

Could William have left the message at the hotel? It wasn't like him—not threats. He'd come to her personally, using his leverage as her closest friend in the family.

Except she was about to destroy their relationship.

"I have a question for you."

"Can it wait?"

She glanced down the hall. "What are you so nervous about?"

"I'm not."

William was most certainly nervous.

"Why didn't you tell me you were at Lindy's house the night she was murdered?" Max hadn't meant to ask the question that way. She'd planned to ask if he'd told the police he'd been there. She'd been questioned, just like all of them—the police asked about the last time she'd seen Lindy, who she'd been with, her state of mind, if she was having an argument with anyone, who did Max think might have killed her. Though she wasn't in the room when William was questioned, he would have been asked similar questions.

"I wasn't," he said without hesitation.

"Your car was ticketed down the street from Lindy's house three hours before she was killed. That never came up in the trial, and it never came up in any of our conversations."

"Shh! Dammit, Max!"

"Why did you hide that information?"

"I knew you didn't come just for Kevin's funeral." He ran a hand over his gelled hair, a bit long, but not too long, like Max always imagined Jay Gatsby would look.

"I did." She caught his eye. "But I changed my mind."

He paled. "Max, please—"

"You didn't answer my question."

"Why does it sound like you're interrogating me?"

"It's a simple question."

Caitlin walked down the hall, her heels clicking purposefully on the tile. "I can hear both of you all the way in the library." She locked arms with William then looked up at Max. Even in her heels, she was several inches shorter. A petite, blond, blue-eyed Kewpie doll with the fangs of a viper. "Hello, Maxine. We're so glad you're not in jail, and that you could make time for your family. Perhaps you and William could save your arguments for later."

If there was a picture next to the definition of "passive-aggressive" in the dictionary, Caitlin Talbot Revere would be it.

One well-placed question at the dinner table and Max would know the truth, but she hadn't seen William with such a deer-caught-in-the-headlights expression in her life, even when they were fourteen and Aunt Joanne caught them sneaking back into the house at dawn after they'd gone to a concert at the Frost Amphitheater, after expressly being told they couldn't go.

If he wasn't hiding something, why hadn't he shared the information with the police?

Maybe he had and they'd dismissed it. But if they had, Kevin's attorney should have brought it up in court because it would have cast doubt on Kevin's guilt as well as highlighted the errors in the initial police investigation. Max had never looked at the case files as a reporter because she'd washed her hands of Kevin twelve years ago. She hoped Kevin's attorney could get her a copy of the files, because it would take much longer for her to pull all the information from the police department and courthouse.

William had locked down his emotions since Caitlin's interruption. He gave Max a half smile. "Truce."

She nodded curtly, but they both knew this conversation wasn't over.

"After you," William said.

Max walked down the hall, passed the elegant white living room with its dark antique furniture, the stately French dining room that was set for nine—who else was coming tonight?—the hall that led to her bedroom suite, the two rooms that had once been her mother's. The library, where the family liked to gather before dinner, was in the far corner of the house, two walls of bookshelves and two walls of floor-to-ceiling windows that looked out onto the infinity pool on the side and a hundred-year-old oak tree in the middle of the large lawn in the back.

The library was Max's favorite room in the

house because it was the most lived-in. Before his death when she was fifteen, her grandfather spent most of his waking hours in this room watching baseball—his one, true love—and reading military history books—his second love. Max had often hidden in here with her grandfather, he at his desk, she on the leather couch with her homework or a book.

Stepping inside brought back a rush of warm memories, reminding her that her childhood was marked with quiet joy she sometimes forgot.

She glanced at her grandfather's favorite chair, half expecting him to be seated there, reading. Of course he wasn't, he was sixteen years buried, but Eleanor hadn't moved it from its original spot. Though Eleanor was a hard woman who was critical of everyone in the family, including her husband, she had truly loved James Revere.

William handed Max a glass of wine.

She sipped. It was a perfectly chilled private reserve chardonnay. "Where's Brooks and Grandmother? Still on the phone with the police chief?" She smiled.

Caitlin tilted her chin up. "You should be more concerned. This is serious."

Max rolled her eyes.

Two little boys, Tyler and Talbot, ran into the room, each carrying a Maltese. "Auntie Max! Grams got *two* dogs!" the older of the two, four-year-old Tyler, exclaimed. He said "auntie" like

"Annie." She adored her nephews, and the worst thing about living so far away was that she rarely got to see them. William had brought them to visit her last September in New York, but she hadn't seen them since.

Last year, her grandmother's precious Pomeranian had died at the old age of sixteen. Before that had been a Maltese, which Max had adored. She'd never had a dog with her mother because they moved around so much, but she missed Eleanor's pups.

"Boys," Caitlin said, "I told you to stay in the playroom."

"But Auntie Max is here—" Tyler said.

"Don't argue with me."

Max walked over and led the boys out of the library. "I want to see the dogs," she said. "Let's hang out in the playroom. Less stuffy." She glanced over her shoulder and caught the glare from Caitlin. Max stuck her tongue out at her cousin-in-law, and caught a half grin on William's face.

The playroom was filled with state-of-the-art toys and classic games. The boys put the dogs down—the pair were about nine months old. The puppies immediately began wrestling and the boys laughed. "What are their names?" Max said, though she already knew because her grand-mother had sent her pictures. She knelt on the floor with the boys and the dogs sniffed her, then licked her hands.

"Winston and Queen Anne," Tyler said. "They're brother and sister."

"I wish I could take them home with me."

"Me, too," Talbot said. His little three-year-old voice had a slight lisp, which Max found cute. She wasn't much for babies, but she loved the innocent sweetness of young kids. She wished Tyler and Talbot could stay this young forever.

"Why don't you get a dog, Auntie Max?"

"I travel a lot for work. It wouldn't be fair to a dog to keep him locked up or in a kennel when I wasn't home."

"Yeah," Tyler said as if he completely understood. And maybe he did.

Max looked up and saw Eleanor standing in the doorway. She had an odd expression on her face, almost wistful, until she saw Max looking at her.

"Maxine," she said.

"Hello, Grandmother." She said to the boys, "I can't play tonight, guys, but I'll come see you before I go back to New York, okay?"

Tyler gave her a spontaneous hug. "Daddy said we can visit you again. Right? Can we?"

"Of course you can." She got up and left the boys to play with the dogs. "Handsome pups." She kissed her grandmother on the cheek. She looked both regal and disapproving. "I hear you've been chatting with the police chief."

"I don't know where to begin," she said, closing the door. "The police, Maxine!"

"Kimberly overreacted," Max said.

"You know better than to talk to that woman," she said. "After the scandal—you should never have been there. You're lucky she didn't insist on having you arrested."

Max laughed. She couldn't help it. "Scandal?" They weren't talking about Lindy's murder. They were talking about what had happened three years before that. "Really, Grandmother. Are affairs even scandalous anymore?"

Eleanor reddened. "What are you doing here?"

"William invited me to dinner."

"You know what I mean."

Eleanor was seventy-nine, but looked and sounded a decade younger, owing her health to remaining active and eating properly. But suddenly she looked weary, and Max felt a pang of guilt for putting the age on her grandmother's face.

"When I arrived yesterday morning, I had no intention of opening an investigation into Lindy's death," Max said as they stepped back into the library. "Circumstances have changed."

Eleanor didn't say anything. Brooks was there, but his wife was not. William glared at her, and the intake in Caitlin's breath sounded rehearsed. Eleanor crossed to the bar and mixed herself a martini. Max waited for her to finish straining the chilled alcohol into her glass. But she didn't sip.

"William," Eleanor said, "take your wife to the dining room."

"But—" Caitlin began. William grabbed her by the arm and half dragged her out. He closed the library doors behind him.

"Grandmother, I don't think this is your business." She looked at Brooks who stood like the Tin Man in the corner. "Nor yours, Uncle Brooks."

"Anything that touches my family is my business." Eleanor picked up her drink and took a long sip. She crossed to the windows and looked out into the lit backyard. "When I heard Mr. O'Neal committed suicide, I feared you'd do exactly what you're doing."

"Kevin didn't kill Lindy."

"You don't know that."

"I do."

"You were always overly confident," Brooks said.

"Why don't you join William and Caitlin in the dining room?" Max said, mimicking her grandmother.

"Watch your tongue, Maxine."

"Don't start with me, Brooks." She wished her grandmother would send him packing, because his presence was making the entire situation worse that it would have been.

Instead, Eleanor ignored the exchange as if it were between two of her children. "Let's assume

172

that he didn't kill poor Lindy," she said. "What good could come from digging into the past? What do you hope to accomplish?"

Max was perplexed on how to answer her grandmother's question. "Isn't the truth a good enough reason?"

Eleanor turned to face her. With her chin up she said, "No."

"I think it is."

"I don't think it's the truth you're after."

"I'm always after the truth."

Brooks stepped forward. "You simply want to embarrass me, embarrass the family."

Max said to Brooks, "You? Yes." She shouldn't have. She should have bitten her tongue, but Brooks always brought out the worst in her. She said to her grandmother, "My goal is not to embarrass anyone."

"Being called by the chief of police is embarrassment enough! But you go beyond the pale. Dredging up the past, hurting people, digging around into other people's business."

Max laughed. "You're one to talk."

Her grandmother looked grossly offended. "I don't gossip."

"No, but you use information to your advantage."

"To protect my family when necessary. That includes you, Maxine."

"I don't need your protection, Grandmother."

"I wasn't going to let you go to jail." Her voice cracked, just a bit, but Max realized that Eleanor was worried about her fate. They had rough patches—many—but Max understood Eleanor. Too well.

"I appreciate that, really, and you know I love you." Family was complicated. She could be so angry with them, with one or all of them, but she still loved them. Her grandparents had treated her the same as William and all her other cousins. She would never forget that. But that didn't mean she was going to let her grandmother cover up a crime.

"Kimberly called the police out of spite," Max said. "She doesn't like me, and it has less to do with Kevin than it does with me exposing her infidelity—"

She looked pointedly at Brooks. Then she smiled.

He took a step toward her and raised his hand.

Hit me. Please hit me.

"Brooks!" Eleanor said.

He turned around and drained his Scotch before pouring a double.

"Hypocrite," Max said to him. "You're just mad that Aunt Joanne walked out and Kimberly's husband forgave her. She probably told him it was just you—while you couldn't very well tell Aunt Joanne that Kimberly was the only woman you screwed—"

"Maxine! Enough!" Eleanor crossed over to her, put a hand on her shoulder. "You need to stop."

She took a deep breath. Brooks always did that to her. Brought out her cruel streak.

"I don't know why Kimberly called the police," Max said slowly. "There was no reason to, other to intentionally try to embarrass our family. Besides, I can take care of myself, I've been a reporter for a long time."

Eleanor winced when Max said reporter.

"You're going to damage our family," Brooks said, his voice vibrating in anger.

"Did someone in our family kill Lindy?"

Her grandmother gasped audibly. "Of course not!"

Brooks added, "This has nothing to do with murder. Leave this alone."

It clicked. "You know about the parking ticket."

Eleanor didn't acknowledge her statement. "I said leave it, Maxine."

"No."

"It's your immature, misplaced arrogance that brought you here," Brooks said "You have a psychopathic need to scratch at old wounds. To prove you are better than others? To embarrass and mock your friends and family?"

"Brooks," Eleanor began, but he was on a roll.

"You're just like my sister," he continued, "selfish to your core. You don't care about the family name, who we are, what we stand for in this community!"

"The only thing I despise about my name," Max said through clenched teeth, "is that I share it with you."

"Enough," Eleanor said. "Please."

"I'm sorry, Grandmother," she said.

"I can't let you tear apart our family."

"Clearly"—Max finished her wine—"I should leave."

"Go back to New York," Brooks said.

"Kevin O'Neal killed himself because his life was destroyed after being accused of murder. After thirteen years he still couldn't exonerate himself. He didn't kill Lindy. I'm not leaving until I find out who did."

Eleanor's hand was shaking. What did she know? Who was she protecting?

William?

Max's chest tightened. Could she do this if her own cousin, her friend, was guilty? Could she put her faith in William that he hadn't killed Lindy, the same faith she'd put in Kevin's innocence?

Why was he at Lindy's house the night she was killed?

Max put her wineglass on the bar and walked out. She heard the boys laughing down the hall and yearned to be that carefree again, to roll on the floor with puppies. She passed the kitchen, where

William and Caitlin were talking quietly, their heads close together. Max glanced at them, wanted to force William to tell her the truth about that night. She wanted to believe anything he told her, but knew that she'd have to prove it. He'd been lying for too long.

She walked out of the house without saying anything.

"Maxine?"

She almost ran into Archer Sterling, her grandmother's brother. "Uncle Archer!" She gave him a hug, surprised. "I didn't expect you."

"You're not leaving so soon?"

"I—it's not a good night," she said lamely. Archer was eighty-one, and though like Eleanor he looked and acted younger, she didn't want to trouble him with the drama with Brooks. "How's Aunt Delia?"

"She wanted to come, but since her hip surgery, mobility is difficult. I hope you'll come to the house and see us before you return to New York."

"I'd like that. Thank you." She squeezed his hands. "I heard about the Sterling Pierce Sports Center. It's wonderful what you and Jasper Pierce put together."

"I wish I could take credit, but it was Jasper's idea. He and Jackson graduated together, I've known him since he was a boy. He had the vision for the project, he needed matching funds. I was glad to do it."

"I'd like to talk to Jasper about the project. Do you have his contact information?"

Archer pulled out his BlackBerry and pressed a few buttons. "Hmm, my eyesight is fading. Can you read this?"

She took the phone and copied down Jasper's private cell phone and address. "Thank you," she said, and handed the phone back to Archer. "Give Delia my love, please."

"You certain you can't stay?"

She smiled but shook her head. She waved good-bye, and walked out to her car.

Max had just turned the ignition when William tapped on her window. She rolled it down.

"Uncle Archer wants me to convince you to stay. What did you say to him?"

"Nothing. He doesn't need to know what an ass your father is."

"Maxine."

She pinched the bridge of her nose. "Jet lag."

"Max, what's going on?"

She looked up at him through the open window. "I want the truth. Now."

He glanced at the house, then back at her. "Don't do this."

She didn't say anything.

"Look, it was a long time ago."

"Did you kill Lindy?"

He blanched. "No! God, no."

There was something in his face that made

Max believe him, but she didn't know if she could trust her instincts when she had been so close to him growing up. She truly liked her cousin, warts and all, and maybe their history was clouding her judgment.

She turned off the car. "Why did you lie about being at Lindy's the night she was killed?"

"I didn't lie. I was never asked."

"Excuse me?"

"Until you brought it up today, I didn't think anyone knew I was there. The police didn't ask me, no one did."

"But you talked to them."

"I didn't kill her. Why would I tell them about seeing her that night and put myself on the hot seat?"

"Because it's evidence. Maybe you saw or heard something—"

"I'll tell you the truth, but it has to remain between us."

Max didn't want to agree, but the reporter in her couldn't help it—she had to know the truth.

"Agreed, unless you lie to me."

He shifted uncomfortably, then squatted next to her car so he could lower his voice. "Lindy and I were sleeping together."

Suddenly, everything made sense. Lindy being so secretive. Picking fights. Not wanting to spend time with her. Lindy knew Max would have been furious, at both of them. Not because she would have cared that they were dating, but because they'd both publicly been dating other people. The dishonesty of the situation would have angered Max more than anything, and she'd have had a hard time keeping her mouth shut.

"How long?"

"On and off—about a year."

A year. During the time Lindy was with Kevin.

"It just kind of happened."

"A year—you went to the prom with Caitlin. I caught you two—" Her stomach rolled uncomfortably. "Shit, William."

"I left Lindy's bedroom at a quarter after twelve. We'd had sex, but she was preoccupied and we fought. She'd broken up with Kevin, I'd split up with Caitlin after the prom, I thought—well, I thought maybe it might work between us. I cared about Lindy, you know that. But—I don't know. She said we were done. We were both going away to college, she said she wanted a clean break. She seemed angry with me about nothing. So I left."

"And the ticket?"

"I paid it, didn't think anyone knew about it. No one asked me about it."

"Eleanor knows. So does your father."

William couldn't hide the surprise on his face. "How?"

"She knew the police kicked me off the Ames property less than fifteen minutes after it happened. Chief of Police Ronald Clarkson has been here for a long, long time. Since before my mother dumped me here over twenty-one years ago."

"You're not going to say anything, you promised," William said as Max put the car in reverse.

"You know, William, that you and Lindy fought makes you a suspect. It would have thirteen years ago."

"I didn't kill her. I swear to God."

She wanted to believe him. She could hardly breathe thinking he could have done that to Lindy.

"As long as you're not lying to me, I'll keep the information to myself. But if you're lying, William, by what you say or don't say, all promises are off."

Chapter Ten

Max parked her rental across the street from Atherton Prep because it was technically in the city of Menlo Park and not Atherton. There was no street parking allowed in Atherton except in rare, designated areas. After her run-in with Grant and Sherman she didn't want to tempt fate. And parking in the construction area after seeing the security in place, no way. She wasn't even certain she wouldn't be caught on camera along the west fence, except that she hadn't seen any outside of the construction zone.

She took off her colorful scarf and slipped on the black blazer she'd worn to Kevin's funeral. No reason she needed to stand out, considering that now she truly intended to trespass.

One of the benefits of having gone to school at ACP was that Max knew all the secret pathways. The school itself was a sprawling campus with six separate, architecturally attractive buildings. The two original buildings, which had been built more than a hundred years ago and renovated to maintain their old, early twentieth-century appearance, housed the administration offices and the English classes. The other four buildings, built over time from the late 1940s until the most recent state-of-the-art math and science lab that had been built during Max's first year at ACP, highlighted the contemporary style of the decade in which they were built, while keeping details of the past.

The sports complex was on the opposite end of the campus, and that's where Max was headed, but she hadn't wanted to park near the construction entrance because of the security cameras she'd noted when she spoke with the project manager earlier. Instead, she walked along the bike path that wove around the perimeter. Max stayed on the side, among the elm and birch trees, until she reached the backside of the old gym.

She surveyed the buildings looking for security

and found it—every door to the old gym was secured with a keypad. Definitely new since she'd graduated.

Max walked around the back of the gym to where a door led to a corridor connecting the other athletic buildings, including the locker rooms and the indoor swimming pool, where Lindy's body had been found.

Max had come for one reason—she wanted to see how close Lindy's backyard and clubhouse were to the pool. She walked from the pool house to the back fence. It was thick with trees, even though the grounds and foliage were well groomed. Fifty feet to the fence.

Max took out her cell phone and retrieved a map of the area. She pinpointed the Ames house and the school. A blue dot showed Max where she was standing, the wonders of GPS. It wasn't accurate to the foot, but it was close.

The Ames property shared a rear property line with the school. The Ames's vast backyard was on the other side of this stone fence.

Max walked along the ten-foot-tall fence. It would be difficult to scale and impossible to see through. Plus, she didn't know if the Ames family had security on the fence, but she had to assume that they did.

She stopped walking and pictured Lindy's clubhouse, her sanctuary, and where it was located in relation to the yard. She looked again at her map and walked back toward the pool house, then stepped away from the fence and looked up.

It was dark, the security lighting from the school building shining down, not up at the trees. But there was a structure there, surrounded by a dense group of redwood trees. The trees were so familiar, Max was certain she was right, but she needed to confirm her memories. It had been a long time since she'd been a regular visitor to Lindy's clubhouse.

Max pocketed her phone and surveyed the area around her. No bright lights, no sign that anyone was around. There were several magnolia trees to the left, not directly behind what Max believed was the clubhouse, but close enough that if she got high enough, she'd be able to confirm she was right.

Climbing trees was like riding a bike, but unwise to do in heels. She slid out of her two-inch pumps and pulled herself up to the first thick branch. Her heart raced, exhilarated, reminding her of when she first became an investigative reporter. When she didn't have the obligation of the cable show, when she didn't have staff who depended on her, when she didn't have any responsibilities to anyone, only to herself and her drive to learn the truth. She'd been reckless, brash, and free.

She missed it.

She climbed higher than she needed to, mostly

because she could and the sensation of height was freeing. The headache that had plagued her since she'd left the Ames house had disappeared and in a moment of clarity, Max saw what she might have been doing had she said no to Ben two years ago. More undercover work. Fewer responsibilities. More freedom.

Max didn't like supernatural anything, from movies to television to the plethora of ghost hunters and paranormal activities people claimed to have witnessed. But she'd been drawn to the television show *The X-Files* because of Fox Mulder's tagline: "The truth is out there." She didn't believe the truth was in outer space or in some military complex doing experiments on aliens, but she did believe that the truth was knowable, that it would set those trapped by lies free.

And from her vantage point halfway up the magnolia tree, Max saw the truth.

Lindy's clubhouse was directly behind ACP's pool house. Behind the clubhouse, Max could see the lights from the Ameses' sprawling home. Ground lighting, lights in the trees, lights from the deck, lights from the windows.

And behind the house, a well-lit, black-bottomed swimming pool.

What if Lindy had died in her own pool and someone moved her body to the pool house? Why? Forensic tests could have proven which pool she'd drowned in. But because her death had been ruled strangulation, had either pool been tested? Television shows showed the cops and CSIs going through every possible permutation of the crime, leaving no stone unturned, but reality was much, much different.

Kevin's attorney had said the Atherton Police Department had bungled the case and not turned it over to Menlo Park for twelve hours after the body was discovered. If there had been evidence in Lindy's clubhouse, had it been removed or contaminated? Not by the cops specifically, but perhaps by someone who shouldn't have had access. There was no way of knowing, short of tracking down the responding officers and asking them. And that would hardly work, considering Max's accusations of incompetence wouldn't make them willing to talk.

Max's instincts twitched again. If William was telling the truth and he'd left Lindy alive at twelve fifteen the night she died, there was no reason for her to go to the high school pool. She had her own swimming pool. Her parents hadn't been home. Her older brother was in college on the East Coast. So why would she leave her property to meet someone?

Yet, if someone had strangled Lindy to the point of unconsciousness on her own property, how would they get her body to the high school? If the killer was trying to destroy evidence, why not dump the body in her own pool? Had he or she intended to make it look like an accident?

What had seemed so clear a moment before was now murky.

Max's vibrating phone startled her. She balanced her body against the trunk and pulled it out.

"Hello," she answered, her voice low and quiet.

"Um, is this Maxine Revere?"

"Yes."

"This is Dru Parker, we met this morning at Evergreen? Why did you call the police?"

Max had pegged the situation from the minute she talked to Nick Santini. She would have patted herself on the back if she wasn't up a tree.

"I'm a reporter. I talk to a lot of people."

"That detective was waiting at my house when I got off of work! Do you know what this means?" She sounded both angry and scared. "You're messing with my *life*. I'm freaked. I told him I didn't know what you wanted, but that you scared me because you were following me."

"I didn't follow you."

"You know what I mean. If they find out the police are talking to me—oh, God, I don't know what to do!"

"So you do you know something about Jason's murder?"

Her voice cracked. "You gotta help me. I'm scared." She sniffed loudly and that's when Max realized Dru was on the verge of hysterics.

"Dru, calm down."

"I can't!"

"Yes, you can. Where do you live? I can meet you there."

"No! I have roommates."

"Dru, listen to me," Max said sternly. "I'll help you, but you have to get your act together. *Calm down.*"

"Okay, okay," she repeated.

"Where's someplace you feel safe?"

"I'll go visit my mom—that's it."

"Hold it. If you have information about Jason's murder, you need to tell someone. If his killer thinks you're a threat, you're in danger *unless* you tell someone what you know."

"I'll tell you—I don't know who killed Jason, okay? But there were some weird things going on the week he died, and I think it might be connected, okay? But I don't know how . . ." Her voice trailed off.

Max thought she'd hung up. "Dru?"

"My mom lives in San Francisco. I'll meet you at the Caltrain station in Redwood City—you know where that is, right? By Sequoia High?"

"Yes."

"Okay. Good. There's a Starbucks there. Twenty minutes."

"Wait for me," Max said. "It'll take me thirty."

She hung up and looked down. Getting down from the tree was going to be harder than climbing up.

Chapter Eleven

It took Max thirty-five minutes to get out of the tree, walk to her car, and drive to the Starbucks across from the Caltrain bus terminal in nearby Redwood City. She didn't see Dru when she entered. She waited a few moments in case the girl was watching from outside, then Max walked to the counter and ordered a half-caff latte.

She asked the clerk, "Did you see a girl about nineteen or twenty with long, straight blond hair and brown eyes?"

He stared at her blankly. "We get a lot of people in here, ma'am."

"She would have been here not more than twenty minutes ago."

He shrugged.

Without looking up from the machine, the barista asked, "What was her name?"

"Dru."

The woman nodded. "Iced white mocha with caramel. First drink I made after my break."

"Did you see her leave?"

"No, sorry."

"Thank you." Max put a five-dollar bill in the tip jar, collected her drink, and sat down at one of the tables where she could watch the door.

A text message from David popped up.

Evergreen was on the verge of bankruptcy before Jasper Pierce put together the deal with Archer Sterling and Cho Architectural. There was no bidding process—seems odd.

Definitely worth noting. And based on what Uncle Archer said tonight, the whole idea was Jasper Pierce's. Archer was just the money guy. She needed to talk to Pierce—there might not be anything to the story, or there might be a secret worth killing to keep. She'd seen it far too many times to make the motive original.

She sent David a note about what Dru had told her over the phone and that she was meeting her at Starbucks.

She tried Dru's cell phone. It rang five times, then voice mail picked up. Max didn't leave a message.

Her phone rang almost immediately. She thought it was Dru; caller ID told her it was David.

"Hello, dear," she teased.

"I looked into the Parker girl, too, after you sent me her last name. Parents divorced. One older sister named Gina who lives in L.A. She lives with two other college girls, all working part time and going to school part time. I'll send you her address and the names of her roommates."

"Thanks."

"One interesting thing I learned—her car is registered to a business, DL Environmental."

"Never heard of them."

"They have a Web site. Not much on it. Pictures of college-aged kids protesting this and that." She could practically hear the eye roll in his voice.

"If you have time tonight, see if you can dig into them a little deeper." She stepped outside of the coffee house and looked around the parking lot. She didn't see Dru's bright yellow VW parked anywhere. Damn, had she really left to stay with her mother? Was she now avoiding Max's calls because she changed her mind?

She asked, "Anything about Roger Lawrence?"

"He's been with Evergreen for over fifteen years. Married twenty years. Two kids, both in high school. Nothing that seems out of place. Doesn't live above his means."

"Hmm."

"You're skeptical?"

"Curious." Max saw a sign that indicated there was underground parking. "Okay, you're officially off duty, Kane. If I hear from you again, you're fired."

"You can't fire me."

"I can make your life a living hell."

He laughed, then said, "Watch your back with Parker."

"Yes, sir."

Max hung up and tossed her empty cup in a

nearby trash can as she approached the parking lot stairwell. It was well lit and there were security cameras on the door. She went down the stairs. The lot, primarily for Caltrains parking, was built under a discount drugstore. She immediately spotted Dru's car next to the stairwell, where most of the cars were clustered.

Dru wasn't in it.

Inside the car was a half-empty Starbucks cup, the ice still solid.

Dru had ordered her drink then what—gone to her car to wait? Why park down here? Max could think of one good reason—if Dru really was scared of someone, her car stood out. Parking down here would minimize being seen.

Caltrains parking. Dammit, she must have left on a train. Max pulled out her phone to find the train schedule. She hadn't heard one since she pulled into the parking lot twelve minutes ago.

There was no train scheduled until after nine that evening; it was eight thirty now. Max walked around Dru's car and looked in the back. There was a suitcase on the backseat.

The hair on her arms rose. Car, suitcase, melting drink—no girl. She dialed Dru's cell phone again.

She heard a musical chime three cars over.

Max took out the stun gun she had carried with her since college. Not the exact same Taser, she'd upgraded, but it was the only weapon she'd ever felt comfortable carrying. She'd only used it once before, but she wouldn't hesitate if she had cause.

She saw the blood before she saw Dru's body, lying between two parked cars. Before she could check her pulse, headlights flashed bright and tires squealed from a car parked directly opposite her.

Max had little time to react. She could see nothing, blinded by the high beams, but while she jumped between the two cars where Dru's body lay dying, she tried to picture the car. Dark. Tinted windows. Four-door sedan.

The sedan turned rapidly to avoid a collision, but fishtailed and the rear driver's side hit the back of one of the parked cars. Max ducked, in case the driver had a gun. She peered carefully over the trunk of the vehicle, blinking rapidly to get rid of the flashes of light the high beams left in her eyes. She couldn't make out more than a B and 8 or 3 in the license plate, and even then she wasn't 100 percent certain she read it right. The attacker drove rapidly out of the parking garage.

Heart pounding heavily in her chest, Max leaned over Dru and felt for a pulse. She had one. Max pulled out her cell phone to call 911, then put the phone on speaker. Carefully, she turned Dru from her side to her back to find out where all this blood was coming from. The girl moaned, but didn't regain consciousness. Blood had soaked her T-shirt, but it seemed to be coming from her lower abdomen. Max took off her scarf, wadded it up, and applied pressure on Dru's stomach while talking to the dispatcher, identifying herself and telling her to send an ambulance and the police.

"Dammit, Dru, why'd you park down here? What were you thinking?" Max muttered.

"Ms. Revere? I missed that."

"I wasn't talking to you," Max told the dispatcher.

"Can you apply pressure to the wound?"

"I'm doing that."

"Is the victim conscious?"

"No."

"Does she have a pulse?"

"Yes."

"Do you know what type of injury?"

"Someone either shot or stabbed her in her lower abdomen, there's a lot of blood, she's going to die if the ambulance doesn't get here immediately." The warm blood had seeped through Max's scarf and coated her hands. She thought the flow had slowed, but she couldn't be sure.

"An ambulance has been dispatched and is en route."

"ETA?"

"Three minutes."

Max didn't know if Dru had already lost too much blood to survive.

She glanced around, making sure there wasn't anyone else she had to worry about sneaking up on her. Her Taser was on, but she'd put it on the ground next to her to tend to Dru. Max glanced under all the cars and didn't see anyone lying in wait. She heard voices coming down the stairwell. Laughter, male and female. When the couple walked by, they jumped at the sight of Max huddled over a bleeding body. The man stepped in front of the woman and said, "Are you okay?"

"Does it look like I'm okay?" Max snapped. She took a deep breath. "Police are on their way." She was definitely on edge. It didn't help that she had a throbbing headache and an edge of adrenaline clinging from the near miss with the black sedan and holding Dru's life in her hands.

Don't die, don't die, don't die, dammit!

Dru was so young, her life just getting started, Max willed her to survive, to be strong.

"If you have a blanket in your car, that would help. And if one of you could run up the ramp and flag down the ambulance so they know exactly where we are, that would be great."

They glanced at each other, then the man said, "Okay."

Dru moaned again.

"Ms. Revere?" the dispatcher said over the cell phone.

Max could barely hear Dru with the noise coming from her phone, so she cut off the dispatcher and said, "Hey, Dru, it's Max. Take it easy."

"S-s-sorry," Dru breathed.

"Don't talk, kid. Help's coming." Max could

hear the sirens in the distance. "Who hurt you?" she asked.

She shook her head, then cried out in pain.

Max wished she could make her comfortable. "Don't talk, conserve your strength." Max didn't know if it was good or bad news that Dru was awake.

"Wore. Mask."

The man returned with a blanket and Max motioned for him to cover Dru's body. She didn't want to let up on the pressure.

"Ask."

"Shh."

"J—Jase—the trees. Holes in the trees."

The sirens were louder, and Max saw the red lights reflecting off the concrete walls of the underground garage before she saw the ambulance turn down the ramp. The woman motioned the emergency vehicle over to the two cars, and the man waved his arms.

"The cavalry has arrived," Max told Dru, but the girl was unconscious again.

Holes in the trees? What the hell did that mean?

Max watched as Dru was loaded into the ambulance. The responding officer ran her license through the system. He'd already talked to the couple who had shared the blanket, and taken Max's statement, but she had to wait for the detective.

She stared at the blood on her hands. Dru was young and strong and healthy, but there had been so much blood.

While the cop was occupied, she called Detective Nick Santini.

"Santini."

"This is Max Revere. Your witness was just stabbed—Dru Parker."

"Where?"

She told him. "She called to meet with me and I found her unconscious and bleeding in a parking garage. She's on her way to the hospital."

"Stay put."

"I don't think the police are going to let me leave," she said and hung up.

The officer said suspiciously, "Who were you talking to?"

Max almost made a flip comment about calling the police commissioner, but decided to say, "It's personal."

"Detective Gorman is on her way, I need you to wait for a couple more minutes."

"I'd like to clean up."

The officer looked skeptical, and Max said, "Really? You want me to stand here covered in that girl's blood and wait for your detective to get her ass here?"

"I don't have a female officer to escort you to a restroom," he said.

"I'm not under arrest. I'll come right back."

"I need you to stay. The detective may need your clothes for evidence."

Max's adrenaline was fading, leaving only a worse headache. If she was at her prime, she would have walked away and let the cop either arrest her or let her go. She had no tolerance for bullshit. Making her stand here with blood all over her hands, arms, and dress was making her both queasy and ornery. She mentally wrote an article. *Asshole cop forces witness who saved victim's life to sit in blood for nearly an hour.*

Her editor would edit out *asshole.* No matter how accurate the adjective was.

She forced herself to regain her composure. The cop was just doing his job. What she really wanted to know was: Were there security tapes? Had someone witnessed the brutal attack on Dru Parker? And dammit, *why?* If she'd just gotten here sooner. If she'd told Dru to stay put in Starbucks where there were people and some degree of security. If she'd looked for her immediately rather than waiting upstairs.

She pulled out her phone again and called David. "My witness was attacked," she said.

"Dead?"

"Not yet. Unconscious, being taken to Sequoia."

"I'll get her status."

"Thanks."

"I can be there in an hour."

"No." She'd have to tell David what happened

eventually, but she didn't need him here now. "This has nothing to do with me."

She didn't want him postponing his trip with Emma. Brittany was such a bitch she was practically a nutcase about his visitation rights.

David had been hired as her assistant, but he often acted like a bodyguard. Or, at least, a protector. Max didn't want a bodyguard, but after a particularly violent trial she covered eighteen months ago that instigated death threats, Ben had hired David. And he'd saved her life in Chicago when a wacko went after her. Now Max depended on him more than anyone else in her life, which made her uncomfortable. Maybe if she'd had sex with him it would be different—she tended to maintain the upper hand once she'd slept with a guy—but David was gay and sex was out of the question. He took both parts of his job—as her assistant and as her bodyguard—seriously. She sometimes missed being completely independent— of the show, of Ben, of an occasionally over- protective assistant.

David said, "Whoever attacked her knew she was meeting with you."

"Not necessarily."

"Don't be dense."

Max watched an unmarked sedan with govern- ment plates drive into the parking garage. A female detective—Gorman—stepped out of the car and talked to the officer who'd irritated Max earlier. They looked over at her. "I'm fine, David. Ben hired you to protect me when I'm working for the show, and this is personal. Really. The cops are here, all is well in the world." She was being sarcastic, but she was tired and worried. "I was just calling to keep you in the loop and ask you to follow up on Dru's condition. If something changes, let me know. But you'd damn well better be on that plane to Hawaii tomorrow."

The detective strode over to where Max had been told to wait.

"If you get yourself in trouble, call," David said.

"If *I* get myself into trouble? Ha." She hung up. David knew her well. She followed trouble because that was her job. But she didn't want him here. She needed the freedom to do her own thing.

Ben wouldn't like her working on the Jason Hoffman murder because it would take time—time he wanted on the Bachman trial. Also, the Hoffman case wasn't "sexy" enough for him. Ben had been trying to get her to write about Lindy's murder and Kevin's trial—if he knew that Kevin had contacted her four months ago, they'd have argued every day about whether she should pursue it or not. So she never told him. And she wasn't going to tell him now—he'd insist she do a show, and she'd have to tell him to go to hell. She didn't want to quit.

Not yet, anyway.

Detective Gorman glared at her. "Who were you talking to?"

"A friend."

"About what?"

Max checked her temper. "It's personal."

"Do you understand the seriousness of this situation?"

"Yes, I do."

"Then you should know better than to talk to anyone until you give your statement to me, got it?"

She bit back a sarcastic comment. "Yes, Detective."

Max didn't like Gorman. One of Max's faults—if one listened to Ben—was that she formed knee-jerk opinions of people. Her opinions were based on her experience coupled with the first impression package. Gorman's first impression package was: tough female detective, angry, competent, chip on her shoulder. From her attire Max suspected she was in debt—cheap shoes and clothes, but with a fondness for jewelry. The diamonds in her ears, for example, were real.

What really irked Max was Gorman's approach. She watched as Gorman waited for Max to elaborate. It was a technique cops loved, letting the silence hang to get a suspect to continue talking—hopefully to send him to prison.

It took Gorman ten seconds before she spoke. Not very patient. Max had remained silent with cops for upwards of two minutes when she'd been questioned in the past. Two minutes was about Max's threshold. That's when she'd say, "I'm leaving." They'd either let her go or ask more questions.

"Do you know the victim"—Gorman looked at her notes—"Dru Parker?"

"Not well."

"But you know her."

"I met her for the first time today."

"So you don't know her."

"I said, not well. I met her at her place of employment, Evergreen—"

"This is rather a coincidence, don't you think?"

"What?"

"That you just show up here and find her bleeding on the ground."

"She called to meet with me. She picked the place—"

"You're telling me that a girl you barely know, who you just met today, agreed to meet with you in a parking lot in the middle of the night?"

"We agreed to meet at Starbucks. She wasn't there, so I started looking for her. It seemed—"

"Why did you start looking for her?"

"Because an employee said she had been in, but left."

"How'd you know she was in the parking garage?"

"I didn't see her car in the lot outside, so I came

down here. She'd mentioned she was going to take the train to her mother's in San Francisco, and I thought—"

Gorman cut her off. "You barely know the girl, but you seem to know a lot about her plans."

"Stop cutting me off!"

"You're telling me how to do my job?"

"Someone has to," Max snapped.

Gorman bristled. "Why did you have a weapon?"

"My Taser?" Max counted to three. "Here's my statement. My name is Maxine Revere. I'm a freelance reporter. I was asked to look into the cold case of Jason Hoffman, who was murdered at Atherton College Prep at the Evergreen construction site last November. I met Ms. Parker at the site this morning, asked her to call me if she wanted to share information related to Jason's death. She called and asked to meet me here. When she wasn't in Starbucks like we'd agreed, I came down here and found her car. I called her cell phone, heard it ring, took my Taser from my purse, turned it on, and followed the sound. I had the sense that something was wrong. I found her lying, bleeding and unconscious, between those two cars." Max gestured. "Then, from that parking space"—she pointed to the spot across and one over from where Dru had been—"a dark, probably black sedan flashed his brights, peeled out of the space, and nearly hit me. The rear driver's side hit the white car," Max pointed, "when he fishtailed, and then he left. I couldn't see the license plate because the high beams temporarily blinded me, but I believe B was the first letter and the last number was eight or three. I then called 911 and administered first aid until the ambulance arrived." She took a deep breath. "You have my contact information if you need to reach me. I'm going back to my hotel now."

"I'm not through," Gorman said.

"I am."

She turned and found herself staring at another cop, this one also in his mid-thirties, with a conservative haircut but unshaven jaw, and sharp green eyes. Six feet two inches, wearing jeans and a black T-shirt. Part of a U.S. Marine Corp tattoo was visible on his bicep. His badge was clipped to his belt and so was his gun. It looked like a .45, but Max couldn't be certain. David was teaching her about guns since she obtained a permit to have one in her New York City apartment. Threats were part of her business, and none of them were viable, but they seemed to keep coming, and David said unless he could be with her 24/7 she'd damn well better learn how to protect herself in her own apartment.

The cop lifted his badge for Gorman, but didn't take his eyes off Max. She couldn't read his expression. Her first impression package was: ex-military, tough, immovable. A man of few words who would take shit from no one.

"Santini, Menlo Park," he told Gorman. To Max he said, "Five minutes."

She wanted to argue with him—she was tired, hungry, crabby, and her head was about to explode. But she didn't. She stood there and watched as Santini pulled Gorman aside. Santini positioned them so he could see Max, but Gorman couldn't. Did he think she was going to leave?

She wanted to. But the night had drained her and she had no more energy. She didn't even think she could handle another confrontation with Gorman.

The conversation between Santini and Gorman lasted less than three minutes, and Gorman walked over to the officer who was standing near the couple who'd stayed to help. Santini walked over to Max.

"Please don't tell me I have to go through this all again."

He shook his head. "I heard everything after you called Dru Parker's cell phone." He handed her the Taser the officer had taken when he first arrived.

She smiled and put it in her purse. "Thank you."

"Gorman doesn't like you."

"I doubt we'll be getting pedicures together anytime soon."

He cracked a half smile. "We need to talk."

"Okay." She glanced around, looking for a place to sit.

"Why don't we go up to Starbucks and you can clean yourself up? I promised Gorman I'd get your clothes for evidence before she leaves."

Max raised an eyebrow. "What's the indecent exposure law in this county? Can I walk around in a thong and lace bra?"

"I wouldn't arrest you." Santini grinned. "Follow me."

Max followed the detective up the staircase, which opened into a courtyard. Everything was closing around them, even Starbucks. Santini knocked on the door and showed his badge. "Can Ms. Revere wash up? Five minutes."

It was the barista from earlier. Her eyes were wide with curiosity, but she nodded and let them in.

Santini turned to Max and said, "I'll be back in one minute. Don't leave."

Max went into the bathroom and turned the water on hot. Looking in the mirror she realized she was a horrific sight—there were blood smears on her pale face, her eyes were bloodshot and droopy, and she looked as crappy as she felt.

There was a knock on the door. "Max," Santini said.

She opened the door and he handed her a large paper evidence bag, plus a pair of sweatpants and a T-shirt. "It's all I have. I need your shoes, too. And the thong and lace bra." He winked.

She took the clothing and bag and shut the door. Nick wasn't as hard-nosed, tough military commando like she first thought. He had a sense of humor. She liked the contrast.

The paramedics had taken her scarf. She removed everything and dropped her clothing in the bag. She wasn't planning on wearing any of it again.

She cracked open the door. "Santini!" she called out.

He stepped in the corridor. She dropped the bag in front of him and closed the door again.

Naked, the tile floor cold on her feet, she washed her hands, arms, face, and neck as best she could with the water from the sink and paper towels. She still desperately wanted a shower. She pulled on the sweatpants—a little big, but workable—and T-shirt. USMC. It was faded, but smelled clean, and fit comfortably.

She breathed deeply, splashed cold water on her face, and felt human again.

Nick Santini was waiting for her, holding two cups of coffee and a small bag. He must have passed the evidence bag off to Gorman.

"I told them to make whatever drink you had earlier," he said. "There's also water and a muffin in the bag."

She was surprised and impressed with his thoughtfulness. "Thank you." She took the coffee he offered. "How did you know I was starving?"

"Your stomach growls quite loudly."

She laughed and they walked out. The barista locked the door behind them. "I'll answer any questions, but I can drive myself back."

Nick opened the passenger door of a Ford Bronco. "In."

She obliged. He closed the door and walked to the back and opened the back door. She didn't know what he was doing, but when he finally got into the driver's seat, he tossed her a pair of white gym socks. "They're clean."

"Thanks." She slipped them on, surprised at his thoughtfulness.

"Tell me what you didn't tell Gorman."

"Parker called me at quarter to eight. She sounded scared. She specifically asked why you showed up at her house."

"So because I wanted to interview her again, she called you, a reporter? Why would she do that?"

"My experience has been that people are intimidated by the police when they think they're going to be questioned and they have something to hide."

"What was she hiding?" Santini was asking himself almost as much as Max.

"She wouldn't tell me on the phone. She planned on going to her mother's in San Francisco—that's why I went down to the parking garage, thinking she'd left before I arrived. She said that the week

208

before Jason died, there were some strange things going on. Now she thinks they might have been connected to his death."

"Any idea what those strange things were?"

"I'll find out." She bit into the muffin. Her stomach rumbled in appreciation. "She said one thing before the ambulance took her away."

"Identify her attacker?"

"I would have told Gorman if she had." Max ate more muffin. "She said that Jason was concerned about something in the trees. 'Holes in the trees,' she specifically said."

"Holes in the trees? What's that supposed to mean?"

"I don't know. But he was spending a lot of time at Atherton Prep and he was there Saturday night for no known reason."

"Is that what she said? Holes in the trees?"

"Yes. Those were her exact words."

Santini didn't say anything. Max continued. "Why did you question Jessica Hoffman in January about her mother?"

He looked at her with surprise. "Jessica told you that?"

"She told her grandparents. She thought it was odd you were asking questions about her mother and Evergreen. What did you find?"

He didn't answer her question, and she hadn't expected him to.

"Does it have something to do with the financial

situation of Evergreen prior to the contract with ACP to build the sports complex?"

Santini had a great poker face, but a small dip of his eyebrow told her she was right.

He said, "Did you offer to pay Dru Parker for information? For her story?"

Max bristled. "No."

"Just asking."

Nick Santini was a hard man to read. A lot of cops were, but he was more difficult than most. He seemed to be pleasant and professional on the surface—even kind, getting her the coffee and muffin—but there was an underlying hostility, and though his posture was relaxed, it seemed that every muscle under his skin was tense and waiting. For what, Max didn't know.

Max wanted this cop to trust her, but she didn't know how.

He glanced down at his phone. "Gorman says Parker is in surgery."

"That's good news, right?"

"That's all it says. I suppose it depends on how much blood she lost and what damage they find when they get in there."

She gave him the last piece of information she had in an effort to earn his trust. "Dru Parker's car is registered to a nonprofit group, DL Environmental. Heard of it?"

"No. How do you know?"

"I'm a reporter. I ask questions."

"Don't pull that bullshit on me. Did you search her car?"

She didn't respond. She didn't like the instant accusation, or the change in tone. She hadn't done anything to deserve his animosity, but that could certainly change.

Her hand on the door handle, she said, "It's been a long day, Detective. And you have a lot of work to do."

"Stay out of this investigation."

She stared at him. "You told me yourself that you just put the case on the inactive sheet, and if it weren't for me, it would have stayed there. No way in *hell* am I walking away. You can either work with me on this or I'll do it myself."

"I could put you in jail."

Max laughed. "I'd like to see you try." She opened the door and stepped out. With her hand on the roof she said, "Thank you for the clothes and coffee. I'll be at the Menlo Grill at noon tomorrow to discuss this case, as we planned. Either bring your appetite, or bring an arrest warrant." She slammed the door shut.

Chapter Twelve

A rap on her door pulled Max from the article she was reading on her computer about the attack on Dru Parker. Half the information was flat-out wrong. The way local news was reported today, especially outside of big cities, was primarily online and had a desk reporter listening to scanners then calling the PIO for information. Whether Gorman intentionally misled the reporter or if she *really* thought Dru Parker had been attacked during the commission of a robbery, Max didn't know. Fortunately, they hadn't named Dru in the paper, so that tidbit was something Max might be able to use. If her friends didn't know she was in the hospital, maybe she could get more information out of them.

It was nine in the morning. She hadn't gotten up until after eight, but after a fitful night, she'd needed the extra rest. She was already on her third cup of coffee from the pot that she'd ordered from room service.

She opened the door.

"David." She looked at the young girl with long sandy blond hair standing next to him and smiled. "Emma! This is a fantastic surprise. Come in."

Emma grinned and ran in, giving Max a hug. "Dad took me to the de Young Museum yesterday.

They had a *really* cool photo exhibit of the national parks. Have you seen it?"

"No, but sounds like something I would like." She glanced at David. He was not smiling. "I'm thrilled to see you, but aren't you supposed to be on a plane?"

"We have time," David said. He said to Emma, "I need to talk to Max, then I have a surprise."

"Tell me." Emma practically jumped. She was twelve, between the age of excitement and teen-age apathy. Max was glad she was less apathetic and more excited about life.

David pulled an envelope from his pocket and handed it to her. She opened it and squealed. "OMG, first base? *Really?* Giants versus the Mets? The night we get back? I can't believe it, you hate the Giants."

"You love the Giants, I love the Mets. One of us will go home happy."

Emma hugged David. "Ten minutes and then I'll be back. Can I have five bucks?"

"Charge whatever you want to my room," Max said.

"Thanks, Max—you know you're in trouble, right?"

"I didn't think your dad drove thirty miles out of his way before a five-hour flight to tell me how much he loves working for me."

Emma left and Max sat back down at her desk. "She's grown two inches since last summer."

"Brittany told her she could get her belly button pierced when she's thirteen."

"You didn't come here to bitch about Emma's mother."

David raised an eyebrow. "You usually enjoy it when I complain about Brittany."

"Am I that obvious?"

David sat down on the chair across from her, but he didn't relax. There were a lot of similarities between David and Detective Nick Santini. Max dismissed it to their military backgrounds. David could have easily been a cop. Max had asked him once why he didn't go into law enforcement, and he'd never really given her a good answer.

"We have a problem."

Max waited for David to tell her what was bothering him, but she feared the worst. "We have a problem" never led to anything good. It led to people quitting on her, or her firing them. "We have a problem" was always an ending, never a beginning.

David didn't say anything, either.

"Don't leave," she said quietly.

"I can't do my job if you lie to me."

"I don't lie."

"You neglected to tell me that you were nearly run over in that damn parking garage, or that you saved Dru Parker's life."

"So she's okay?" She'd tried getting information

from the hospital this morning, but they gave her the runaround and she grew impatient.

"Don't."

"David, I didn't want you doing *this*."

"What? I don't get it, Max. What am I doing that pisses you off?"

"Nothing."

"You told me that I was your right hand."

"You are. You know I don't trust anyone else."

"And that's a lie." He stared at her. "You don't trust anyone."

"David—"

"I need to be in the loop, Max. The *need to know* loop. Always. I have to be able to trust you to be honest with me."

"This coming from the man who's told me more than once that I'm *too honest?*"

"You know exactly what I mean."

How did Max explain to David what she wanted? What she needed? "For years I investigated on my own, wrote articles *on my own,* did research *all by myself.* I can work all day and all night and live off caffeine and chocolate and it doesn't impact anyone but me. You have a daughter you never get to see."

David leaned back. "Now I'm clueless."

"This is your time with Emma. You get only four weeks with her a year. I'm not helpless, and I've already had you working when you should be ignoring my calls."

David didn't say anything. Max couldn't stand it. "Dammit, David, you're a good father. I'm not going to ruin that."

"You couldn't. I'd much rather Emma have you as a role model than Brittany."

Max was surprised. "I'm not a role model for anyone."

"You have your moments." But he smiled, and for the first time since David sat down, Max relaxed. But his smile disappeared and he leaned forward. "Next time, don't leave out the details."

"All right."

He seemed to assess her sincerity, and Max wished she could promise more, but all she could do was try. She didn't want to lose David—as an employee or a friend.

"I have some information." He handed her a sheet of notes written in his small block letters. "Here's the financials details on Evergreen, and the agreement with ACP. Evergreen would have filed bankruptcy by the end of the fiscal year, no doubt, if this didn't happen."

He glanced at her two trifold boards. "You have a lot of information already."

"Not enough. But my uncle is financing the sports complex, so I have an in with Jasper Pierce. I'll find out exactly what his connection is with Evergreen and the Hoffman family. No one hands over a multimillion-dollar contract with no bids for no reason."

"And the Lindy Ames board?"

"That's just personal."

"Hmm."

"Don't do that."

"I'm not doing anything."

"It's your disapproving grunt."

"I don't disapprove." He looked back at her. "I think you need to find out what happened or it'll be one more thing that keeps you awake at night."

"Go," Max said. "Enjoy Emma. Have a safe trip. And *please* don't worry about me. I'm okay."

He looked like he wanted to say something, but didn't, and Max was relieved. She wasn't used to having a relationship like the one she had with David.

He opened the door. "I'll see you Saturday."

"Saturday? I'll be back in New York."

He smirked. "We're flying home Friday afternoon, going to the Giants-Mets game that night, and Emma has to be back to her mother's by noon Saturday." He nodded toward her boards for Jason Hoffman and Lindy Ames. "You won't be leaving until you solve both cases. And I think it's going to take you all week."

Max almost thought Nick Santini wouldn't show. It was Sunday afternoon, she was a reporter, he was a cop. David had called one of his buddies in the Marines and learned that Nick was a decorated veteran who'd served in both Iraq and

Afghanistan as part of a Special Forces unit. He was still in the Reserves, like David. David was Army, but as far as Max was concerned, military was military.

Max sat in her favorite booth in the bar. Her phone vibrated again with another call from William. He'd left a message for her last night, which she'd ignored, and called again already this morning, which she also ignored. Maybe now he understood that she was serious about that parking ticket.

She answered the phone.

"I thought you were going to send me to voice mail again," William said.

"What do you want? We said everything that needed to be said last night—unless you were lying."

"I didn't lie to you. Why can't you trust me on this?"

"I want to," she said.

"I was calling to warn you—Andy knows about what happened at the Ames house last night."

"Why does Andy care?" But he *had* come to see her Friday night, and their conversation hadn't been all that friendly.

"I told him you weren't looking into Lindy's death, and now you're making me a liar."

"I never told you to lie."

"You brought me into it last night!"

"Me? You're the one who had the secret parking

ticket and didn't tell anyone. All I did was call you on it. So I repeat, why are you now a liar?"

"Andy asked me point-blank what you were doing at the Ames house last night. I played dumb, like I didn't know what he was talking about."

"You don't. I never told you."

"I can guess."

"You'd be wrong." Max shifted uncomfortably. She hadn't told David about the call to her hotel yet, and he wouldn't like that she'd kept the information from him, especially after their heart-to-heart this morning. And she didn't know if she'd honestly forgotten to mention it, or if subconsciously she knew David would have canceled his vacation with Emma if he knew there had been a threat, however subtle it was.

"Then why?"

Max might have told William about the threat, except that she saw Andy walking briskly toward her. He looked as happy as Brooks and her grandmother had last night.

"Your best friend is paying me a visit. Is that why you really called? To warn me that Andy was on his way?"

"He's there?"

"Good-bye." Max hung up on William. Andy leaned over, his palms flat against the table.

"What the *hell* are you doing harassing Kimberly Ames?"

"Hello, Andy," Max said. "I'd invite you to sit down but I'm expecting someone."

Andy sat and Max's temper went up a dozen degrees. "I told you to leave Lindy's murder alone."

"I don't take orders from you."

"You don't take orders from anyone. You never did. I came to you as a friend the other night—"

"I'm not going to repeat myself."

"What did you say to William that got him all upset?"

"Why don't you ask William? He's your best friend."

"I did, and he talked around it, but he can't lie to save his soul, and the more I pushed the more upset he became."

Max stared at Andy. "Why do you care so much?"

"Because Kevin O'Neal killed Lindy, and you're stirring up shit that doesn't need stirring."

"How do you know I was at the Ameses' house last night?"

"Everyone knows!" He slammed his fist on the table, causing water to slosh from her glass.

Max noticed that Nick Santini was approaching. His eyes weren't on her; they were fixated on Andy, as hard as his expression.

"Hello, Nick," Max said with a half smile.

Andy had been so engrossed in trying to intimidate her that he didn't notice Nick until he

220

was standing right next to the table. His manners battled with his anger. Manners won, barely.

"I'm sorry if I interrupted your meal," he said through clenched teeth.

"Good-bye, Andy," Max said.

Andy stood, turned back to her and said, "We used to be friends. If that means anything to you, you'll just stop this nonsense and go back to New York."

"I think you know me well enough to know that I like running with scissors."

For some reason, that infuriated Andy. "Be careful which way you point the scissors."

Nick said, "Is that a threat?"

"Back off," Andy said. "This doesn't concern you."

Nick showed his badge. "Everything concerns me."

Andy wasn't fazed by Nick's shield. He smirked, glanced at Max, then said to Nick, "Watch out. She bites." Then he left.

Nick watched Andy leave the restaurant before he sat down. He looked at Max and said, "You don't look intimidated."

"I've known Andy for a long time."

"Ex?"

She shrugged. "High school sweethearts."

"That's right. You graduated from Atherton Prep."

The way he said it made Max wonder how much

research he'd done into her background. It was mostly an open book—she had a detailed bio on the "Maximum Exposure" Web site and there were interviews she'd given that spilled most of her secrets. How she was raised by her grandparents, didn't know who her father was, and her mother disappeared when she was a kid. Oh, and that she'd been left millions of dollars by her eccentric great-grandmother and her family sued to try and null and void the will. They lost, she won, and the rest is history.

If Max could take on her family and win, she could take on Andy Talbot and anyone else who interfered with her pursuit of the truth.

"Yep, I've lived here since I was nine-and-a-half when my mom dropped me on my grandparents' doorstep. I didn't even know I was the greatgranddaughter of one of the wealthiest women in California until then. But you didn't come here to talk about me."

"I didn't?"

She didn't quite know how to take his comment. "I'm an open book. Ask me what you want to know."

"Was your ex-high school sweetheart Andy talking about my case?"

"No."

Nick didn't say anything, waiting for Max to continue. She didn't. She didn't know if he would change his mind about helping her with the

Jason Hoffman investigation if he knew she was also pursuing a cold case one of his colleagues considered closed. Juggling the two was becoming increasingly difficult.

"You don't ask for help, do you?"

"That's a question out of left field."

"Which you smoothly avoided."

"I did?" She smiled. The waiter came over with two menus. She ordered a pinot grigio and Nick ordered a beer.

She gave him an olive branch. "Sometimes, asking for help comes with strings. That's why I prefer a trade. Like this."

"I didn't agree to anything."

"But you will." She hoped. "Unless you have an arrest warrant in your pocket."

"If Harry Beck had his way, you'd be in jail."

Her stomach dropped. Nick Santini knew far more about her and why she'd returned to Atherton than she realized. Why was she surprised?

"Harry Beck is a prick."

"I can't argue with that."

"He has nothing to do with the Jason Hoffman homicide."

"But that's not why you're here."

"You obviously know why I'm here; you talked to Beck."

"I wanted to hear it from you. If I believed Beck, you'd be an accessory to murder or something. He was a bit irrational when he spoke of you."

"I'll bet." She assessed Nick's interest; it seemed genuine. "If you talked to Beck, you know I'm in town for a friend's funeral. Kevin O'Neal was tried for the murder of my best friend, Lindy Ames. I never believed he did it. He committed suicide last week, I suspect because he never could shake his reputation. The jury was hung, and Kevin lived with everyone in town thinking he was a killer. Including Beck."

"If not Kevin, who?"

"I wish I knew. But I didn't originally return to investigate Lindy's murder. I came to help his little sister come to terms with his suicide. I owed him that much."

"Why?"

Nick's probing questions irritated her. The complexities of her feelings about Kevin and Lindy were just now becoming clear to her, and she was still twisting them around, trying to understand. She wasn't ready to discuss them with anyone, especially a virtual stranger. The waiter returned with their drinks and they ordered lunch. "I'd prefer to talk about what I know about Jason Hoffman's murder."

"Go."

That was too easy. Max suspected that the conversation wasn't over. "I told you his grandparents contacted me—"

"How?"

Max uncomfortably felt like she was the one

being interviewed. Or interrogated. No one had ever made her feel this way—in fact, she had fallen into responding without even knowing it.

She smiled. "You're good."

"Generally."

"I slipped right into the role you wanted me to."

"Does that mean you don't want to share your information?"

She leaned back and sipped her wine. "Henry and Penny Hoffman saw me at the airport Friday morning."

"They recognized you?"

"They watch my show."

His face clouded just a bit, but then it disappeared. She had a feeling he was hiding his true opinion about her and her career. She'd have to come back to that.

She continued. "They'd written me earlier, but one of my former assistants didn't forward me their message. I told them Friday I would look into it, but with no promises because I was only going to be here for a few days."

"And now?"

"And now I finagled a bit more time. Jason was killed at my alma mater. I would have been interested even if he wasn't, but it makes the connection not easily avoidable. It helps when you don't need the job to force your boss to be flexible."

"But you like what you do."

"Mostly. I miss the freedom of being an investigative reporter."

"Isn't that what you do for that show?"

"Yes, but people usually know why I'm asking questions. I used to do more undercover work. More like a private investigator who wrote exposés rather than broadcast them."

"And books."

"A few."

"Working on anything new?"

"I haven't had time." She had a few ideas, but true crime books took a long time to research and work, to fact-collect and fact-check. "Ben, my producer, wants me to write a collection based on the stories I've covered for the show."

"But you don't want to."

"I've already told the story. I'm not interested in writing about them as well." She didn't want to talk about her job or the show. "I met with the Hoffmans yesterday morning and was going to tell them I couldn't help, except I have a feeling there's something to the case—something is pulling me, not just the connection to Atherton Prep. They told me about what Jessica Hoffman said, you interviewing her about her mother, and after a little research into the crime rates on construction sites—"

"Which is high."

"But not homicides."

Their food arrived—a Cobb salad for Max and a

club sandwich for Nick. She filled him in on what had made her suspicious at the construction site, how she met Dru, and what Dru had said when she called to meet.

"The thing that really bugs me is that Jason was killed for nothing. There was nothing to steal. That suggests that it was personal. Someone who wanted him dead followed him to the school, or knew he planned to go there Saturday night. So when the Hoffmans told me you questioned Jessica Hoffman about her mother, I thought there might be a family connection. Put that with the financial trouble of Evergreen before the fairy godfather in the persona of Jasper Pierce took it all away with the sports complex. But Dru's comment about Jason's obsession with the trees . . . well, that seems out of place."

Max sipped her water, then continued. "However, I don't know any more. Dru said that odd things had been happening that week. He was at ACP for a specific reason the night he was killed. And that makes me wonder if there's a completely different reason, not personal, but tied to money—either the funding or an environmental consideration. Holes in trees. That doesn't make sense. What do you think?"

What was going through Nick's mind was likely what went through the minds of all the cops who ended up working with her. Should he or shouldn't he work with her? What should he tell her? Was she going to screw him and make his department look bad? Was she going to jeopardize his case? Would his lieutenant reprimand him? Would the DA get mad?

Scratch that. Max suspected Nick didn't care what the DA thought.

"I have some ground rules," Nick said.

"Lay them out."

"Write nothing about this case without talking to me first."

"I'm not planning to write about the case, but if I do, I agree."

"You may not quote me, unless I give you express permission and I approve the quote."

"Agreed."

Nick waited until the waiter removed their plates before he told Max anything important.

"I have some suspicions about the financial dealings between Evergreen and Jasper Pierce. Something you didn't mention in all your research, but Pierce is a silent partner of Evergreen. He profits from the building of the sports complex, which makes it seem like a scam, except he'd disclosed it to the school before they agreed to the contract. Still—he's also funding the project, along with this guy named Archer Sterling."

"Archer is my uncle," Max said.

Nick stared at her. "Why didn't you say so?"

"It didn't come up, until now."

He still looked unhappy. "No matter how hard

we looked, me or the FBI fraud task force, there's nothing to it. I just don't like when I learn something important that my witnesses neglected to tell me."

"Did you talk to Pierce?"

"Yes, initially, and he was cooperative, but less so during follow-up interviews. He was irritated that we weren't doing more to find Jason's killer." Nick's jaw clenched, but he hid his temper well. "I was mad that I was stuck. I interviewed Dru Parker twice—she didn't say anything about odd behavior or why Jason was hanging out at the site that night. His uncle, Brian Robeaux, was the only one who mentioned it. Robeaux said that Jason walked the grounds repeatedly, but thought it was his way of communing with the earth or something. Jason was apparently big into building structures that blend into the natural environment. He and the architect were friends—Gordon Cho— who'd also been his mentor and boss when Jason interned at Cho Architectural. Robeaux said nothing about any obsession with trees or holes."

"Maybe," Max said, "Dru didn't think anything was wrong until something spooked her yesterday."

"On Friday I put the case in the inactive file, so when you called me Saturday I was both irritated and interested. Dru Parker was a part-time secretary and didn't seem to have any useful information. I should have pushed."

Nick was blaming himself for missing something. For some reason, that endeared him to Max. "She was definitely worried when she called me. She didn't want her roommates knowing that she was meeting with me, and she planned on visiting her mother for an extended stay. Maybe someone else spooked her."

"Who else did you talk to?"

"Roger Lawrence. I thought he acted belligerent when I was talking to Dru, but that could have been his personality."

"He didn't kill Jason, that I'm certain about," Nick said. "His alibi is rock-solid. He was in the middle of his twentieth anniversary cruise to the Caribbean. Jason's parents were home together. Brian Robeaux was at a party in San Mateo. He told me Jason was supposed to join him there, and they were going to drive back together, but Jason didn't show. Jasper Pierce was home alone, but I couldn't find any motive as to why he would want Jason dead. Still, he's the only one who doesn't have a witness to verify his alibi. We looked at friends, neighbors, even his sister and her fiancé—there was no one with the motive or opportunity to kill him."

There was a long silence before Max asked, "Did you learn anything about DL Environmental last night?"

"Just an envirogroup. Harmless. They don't seem to do much of anything except organize petition drives."

"Then where did they get the money to buy a car?"

"People give money to those groups all the time."

"Maybe you can subpoena their records."

"For what cause?"

"The car was present in the commission of a felony."

He laughed. "The DA would laugh his ass off."

"Maybe Dru will give them to you, or tell you what the group does."

"I doubt she'll talk to me. As soon as she regains consciousness, she'll lawyer up."

"She can't lawyer up with me." She tilted her head and smiled. "I can get her to cooperate."

"I can offer her police protection."

"I can offer her a voice. The ability to control the message. I'll convince her to help, and then you can give her protection."

He grunted and responded snidely, "She can be a hero."

Max shrugged. "She might think so."

"I haven't done this before," Nick said. He gestured at her. "Worked with a reporter."

"I'll be gentle with you," she said lightly.

But his tone wasn't light when he said, "I'm not really comfortable with this."

"Then why?"

"I'd considered getting the arrest warrant," he said and it was only a beat later that Max realized he was joking. Possibly. "But after getting an earful from Beck about you, I watched a couple of your shows. Honestly, you have an underlying disdain for law enforcement that grates on me."

"I like cops who do their job well." She didn't want to argue with Nick, not when they'd be working together. She'd done it before, had a cop who didn't want to work with her but was forced to by his boss or the PR department, and the tension of the situation made her irritable and ill. She didn't want to work like that again.

"Do you know any?"

"A few. I don't want to argue—"

He cut her off. "But there was something else about your style that surprised me. You have a way of protecting the victims and their families even while exploiting the crime."

"That's a backhanded compliment if I ever heard one."

"It's like you have this big bubble around you that says, 'Fuck with me, fuck with these people, and I'll destroy you.'"

"I'll run that by Ben for our new tagline."

"I want to put Jason Hoffman's killer in prison." He reached into his pocket and pulled out a folded piece of paper. He handed it to her. "I don't know how much research you did on the kid, but he was a good kid, twenty-three, the whole world open to him. He shouldn't be dead."

She opened the paper. It was a copy of Jason's bio, of sorts. Honor student, high school football star, volunteer. She'd already found all that, and more.

Nick nodded, took the paper, without her having to say anything.

"And that's why I'm going to work with you."

"Maybe I'm slow on the uptake here."

"Because you already knew everything about Jason that's important to his friends and family, but not important in the investigation. You care."

"I want justice the same as you. The victims need a voice. The families deserve peace. You can't have peace if you don't know what happened."

"Some people do."

"Not me."

"Why?"

"You don't want to hear about all my baggage."

"Then I'll ask this: why don't you like cops?"

"I have no problem with law enforcement. What you see on my show or read in my books are the failures of the system—that they couldn't solve a crime, for whatever reason. I have access where you don't. People talk to me and I'm pretty good at weeding out the bullshit. I have the time and energy and resources to do things you can't do. I portray cops as I see them—some are good, some are bad, most are overworked and I don't blame them for filing a case cold when they get dumped a dozen more before the end of the first week of investigation. But I'm not going to sugarcoat garbage when I see it. And as far as exploiting crime—maybe I do. But sensationalism is not my goal. I don't need the attention, and I certainly don't need the money."

"I'm going to be talking to Dru Parker as soon as she's conscious," Nick said after a moment. "Gorman is handling the initial interviews with Parker's employers at Evergreen, and her roommates. If the killer thinks that we've made the connection between the attack on Parker and Jason's murder, they'll be on guard. I'm hoping Gorman can get statements, and then I can go in and raise the temperature. I'm pretty certain whoever attacked Dru saw or called her yesterday. We just have to figure out who."

Max was only partly listening to Nick. She had an idea and wanted to run with it—and she wasn't sure he would agree.

"You don't like the idea," he said.

"No, it's fine. I'm going to talk to Jasper Pierce."

"You're not a cop."

"What did you think I was going to do in this partnership? Give you all my information and then sit back while you follow the rules and hope to find a suspect? Maybe this was a mistake. Roger Lawrence knew I wanted to talk to Dru; I should have gone to confront him this morning, put him on the defensive immediately. You'd be surprised how fast stories change when people think they're cornered."

"That's also a very dangerous approach."

"Reporters are generally safe from crossfire—unless we're covering conflicts overseas." She thought a moment. "I think, in hindsight, that it's best we each approach this case from our own angle, and if I learn anything important, I'll let you know."

Nick wasn't sold on that idea. Whether he doubted she'd tell him what she learned or just didn't want her in the mix, she wasn't sure.

Nick said, "Think you can do a better job than me?"

"That depends. Is this a competition?"

"That wouldn't be very professional of me." He gave her a half grin. "It might take you time to get in to see Pierce."

"Don't count on it."

He gave her a quizzical look, then groaned. "Your uncle."

"Bingo." She smiled and signed the check to her room. She put her hand on Nick's arm. "I have to go." She slid out of the booth as Nick's cell phone vibrated on the table. "I'll call you."

As she was about to walk away, Nick took her wrist. She was startled and looked at him. "If you need help, just ask."

"I'll keep that in mind."

He dropped her arm. "And watch yourself around Beck."

Where had that come from? But Nick was already on his phone, so Max didn't ask.

Chapter Thirteen

Max realized during her conversation with Nick Santini that if he knew what she planned on doing, he would legally have to try and stop her. Or if he knew that she planned to break the law, he might have to arrest her. She didn't want to put him in that position, and she really didn't want to spend the night in jail. She'd spent a few days in jail in the past, and it was never fun, even when the charges were dropped. And they always were.

Plus, she liked Nick. He was intellectually challenging and she suspected there was a lot more depth to him than most of the cops she worked with. Maybe that was because most of them kept her at arm's length, as if by definition, reporters were poison. Sometimes she didn't blame them, but sometimes it just made all their jobs more complicated.

Job. This wasn't a job for Max, and maybe that's why she rubbed people the wrong way. This was a vocation, a calling she couldn't avoid if she wanted to. Not knowing the truth about what happened to her mother, what happened to Karen

Richardson, who her father was—she knew what drove her. She could give answers to others, even if she couldn't find them for herself.

Max went up to her room and first called Jasper Pierce. He didn't answer his cell phone, so she left a message with her name and number and suggested they meet for dinner to talk about the Sterling Pierce Sports Center. Then, she changed into jeans and Nick Santini's USMC T-shirt. She didn't have a lot of options with her limited wardrobe, and her workout clothes needed washing. But this would work for what she wanted. She scrubbed off her makeup, then reapplied just a hint of mascara and concealer, put her hair up in a sloppy ponytail, and figured she could pass as a college student if confronted.

She drove to Dru Parker's small house in Redwood City. Max had researched the property and Parker's roommates the night before. House managed by a property company, two female roommates, all three students at Cañada Community College. Max parked and rang the bell, then knocked. It was clear no one was home.

Max picked the flimsy front lock and slipped in. The house had an empty feeling. The only sounds were the low hum of a refrigerator, a ticking clock, and a faint scratching sound. Max looked around the living room and realized the scratching was coming from a hamster who scurried through a tunnel that connected one plastic cage with another. When he got to the end, he turned around and went back, then jumped on a wheel and started running.

There were three small bedrooms and one bath in the tiny house. It was marginally clean, but dishes were unwashed in the sink and junk mail was piled high on the kitchen table. Max ignored the living quarters and looked in each bedroom, quietly, in case someone was sleeping. Empty.

Dru had the smallest bedroom, in the back of the house, hardly larger than an oversized closet. Max could tell it was hers because the walls were decorated with save-the-earth posters and pictures of cute baby animals. And the pictures of Dru pinned to the walls. Unmade bed, dresser with a television on the top, desk with a laptop computer.

She hadn't brought her computer with her last night? That was odd—or was it? What if she wasn't really planning on going to her mother's house? Or what if she bolted before she could go home? Or didn't think she'd need a computer because there was nothing important on it?

Max turned on the computer. While it booted up, she searched Dru's room. In fact, she had been here last night—her top drawer was partly open and it appeared as if half the contents were missing. Her pillows were also missing from her bed—Max used to travel with her favorite pillow, until she forgot it in hotels too many times.

Dru had come home from work, found Nick

waiting for her with questions, got scared, packed quickly, and left. Where'd she been when she called Max? Had she been packing up? Already driving? She'd said she could be at the Caltrain station in twenty minutes; her house was less than fifteen minutes away. Max guessed she was here, packed and ready to go.

The computer was on and there was no security or passwords required. Max first looked at her browser history. Dru had indeed looked up train times to San Francisco right before she'd called Max. She'd also checked her e-mail.

Because she used an SMTP protocol, all her e-mail popped up into her computer. Max didn't need a password to access it.

More than half the messages were from makeup and clothing stores with 25 percent off coupons or one-day-only sales. Most of the others were from environmental groups. Few seemed personal. Nothing had come in yesterday or today that looked odd or suspicious. Max checked the deleted items folder; nothing was there, either. She searched the mailbox for messages from anyone at Evergreen; nothing except a woman named Janice Platt who sent weekly messages about schedules. She searched for Roger Lawrence; nothing. Brian Robeaux; nothing. Sara Hoffman; nothing. But people often didn't use their full or real names in e-mails. She searched "Hoffman" alone and immediately hundreds of messages popped up—all from Jason Hoffman, they were dated more than a year before he died and up until the morning of his murder.

Max started reading them.

It was immediately clear that Dru and Jason were more than casual acquaintances. They might have had a relationship, but they were also friends. The last message he sent, the morning he died, was cryptic, because there were no messages before or after in the thread. It was as if he was continuing a verbal conversation.

> Dru, thanks for understanding. I'll make it up to you tomorrow, tonight I have something to do. Jase

Why hadn't Dru come clean about their relationship? Why hadn't she told Nick that Jason had canceled plans with her the night he was killed?

Two nights before he died, Jason sent Dru another cryptic message.

> Dru, you know plants better than I do. I need you to look at something for me, but you can't tell anyone.

Dru had e-mailed back: Sure, when and where?

Jason responded: I'll call you.

All the other messages were while Jason was away at college, talking about his classes, sharing some of his design projects, asking how various construction projects were going. Dru told him about her friends, her classes, and vented about how one of the guys at the site would touch her whenever he came in for his paycheck, and that he was creepy. Jason wanted to know who, she wouldn't tell him.

> Roger said he'd talk to him—I don't want you getting in the middle of it. It's really not a big deal, I just don't like grabby hands.

The more Max read, the more she thought that Jason and Dru were just friends. There was nothing romantic in any of the messages, no "I love you" or "I miss you;" mostly chitchat. A lot about the sports complex.

She almost missed it because it was an old message, but one thread caught Max's attention. Jason sent it almost a year before he was killed.

> I might be able to save Evergreen. Jasper and I talked about working with Gordon and bidding on the Atherton Prep Sports Center. Jasper can get us to be considered because he's the one who put together the financing for half the project. Still, Gordon and I have lots of ideas that we think will work. I wish my uncle had the vision. Don't say anything to anyone, I don't want Uncle Brian finding out I'm working behind his back on this.

Dru never responded, but three days later Jason sent a second message.

> Wow, thanks for all the information. Lay low, I'll check into it after I graduate. In the meantime, Jasper talked to Brian and they're working up a bid. Gordon already has a winning design—I'm certain he'll get it. If Gordon's in, I'm in. I just don't know if Evergreen will make it. Cross your fingers.

There was no printer in her room—odd, considering she was a college student—so Max took a picture of each of the e-mails with her cell phone.

So Jason and Jasper were working behind Brian's back. Maybe Jason's murder was personal. At the least, Nick should follow up with Brian Robeaux, maybe check out that party again.

Max looked around. If someone was worried that Dru knew something about Jason's murder, why hadn't they come in here and searched? Unless they knew exactly what they were looking for. Of course, it could simply be that she had information—and if that was the case, she was still in danger.

Or, maybe, the killer just *thought* she knew something that would trigger a closer investigation into Jason's murder.

How did they know that Nick Santini had come to talk to her? Unless it was Max's presence yesterday morning that spooked them.

She made a note to ask Jasper Pierce, when she finally met with him, about the e-mails Jason sent to Dru, as well as the financing and no-bid project. Then she went to work searching Dru's drawers, desk, and closet. It was under her bed that she found the jackpot. A file box of all Dru's personal information—her school transcripts, grades, bank statements, insurance payments.

Max quickly photographed all the bank statements, but immediately something jumped out at her: *DL Environmental.*

Every other week, DLE deposited between four and five thousand dollars into Dru's bank account through a direct deposit. Then, three days later, the money was wire transferred to a company called R4E, minus three hundred dollars.

Once or twice wouldn't have caused Max's radar to go wacky, but twice a month for nearly two years—twenty months total. The odd deposit and withdrawal history started three months after she started working for Evergreen. Coincidence? Or was there something wonky going on? Dru, essentially, made six hundred dollars a month for allowing her bank account to be used as a pass-through. For what? And did it have anything to do with the knife attack on Dru or Jason's murder five months ago?

The front door shut, and Max quickly boxed back up the personal information. She grabbed her backpack from where she'd put it next to Dru's door, and unzipped it, as if she were unpacking.

"Dru?" she called out. "Is that you?"

"No," a female voice said.

Max stepped out into the hall. A petite blonde who looked like she'd just rolled out of bed was going through the mail on the kitchen table. "Hi," Max said. "I'm Max, a friend of Dru's. She said I could crash with her for a day or two, since my boyfriend is being an ass."

"Whatev." The girl glanced over at Max. "How do you know Dru?"

"High school. We haven't talked much lately. Which roommate are you? Amy or Whitney?"

"Whitney. Dru's not here?"

"She gave me a key yesterday and said she was going to be out all night."

"Huh. She must be shacking up with J. C. for the weekend."

"She didn't say anything to me." Who was J. C.? Max hadn't seen any e-mails from a boyfriend, but with all the messages going back and forth via texting and Twitter and other social media, it would take Max a while to find it. She wondered if Nick had access to Dru's phone, or if Gorman was going through the calls and logs.

"Talk about a jerk, but she's all into him. He's hot, but a wacko. I thought they weren't together anymore, but it's back and forth." She rolled her eyes.

"He's not from work," Max said as if it were a fact.

Whitney snorted. She walked over to the refrigerator and grabbed a Diet Coke. "Hardly. Want one?"

Max rarely drank soda, but she also knew that sharing a meal or drinks loosened tongues.

"Thanks." She took the can and opened it.

Whitney sat at the table, one leg under her body, and leaned back. "I should go save her."

"Maybe she doesn't want to be saved."

"That's the problem. Dru is such a sweetheart, she gets sucked into all these wild causes and J. C. is the worst. Was she like that in high school?"

This was going to get tricky. It didn't seem that Whitney was setting her up, but Max couldn't quite tell. Fortunately, she knew the basics about Dru's family life. "I'm a couple years older. I was friends with her sister."

"How is Gina?"

Max shrugged. "We lost touch when she moved to L.A. We just keep up on Facebook."

"I know. My best friend, Tiff, she got a full-ride scholarship to play volleyball in Texas. I never see her, we never talk. It's like I don't exist."

Bitter. Best friend going to a four-year college, Whitney stuck at a community college and working to pay her way.

Max said, "I'm going to leave a note for Dru, but I have to run."

"If you come back tonight, just be quiet. Amy and I have to be at work at six, so we crash early."

"Promise. Thanks." Max went back to Dru's room. She sat down at the computer and looked for any e-mails from a J. C. She found nothing. She went back to the browser history and found Dru's Facebook page. She was still logged in—a bad but easy habit to get into when one didn't share a computer.

She scanned all Dru's friends and found one that matched.

J. C. Potrero, San Mateo. She clicked through and found pictures of him, Dru, and others at a variety of protests and parties.

J. C. Potrero's page indicated that he was the owner of DL Environmental, the business that was depositing nearly $9,000 a month into Dru Parker's account in small, hard-to-track amounts.

Maybe this scheme had nothing to do with Jason Hoffman's murder.

Or maybe it was the reason.

Max sat in her car down the street from the legal address for DL Environmental, which was a mail drop. She pulled up all the information she could find for the business on the Internet. DLE appeared to be an environmental watchdog group that gathered petitions on a myriad of causes.

They seemed to be advocates of all things green, but it was all surface—she couldn't find anything specific that they had done other than write letters and petitions to politicians. They solicited online donations and had a fancy Web site, but no substance.

She called a friend of hers in Washington, D.C. Shelley Abbott, a legislative aide, had a finger on the pulse of all things environmental.

"Shell, it's Max."

"Maxine?" Shelley squealed. Then she laughed. "It's been three, four—no, *seven*—months since you called me. You must want information."

"You know me too well."

"Too damn well. Some day, I'm going to tell you to fuck off."

"I know too many of your secrets."

"That you do, Maxie."

Max cringed at the nickname Shelley knew she hated. They'd gone to college together and used to have brutal arguments about nearly everything, which Karen had mediated. Karen's murder had hurt Shelley as much as Max, and Shelley was one of the few people Max still talked to about Karen. Max loved Shelley like an annoying but fun sister; she was pretty sure Shelley felt the same about her.

"What do you need?"

"DL Environmental. It's an activist group in California."

"Never heard of them, but they're really a dime a dozen. It's not one of the big groups."

"Can you check your database?"

"It's Sunday night."

Max glanced at the clock on the dashboard. Four in the afternoon—seven in D.C.

"Sorry, babe."

"Don't call me babe."

"Don't call me Maxie."

Shelley sighed. "Yeah, yeah, I'm getting off my ass and walking to my computer. What are you up to?"

"I'm in California for a funeral."

Shelley's voice softened. "I'm sorry."

"Old friend I haven't seen in a long time."

"Still."

"Thanks."

"Okay, I'm logging into my network. DL . . ." she typed, mumbling to herself. "I have nothing."

"Nothing nothing?"

"I have the group logged as a tier seven."

"You're talking in-speak again. Pretend I can't read your mind," Max teased.

"Sorry. Just my personal shorthand. That means they're a letter-writing group. No ties with any state or national group. I suspect they're run out of someone's house. Don't give political or nonprofit donations. They are a registered nonprofit, which is the only reason they're in my system at all."

"You're not helping."

"Tell me more."

"A guy named J. C. Potrero says he's employed by them."

"Maybe." Max heard the shrug in her voice. Shelley continued. "A lot of these little groups will raise money for a local issue, like saving a park or protesting a development that impacts a river, things like that. They hire someone, usually a relative or friend of the organizer. I wouldn't call them a scam, but the employee does little more than maintain a Web site or organize a letter-writing campaign. Nothing illegal, nothing that helps except for their one pet cause, often they're absorbed into a state group when it's done. But there's nothing on DL or this Potrero person."

"What if I told you that DL was depositing between eight and nine thousand dollars a month in a college student's account and then that student was sending a wire transfer of almost the same amount out to another group?"

"Sounds like money laundering to me. Why don't you call your hot Cuban G-man? What's his name? *Marco.* Even his name sizzles smoothly off the tongue."

Max laughed. "He's not my hot Cuban, not anymore."

"That's what you said last time he pissed you off. And the time before that. And—"

"Cool it, Abbott."

"Touchy."

"I can't think of a reason for the money laundering," Max said to get the conversation back on track.

"Could be a fund-raising scam. The FBI would be all over that if you get a whiff of something underhanded."

"Maybe," she said, thinking. Very possibly right, but then why the laundering through Dru's account?

"I'll dig around if you want. Where in California?"

"They're based in San Mateo."

"I have a friend in San Francisco who knows everything about anything green. I'll call him and let you know what's up."

"Thanks, Shell."

"Anytime. But seriously, Max, don't wait until you need something to call. I miss you."

"Hey, the phone lines go both ways."

"Touché." Shelley laughed and hung up.

Shelley had a point. Max tended to keep her friends at a distance, and she wasn't sure why. She really didn't like psychoanalysis, but she suspected her need to avoid close attachments was related directly to Karen's death as well as her mother's disappearance. No-brainer, she was sure any first-year shrink would diagnose her as having abandonment issues or some such nonsense. *Whatev,* as Whitney said earlier.

Sitting down the street from a mail drop wasn't going to help her find J. C. Potrero. There had been nothing in Dru's room with his address or phone number—that information was likely in her cell phone. If the police had recovered her cell phone, Nick might be able to get it, but then she'd have to explain why, and she wasn't certain there was anything to this theory. In fact, she didn't even *have* a real theory. Nothing that connected to Jason Hoffman.

If Potrero's mail drop was in San Mateo, it was reasonable to think that he lived or worked in the area.

She logged into a public files database that was used primarily by private investigators. She did a variety of searches, but it wasn't until she went back to his Facebook page and learned that his full name was John Carlos that she was able to find his home address.

John Carlos Potrero was twenty-one, a year older than Dru, and lived in a pricey condo west of El Camino Real in San Mateo. Just up the hill from the complex were some of the most expensive homes in the region and Crystal Springs School, which had been a rival of Max's own Atherton Prep.

Family money—maybe. But when Max did an ownership search on the address, the condo was owned by DL Environmental. And she couldn't find anything on a Potrero family trust or a DLE trust. Didn't mean there wasn't family money, but if there was, it wasn't obvious.

Max sent the information she'd uncovered to Shelley, then approached the building.

The apartment building was a combination of condos in a three-story structure and bungalows, which surrounded the main building. She pulled a flyer from a unit that was for sale and was surprised it was listed for more than half a million dollars. J. C.'s property was a bungalow in the back, likely worth more than the condos. There was a single car garage attached. Max couldn't see in through the shuttered windows.

She knocked on the front door and there was no answer. She considered breaking in like she'd done at Dru's house, except here was a lot more dangerous and she didn't have a plausible excuse. All the shutters were closed and she couldn't see into the unit. She turned to leave.

"You're trespassing," a guy said behind her.

She turned back and faced who she knew to be J. C. Potrero from his Facebook profile. "J. C., right?" He wore jeans and a red windbreaker. He looked like he was leaving, but he hadn't answered the door. Odd.

"What do you want?"

She extended her card. "Maxine Revere, free-lance reporter. I'm writing an article about the attack on Dru Parker last night. She's a friend of yours."

"Why would a reporter care?"

"Because she had a meeting scheduled with me

last night, but was attacked before we could meet."

"That's none of my business."

"But you're her employer."

"She works for a construction company in Redwood City."

"But you own DL Environmental."

"It's just a small nonprofit."

"Small? It paid for this condo. And nearly one hundred thousand dollars of annual income to Ms. Parker over the last two years."

"Where are you getting your information?"

He was edgy, bouncing on his feet, and belligerent.

"DLE also has the title on Ms. Parker's car." Max took a leap. "I can't help but think she was attacked because she had planned to meet me. Do you know what she wanted to tell me? Do you know why someone would want to kill her?"

"I haven't talked to Dru in months. Now leave."

"Months? Then why would her roommate have suggested she was spending the weekend with you?"

"Get the fuck off my property or I'm calling the cops."

That would be interesting. "Do you own a black sedan?"

His face was red. He couldn't speak. He pulled out his cell phone.

She doubted he'd call the cops, because she

had a lot to tell them if he did. But she walked back to her car and drove down the street. She stopped at the end of the block and waited.

She didn't have to wait long. A motorcycle with a rider in a red jacket identical to the one J. C. had been wearing flew past her.

She quickly wrote down the license plate while she followed the bike.

He didn't go far. Four miles up the road, in Burlingame, he turned off El Camino Real and wound through a neighborhood until he was at the top of a hill. Another nice neighborhood, though not as pricey as the Crystal Springs area where J. C. lived. He parked in the driveway and strode up to the door. A woman answered and he started shouting at her, then the door closed and Max couldn't see or hear him.

She ran a title search. The house was owned by Rebecca Cross, and had been for the past three years. No husband on the title. A Google search told Max that Ms. Cross was an instructor at Cañada College.

The circle was complete. Cross was a professor at Cañada and Dru was a student. J. C. Potrero— whether he was her boyfriend or employer or something else—knew both of them. And he certainly hadn't been overjoyed with Max's interest in DLE or the attack on Dru. Now Max had to figure out what DLE really did, and how Jason Hoffman's murder figured into the scam.

Maybe Jason found out about DLE and confronted his friend Dru. She tells him what's going on, he tries to help her get out of it, and gets shot.

From everything Max had learned about Jason, he was a helper. He helped his family, he helped his friends, he was generous with his time and money. It would fit his profile that he would help Dru. Except it wouldn't be why Dru wanted to meet with her. Unless she felt that Max was getting too close and guilt made her want to come clean. It had happened to Max several times in the course of a cold case investigation—guilt motivated a witness to come forward.

But when Max talked to her, Dru didn't seem like the type of person who could lie so smoothly about a friend's murder. More likely, she didn't make the connection until Max asked questions and had her thinking.

Except . . . Dru hadn't called Max until after Nick Santini came to question her again. Had his questions prompted a recollection?

Max parked down the street and walked to the house. J. C.'s motorcycle was still there. She walked along the side to peer into the garage. As her eyes adjusted to the dimness of the garage, she saw a black BMW. The rear driver's side was damaged.

Bingo.

She jogged back to her car and called Nick.

"I found the car that nearly hit me last night."

He didn't say anything for a moment.

"Are you there? Nick?"

"Where are you?"

She told him, then explained what she'd learned through Dru's banking statements, how she tracked down her boyfriend, and then followed him to Rebecca Cross's house.

"Maybe you should have been a cop, not a reporter."

"Um, you wouldn't have been able to get the information the way I did."

"I need a plausible reason to get a warrant."

"I gave Gorman a description of the car."

"Color and general size. Black is rather common."

"Sarcasm doesn't become you, Detective. You have Dru's phone. You grabbed J. C.'s name off her Facebook profile. Her roommate confirmed they were dating, at least had been dating recently. You tracked him to Rebecca Cross—followed him like I did. Now you have questions." He didn't say anything. "Or I can simply go in and interview them for an article I'm writing."

"No," he snapped. "I'm on it, do not do anything, Maxine. Promise me."

"Define what you mean by 'anything.'"

He abruptly ended the call.

Max was confident that Nick Santini would take care of this. And if not, she knew where

Rebecca Cross lived and she would be back to talk to her.

Besides, she had another errand. Jasper Pierce had returned her call. His voice mail said he would love to meet for drinks—or dinner—at seven that evening. He suggested Evvia, a Greek restaurant Max had been dying to try.

She had just enough time to shower and change.

Chapter Fourteen

Jasper Pierce was everything a wealthy entrepreneur should be—attractive, well dressed, charming, and a flirt. His short sandy blond hair reminded her a bit of Daniel Craig, until she approached and she noted that he was well over six feet. The restaurant was warm and hospitable with a large hearth fireplace and the wonderful, rich smells of Hellenic cuisine. Max's mouth practically watered. Though the place was crowded, Jasper had procured a large, round corner table near the front that could have comfortably sat four. Other two-person parties were at much smaller tables.

He took her extended hand in both of his. "It is such an honor to finally meet you, Ms. Revere."

"Thank you." He pulled out her chair for her. "I have wanted to eat here since they opened," she said, "but I'm rarely in town. Call me Max."

"I've been friends with Jackson Sterling since high school. He speaks highly of you."

Max laughed. "He's probably the only one in my family who would."

"I'm sure that's not true." He gestured to the wine. "I ordered a Rapsani red, one of my favorites. The grapes are grown at the foot of Mount Olympus. But I can also recommend a white, if you prefer."

"I'll trust your judgment."

He smiled and poured the wine. She sipped. It tasted like it had been cultivated for Zeus himself.

They chatted about mutual friends and ate a full meal—the owner obviously knew Jasper and kept bringing out plates for them to share. Max didn't remember ordering anything, but felt like she sampled half the menu.

They were on their second bottle of wine when Max said, "You've been very hospitable, and I almost feel guilty that I need to ask you some questions."

Jasper smiled. "*Almost* guilty?"

"It *is* my job."

"I'm all yours." He leaned back and smiled. Definitely turning on all the charm.

"Did you hear about Dru Parker?"

"Yes. The receptionist. She's been with Evergreen since she was a senior in high school. Works hard, has poor taste in boyfriends but a strong work ethic, and that's really all I care about. Jason was friends with her. I thought they might have dated now and again, but I can't be sure."

"She planned to meet with me the night she was attacked. I am certain she knows something about Jason's murder, even if she doesn't realize she knows something. She's still in recovery at the hospital, but I'm hoping she'll be up to talking tomorrow."

"Why do you think she knows anything?"

"She said something strange had been going on at the Atherton Prep construction site the week Jason was killed. Jason was preoccupied about holes in the trees. Do you know what that means?"

"Possibly. Jason said someone was digging on the site, and he was worried that there was an environmental issue that would impact our ability to get the final building approval and break ground on time. I assured him that all the EIRs had been filed, that there was nothing to worry about. And when I went out to the site, I realized he was concerned about the grove of redwoods on the west side of the property—more than a hundred yards from our construction perimeter. I didn't pay much attention after that—haven't even thought about it until you brought it up."

"You were close to Jason."

"Yes. Gordon Cho and I have been friends since we were kids. His parents sent him to Bellarmine, not ACP, and we lost touch then and during college, but we both settled back here and I'm his daughter's godfather. I knew Jason had a gift, he was very talented, and I hooked him up with Gordon to intern as soon as he was in high school. He would have made a wonderful architect. It's truly a great loss that he's gone."

"The Robeauxs—Brian and Sara—come from modest means and, honestly, you come from money. You weren't raised in the same town, didn't go to the same schools, and they're older than you. How did you become a partner in Evergreen?"

"You've done your research."

"That's a comment that usually means you don't want to answer my question."

He sipped his wine. "Hardly. I hired Evergreen ten years ago on one of my first buildings—it was a renovation project, and Brian underbid. I was skeptical that he could get it done at cost, but I liked his no-nonsense attitude. He did an amazing job, and after the fact I learned he hardly made any money on the project. He's not a money guy. I made a proposition that I'd be a silent partner and help with his financing and bids—I know how businesspeople think, I know the market. The problem was that Brian, though gruff on the outside, has a soft streak. The economy really hit him harder than most. So I approached Jackson about putting together the funding for the new sports complex, and he hooked me up with his grandfather, Archer, and the rest is history."

"And the no-bid project?"

"Evergreen was cut a break. It happens all the time. Brian didn't know until after the fact—Jason and I kept it from him. If he thought it was competitive, he would have completely undercut the project and Evergreen would have completed it, and Brian would never earn a dime. I have an interest in the company, but it's small compared to my other businesses. ACP is getting a fabulous project and a very good deal. You know how it is—business is about who you know."

"How did Brian feel when he realized you and Jason had gone behind his back in bidding on the ACP project?"

Jasper stared at her. "How do you know about that?"

"Confidential sources," she replied.

He assessed her before answering. "Brian was upset at first, but I convinced him it was best for the company. Jason had graduated from college with a degree in architectural design and a minor in environmental impact, he had experience with Gordon Cho, one of the most respected design firms in the country, and, to be blunt, me. I couldn't continue to funnel money into Evergreen if Brian was going to turn down clients because he didn't like their politics or because he didn't like how they talked to him. Jason had a personality that made everyone like and trust him. I really liked the kid—I hope to someday have a son just like him."

He had an odd look in his expression as he looked at the candle flickering on the table. Forty, single, lamenting the lack of a prodigy. Max's urge to fall into bed with him for a brief fling went from hot to cold in a snap.

She asked, "Could Brian have killed him?"

"Why?"

"You didn't say he wasn't capable."

"Anyone is capable of murder under the right circumstances," Jasper said. He poured the rest of the wine into both of their glasses. Max stopped him before he finished with hers. Jasper sipped, then said, "Brian didn't kill Jason. I would stake my reputation on it. He loved Jason like a son. Jess and Jason were like his own children. He's truly only a nice guy around them, and Sara. He's angry and bitter about the economy and his struggling business, but he works harder than anyone I know. Physically hard labor that he's not up to anymore, but he does it anyway. He can be judgmental and rigid, but when it came to Sara and her kids, he was kind and even flexible. Honestly, if I didn't admire his work ethic and job quality, I would never have put up with Brian all these years. But I understand him now, after working with him for so long. He had the patience of a saint teaching Jason the tools of the trade. If

Brian had killed him, it would have been an accident, heat of the moment, and he would have confessed immediately. He'd never forgive himself. I just don't think he could do it. Not that he couldn't kill, but he couldn't kill Jason."

Jasper's assessment had a ring of truth. More, he had an insight into people that Max appreciated.

"So, are you done?" His eyebrow arched, making him appear even more charming and handsome.

"I'm certain Detective Santini asked you all the standard questions—did Jason have any enemies, was he worried about anything specific or vague, how was his relationship with the employees, et cetera."

"Yes, he did."

"Anything come to you now, five months later, that you didn't think about then? Particularly in reference to the trees that Jason was obsessed about."

"I wouldn't say obsessed."

"Dru Parker thought she was dying—and she's still not out of the woods—and the last thing she said to me before she lost consciousness was about how Jason thought there was something odd about holes in the trees. Maybe that's why he was there late Saturday night."

"Maybe we should go look at them."

"Can you show me what he was looking at specifically?"

Jasper nodded. "He took me out there but I didn't see anything that caused me to be suspicious. Someone had been digging around, but it didn't look like a big deal. A few holes in the dirt under the redwood trees. He asked me to talk to the school and find out if they had a science class or someone working on a school project. I asked; they said no. They'd banned students from that side of the campus because of the pending construction. We'd already put the fences up."

Max wanted to do it first thing in the morning, but she needed to talk to Dru first. "I don't know what my plans are tomorrow, but the morning is shot," she said.

"Tuesday I'll be at the site meeting with alumni who are planning to invest in the interior of the sports complex. I'll be done with them around noon."

"I'll be there. I appreciate it." Maybe she could get Santini to meet her there—it was worth a few minutes of his time.

"And then perhaps we could have another meal together."

His eyes were sparkling and Max smiled. Jasper was attractive, very smart, and educated, the type of man Max enjoyed spending time with. But most of the men she dated thought they could handle her independence and drive, but within weeks they were clingy and urging her to spend more time with them and less time with work. Which meant they'd never listened to her, let alone understood her. They paid lip service to her dreams and her career drive, all the while thinking that great sex would keep her chained to them. It's why she maintained the long-distance relationship with Marco—no strings, great sex, and she would never in a million years move to Florida, and Marco would never leave. It was perfect. Until it wasn't.

Jasper was looking for a wife, it was clear as day. His wistful expression thinking about Jason as a sonlike figure, lamenting his own lack of a family. This was a man with an agenda, and Max needed to steer clear. He might say he was worldly and cherished her independence, but he wouldn't remain that way for long. She pictured them in bed together, and all she could see were little sperms defeating all her birth control measures and invading her eggs.

But she had to admit that she liked Jasper and found him to be both sincere and honest; rare qualities.

"Maybe, but I'm trying to wrap things up so I can get back to New York."

"Wrap things up? Like what?"

"Like finding out who killed Jason."

It was well after ten by the time Max arrived back at her hotel and the desk clerk approached. "Ms.

Revere? You have a guest waiting for you in the bar."

If it was Andy, she was going to ignore it.

"Who?"

"He didn't give his name, but he was at your table yesterday."

"Blond or brunet?"

"Brunet."

Nick. "Thank you," she said and walked into the bar.

He was sitting in the far corner with both a folder and a beer in front of him. She had no opportunity to sneak up on him—his eyes were on her as soon as she stepped into the bar.

She asked the bartender for her favorite wine, and slid into the booth next to Nick. He closed the file he was reading. The tab referred to Jason Hoffman.

"If I'd known you wanted to see me," she said, "I would have rushed through dinner. Good news, I hope."

"Neither good nor bad," he said. "But since you gave me the tip on Parker's boyfriend, I thought I'd fill you in, at least as much as I'm able to."

"Is she awake?"

"Not yet, but they expect her to be conscious tomorrow."

Max was relieved. "Good."

"I spoke with Potrero. He has an alibi for the time of the attack."

"Did you check it out?"

He stared at her, his green eyes narrowed like a cat about to pounce.

She smiled. "Of course you did."

"But he was definitely squirming when I spoke to him. I'm checking out his employer and I hope Parker is forthcoming tomorrow."

Max knew better than to ask if Nick could get a warrant for Dru's house or Rebecca Cross's car—Max's statement wasn't going to get him anything. He needed probable cause, which he might get if Dru told him whatever she had planned to tell Max before the attack.

"I have a friend of mine digging around on DL Environmental."

"Maxine—"

"Just trying to find out how much money they're pulling in, what they're doing. They could be totally legit, but paying for Dru's car and Potrero's condo—"

"How the hell did you—never mind," he interrupted himself. "Don't tell me."

"I didn't break any laws." *At least not while I was investigating Potrero.* "I'll share with you what I learn, but Shelley thinks it's fishy. She knows everything there is to know about environmental fund-raising, so if they're kosher, she'll know." She sipped her wine and smiled at Nick. "I did good."

"You think very highly of yourself."

"When warranted. Come on, admit it, you wish you could do what I do."

He shook his head, but she caught a half grin. "It would be nice, but the rules are there for a reason. If I break the rules, a killer could get off on a technicality. It won't happen on my watch. So don't make me shut you down."

She leaned close to Nick. "Sweetheart, you couldn't stop me if you wanted. But I've been doing this for a long time. I know the lines I can't cross."

She wasn't going to tell him that *can't* is subjective. Some causes, some cases, she was willing to cross any line.

His eyes darkened and Max wanted to kiss him.

Max always went after what she wanted.

She leaned forward but before she could kiss him, his left hand was on her wrist. He shook his head slightly, but she ignored his hesitation. Her lips parted and his right hand went behind her neck and pulled her lips to his. The sudden lust jolted her, unexpected but very much wanted. Her hand found his hard bicep and squeezed as their kiss deepened to the point where she wanted to take him upstairs without delay. Their attraction was mutual, and by the one kiss it was clear to her that they would be very compatible in bed.

He pulled back first. He didn't have to tell her he was leaving; she saw it in his eyes.

"I don't want this," he said.

She managed a sly smile, even through her racing heart. "You don't?"

He got up, picked up his files, and stared at her. That's when she realized it was that he didn't want the feelings of attraction, not that he didn't want to have sex. Her confidence regained its foothold.

"Max—" He stopped. He leaned over and gave her a last, quick kiss. "Be good." Then he left before she could say anything in reply.

Chapter Fifteen

Max's cell phone rang at five thirty in the morning. It was Shelley from D.C.

"You know I'm in California," Max grumbled as she pulled herself from a deep sleep.

"Good morning, sunshine," Shelley chirped.

Max groaned.

"Nice way to thank me for working all night for you."

"Thank you." Max was still confused, but put it off to being jolted from a hot dream that involved strawberries, chocolate, and Nick Santini.

"You don't sound excited."

"You're excited for the both of us."

She swung her legs over the edge of the bed, stretched, then walked over to her desk and turned on her computer.

"Not excited—just pissed off. I've spent all my

life working to protect the environment, you know? It's my *calling*. So I really hate it when people scam the system. It makes us all look bad, right?"

"Right," Max agreed, though she was still catching up with Shelley.

"So I called a friend of mine high up in Cal-EPA—someone who knows everything about every environmental group in California. He never heard of DL Environmental. He has access to a database of nonprofits, and DLE is registered, but no sign of that kind of donation history. Have no idea what's going on with them, but they file a simple tax filing stating that they receive less than $50,000 in donations. Tommy thinks that they're running a scam—you know, donate to this cause and feel good, but they don't use any of the money for the cause."

"Hmm."

"You don't think so?"

"I think it's bigger than fraud."

"How so?"

"They own a half-million-dollar condo in San Mateo and a new car that one of their people is driving. They have a mail drop for a business address."

"Well, just so you know, they're not a player at all, never raised a finger or given a dollar to any of the legit causes."

"Good to know. Can your friend Tommy get

their filings? The nonprofit paperwork, and public tax information."

"Because they're nonprofit, most of the stuff is available to the public if you know where to look. I can get it for you. Give me an hour and I'll e-mail what I find."

"Thanks, Shell."

"So it helps?"

"Yes." It confirmed what Max had been thinking, but she still didn't know where DLE was getting their money. If it was an Internet financial scam, that was under the FBI. "Can you please cross-reference any paperwork with the names John Carlos or J. C. Potrero and Rebecca Cross?"

"Wow, you said please. I don't think I've ever heard that word cross your lips." Shelley laughed heartily.

"You're not funny."

"I'll be in New York for a conference this summer. I expect dinner and a show and lots of drinks."

"You're on. E-mail me the dates and I'll clear my calendar."

Max hung up and ran through all possible scenarios, but it seemed pretty clear based on the evidence she saw at Dru's place that she and Jason were friends. Maybe she told Jason what she was doing with DLE, and Jason being a smart guy knew it was illegal. Perhaps he tried to help her, and got a bullet in the head for his effort.

Except, that meant she lied to Max when she

said that there were weird things going on at Evergreen the week Jason was killed. That could have been a cover for Dru, feeling guilty and wanting to point a finger at J. C. and his buddy Rebecca Cross? Dru didn't seem like a killer, but she might have kept quiet about the murder. Yet when both Max and Nick started asking around about Jason's murder again, she panicked. And would she have really kept quiet, considering her and Jason's long-term friendship?

Murder over a financial scam? People have been killed for less, but it didn't feel right to Max. And would Dru have told J. C. that she planned to talk to Max about whatever was going on? Doubtful. Not if she thought J. C. was a killer. Maybe he followed her. Or . . .

Or someone Dru trusted knew about the arrangement. Like her roommates, Whitney and Amy. If one of them were home when Nick came over, and then Dru bolted, they might have alerted J. C. or Rebecca.

Too many what-ifs and not enough answers. She ordered up coffee from room service because she had a lot of work to do.

A text message from David popped up on her phone: Parker is conscious. Being moved to Room 242.

It was 3:00 A.M. in Hawaii. Did David never sleep? She responded with a smiley face.

Max needed to talk to Dru. She could put all this

together if Dru would admit to what was going on with the money and DLE and tell her if Jason had found out about it.

She frowned. That still didn't explain Jason's obsession with the trees at Atherton Prep. Maybe Dru had said the wrong thing. She had been bleeding and in pain.

Max waited for her coffee, drank a cup, dispensed with e-mail, then quickly showered and dressed. Today called for professional, because she might have to talk herself into Dru's room. As she was about to leave, her e-mail popped, a message from Shelley. She'd attached a list of property owned by Rebecca Cross, DL Environmental, or R4E. There were only four, two owned by Rebecca Cross, and two owned by DL Environmental. DL owned the house Dru and her friends rented and J. C. Potrero's condo. Cross owned the house Max had followed J. C. to yesterday, plus a remote property off Phleger Road. It was in the country, in the mountains west of Woodside. The area was mostly open space and protected land, but any original property ownership was grandfathered in decades ago, with right of survivorship.

It was less than thirty minutes from a town, but remote nonetheless. Few people lived up there full time.

It might just be time for a day trip.

The case had become far more interesting. Lies, money laundering, murder. Ben would be furious with her because this was going to take time, but she didn't care. Jason's murder had grabbed her and she wouldn't be able to let go until she solved it.

Max left her hotel and drove toward Sequoia Hospital. Almost immediately, she noticed that she was being followed. Or was she being paranoid? Maybe the break-in while she'd been in Kevin's apartment had thrown her for more of a loop than she thought.

After a couple of turns, she didn't think paranoia was to blame. The car was a white Mercedes with partially tinted windows. With the angle of the early morning sun, she couldn't make out any distinguishing characteristics of the driver. There was no front license plate, a violation of state law unless it was a new purchase. The car looked new, but she wasn't a good judge with cars.

She drove straight to Sequoia Hospital. The Mercedes passed by, but she still thought it had been following her.

Max checked in at the desk for a visitor's badge. She had to give the name and room number of the person she was visiting, but no flags were raised. The desk told her to check in with the second-floor nurse's station, but Max ignored that request. She didn't want anyone questioning her right to be there.

She caught the nurses at a busy time as meals were being cleared and visiting hours had just started. Max slipped into room 242. It was a two-bed room, but right now Dru was alone. She looked small and pale on the stark white sheets. She had a breathing tube in her nose. Max had a flash of sitting next to her in the parking garage, holding her scarf on the girl's abdomen, blood seeping through her fingers. That she'd survived defied the odds. She was a fighter, and Max hoped she still had fight in her. If Dru came clean, Max would move heaven and earth to help her.

Max looked at the chart in the slot next to the bed. Dru had been downgraded this morning from critical to serious. Max couldn't read everything, but it appeared that the surgery had lasted six hours to repair damage, her lung had been punctured but after twenty-four hours in recovery she'd regained consciousness.

Dru opened her eyes as if sensing there was someone watching her. "Hey." Her voice was low and gravelly.

"Don't talk." That was a dumb thing to say. Max planned to ask questions. She sat down on the chair next to the bed. "I'm glad you're okay."

"You. Thanks."

"Dru, I need to ask you some questions, but I think I know the answers and I don't want you to get upset or work yourself up, okay? So I'm going to tell you what I think happened, and if I'm wrong, squeeze my hand."

She nodded. She looked defeated but emboldened. Someone had tried to kill her but she survived. That changed a person, and Max was counting on that change to be for the better.

"Your ex-boyfriend J. C. Potrero used you to launder money from DL Environmental. I haven't figured out what his scam is, but I will. The car that nearly ran me over in the parking garage, driven by who I think stabbed you, is owned by Rebecca Cross. She's a teacher at Cañada College. Do you know her?"

Dru nodded once.

"I think that J. C. or Rebecca found out that Detective Santini came to talk to you and felt you were a liability. You know something they don't want the police to know. Did J. C. kill Jason?"

Dru squeezed Max's hand. "I don't know," she whispered.

"That's okay. Was this money laundering scheme to hide donations to DLE?"

She shook her head.

"Were they getting money somewhere else but saying it was from DLE?"

She nodded.

Max's stomach flipped. She was close. She thought about Evergreen—construction was ripe for graft and corruption. Maybe they planned on robbing the construction site and Jason got wind of it—but that didn't feel right. Still, she asked, "Were they robbing construction sites using DLE to launder the money?"

"No. No."

The machine Dru was attached to started beeping as her heart rate rose.

"Shh, Dru, don't get yourself upset. Okay?"

"Pot."

"Potrero?"

Dru shook her head. "They have a pot farm. I don't know where."

Drugs? This was all about *drugs?*

"And Jason found out? Maybe tried to help you?"

She shook her head again. "Jason didn't know. I don't know why they'd kill him."

"But they did kill him, right?"

"I don't know. I swear."

Her heart rate was going up again.

"I believe you." Max did—she believed that Dru didn't know whether J. C. or Rebecca killed Jason. But Max could see a possible scenario unfolding, where Jason found out his friend Dru was doing something illegal and confronted her ex-boyfriend. It was something an overprotective big brother might do, and from all the e-mails she'd read between Dru and Jason, that fit their relationship. She wanted to ask about the documents Dru had sent Jason before he graduated, but Dru was fading, and Max didn't want to jeopardize her recovery. Still, she needed to find out what Jason meant about the trees.

"You said that Jason was obsessed with the

trees at Atherton Prep. That something was odd, holes in the trees."

"Trees? I said that?"

"Yes, Saturday night when I found you."

Dru took a moment to collect her thoughts. The machine that monitored her heart and breathing also seemed to slow down. Good.

"Jason was acting weird all week," Dru said slowly, her voice scratchy. "He spent hours at ACP, walking the campus, doing nothing."

"You know this how?"

"I heard Brian and Roger talking about Jason's strange behavior. And I saw it myself. Brian said he thought Jason was on drugs, but I think he was just mad at Jason."

"Because Jason went behind Brian's back to bid on this project with Jasper Pierce and Gordon Cho?"

Dru stared at her as if she were a mind-reader. "How did you know?"

"Research." No sense telling Dru she'd broken into her house.

"So Brian said to Roger that Jason was talking about the trees, or something that was happening under the trees. Holes in the ground."

"Do you know which trees?"

"Not then, but later, when I moved my desk to the site, Roger told me it was the trees along the west fence, Jason would walk through them then ask Roger if anyone from his crew had messed with them. Roger said no. He didn't really even *have* a crew then."

That confirmed what Jasper had told her the night before.

"Do you think that's why Jason was at ACP the night he was killed?"

Dru thought for a long minute. "Yes. He was waiting for something. He said something like . . . I'll figure out who's messing with my site. I think that was it. But that was days before Thanksgiving. I didn't think about it."

"And you never told the police this."

"I didn't really remember, or I didn't think it was important." She looked pained. "Believe me, I cared about Jason. I wish I'd fallen for him instead of J. C. Jason wanted to get together, but . . ." Her voice trailed off. Max knew exactly what she'd been thinking. Jason was the good boy, the college grad, the straight-and-narrow boyfriend who was marriage material. J. C. Potrero was the bad boy who excited her and made her feel powerful and on the edge.

Max had been there, done that. She completely understood.

"One more thing. How did J. C. and Rebecca find out Nick Santini came to talk to you?"

Dru closed her eyes. At first Max thought she'd fallen to sleep. Then she said, "Whitney and Amy. All of us were getting paid by DLE."

• • •

Max loved spring in the Bay Area. Seventy-five degrees, light breeze, blue skies. While she loved living in New York City, nothing beat the California climate. The drive up to Phleger Road reminded her that sometimes, she needed a break. Even if it was a short drive into the mountains.

She looked around for the white Mercedes, but she hadn't seen it in the hospital parking lot, and it wasn't following her now. She debated telling David about it, and decided she would—when they talked or when he returned, whichever came first. If she saw it again, she'd reconsider.

She realized that the college where Cross taught was only fifteen minutes from her property. To get to her home in San Mateo was less than thirty minutes in the other direction. If they had a pot farm up here, it was bold—though the mountain wasn't extensively populated, there were plenty of homes and weekend cabins, bikers and hikers.

As soon as she turned onto Phleger from Cañada Road, she realized she had a problem. It was not only a private road, but gated as well.

The road itself was about three miles from Cañada to Skyline Boulevard, but completely uphill from where she was. The property in question was one mile east of Skyline, and from there had a more or less even terrain.

She drove to a strip mall and found a sporting goods store. She had sneakers in her bag, but no clean running clothes. She bought a fanny pack, sweatpants, T-shirt, and windbreaker, changed in the bathroom, and drove up to Skyline Boulevard. There was no place to park on the edge of the road, but less than two hundred feet from the private road was a high-end restaurant. She'd eaten here before—delicious food and an amazing view. That it was both remote but close to the city made it doubly attractive for special nights.

It was closed on Mondays, which was good for Max, so she parked in their lot and stretched.

She jogged down Skyline until she reached the private road. Based on the parcel map she'd downloaded to her phone, there were only six property owners off Phleger. Like she suspected, most of the mountainside was owned by the county or state, and the owners maintained the road because it was gated. Cross's property, which had been gifted to her by her grandparents years ago, was less than a mile down the road. Max tucked her phone into her fanny pack, along with a water bottle, Taser, and identification, glanced around for any nosy observers, then quickly hopped the metal gate.

If anyone questioned her, she would simply saying she was jogging the five miles down to Cañada Road—she checked her map and while it was three miles as the crow flies, it was definitely longer with the twists in the road. She was pretty certain they'd had trespassing joggers and bikers on this narrow road—so narrow that there were stretches where two cars couldn't pass.

She spent so much time on a treadmill at the gym she forgot how much she enjoyed running outdoors in fresh air. She kept an easy pace, not knowing what she might encounter.

She heard no one, saw no cars or people or bikers or joggers. She was twenty minutes from Redwood City, but she felt like she was in the middle of nowhere. It was truly awesome, yet at the same time a bit disconcerting. She'd broken one of her rules—loose as it was—that she'd always let Ben or David know where she was headed when she was following an investigative trail. A few times she'd been in sticky situations, but she'd always managed to get herself out just fine. She was smart and resourceful, and this was her life. She knew it the minute she started the journal when Karen disappeared in Miami. In fact, the anniversary of Karen's disappearance had just passed while she had been with Marco in Miami. Karen was never far from her thoughts, which both bothered Max and comforted her. If she didn't forget what happened to Karen, if she was still looking for evidence, still looking for her remains, then Karen would never be forgotten.

The road Max ran down gently inclined, with a few slight hills and steeper dips. Nothing she couldn't handle, but she had to watch her step. The road wasn't well maintained and there were potholes and rocks in her path. Worse, there was a steep drop-off to her right. Max wouldn't say she was afraid of heights—she was more afraid of falling.

Max turned along a forty-five-degree curve and saw a steep driveway up the north side of the mountain. It, too, had a gate on it and no address, but based on her map this was the Cross property.

There was barbed wire fencing along the top of the gate, making it impossible to climb. There was no easy way to get around it.

She walked down the road until the mountain-side was less steep. Looking carefully for poison oak—it was common here, she remembered from her youth—she found a place she could scale without too much effort.

There was fencing here, too, but most of it had fallen down. Still, Max was careful as she climbed over the half-buried barbed wire.

Five minutes later she found herself looking down onto the curving driveway. The trees on this side of the mountain were dense, providing a natural canopy, while the mountain side wasn't as steep as on the south, making the land easier to access.

Max wasn't an expert on the drug trade, but she knew that pot farms were big business, especially in the far northern reaches of California. Here, so close to a big city, it was rarer to find outdoor farms, which made this area strategically located.

They'd need a storage shed that could be used for drying out the plants when harvested. Which meant electricity or generators.

She suspected that there would be some sort of surveillance system unless Cross and Potrero had a caretaker. Or both. She wanted to find evidence of the pot farm, take some pictures, and then get out of here. Confronting drug growers wasn't a smart move.

She listened to her surroundings. It wasn't as quiet as she originally thought. Birds mostly, a distant motorbike or quad that faded away to a faint echo as she listened, and the rustling of trees as the breeze gently moved the air. Fortunately, she'd be able to hear any vehicle long before it approached, so she felt confident about walking along the driveway.

Max scrambled down the side and started walking along the narrow, unpaved road, hyper-alert for any sounds. She was startled when she soon came upon a small, rustic cabin. She pulled back into the redwood trees and surveyed the place. No cars, no people, nothing to suggest anyone was here.

Confident she was alone, she left her hiding spot and walked up the porch. All the blinds were closed. Through one narrow crack she made out a table and chairs, a couch, a door on the left. She heard a faint hum and, for a time, thought it came from the house—but it sounded too loud to be a refrigerator. She walked around the house then noticed a barn on the far side of an overgrown clearing, half-concealed by redwoods and birch trees of all sizes. She approached the barn and the hum grew loud enough that Max recognized it as a generator.

The windows on the barn were better camouflaged; they were all painted black on the inside. There was also a heavy-duty chain on the door. She walked around and found a second entrance in the back; it was locked from the inside.

But this was her only chance of confirming her theory. She found a rock and broke the window next to the door. Though the window here was also painted, a thick curtain had been nailed over the opening as well. She pulled the curtain from the nails and it fell aside.

The barn housed a full drug operation—thick bunches of marijuana hung upside down to dry under low-wattage heat lamps, fueled by the generator that was operating next to her behind the barn. There were tables for cutting and sorting and whatever else they did with the dried pot.

She snapped several pictures with her phone camera, sent them to her cloud server, hoping they went through with the sketchy cellular connection, then pocketed it. She considered crawling through the window, but she'd then be trapped if anyone came. And what she had documented was good enough for the authorities.

Because she was right next to the generator, she didn't hear anyone coming until a motorcycle had driven up to the barn. She dropped down from the broken window and flattened herself against the back of the barn.

Shit.

She peered carefully around the corner. Behind the motorcycle was a truck with a camper shell. The motorcycle was a black BMW bike, property of DLE and ridden by J. C. Potrero—confirmed when he whipped off his helmet and started yelling at the woman driving the truck. "We don't have time," he said.

"You're being paranoid," the female said.

"That reporter was in your house. She found me, we don't know what Dru told her. The cops talked to Becky this morning. We're clearing out."

"We still have another crop to cut—" the girl said.

"Dammit, Amy, leave it. If they find this place, they can't prove we knew anything about it. It's only Becky's name on the title, and she hasn't been up here in years. She'll deny knowing about it, and no way can they prove she did. And if they don't find it? We'll come back in a couple months for the rest."

The chains on the front of the barn rattled and the doors opened. She didn't know how long it was going to take for them to clear out; she needed to get the authorities up to the mountain fast. No way could she go back using the driveway—at least not until she cleared sight of the house.

She checked the cell reception on her phone; none. That meant the pictures hadn't been uploaded either. She'd have to get back up to Skyline in order to call the police.

She didn't want to wait, but she also didn't want to get herself killed. She looked around. Behind the barn was a wide, worn path that disappeared down a gentle slope into a copse of trees. She didn't see where it led—probably to the remainder of their crop. She didn't much like the idea of trying to get back to Skyline via the mountain side. She had no idea what kind of terrain she was looking at, but it would be uphill most of the way, some of it steep—possibly too steep to walk.

Max had one option that seemed the most viable—walk around the opposite side of the barn and into the trees, keeping to the shade, and going back up the hillside toward Phleger Road. She would be exposed for a short distance, but she didn't see an alternative.

Ticktock, Max, make a decision.

"J. C. come here." Amy's voice was right on the other side of the broken window.

Her imminent discovery made the decision for her. Max moved quickly around the side of the barn and back toward the house. She grabbed her Taser and flipped it on, just in case, and stopped only when the house blocked the view from the barn. She had to wait, hoping they hadn't seen her.

She heard commotion at the barn. Max could only make out a few words, most of which had to do with J. C. barking orders at Amy to hurry; he wanted to be out of here with or without the pot.

Then J. C. started toward the house. He unlocked the front door, Max just on the other side, her body up against the wall, making herself as small as possible. Hard to do when you were five feet ten and a half inches tall.

She heard his voice. There must be a landline inside, because Max still had no service on her cell phone.

"No, it wasn't a fucking tree branch. The curtain was pulled out," J. C. said. He was standing inside the house, right on the other side of the wall.

As much as Max wanted to listen to the conversation, she knew this was her best chance to get to the tree line and escape while there was still time to bring the police in to stop them.

Staying as low as possible, she ran toward the trees and up the slope.

J. C. spotted her.

"Stop!" He shouted behind her. She didn't stop; she ran as fast as she could up the hill, her hamstrings burning.

Please don't have a gun, please don't have a gun.

She heard a gun go off. Of *course* he had a gun. But she still had distance in her favor, and she appeared to be in better shape than her pursuer. She hoped. He was ten years younger.

The slope was too steep for her to keep going in a straight line; she began to slide backward, losing ground. She turned and went up at a diagonal, using the trees to brace herself as needed. She spared a glance back and couldn't see J. C., but there was another gunshot and Max didn't slow down to figure out where it came from. She didn't see the bullet hit anything around her. Was he shooting to scare her? Had he recognized her?

Max kept going at a brisk pace, even though she didn't hear anyone pursuing. Her lungs and calves burned. Then, in the distance she heard a motorcycle, and that's when she stopped and gave herself a minute to catch her breath.

She willed herself to control her racing heart. She took out her water, drank half of it, and bent over, taking long, deep breaths. She was light-headed and dizzy, but knew that would fade. While her run had been steep and treacherous, she'd run much longer in marathons. Too bad she hadn't been in the middle of training for a marathon, she'd probably have been able to take the mountain with no problem. But it had been years, and it showed.

The echo in the mountains made it difficult to gauge the direction of the bike, but she guessed he was on the driveway going from the house to the road. Either he was making a run for it, or he was attempting to intercept her.

She used the sound to help her with direction. Soon she found the trees she'd marked when she first left the road, then she went through the broken fence. She no longer heard Potrero's bike, but she sat behind a tree and listened for several minutes before she felt comfortable leaving her hiding spot.

She walked briskly up the road, toward where she parked her car, and pulled out her cell phone. She had one bar. She tried calling Santini, but the call wouldn't go through. Instead, she sent him a text message, knowing it was easier to get one through than a call.

> On Phleger Road in Woodside, heading toward Skyline Boulevard where I left my car. Found a pot farm and drying facility at Rebecca Cross's property. They're clearing out now. They spotted me, but I lost them. Get the authorities up here before they disappear with the evidence.

She then forwarded him the photos that she'd taken. They were going through very slow, and she pocketed her phone.

She walked fast instead of running, because if

she spotted J. C., she needed to be able to sprint.

Like you can outrun a motorcycle. Just don't be spotted.

She could see the headline now: INVESTIGATIVE REPORTER MAXINE REVERE FELL TO HER DEATH AFTER UNCOVERING A MARIJUANA FARM.

She pushed the macabre thoughts of dying from her head as she approached the gate that led to the main road. It was closed, which meant he had gone east, or he'd taken the time to lock it behind himself.

She hopped the gate and turned toward the restaurant where she parked her car.

That's when she saw J. C. Potrero's motorcycle partly hidden behind a thick tree.

Earlier, cars had passed her intermittently on Skyline Boulevard. Right now, Max saw and heard no one, and a killer was waiting for her.

She looked around, her Taser in hand. There was a house up the road in the other direction, but the chances that someone was home in an area that was mostly weekend cabins was thin. She didn't want to be trapped, and had to assume that J. C. knew this area better than she did.

She heard a car coming from the north. She didn't want to endanger anyone else, and she didn't know how stable J. C. was—would he kill an innocent bystander just to get Max?

She went toward her car. There was another

house between the restaurant and the gate, but there were no cars in front and it didn't look like anyone was home.

"You fucking bitch," a voice said behind her.

Max slowly turned around. J. C. Potrero had a gun pointed at her. He heard the car as well, and lowered the gun, keeping it in front of him so the driver wouldn't be able to see.

"The police already know."

"Like hell they do."

"Why did you kill Jason Hoffman?"

He stared at her, seemingly baffled. He might be innocent of murder; it had most likely been Rebecca Cross who'd stabbed Dru.

"You know that's why Dru was meeting with me, to tell me something about Jason Hoffman's death. I didn't know about any of this until your girlfriend nearly killed her."

The car passed and J. C. raised his gun.

Max had her Taser up the sleeve of her windbreaker. She fired as she sidestepped. He didn't get a round off, but fell to the ground, dropping his gun.

She kicked the gun away and ran to her car. She got in, locked the doors, and pulled out her phone to call Nick Santini.

Only then did she realize she had six missed calls. She'd had her phone on silent.

"What the fuck is going on, Revere?" Santini asked.

"Your suspect is down. Tasered. Don't know how long he'll be down."

"Stay away from him."

She glanced over to where J. C. was lying on the ground.

"I kicked his gun away and he's still down."

"Where are you?"

"Outside the Bella Vista Restaurant on Skyline Boulevard. Nice place. Maybe we can have dinner here when I help you wrap up your case."

"You're a piece of work."

"Thank you," she said. She was trying to diffuse his anger, but it wasn't working.

"Stay put. And you might want to call your lawyer, because I'm planning on putting cuffs on you."

Max swallowed her sexy retort about how she didn't do threesomes. Now she was pissed. "I broke your case wide open."

"You screwed my case. Don't. Move." He hung up.

She glanced over to where J. C. was lying on the ground. He was trying to get up, but had no balance.

A car was approaching from the south. She got out of her car and flagged them down. "Do you have any rope?" she asked with a smile.

Chapter Sixteen

Max ordered a second glass of wine as the Menlo Grill waiter took her plate away.

The police had taken J. C. Potrero into custody and found Amy Benson still at the house with a truckful of marijuana. The evidence was solid. Rebecca Cross was being interviewed, and the detective in charge—not Santini—said that Amy was talking, and they should know in short order how the entire operation worked.

Not bad for a day's investigation.

Nick Santini hadn't spoken more than two words to her when he first arrived. They were, "Explain. Now." She did. He wrote everything down and walked away. At least she didn't need to call her lawyer. Arresting a reporter was never a good idea—she would be able to control the public message.

No one—J. C. or Rebecca—had admitted to Jason Hoffman's murder or the attack on Dru Parker, but it was clear that Rebecca Cross's car was the one that had nearly hit Max in the parking garage. Max hoped that the multiple jurisdictions didn't mess with the case—the most important thing, from her point of view, was finding out who killed Jason Hoffman and why.

She hadn't picked up on much of anything—

after taking her statement, Nick and the other cops had stayed away from her—but she overheard Nick tell someone on the phone that Dru Parker was cooperating. Max was pleased—she thought the girl was remorseful and she could use a fresh start. Punish her, but not where it would ruin her life. Her efforts to help catch her attacker and Jason's killer would go a long way with a jury and judge. Max hoped she had a good attorney. She might be able to help with that. At least get her someone good, who wouldn't put the girl in debt for the next decade.

She didn't think that Dru knew or even suspected that J. C. or Rebecca killed Jason until recently. Max liked to believe that Dru would have come forward, even though it was plausible she might have remained silent out of fear. Max certainly hadn't pushed her hard this morning at the hospital for information, though nearly dying might have had something to do with her willingness to talk.

The problem, Max realized, was that she had doubts that the drug money laundering scam was the root of Jason's murder. Dru had seemed nervous around Roger Lawrence, the general manager of the Evergreen project, and Lawrence had been the one to send her on a worthless errand when Max started talking to her. Max wouldn't have been surprised if Lawrence had been the one to knife her—that it was someone completely different, with no apparent connection to Evergreen, made Max skeptical that the two cases were connected.

She didn't want to be skeptical. Skeptical meant that she still had questions that hadn't been answered. Questions she couldn't even guess at.

She couldn't forget what Dru said on the phone. That strange things had been happening at Evergreen the week before Jason's murder. And later Dru talking about holes and trees. And since the farm had nothing to do with the construction company—at least from what Max could tell so far—these "strange things" might not be related to the drug money, either.

She needed to talk to Dru again. But not tonight.

Max signed the check and went upstairs to change into her swimsuit. She needed to decompress. Her muscles were already so sore she could hardly walk up the stairs; the spa would work wonders to loosen her up and help her sleep.

She changed into her blue one-piece suit, pulled on a hotel robe, and grabbed a towel. She swung by the bar for another glass of wine, this one in a plastic cup for the pool, and went outside. The night had cooled off substantially and steam rose from the spa. There was a couple enjoying the warmth but Max had no problem slipping in and relaxing. She said a polite hello, then closed her eyes and put her head back. A few minutes later she heard the couple leave, and then she put her feet up on the seat. The cold wine went down beautifully and for a few blissful minutes, her mind was completely clear.

Then her thoughts drifted back to Lindy's murder and the key she'd found in Kevin's apartment. Jason Hoffman's case was far from closed, but she'd handed everything over to the police. Though she still had some questions—that she hoped Dru could answer—she didn't have another angle to follow. And while the pot farm had been a big distraction, Lindy and Kevin hadn't been far from her mind.

Though Kimberly Ames had kept Max from talking with Gerald Ames on Saturday, she wouldn't be at Gerald's office tomorrow morning. Max would ask him point-blank whether he'd left the message for her at her hotel. And then, depending on the answer, she'd ask for his blessing. Lindy had problems with her parents—what teenager didn't?—but she'd truly loved her father, and Max wanted to give him peace of mind.

She considered her motivations. Was it Gerald Ames she cared about or herself? Did she need to know, regardless of who else wanted the truth? Would she continue pursuing answers even if Lindy's father wanted her to stop?

She wouldn't know until she asked him.

Max heard someone approach and opened one

eye to find Nick Santini standing over her. She smiled; he frowned.

"Detective," she said.

"What the hell were you thinking?"

She closed her eyes again. "You can go," she said.

"Not until you explain yourself. Risking your life for a damn story?"

She sighed. "I'm trying to relax. Don't yell at me."

A chair scrapped along the tiles and Nick sat down. He said in a low voice, "You could have gotten yourself killed."

"You're a cop. It's part of your job."

"You're not a cop."

"Until I took the host position with 'Maximum Exposure,' I was an undercover investigative reporter. I sometimes got into scrapes that were hard to get out of, but aside from a broken arm a few years back, and the occasional bumps and bruises, I've been fine. Going out to Cross's place on Phleger Road brought back all the reasons why I love my job. Besides, no cop could have gone where I did without a warrant."

"There's a reason for the rules."

"And there's a reason to break them." She opened her eyes again. Nick sat close to the edge and she had an overwhelming urge to pull him into the spa with her. After last night's kiss, she wanted more.

But he still looked angry.

"You talked to a suspect."

"Dru? She would have lawyered up if you went in all hard-nosed cop on her. I got what you needed, and she's cooperating. You're welcome."

"You think you're some catalyst for truth, justice, and the American way?"

"I'd use the slogan, but that would be plagiarism."

"You have an answer for everything, don't you? It takes time to build a case. We had to arrest them because of what you found, but now they've called their lawyers, I have no proof that either of them killed Jason Hoffman, and if the DA or the U.S. attorney—because hell, right now there's such a big jurisdictional fight that I don't know if I'll even get to talk to any of them again—cut some fucking deal, there goes any closure for the Hoffman family."

"Rebecca Cross stabbed Dru. I saw her damaged car."

"Her car was definitely in the parking lot. We have it on surveillance. But we don't have *her* on tape. The angle is wrong. And she's not talking, not one word. Neither is Potrero. The only thing Potrero said when I put Jason Hoffman's murder on the table was that he didn't kill Hoffman, didn't even know him."

"You believe him?"

"Potrero is an ass, and he's definitely capable of

killing someone. Possession with intent to sell is a far lesser charge than murder and attempted murder. We'll see."

"Cross?"

"Cold. We now have to build a rock-solid case." He ran his hands over his face. "I don't think you understand the position you put us all in today."

"I got you proof of their operation."

"They're going to make bail. We just found out about the drug operation—usually, we work for weeks, sometimes months, to build a case to turn over to the district attorney. We don't have that kind of time now—we have to show our cards and build the case after the fact. That makes it harder on everyone, and we're going to miss things. Some damn lawyer will get them off on some fucking technicality and that's all on you. It's out of my hands now. The FBI and DEA are taking it over."

"And that's why you're mad."

"I couldn't care less if the feds take over the drug charges. But one of our suspects may have killed Jason Hoffman. I had my shot today and that's it. The feds know it's a concern, but they're not going to care like I do. I want Jason's killer to go to prison for the rest of his—or her—life. And now—I just don't think I can do that."

"I'm sorry," Max said.

Nick stared at her. "You don't seem to be the type of woman to say she's sorry about anything."

"I'm usually not. But I understand how important it is to you to see justice done."

"You're a piece of work, Revere. You can relax there in your hot, bubbling water and lie to me. You're not sorry. Not at all."

Through clenched teeth she said, "Don't tell me what I am."

"I know what you are. You're a ruthless, reckless, story-chasing reporter who doesn't care whether she screws a major case, as long as you get the byline. Or the face time. But you're good."

"Yes, I am." She was on the defensive, but she wasn't going to let him see it.

He smiled, but it was cold. He rose from the chair and towered over her.

"You had me sucked in. Yesterday, I was willing to work with you. I saw something in you Saturday night . . ." His voice trailed off and then he shook his head. "What was I thinking? I know better than to trust a reporter. Especially one like you."

He started to walk away. Then he turned back and said, "If Jason Hoffman's killer goes free, it's on you. Tell that to your viewers."

Max watched Nick leave, seething. He had no idea who she was or why she chose this life. Did he think she was a reporter for the fun and glamour? Hardly. It was *damn* hard work, often unrewarding. But when her efforts paid off and the truth was set free, all the disappointments disappeared.

She wasn't going to explain herself to someone who had already judged her.

Max closed her eyes and leaned back into the hot water, but the tension had returned and turning into a human prune wasn't going to fix anything.

It would have been a hell of a lot easier to accept Nick's tirade if she didn't already like Detective Santini.

Chapter Seventeen

Lindy's father, Gerald Ames, was a businessman with an office in Silicon Valley. When they were kids, neither Lindy nor Max really knew what Gerald did for a living or how he made his money, but he went to the office every day and he brought home a substantial income. Now Max understood that he was the business end for a major computer software company and traveled all over the world brokering agreements with countries and corpora-tions. But it was really his stocks, investments, and shares in the company that gave him his sizable wealth.

Max knew that Mr. Ames would never agree to meet with her, especially in light of her con-frontation with Kimberly on Saturday night. She didn't particularly want to be tossed from his office building by security. She couldn't access the secure employee parking lot with her car, but walking in proved to be easy. There she stood under one of the cameras near the elevator and hoped she wasn't visible at the guard station. Considering no one came and arrested her the ten minutes she waited, she was in the clear. It helped that she'd dressed like a businesswoman—she'd bought the suit the night before at Macy's. The fight with Nick Santini had put her in a rotten mood; an evening shopping spree perked her right back up.

It was amazing what new clothes and shoes did for her attitude.

Mr. Ames's cherry red convertible BMW pulled into his assigned parking place a few spaces away from Max.

He looked far older than he had at Kevin's trial, which was the last time Max had seen him in person. He didn't recognize her until he was only a few feet away.

"Maxine," he said in surprise.

"Hello, Mr. Ames. May I have a moment of your time?"

"I'm not going to talk to you."

"But you can threaten me?"

He gave her a look of such shock that she knew immediately that he wasn't the person behind the threatening phone call over the weekend.

"I've never threatened you, Maxine. You and

Lindy were friends, and I dismissed your loyalty to the boy who killed her as youth and inexperience. I forgive you, if that's what you're looking for."

"I'm not." But it felt surprisingly good to know he didn't harbor resentment. Or so he said. "I think we've both been used, Mr. Ames."

Mr. Ames sighed. "Because Lindy always admired you, I will give you ten minutes. But that's it. And nothing I say can be used directly or indirectly in the media."

"I'm not doing a story," she said. She would have said more, but she was stunned with his belief that Lindy somehow looked up to her. Yes, they'd been friends, but Lindy never looked up to *anyone*. In her eyes, no one was better than she was. It wasn't just narcissism that had made Lindy so arrogant; it was the people who'd disappointed her.

As Max once told her, if she looked for secrets, she would find them, and they couldn't be unfound.

The only person Lindy had ever truly loved and respected was her father.

They rode up the private elevator to the top floor of the twenty-story glass building. The silence was welcome; Max had to change gears now that she knew Mr. Ames wasn't behind the phone call. She was also relieved that he seemed to want to talk about Lindy. Everywhere she went, it was always Kevin's guilt or innocence that was debated, never Lindy's final moments. Max didn't even know the truth about her death because she still hadn't received all the files from the Menlo Park PD or Kevin's attorney. That was, in part, her fault because she'd spent yesterday following the lead in Jason Hoffman's murder. Today would be different.

Mr. Ames told his secretary not to disturb him for the next ten minutes, then ushered Max into his office.

"Office" was an understatement. The room was larger than her New York apartment, in a corner, glass on two sides with a view of the San Francisco Bay. The Dumbarton Bridge was visible in the clear morning. The furniture was modern, leather and glass, but with warm accents of plush burgundy rugs and attractive classical art that Max suspected were either originals or damn good reproductions of originals that Mr. Ames owned but kept in a more secure location.

Though considering the security in this building, Max couldn't imagine his house was more secure.

He motioned for her to sit on the couch. He put his briefcase on his desk, but came back to the grouping of couches and sat across from her.

"I'm sorry about Saturday night."

He looked at her, perplexed.

"The police?"

"I don't know what you're talking about."

Kimberly hadn't told Mr. Ames that she'd visited.

"I'll backtrack. On Saturday, I received a message that implied it was from you, essentially threatening me not to look into Lindy's death."

His face clouded almost imperceptibly. He was still grieving over the loss of his only daughter.

"I didn't come back to investigate Lindy's murder," Max said. "But I have some questions that were never answered at the trial, and, simply, I need to know who killed her. I'm really sorry if you don't want to know, but I feel like I have an obligation to clear Kevin O'Neal's name, to find the truth, so everyone—your family, me, Kevin's family, all our friends who've been divided over this for thirteen years—can finally put it to rest."

He didn't say anything for a long minute. He wasn't even looking at her, and it wasn't until later that Max realized he had been staring at a picture of Lindy on the bookshelf behind her.

"I never left a message for you, nor do I know of a message," he said. "I don't threaten people. Everyone, including the police, believed Kevin killed Lindy. Everyone but you."

"I know."

She wished she could read his mind, but Mr. Ames had a poker face. Sad, but still unreadable.

"I liked Kevin," he said.

Max didn't push or question. Mr. Ames had

things he wanted to say, and maybe he'd never felt comfortable saying them before now.

"I'd always felt there were so many unanswered questions. Why? Jealousy? It seemed so . . . common."

Perhaps, but jealousy—envy—was the root of so much evil in the world.

"If there's a chance he didn't . . . didn't *hurt* my daughter, that means someone else did," Mr. Ames said.

"Yes." Max didn't want to hurt Mr. Ames. But, if he told her to back off, could she? *Would* she? Was the truth more important than this man's grief?

"I can't give you my blessing," he said, "but I'm not going to ask you to stop looking. I want to know what happened, even though I don't want to relive the pain." It was a conundrum faced by many survivors.

"Sir, if I may, you're still in pain."

He rose and walked around to his desk. "I don't think you can possibly understand how I've suffered these thirteen years." He sat down, putting physical distance between them, a way of self-protection and exerting his authority. "Jerry and Lindy are my children. Now Jerry is working for Doctors Without Borders in countries where he is in danger because he's trying to help people, and I worry about him as much as I'm proud of him. And Lindy's gone. My daughter. My princess. You can't know."

"You're right." Max left it at that. She'd been accused by many of not being able to understand grief. It was a defensive mechanism on their part, a way to separate themselves from others as well as to try and bring others closer, a way to say, *You can't understand, but I wish you could so you would know what I feel.*

But Max did understand. She hadn't lost a child, but she'd lost a mother to the void—a place where she just disappeared and Max didn't know what happened to her, whether she was dead or alive. She'd lost her best friend Karen, whom she knew was dead. The blood and violence—but there was no closure. No body, no witness, no conviction. She'd lost Lindy, a friend she'd had for years, who'd pushed her away for no reason Max understood, only to end up dead and leaving Max in the position of defending the man accused of killing her.

She understood loss, violence, death, as much as anyone. But she wouldn't say it, because Mr. Ames, or the other survivors she faced, wouldn't believe that she knew how they felt.

"What do you want from me?"

"I already got it. I wanted to know if you'd threatened me."

He tilted his head quizzically.

She didn't answer his implied question. Instead, she got up and sat in the chair across from Mr. Ames. "I came to talk to you at your house on

Saturday before I went to visit my grandmother. Kimberly called the police, who told me to leave or they'd arrest me."

Mr. Ames frowned. "I'm sorry about that. Kimberly thinks I need protecting."

She wondered if Kimberly was protecting him from memories of Lindy, or from remembering her infidelity. Obviously, he'd forgiven his wife and they'd made their marriage work, unlike Max's Aunt Joanne who'd walked out on Brooks. Maybe Kimberly had been telling the truth, and Brooks had been her only indiscretion. Unlike Brooks, who had repeatedly cheated on Joanne.

"Mr. Ames, Lindy's murder affected everyone in Atherton. There were mistakes made by a lot of people."

"Is this why you're a crime reporter?"

He sounded genuinely interested, and Max found herself being completely honest. "No, it's not. In fact, I wanted to get as far away from murder and police and lawyers because I thought the system was a failure and I wanted no part of it. But my senior year in college, my best friend disappeared in Miami while we were on spring break. There was extensive evidence that she'd been murdered, but there was no body, and the police had only circumstantial evidence against the person they thought responsible. I stayed in Miami for a year searching for proof and answers, and never got what I needed. I discovered I had a knack for writing, and wrote a book about what happened to Karen."

She'd written the book from the journal she'd kept the year she lived in Miami investigating Karen's disappearance and murder because the police couldn't. Couldn't because there was no solid evidence. Thinking about the journal she'd kept that year, she couldn't help but remember Lindy's diary, and the arguments she and her best friend had over the information Lindy wrote down.

"I have a meeting shortly," Mr. Ames said, his eyes solemn. "If you want to talk to me, call my cell phone." He handed her his private business card.

"Does Mrs. Ames still have the antique store on Oak Grove?"

"Yes, it's been her sanctuary these years." He walked Max to the door. "Kimberly has always been particularly troubled by Lindy's death. They had a fight before Kimberly and I left for my business trip, and it still hurts Kimberly that their relationship ended with that cloud."

Max wasn't certain that was completely true, not after her confrontation with Lindy's mother, but she didn't comment. If Lindy had still kept a diary, she wouldn't have told her mother about it. Would she have told her father?

She turned around and asked, "Do you remember when Lindy and I were freshmen in high school and she got in trouble for writing in a journal?" In trouble was an understatement. Lindy had put everyone's secrets in a journal and someone at school found and shared it. Like the fictional *Harriet the Spy*, only much, much more scandalous. It got out, and she stopped writing.

"I remember. She didn't mean to hurt anyone— the journal was for her only."

Max didn't know if it was just for Lindy—Lindy had shared some pages with Max and undoubtedly others when she wanted. When she thought she could benefit, heap rewards on those she liked, or inflict pain on those she didn't. "Did she ever keep another diary?"

"No. She was truly devastated by what happened. Kimberly was furious, but I never read it. I didn't want to. They had a ceremony where they burned it and Kimberly said, 'Some things should never be immortalized on paper.'"

Just because her parents didn't know if she kept one, didn't mean she hadn't. Olivia would, hopefully, know the truth.

Max was torn—who first, Kimberly Ames or Olivia Langstrom Ward? She wanted to talk to both of them, but Kimberly would be the most challenging. She chose Olivia because Palo Alto was on the way to Atherton. It was nine thirty in the morning, and Max had a meeting with Jasper at Atherton Prep at noon. Kimberly owned a small antique store in Menlo Park near the Atherton border. It was more a hobby than to make any substantive income, but the word was Kimberly could get anything for anyone.

Similar to how her daughter Lindy knew everything about everyone.

Max hopped on to the freeway toward Olivia's house in Palo Alto and mentally catalogued her day. After Olivia, Kimberly. After Kimberly, Jasper. Last night she'd printed a list of the local storage units and ranked them in order closest to Kevin's apartment. She hoped she had time after Jasper to hit at least two units before closing.

A car she'd seen outside of Gerald Ames's building followed her on the freeway. She hadn't seen the vehicle follow her from Mr. Ames's office, but now she couldn't be sure. She'd been on the phone with Ben giving him the details of the drug bust and the possibility that Jason Hoffman was killed by Dru's ex-boyfriend or Rebecca Cross, and then David had called to check in. She should have been paying more attention, especially since she'd been followed yesterday.

Except, she'd thought that was related to Dru Parker, not Lindy. That car had been white, not black.

This car was a dark, nondescript late-model sedan. Max didn't do well with models, but this looked like an American make. Feds? Was the FBI following her? There were no government plates on the vehicle, but that didn't mean anything.

Any other time, she'd have called Marco and asked him to look into it. But after the way she'd left things with him in Miami, she wasn't going to ask him for a favor. She had other friends in the FBI, but no one she was close enough with to ask if they could call the local office and find out if she was under surveillance.

And why? Why would the feds be following her? Because she found the pot farm? That didn't make sense. But truly, sometimes law enforcement did things that made no sense to her.

Or had Gerald Ames sent someone to track her? Why? He'd been polite, although sad; why would he have her followed?

The person who'd threatened her Saturday might not have wanted her to talk to Mr. Ames.

Max wanted to confront whoever was following her, but she wasn't stupid. She didn't know who or why, or if they had a weapon. She didn't know if the person tailing her was the same as two days ago. Different car, but how could she have fallen under the watch of two different people? Chances are, the two incidents were connected. It was clear she was going to have to rent another car.

She decided to lose him, then go straight to Olivia's. She didn't want anyone following her there, or while she searched for Kevin's storage locker. Though she originally thought her pursuer was related to Dru Parker, now she wondered if she'd been mistaken.

Did this have something to do with the threat that ostensibly came from someone close to Gerald Ames? Had Gerald Ames manipulated and deceived her? She had pegged him for being honest in their conversation—he hadn't promised her his cooperation or blessing, but he definitely hadn't asked her to stop what she was doing.

The car was keeping pace with her. Max sped up; the sedan sped up. She pulled out her phone and did a quick search for the closest police station. David would have slapped her hand—but this was an emergency.

She exited on El Monte and headed toward the Los Altos Hills police station. The sedan followed, but when she drove into the parking lot, he passed by. She tried to catch a glimpse of the driver, but saw little. Her impression was of a male driver, but other than gender, she couldn't give a description.

She mapped out an alternate route to Olivia's house before pulling back onto the road. She didn't see the sedan and no other car appeared to be following her. She made a few loops just to make sure, and ended up at Olivia's house thirty minutes later.

Olivia's husband, Professor Ward, should be at campus, based on his class schedule that Max downloaded off the Internet. She knocked on the door. No answer. She walked around the porch and peered in the windows. The house was immaculate. In the back, a sporty but practical gold BMW was housed in the detached garage.

Max wasn't in the mood to be ignored. She rang the bell and knocked—loudly—on the door. "Olivia, it's Maxine."

The door opened. Olivia stood there dressed like a Stepford wife, but with glassy eyes and a distinct odor of alcohol. Champagne. Max glanced at her watch. Not even ten in the morning.

Olivia tilted her chin up, looking both haughty and regal. "You know, you're really a bitch, Maxine."

Max laughed. "Well, aren't you a surprise. Your husband is at work, you crack open the champagne."

She didn't wait for an invitation, but walked in. The house was elegant and far too picture-perfect for Max. While she liked tidy, this was beyond neat—it was obsessively clean.

"Christopher left this morning to guest lecture in Boston."

"And you didn't want to join him?"

Olivia laughed, but there was no humor. In fact, she sounded almost crazy. "And come between him and his mistress?"

Max had picked the wrong time to visit. Or . . . maybe not.

Max closed the front door because Olivia didn't

seem to care whether it was open. She followed her "host" through the house to the back. As she watched, Olivia touched each perfectly aligned picture, moving it just a fraction so it was out of balance.

Hilarious. Christopher Ward, older husband with a mistress three thousand miles away, was a neat freak, and Olivia rebelled by misaligning his artwork and drinking before noon. Max wondered what other rebellions Olivia had. Was that why she'd really met with Kevin at the lake the night Lindy was killed? Maybe growing up she hadn't been as perfect as everyone thought.

Olivia sat down in a chair on the sun porch, in the back of the house overlooking a pristine pool and rose garden. The champagne bottle, which was chilling in a silver bucket, was half-empty. She pulled it out, refilled her glass, and offered one to Max.

Max was tempted—Olivia was drinking a bottle of Perrier-Jouët Belle Epoque, one of Max's favorite champagnes. She couldn't see the exact year, but it was 199-something. Worth more than $1,000.

But it was ten in the morning, and Max had a lot to do. She declined, and Olivia shrugged, a physical mannerism that seemed ill suited for the trim, perfect, wealthy housewife.

"We had these at our wedding. Ordered a couple extra cases and every year on our anniversary, we open a bottle. It's gotten better with time." Olivia sipped. "Sit. Ask your questions."

"You've changed."

"We all have," Olivia said.

"In three days."

She laughed. It sounded bitter. "That's what good champagne will do for you."

"I don't buy it. We don't change that much. We do, however, wear masks. Is that what you were doing on Saturday? Putting on a mask for your husband?"

"Think whatever you want. I don't care."

Max switched tactics. She wasn't here to save Olivia from her husband or her own bad choices; she was here for answers.

"You told me on Saturday that Kevin talked you out of running away. Why did you want to leave?"

"Lindy always thought my father was molesting me." Olivia reddened and didn't look Max in the eye. No wonder Lindy thought that—Olivia acted like an abused woman. "He didn't, but he was cruel in other ways."

"How?"

"I don't want to talk about it." She stared at Max, her eyes icy marbles. "It's irrelevant."

"I don't think it is." Max leaned forward and said, "You could have cleared Kevin and stopped the farce of a trial. You remained silent and lifelong friendships were destroyed. An innocent man sat on trial. Lindy's killer is still free. Kevin lost everything to protect *you*. Why?"

"I don't know why," she said. "I kept waiting for the police to come and ask me if Kevin was with me that night, but they never did. Not until after the trial, and by that time it wasn't important. I asked him not to tell anyone, but when things got serious—he said that he didn't kill Lindy, so he wasn't going to break my confidence. Maxine, I was scared and angry and worried."

Now the alcohol had Olivia making no sense. Max decided she might never know why Kevin and Olivia hadn't come forward about his alibi. Before Olivia poured another glass of the thousand-dollars-a-bottle champagne, Max asked her the most important question:

"Where is Lindy's diary?"

"I don't know."

Bingo. Max figured that someone as diligent about keeping a diary for years wouldn't have just stopped writing after her mother burned it. She'd just become better in hiding it.

And she'd never told Max. Max tried not to let that truth sting, but it irritated her like sand in her shoe.

"It wasn't part of the evidence," Max said. "Her father doesn't think she had one. Lindy and I—" She couldn't explain how they argued about secrets, how they'd fought over whether to expose Brooks and Kimberly's affair to the world. It was a cloud over Max, that she and her best friend had so many fundamental disagreements . . . but Max had never turned her back on her. Or, she hadn't thought she did. But in the last months before Lindy was killed, they'd been estranged. Distant.

Max wished it could have been different.

"I never saw it," Max said.

"She wrote in code. I never read it. She hid it. She told me some things—like how she was going to get back at the people who burned her."

"Who?"

"I thought she meant Caitlin or her mother."

"Why? She and Caitlin were best friends."

"Lindy always believed that Caitlin was the one who left her diary in Mrs. Frauke's classroom."

When they were freshmen, Lindy had brought the diary to school to show a picture she'd taken of Mr. Bonner, the freshman English teacher, and Mrs. Frauke, the advanced French teacher. Back then, cell phones with cameras were rare for most of the world, but not the affluent in Atherton. Lindy would take pictures, print them out on her computer, and delete them so her mother—who was prone to going through her phone to see who was calling her—would never see them.

It was that scandal—with Mrs. Frauke finding the picture and going to the headmaster with the accusation that Lindy was blackmailing her—that had Lindy suspended for a week and Kimberly reading and burning her diary.

Max didn't know whether Lindy had black-mailed Mrs. Frauke, though she wouldn't have put it past her. Lindy had a cold streak, especially when things didn't go her way. But Max had never heard that Caitlin had anything to do with the diary's discovery.

"What was in this diary?"

"I said I don't know!"

"But you have an idea."

"I think," she said, "she wrote everything she knew. Lindy Ames was Jekyll and Hyde. When Mrs. Ames burned her diary, she realized that her mother was scared that Lindy knew something about *her.* Lindy made it her mission to find out all of her mother's secrets."

Like her affair with Uncle Brooks.

Olivia smiled. "Everyone has secrets. I'd think you more than anyone would know that."

Chapter Eighteen

Max changed her mind a half-dozen times about her next step after leaving Olivia's house but decided to visit William at his law office. She sent Jasper a message that she would be thirty minutes late meeting him.

William practiced corporate law for one of the most prestigious law firms in the country. Probably the world. At thirty-one, he was a junior partner after only five years with the company, which he joined immediately after graduating from law school. He was the pillar of perfection in the eyes of most everyone: attractive, wealthy, intelligent, with an attractive, wealthy, and (marginally) intelligent wife. He had two perfect sons to carry the Revere name into posterity.

To see him rattled that she showed up at his office right before the lunch hour had Max wanting to laugh.

"Maxine." He glanced around to see who else had seen her come in.

"I checked in with the guard. The Revere name opens doors, as I'm sure you know."

"I—"

"I'm here as your cousin, not a reporter."

He breathed easier. She felt bad about giving him that little white lie, but if anyone was eavesdropping, she didn't want to start rumors.

"I have a lunch meeting," he said, "but I'll delay." He turned to his secretary. "Minnie, can you call Josh and Doug and tell them I'll be a little late?"

"Of course, Mr. Revere."

Max saw a brief exchange, a special look, between Minnie and William. She might not like Caitlin, but she sure as hell hoped that William wasn't sleeping with his secretary. How . . . *common*. How . . . *typical*. William had many attributes; fidelity had never been one of them. Like father, like son, Max thought. She was surprised that she was more disappointed than angry.

William's office wasn't as spacious or subtly rich as Gerald Ames's, but it was grand nonetheless. Dark furniture, a complete set of law books in built-in bookshelves, immaculate desk. A conference table that could seat eight comfortably, along with a leather couch and two matching chairs

"So, how long have you been sleeping with Minnie?" she said as soon as the door closed.

William blushed ten shades of red and Max swore under her breath. "It was a guess, *cuz,* and you reminded me again why I always beat you at poker."

"What do you want?" he snapped. He crossed his arms and stared at her.

"Sit down," she said.

"This is my office. You haven't been home in two years, and after what you pulled at Grandmother's house?"

"What did I pull? Confronting our grandmother and your father for obstruction of justice?"

"They did nothing—"

"I'm not here about that. I'm here about Lindy's diary."

He rubbed his face and sat down. "I don't know what you want from me."

"The truth."

"I told you exactly what happened. I didn't

know anyone knew about the ticket, or that Grandmother intervened. She told me everything after you left Saturday. She's very upset, Maxine. She's not young. She'll be eighty this summer."

"She's upset because I called them on it." Max was deviating from her plan. She hadn't wanted to fight with William about the parking ticket or family. "William, I need to find Lindy's diary."

He stared at her as if he hadn't heard her. When she stared back, he asked, "What diary?"

"The secret diary that Olivia Langstrom just confirmed Lindy kept after her mother burned her first one."

"The one with the picture of Mrs. Frauke screwing Mr. Bonner." He smirked.

"William, this is serious."

"I don't know what you're talking about." But he wasn't looking *at* her. He was looking at her shoulder.

She snapped her fingers. "Dammit, I don't have time to play twenty questions. You said you were bed buddies with Lindy for a year, a totally secret relationship that no one knew about, not even *me,* and you didn't ever see her write in a book? She was *that* discreet?"

William sighed and his shoulders sagged. "She might have had something, but I have no idea where it is. She didn't share it with me."

"But you've seen it."

"A couple of times I saw her writing in a black

leather book. In her clubhouse. For all I know, it's still there."

Or the killer took it. Or the police have it. Why wasn't it part of the evidence?

"I need to find it."

"After thirteen years?"

"It has to be somewhere."

"Maybe her father has it."

"He doesn't."

William blanched. "You talked to Mr. Ames?"

"Yes. And he was far more cordial than anyone else."

William seemed stunned. "But you sided with Kevin."

"He, too, has his doubts."

"He's old—"

"Oh, jeez, William. He's your father's age. And for the record, Kevin lied about his alibi."

"We all know that. He couldn't have been home if he killed Lindy."

"He was with Olivia."

The information shocked her cousin. "Olivia *Langstrom?*"

"Yes. She confirmed it. So get off your high horse and either help me, or stay out of my way. Because I'm not leaving town until I find out who killed Lindy."

Max was even later than twelve thirty when she arrived at Atherton Prep. She quickly slipped out of her heels and into sneakers so she could comfortably walk the grounds.

Jasper was talking to the headmaster, Greer Bascomb, who hadn't seemed to age since Max graduated thirteen years ago. He'd looked forty-something then, he looked forty-something now. She knew, however, that he was fifty-eight. Bascomb had been the headmaster of Atherton Prep for nearly twenty years. They were having a big fund-raising gala in his honor next month to celebrate this milestone. Fortunately, Max wouldn't still be in town. Ever since Lindy had told her that his secretary gave him head under his desk, when she saw the diminutive man she wanted to laugh.

With Jasper and Bascomb was also a woman who looked familiar, but Max couldn't place her.

"Maxine Revere," Bascomb said and extended his hand. "Good to see you again."

She shook his hand, then turned to the woman next to him. She wore little makeup, and her light brown hair was cut in a stylish bob. "Hello, Maxine Revere—did we go to school together?"

The woman seemed surprised that she recognized her. "Yes, I'm Faith Voss, I graduated the year after you."

"Volleyball—I should have remembered."

She laughed lightly. "I was a benchwarmer most of the time I played."

Voss—she had a sister, too, who'd graduated the year before Max. Carrie. She had a far wilder reputation than her sister. Faith had always been smart and sweet, from what Max remembered.

"Do you work for Jasper?"

"I'm the admissions director for ACP."

Max couldn't imagine working at her alma mater. She hadn't liked high school much.

"What's Carrie up to these days? She went to Berkeley, right?"

"Good memory. She dropped out and moved to Europe." A hint of sadness clouded her expression.

"Carrie always was spontaneous."

Bascomb said to Max, "We are so fortunate that your uncle, Archer Sterling, and Jasper have given so much to Atherton Prep. We were in dire need of a new gym, and the Sterling Pierce Sports Center is the perfect solution."

That was his subtle way of telling her she *hadn't* given to her alma mater.

"I agree," she said.

"You should visit more often," Bascomb said. "Career Day in October, perhaps. Faith, make a note."

Faith wrote quickly in her notepad, the charms on her bracelet clinking. Admissions director and personal secretary, it seemed. Max handed Faith her business card. To Bascomb, she said, "You could always invite me to keynote graduation."

"I, um, of course, I'll bring that up to the board, but as you know, it's both a board and student decision on which alumnus is asked to give the commencement speech."

He was talking so fast Max wanted to laugh, again, at the weasel. He was such a glad-hander it made her cringe.

"That's right—my uncle Brooks is on the board. I guess I won't expect an invitation anytime soon." She winked at Jasper, who looked bemused at the conversation.

Bascomb couldn't leave fast enough. He thanked Jasper for talking to the donors, then made a lame excuse and walked back to the main campus with Faith on his heels. She glanced back at Max and rolled her eyes. Max laughed.

"I hope Faith gets paid well to work for that sycophant jackass," she muttered.

Jasper laughed. "He wasn't here when I was in school, but his credentials are impeccable."

"I'm sure they are. For an administrator and fund-raiser, he's done well for the school, so I have no complaints there."

"But?"

"But nothing. Let's go for a walk."

Jasper waved over a short, burly man in a flannel shirt and faded jeans. He introduced her to Brian Robeaux. Brian shook her hand firmly. He said, "I can't tell you how much I appreciate you taking the time to look into my nephew's murder.

I haven't slept well since it happened. I knew I should have come here with him that night."

"What happened?"

"Jason was convinced that someone had been digging around the site. There was some unexplained loose dirt, like someone had filled a hole about this size"—he put up his arms like he was carrying a sack—"but we dug up one of them and nothing was there. I think it was some of the kids at the school messing around. Still do. Except—what if I was wrong?"

"Can you show me one of those holes?"

"They won't still be there," he said. "Not after five months. With the rain and everything."

"Maybe it's still happening."

"Nah, I think I would have noticed." Brian glanced at Jasper. He looked undecided.

"It can't hurt," Jasper said.

They walked around the construction site and toward the back fence. Brian said, "We still miss him."

"You always will," Max said. "But time helps," she added. It sounded like a lie sometimes, and this was one of those times. Jason's murder was senseless.

"Jasper said Michael's folks wrote to you about Jason?"

"Yes." She didn't feel it necessary to go into details. "I met with them Saturday and they filled me in."

"They're good people. Considered me family, too, ever since Sara married Mike. Practically adopted me. Our folks have been gone for some time, it was just Sara and me for a while." Brian stopped at the edge of a line of redwoods. He glanced back toward the construction site, then looked at the trees.

The redwoods were two and three deep, all along the west fence, from the edge of the old gym all the way to the far north property line. Max could see the tree she'd climbed on the other side of the old gym, where the trees were a mix of magnolias, oaks, and elm.

"Well, shit," Brian said, then glanced at Max. "Sorry."

"What's wrong?"

"I really don't remember where they were. Jason pointed out three, maybe four. But this is a hundred-yard stretch of trees here, and it was someplace in the middle. Close together—I remember that. But they could have been made by anyone, even an animal, like I'd told Jason."

"I'll walk through here and see if anything pops out at me," Max said. She picked up a long stick and poked at the ground. There was a lot of soft ground here, mulch and needles from the redwood trees. And Brian was right—five months of rain and drainage, the ground would have settled.

But if the holes were deep or big enough, there might be remnants. With the clear sky and sun nearly straight up, this was the best light of the day. And if she didn't find anything now, she'd be back tomorrow.

Brian said, "Jasper, I have to call the cement contractor about tomorrow's pour."

"Go. I'll keep Ms. Revere out of harm's way."

Brian left, and Max glanced at Jasper. "You will?" She walked slowly, eyes cast downward, poking the stick into the ground periodically.

"Wouldn't want you falling down the rabbit hole," Jasper teased.

"You don't have to stay with me," she said. "I'm okay on my own."

"I have no place I need to be."

"Why is it that neither Brian nor you mentioned Jason's interest with these trees to the police? That Jason found evidence there had been digging?"

"Honestly, it wasn't on our minds. Jason was very detail-oriented. He noticed things that other people missed all the time. Very focused. Brian and I thought he was being quirky."

Max squatted to check out a mound of dirt; it was an anthill. She moved quickly away from it.

Jasper grinned. "Don't like bugs?"

"Not particularly, but I'm not squeamish, if that's what you're getting at." Not generally squeamish. However, there were a few situations over the years she'd found herself in that she hoped were never repeated.

They walked all the way to the corner and found nothing suspicious. Max took a heavy-duty Maglite from her purse.

"Do you always carry a two-pound flashlight in your purse?"

She laughed. "I thought it might be a little dark here. Maybe the light will reflect something." She handed him her stick. "You poke this time."

They walked back just as slowly as they'd come. Max was glad that Jasper didn't feel the need for a constant stream of conversation. She had the distinct impression he was still trying to convince her to go out with him.

"There's probably nothing here," Jasper said five minutes later. They were near the middle of the section of trees.

"Jason thought there was."

"Five months ago."

Max wasn't deterred. Jason was killed for a reason; it wasn't just a random crime. At least, it didn't feel like a random crime.

"I'll come back in the morning," Max said, "at dawn. The light will be different."

"You shouldn't be out here a—" Jasper's voice cut off and he yelped. She would have laughed at the sound if he hadn't sworn a blue streak right after.

She turned and found Jasper on the ground. His foot was buried in dirt. "Shit, that hurts."

"What happened?"

She shined the light around Jasper.

"A sinkhole. As soon as I put my weight on it, my foot went in."

His foot was deep in the hole, halfway up his left calf.

"Is it broken?" Max asked.

"No, but it hurts." Still sitting, he pulled his foot from the hole. He felt the ground. "This soil doesn't seem any different from the rest."

"Except for a hole." She tilted her head. "Don't move."

"What? Is something crawling on me?"

"No, just trust me."

She walked to the edge of the trees. The hole that Jasper had stepped in was in the middle of a slight concave. Almost imperceptible. She took out her cell phone, made sure the flash was on, and took a picture of the ground. With the flash, it was obvious that the ground had sunk in. It was narrow, but several feet long. She showed Jasper the image. "What does this look like to you?"

"I don't know—a sinkhole?"

Max frowned. Was she the only one who saw something more sinister?

Jasper got up and winced. "Twisted my ankle."

"Sit—I want to do something." She took several pictures, then shined her light all around the area. She got on all fours and crawled around the sinkhole, moving the dirt with her hands. "Here," she said. "There is an obvious cut in the earth here from a shovel. It's been filled in, but someone dug a hole here."

"That's odd."

Max didn't say anything as she continued to inspect the area. Her knee pressed against something hard, and she reached down. She picked up what she thought was a gray-white stone and almost tossed it, but it had very little weight. She shined her light on it. A thrill of discovery sent butterflies through her stomach.

"I'm ninety-nine percent certain that this is a bone. A finger." She held it up for Jasper to see.

"Animal. It has to be an animal."

"I'm going to call Detective Santini. He's got to get a forensics team out here immediately."

"You don't think—"

"Yes, I do. I think that somehow Jason found out about a crime, and someone killed him to keep him quiet."

Jasper paled as he stared at the ground where his foot had plunged. "Dear Lord, there's a body down there?"

"No."

"How do you know?"

"It's concave. That means something was removed. I think when the sports complex was approved, a killer came here to remove his victim." She held up the bone. "And Jason caught him in the act."

Chapter Nineteen

Nick Santini showed up at Atherton Prep nearly an hour after Max called him. Alone.

Max was standing at his door before he even turned off the ignition. "You took long enough—where's everyone else?"

He didn't say anything but got out of the Bronco. He looked at her from head to feet. She glanced down at her torn panty hose, dirt-stained knees, and formerly white sneakers, then caught his eye. "I told you we found a grave."

"Yes, you did."

Jasper limped over. "Detective."

"Pierce. Explain what you two were doing here."

Why was Nick addressing Jasper? Max didn't give Jasper a chance to respond. She said, "As I told you the other day, Dru said that Jason was concerned about holes in those trees." She pointed to the redwoods. "I asked Jasper to come out with me and inspect the area. I thought he might have an idea of what was off about the trees that had Jason so concerned. Brian Robeaux said there were a couple of small holes in the ground, not in the trees specifically but *around* the trees. Brian didn't think it was important, but Jason thought it was strange. Because Jason was killed here, next to the trailer, Brian didn't think to mention anything about Jason's interest in the holes. He said he didn't make the connection at all.

"While Jasper and I walked through the area looking for evidence of the holes, Jasper stepped into an area of loose dirt and twisted his ankle. I took a picture." She handed Nick her phone with the pictures of the concave area. "That looks like a grave. And considering I found this"—she handed him the finger bone—"I think I'm right."

Nick stared at the bone, pulled an evidence bag from his pocket, and put the bone in. "You think you found a grave and yet you removed evidence."

"I was crawling around the area and knelt on it. I didn't know it was a finger bone until I picked it up. There could be more, I didn't look. Once I knew what was there, I stopped searching. So now, why don't you have a forensics team with you? It's going to be dark in a couple of hours."

"I want to look at it first," Nick said. "You can leave."

"Leave? Hell, no. I found this grave. This is why Jason Hoffman was killed. You know it, I know it. I'm not going anywhere."

Nick took out his handcuffs and cuffed her to his door handle. He did it so fast that by the time she saw it coming, she was too shocked to stop him.

Without a word, he motioned for Jasper to follow him to the trees. Jasper gave her a surprised look, then shrugged and followed Nick. Damn them both.

Max was more than a little furious. She jerked her wrist, watching Jasper and Nick talk as they headed over to the grave that Max had marked with a construction cone.

Damn cop.

She reached into her hair and took out a bobby pin. David had taught her how to pick locks, but she'd never had to do it with her left hand before. And handcuffs were different. She dropped the pin and had to pull another from her hair. It took a minute, but she got the cuffs off.

That was a trick she was going to have to practice a few times. It was a useful skill.

She rubbed her wrist and glanced in Nick's Bronco. She sat in the driver's seat and went through a stack of files on the passenger seat. The top file was the Jason Hoffman case. Most of the stuff she already knew. Except for one tidbit.

Nick had taken notes, apparently from a conversation he had with one of the federal agents. Since Amy was talking in the hopes of getting a lighter sentence, she'd admitted that she'd called Potrero when Nick was outside the house talking to Dru. Potrero's cell phone history confirmed he'd called Cross immediately after Amy called him, not long before Dru was attacked. It was obvious to Max that Potrero and Cross thought Dru was going to expose their pot farm and money laundering scheme, which is why they went after her. While both of them had lawyered up, they each emphatically denied killing Jason Hoffman, and each had an alibi for the night Jason died, which Nick had verified.

Nick had several sticky notes on the inside of his file. One caught her eye: *Follow up on Max's theory about the holes/trees at the construction site.*

He'd planned on coming out here anyway—why was he giving her such a hard time?

She was so engrossed in the files that she didn't hear the men approach until she felt Nick's stare.

She turned to him and smiled. "You locked me up, what was I supposed to do?" She closed the file she was looking at and put it back on the passenger seat.

Nick held up his cuffs, which she'd draped over the door. "I see you have many talents."

"And? Do you agree that there was a grave under those trees?"

"It appears to be, but it could have been a pet dug up by scavengers. It might not be human."

"Who digs a five-foot-long grave for a family pet?"

"You measured."

"Of course I measured."

He jerked his head toward Jasper. "Your boyfriend is going to make sure you get back to your hotel safely."

She hated being kept in the dark.

"He's not my boyfriend." Max got out of the Bronco and punched a finger in Nick's chest. "And the next time you put cuffs on me, it had better be part of a sex game, otherwise I'll skewer you on the front page of *The New York Times*."

Max started to walk away.

Nick said, "I'll take it under advisement."

He looked at her a moment too long, long enough for Max to realize she was going to get herself in a heap of trouble if she got involved with yet another cop. Look what happened with her and Marco. And it was more than obvious, even with his initial flirting, even after that kiss in the restaurant, that Nick didn't like her. The men she got involved with, at a minimum, had to respect her.

Though there was an added benefit that Nick Santini lived three thousand miles away, she would never sleep with a man who didn't like her or respect her career.

Jasper followed Max to the Stanford Park Hotel, but didn't get out of his car. "You okay?" he asked.

"I'm fine. You're the one with a sprained ankle."

"No racquetball for me this week."

"Too bad, I would have taken you up on a game." She leaned into his car. "Thanks, Jasper, I mean it."

"I should be thanking you. We're one step closer to finding Jason's killer."

"I hope so."

"You're skeptical."

"I think we have the motive, but beyond that? I don't know."

"It's more than we had yesterday."

"Santini really ticks me off. I'm not backing down off this, just because he's the one with the badge."

"I don't think he would have minded if you stayed."

"He kicked me out." She eyed him. "Unless you know something I don't."

"There's a cop named Beck who has it out for you. You know him?"

"Yes," she said through clenched teeth.

"Santini said that when he calls in the gravesite, he has to report who discovered it. He said Beck will be all over the place, and he didn't want you there in the middle of it."

"I can handle Beck."

"It's a distraction for Santini." Jasper hesitated, then said, "It's pretty clear he's interested."

"In the grave? He damn well better be."

"In you."

She blinked. "Well. You would be wrong. He had some choice words to say about my profession, and me personally."

"I've been wrong, on a rare occasion." Jasper

grinned. "I'm going back. If I hear anything interesting, I'll let you know." He drove off.

Max dismissed what Jasper said about Nick Santini's interest in her. There was no denying the mutual attraction, but what he said last night really bothered her, far more than she'd admitted even to herself, until now. She *was* her job. Hate her job, hate her.

She walked up to her hotel room, showered and changed. Her suit needed cleaning, so she left it in a bag with a dry-cleaning tag, and changed into slacks and a blouse. Neither formal nor casual, because she wasn't quite sure what her plans were.

She updated her two boards. On Jason Hoffman's, she put a sticky note under her "motive" heading related to the grave.

What did Jason find that no one wanted him to talk about?

Brian Robeaux had said that he'd seen three or four small holes, the size of a bucket, that had been filled in. The one she and Jasper had found was huge in comparison. Had Jason found the grave? If so, did he tell someone? Maybe someone at the school? Why wouldn't he call the police?

Unless he hadn't found the grave, but someone feared he might.

She had to let Nick and his team do their job—for all she knew they would find a full skeleton, and once they identified the remains, they might have all the answers they needed. Until then, she could do nothing but sit and wait.

She preferred action to waiting.

She turned her attention to the board she'd been working on for Lindy. She added a sticky note about her conversation with Gerald Ames and her follow-up with Olivia.

Max looked back at Jason's board.

There hadn't been two murders at Atherton Prep.

There had been three.

Max pulled out a third trifold board that she'd stuffed behind the television and wrote on the top: *Unidentified Victim: Grave*

The grave was on ACP property. Jason Hoffman was killed on ACP property because he was suspicious—but not so suspicious that he'd shared any specific concerns with anyone, other than being interested in who was digging around on his site.

And Lindy was killed on ACP property.

Max couldn't see any connection between Lindy and the other two murders, the unknown victim and Jason, but that there were three people killed at the same location made Max's instincts do more than twitch. They were ringing bells in her head.

She did a quick search on persons who went missing more than a year ago. She wasn't certain how quickly a body would decompose if buried in the ground unprotected, but she would imagine for a finger bone to be devoid of all flesh and muscle, it had to be there at least a year.

There were about a dozen people reported missing, from Atherton and Menlo Park but no one she knew, and no one who had a connection with Atherton Prep—at least a connection that was obvious. No alumni, no students, no teachers, no parents, no employees.

Maybe she was thinking about this the wrong way.

Still, she made a list of the missing people to ask Santini about later—if he planned on talking to her again. Until they had the identity of the victim, or confirmation of how long the victim had been in the ground, all she was doing now was speculating.

She turned back to Lindy's board and added the information she'd learned from William and Olivia about Lindy's secret diary.

Where was it?

Max had always suspected that Lindy had kept another diary after her mother burned her first one, but after the argument Max and Lindy had about Lindy's propensity to gather information— and then not use it to help anyone—Lindy hadn't shared anything else with her.

And they'd had a huge fight over how to reveal the information about Brooks and Kimberly's affair. Lindy had uncovered the affair in the first place, but after she told Max, Max had followed

Brooks for weeks in order to see for herself. She didn't know why she didn't want to believe it— she and Brooks had never gotten along—but she wasn't going to say a word unless she had proof.

Once she saw them, Max had wanted to document the affair and show the evidence to Aunt Joanne and Lindy's father; Lindy had some devious plan to get back at her mother. In the end, Max had gone for bold: she'd announced the affair at a family dinner. Lindy had been angry with her for a long time after that, and in some ways Max couldn't blame her. They'd had a fundamental disagreement about what to do with the scandalous information. Max believed the truth needed to be out there. Lindy wanted to manipulate her mother instead. Max won because she refused to keep the secret. She hated secrets. What good had ever come from them?

Max rubbed her temples, then swallowed two aspirin with half a bottle of water. She picked up the key she'd found in Kevin's apartment. Why couldn't he have made this easy and told her what it went to? Was he worried someone else would find it?

She pulled out the letter he'd written and read it again, looking for a clue, but nothing jumped out at her.

Kevin had put the letter in her first book, the story about Karen's disappearance. Was that a clue? Max didn't think so—but maybe.

Missing in Miami didn't compare with the names of the six storage facilities in Menlo Park. Max looked at the list of storage units. She'd already called all of them. Five had a locker 110. None would tell her if it was rented to Kevin O'Neal. Two she manipulated into telling her that the registered owner *wasn't* Kevin, but that didn't mean he hadn't used an assumed name.

It looked like she was going to have to try all five, but she didn't have time today. She picked the closest to Kevin's apartment and left.

It only took ten minutes to get there. It was small and dark. The guard let her into the main area when she flashed a smile and told him she forgot the door code.

Unfortunately, the key didn't work on the door. These units all had their own lock, brought by the owner. She hadn't thought to ask that question.

Max called the remaining four storage lockers. She asked each manager if they provided a lock and key, or if the renter was required to bring a lock. Only two provided locked doors—and one of those was all electric. The renters didn't even have a key, they set their own PIN number.

Palm Storage and Lock. Palm . . . palm trees. Could have been a clue related to Miami, or just a coincidence, but Max didn't care. It was also the farthest away. By the time she arrived, she only had ten minutes before they closed.

She walked into the office and rang the bell. A frizzy-haired woman in a bright muumuu came in from the back room. "We're closing in ten minutes," she said. "I can get you situated with a storage unit, but you can't move your stuff until tomorrow."

"Locker one-ten, please."

"Go right in. But, like I said, ten minutes."

It was a two-story facility with small, cinder block rooms. Still, it smelled stale with artificial air and the scent of old. Like some of these treasures had been locked in their rooms for decades. The building looked like it had been built before World War II, and for California that was ancient.

Kevin's unit was stifling and musty. The temperature was cold enough to raise goose bumps on her arms, and she had no time to retrieve her blazer from her car. When she turned on the light she saw a desk stacked with files— the missing files from Kevin's apartment. There were odds and ends of things—old skis, boots, textbooks. Why had he moved his files here? His apartment would be far more comfortable to work in.

She looked through the boxes, stunned with the volume of research Kevin had done. Maps, books, newspaper articles, and all the files on her family, the Talbots, and from his lawyer. More information than she could possibly digest tonight.

More information than she could go through in a week.

Over the loudspeaker the manager said, "Palm Storage is closing in five minutes. Please lock up your unit and exit the building."

Max frowned. Why couldn't Kevin have picked a storage facility that had twenty-four-hour access?

She didn't have time to go through everything. It would take several trips from the unit to the car to bring all the files. She grabbed a shoe box in the corner, dumped the shoes on the floor, and took the files that seemed the most relevant to Lindy Ames's murder. She quickly opened the desk drawers. They were empty except for a letter and a leather journal.

The letter was addressed to her.

The speaker came on again. "Palm Storage is now closed. Please exit the building immediately."

Max put the letter and leather book on the top of the files in the box. She left the room, locked it, and hurried out.

The woman glared at her. "I have a life, too, you know."

"I'm sorry," Max said without an ounce of remorse. This was a business—where was the customer service?

Max put the box in her backseat, but brought the letter and journal up front. The woman made her

leave the parking lot—she had to lock the gate—
and Max parked down the street.

She opened the letter. It was after seven, and the
sunlight was nearly gone. She turned on the
overhead light in the car.

Max—

I'm sure you remember Lindy's diary
and what a scandal it caused when Mrs.
Frauke found it. It's a double standard,
you'd say. It's expected that men have
affairs, practically tolerated, but women
wear a scarlet letter for life.

Lindy started another diary after you
exposed her mother's affair with Brooks
Revere. I don't think she could help it—
she was obsessed with information, with
knowing who was doing what, who was
lying, who was cheating. It was like . . . a
religion for her. Every time she found out
something bad, she'd tell me, "See, so-
and-so is a hypocrite, just like I said."
She'd be high-and-mighty, but deep down
she was hurt. It's like she wanted to hurt
herself knowing all the bad shit about
everyone.

I always assumed that the diary was in
police evidence and nothing ever came of
it. But last summer, when I finally cleaned
up my act enough to ask my attorney for

his records, I learned they'd taken every-thing, but never logged in her diary.

If it was still around, I thought it would be in her clubhouse. When Gerald and Kimberly were out of town, I used the old gate and searched, but the journal wasn't in her clubhouse. So I put myself in Lindy's shoes. Where would she hide it?

It took a while for me to find it, but it was in plain sight—in Gerald's private study among the old books. He probably didn't even know it was there.

I don't understand most of it. It's in code. I know what she's saying, but not who she's talking about.

But if you look at the last entry, it says that Hester is back. Lindy saw her going into a doctor's office and followed her. I thought she might have meant Mrs. Frauke, but I tracked Mrs. Frauke down and she's retired and living in Vermont. All her entries were like that. She was obsessed with *The Scarlet Letter*, remember? She'd spray-painted a red A on her mother's new Jaguar when she first found out about her affair with your uncle.

Kimberly was having another affair, but she didn't name names—she called the participants by nicknames. I only knew she was talking about Kimberly because she called her Joan Crawford. You know, from *Mommie Dearest.* Someone was embezzling from her father's company, but Gerald wouldn't listen to her. She had been cheating on me almost the entire time we were dating, but she wrote, "There's a phrase in the Bible that says you reap what you sow. I cheated, so I'm not surprised I'm being cheated on." That was two weeks after we broke up.

You have to read it. I was going to send it to you, but I didn't want it to get lost, and I was afraid you'd throw it away without opening it.

I'm sorry about everything. I should have told the truth from the beginning.

—Kev

P.S. Consider my suicide a mercy killing. I destroyed my body with drugs, and there's no coming back. I would have been dead by the end of the year.

Dead? Was Kevin *dying?* How? He was hardly old.

But she couldn't think about that now. Her heart beat rapidly as she realized exactly what she had in her hands. This was what she needed. She knew Lindy better than anyone, and she knew she could figure out Lindy's code. It was a puzzle, and she would put every last piece in place and finally know what happened thirteen years ago. The diary was Lindy's last days, what she knew and who she knew it about.

What if she hadn't been raped? What if the police assumed she'd been raped because she'd had sex with William before she was killed? Max's heart thudded. Was William the one cheating on her? William said she'd broken up with him because she didn't want to go public with their relationship—was that the real reason? Or an excuse?

Max needed to do this at her hotel, with better light and room to spread everything out. She put her car into gear and glanced in her rearview mirror.

A van was speeding up the street and looked like it would sideswipe her. She waited for it to pass, and then the van's lights temporarily blinded her as the driver turned and aimed right for her car. She had no place to turn, no time to get out of the way or get out of the car.

The van slammed into her trunk. The air bag popped open and her face slammed against it at the same time. All air left her lungs, and she took a deep breath and started coughing from the powder in the air.

Diary.

She felt around but it had fallen from her hands. She tasted blood as it dripped down her nose.

A shadow crossed her window. A quick glance showed a masked man. He tried the door and found it locked. She saw the hammer just in time to turn her head and shield her eyes as the glass shattered.

He reached in through the broken window and opened the door, then grabbed her and tried to pull her from the car. Her seat belt resisted him. He grunted, leaned over, and unbuckled it.

Max wasn't going to let him take her without a fight. She pounded his body with her fists as he yanked her from the car. She tried to scream, but her throat was raw from the air bag's chemicals and it came out raspy. She saw the hammer coming down toward her head and grabbed his wrist. She was strong, pumped with the adrenaline of survival, but he was on top and had muscles that didn't seem evident from his slender build.

She kicked him in the groin, but didn't get close enough to do serious damage. He backhanded her, her head hit the pavement, and she lay stunned. Her attacker went back into her car, and then sped away in the van that had hit her.

She pushed herself up on all fours, but fell back down, dizzy. She shook off the vertigo and crawled to her car. Her purse was still there.

Lindy's diary was not.

This wasn't a robbery.

You were followed twice this week!

She'd been so stupid. She'd hit herself if she wasn't already in such pain.

She took out her phone and her vision was fuzzy. Jasper Pierce must still be in the area. She hoped. She hit redial.

"Santini."

She was confused. Was he the last person she'd called? She couldn't remember. She needed to focus.

"Max? You there?"

"Yeah." Her voice was not her own. She took a deep breath, sat on the sidewalk and leaned against the car. "I—um—r-r-remember when you said if I needed help just to ask-k-k?" Her words sounded funny. She spit blood onto the sidewalk and felt her teeth with her tongue. They seemed to all be there. What an odd thing to think about. But she had nice, straight, white teeth and the thought that some bastard might have dislodged one made her angry.

"Are you drunk? You're slurring."

She laughed. She couldn't help it. "I wish I were. I need a ride."

"Where are you?"

She gave him the address of Palm Storage. "But I'm down the street. Someone hit my car."

"Are you injured?"

"Not serious. Just shaken."

"I'll call a patrol and ambulance."

"No ambulance. Dammit, can I just get a ride

back to the hotel and I can tell you what the bastard stole?"

"Your car was stolen?"

"No, Lindy's journal."

"Who's Lindy?"

"We have a lot to talk about."

Chapter Twenty

Nick could not be trusted. He called a patrol *and* an ambulance, and Max sat in the back of the ambulance while the paramedics cleaned up the cuts on her face and hands. She felt sore and stupid and irate.

She glared at Nick as he talked to the patrol officer. She'd already given her statement and all she wanted to do was go home.

Home. She didn't have a home to go to. She had a hotel.

While she knew that she could go to her grandmother's and curl up in her old bed and have Regina prepare her favorite comfort foods, she would also be subjected to a lecture, an argument about tracking Lindy's killer, and a cold shoulder. It wasn't worth it.

Stop it, Max. You're feeling sorry for yourself.

"Where's my phone?" she asked the paramedic.

"The police have all your personal effects. You should go to the hospital, Ms. Revere."

"No, thank you." She closed her eyes.

"You might have a concussion. You have a pretty big knot on the side of your head."

He touched it as if to prove a point, making her yelp.

"I'll have the front desk call me every two hours and wake me up. Happy?"

Nick said, "I'll watch her."

She hadn't even seen him approach.

"I just need a ride, Detective."

Nick ignored her and spoke to the paramedic. "What's the story? Anything broken?"

"No," he said. "She'll be bruised and sore in the morning, more from being rear-ended. A few cuts, but that lump on her head is nasty. I got most of the glass out of her hair, but Ms. Revere, when you shower be very careful. Even though it's safety glass, it can still cut you."

"I will. Thank you."

Nick helped her stand and they walked over to his Bronco. He opened the passenger door for her. "Nick, there's a box in the backseat of my car. Can you please get it?"

He closed the door without answering. A few minutes later, he put the box of Kevin's files in the back of his Bronco and then silently drove to her hotel.

She expected him to leave her in the lobby; instead, he carried the box to her room.

"Thank you," she said.

He followed her in and put the box on her desk. "Nick, I don't need to be babysat."

He was staring at her boards. She'd meant to close them up—that's why she liked the trifolds, easy to hide. But she also hadn't expected to bring anyone to her hotel room.

"Nick, please—I want a shower." She held the door open for him to get the hint. She wanted to be alone. To lick her wounds.

Her head pounded. She considered everything she'd found, and lost, today. Losing Lindy's diary was not only heartbreaking, she'd never see it again. The killer would destroy it and she'd never know the truth.

She didn't know if she could live with that.

For too long she'd lived with not knowing where her mother was, not knowing who her father was, and not knowing where the bastard who killed Karen dumped her body. And, if she was being so honest with herself, she realized that not knowing who killed Lindy had been like a cancer in her soul, eating her up, driving her forward while holding her back. She hated unsolved crimes, but her life was one big unsolved mystery with partial clues and lots of doubts.

"Nick, you can leave. I'm going to be fine."

"I have no doubt." He turned to assess her. She couldn't read his expression, whether he was angry or worried or annoyed. All of the above. "After you explain to me why you lied."

She let the door close and rubbed her eyes with her fingertips, trying to relieve the building pressure. "I don't lie, Nick."

"Bullshit. When I was on the phone with you, you specifically said he took *Lindy's journal.* But when the officer asked if the attacker took anything, you said you didn't think so." He gestured to the three trifolds. "I didn't make the connection then, but now—Lindy Ames. We talked about this the other day, but you changed the subject. I let you change it then, but no longer. Beck has it out for you because you testified for her killer, that much I figured out. But why this?" He tapped the board. "And you had her journal? Tell me why I shouldn't tell him you're withholding evidence in a capital case."

"I'm *not.*" She closed her eyes. "Kevin O'Neal didn't kill Lindy."

"So you've said. Beck is confident that he did."

"I know. They never looked at any other suspects because an anonymous caller placed Kevin at the school during the time that Lindy died. And Kevin lied about his alibi."

"He still walked away."

Max sat down, realizing her shower was going to have to wait, and that she was too sore and tired to stand.

Nick walked over to her minifridge and took out a water bottle. He handed it to her, then sat on the couch across from her.

"Thanks," she said and drank. Then she told him the abbreviated version of Kevin's trial, Lindy, their friendship and her secrets, and how Max found the storage unit.

"It's my fault," she said. "I'm usually smarter than this. I knew someone was following me, I should have been more diligent today."

"You were being followed?"

"Monday morning by a white Mercedes with no front plate while I was on my way to see Dru Parker. I thought it was connected to her, and I lost the car, so I wasn't really concerned. Then this morning, coming back from a meeting with Lindy's father, Gerald Ames. A black sedan. I lost him too by driving to the Los Altos Hills Police Department, then taking a circular route to my next destination."

Nick smirked, then cleared his throat. "Why?"

"It's clear—Kevin didn't keep it a secret that he was looking for Lindy's killer. I'm in town for his funeral, and my job is to look at cold cases. I'm good at it. Fresh eyes and all that. I tracked down the storage unit and got there right before closing. It's a small room, not much bigger than a closet, with a desk and a bunch of files Kevin had on Lindy's investigation. I grabbed what I thought would be the most important, but there's five times more there than I took. I found Lindy's journal and a note from Kevin."

"Note?"

"Did my attacker take it, too?"

"I have all your personal effects here." He walked over to the box of files and removed a large paper bag. "Purse, iPad, phone, and this." He took out the letter from Kevin.

"I can't believe I lost the diary."

"You could have been killed. The good news is that we have the hammer, could have prints on it."

"He wore gloves."

"He might not have worn the gloves when he first touched the hammer. Most criminals aren't masterminds. We're also pulling surveillance tapes from the storage facility and any businesses on the street that have exterior security cameras. If he followed you from the hotel, he might have driven past the place. We may get a plate number, or a shot of his face. And if he's been hanging around here, they may have him on security."

Nick sat back down and said, "Anything else you want to tell me? Now's the time to come clean."

"Come clean? I haven't been doing anything. This isn't your case, and as far as Beck is concerned, it's closed."

"You can tell him about O'Neal's alibi."

"I told Beck after I found out, twelve years ago, and according to him, he interviewed Olivia Langstrom, the girl Kevin was with, in front of her father, who she was terrified of. She denied being with Kevin. That was that."

"That doesn't make sense. Why would Kevin say he was home alone, and then tell you after the trial that he was with a girl? And why wouldn't she come forward?"

"Her father is powerful and, according to Olivia, emotionally and physically abusive. You can talk to Olivia, now. She's not going to lie anymore."

"Why do you think so?"

"I just know. Reporter's intuition."

"What else do I need to know?"

"The only other thing is that someone called the hotel on Saturday and sort of threatened me. Very subtle. Leave the Ames family alone. I thought maybe Beck, but he'd already gotten into my face at Kevin's funeral. Then I thought Gerald Ames, Lindy's father, put someone up to it. I hadn't planned on talking to him—his wife hates me—but hell, at that point I wasn't even planning on investigating Lindy's murder. But now I know it wasn't Gerald. I think it was someone who thought I'd back down if the victim's family didn't want me investigating."

"And what did Mr. Ames say when you talked to him this morning?"

"He wouldn't give me his blessing, but he didn't tell me to stand down. He said he wants the truth."

"What about your ex?"

"Andy?" She shook her head. "He's just like my family, doesn't want any scandals tainting the Talbot name."

"He's not harmless."

"No." She considered Andy for a moment. "He could have made the call," she admitted. "He didn't want me stirring the pot."

"And why is that?"

"He's always thought Kevin was guilty."

"But you believed from the beginning he was innocent. Did you ever doubt him?"

Max considered. "Not once, until he told me he was with Olivia the night Lindy was killed, and I didn't understand why he lied about it. It made no sense to me. It still doesn't, and I've talked to Olivia twice. But what really destroyed our friendship was that I blamed him for Lindy's killer going free. Both of them—if Olivia and Kevin had told the truth from the beginning, the police would have focused on other suspects."

"That's a valid point. And Andy?"

"Our disagreement over Kevin is what split us up, Nick. It wasn't a minor argument. In his eyes, I was defending the person who killed our friend. She was my best friend. Until our senior year, we did everything together. Kevin, too. In my eyes, Andy had already convicted one friend of murdering another friend. We were eighteen. And temperamental."

"*Were* temperamental?"

It took Max a moment to realize Nick was teasing her. She smiled and pulled herself up. "I'm going to shower now." Nick didn't make any move to leave, so she said, "If you want to order food, go ahead. I haven't eaten since breakfast."

Max really wanted to soak in a hot bath with bubbles and an oversized glass of wine. But she was pretty certain Nick wasn't going to leave, and drinking alcohol with a possible concussion wasn't smart. So she showered, carefully washing her hair in case bits of safety glass remained. Her face was too pale, and with all her makeup gone she looked beat-up. A nasty scrape on the side of her face and big fat bruises on her nose and above her eye—just great. She hoped they would fade enough that she could conceal the damage with makeup before Ben or David saw her.

She dressed in the wonderful plush bathrobe the hotel provided and in the privacy of the suite's adjoining bedroom called David and told him what happened. She didn't want to, but she'd promised, and she wasn't going to lose her one trusted friend.

She downplayed the accident, but didn't lie to David. He listened, asked a few questions, and then said, "Be careful, Max."

"I promise."

She felt a hundred times better telling David the truth, and knowing he wasn't going to abandon his vacation. She stepped out into the living room and the comforting aroma of chicken noodle soup greeted her. Nick had put a tray on her desk. He was sitting at the table, talking quietly on his cell phone, a half-eaten sandwich in front of him.

She took the lid off the soup and ate happily, half listening to Nick's conversation. As soon as he mentioned "bones," her ears perked up, but she only got bits and pieces. Then she heard "thirteen bones."

Nick was off the phone a few minutes later. She waited for him to say something. He had to have known she'd heard part of his conversation. She said, "The soup was perfect."

"My mom used to make me chicken noodle soup when I was sick."

Martha had never cooked, Max realized. For the first ten years of her life, they'd lived a nomadic lifestyle, moving from house to hotel, all over the world, depending on Martha's whims. She had a monthly allowance from her trust fund that kept them living well, but Martha had always spent down to the last dime. She'd be staking out her bank for her next allowance on the first of every month, so she could clean out her account and move somewhere else.

Max once asked her mother, "What are you running from?"

"Nothing, Maxie. I just like moving."

That answer had never satisfied Max. When she got her first apartment in New York, when she and Karen were juniors, a year before she disappeared, Max took cooking classes at a top culinary school. She'd learned the basics from Regina, her grandmother's longtime house-keeper, but Max wanted to know more. She now rarely ate out when she was home, finding cooking both relaxing and fulfilling. She understood it was her need to create something she hadn't had as a child. She wasn't so blind to her own psychology that she didn't know that she longed for what she'd never had.

Nick didn't ask her why she was silent, and Max was relieved. She was an open book—except about her mother. She didn't want to talk about Martha Revere with anyone.

"So, any news?" she asked after several bites.

"You were eavesdropping, you tell me."

She frowned. "You're in my hotel room. I wasn't going to leave the room."

He looked around. "I don't see a bed."

"It's a suite."

"Nice."

"They found thirteen bones?"

"Very good." He sat across from her. "Forensics sifted through the dirt and found what appear to be thirteen human bones. They've pulled soil samples from the grave site and the surrounding area for comparison. They also found a small diamond earring. Everything is going to the county lab."

"When are they going to have results?"

"It won't be tomorrow. This isn't television."

"No need to be sarcastic," she said. "I've

worked enough of these cases to know how it's done and law enforcement limitations. I have a private forensics lab I've used on some of my investigations. They're in Sacramento, two hours away. They have all the necessary state and federal certifications."

"Conflict of interest."

"There is none. It's not my personal lab. I'll hire them."

"You can't pay for it."

"I have a nonprofit foundation that—"

"No," he interrupted. "We're going through the county lab. They know this is a priority. I told them it ties in with an active murder investigation." He hesitated. "I know the head of our CSI unit well. He didn't want to, but he told me—off the record—that the bones are human. He can't *say* that until it's verified in the lab, but it gives me something to work with. The earring—it most likely came from the victim—there was an intact back on it. Gold. I'm making an assumption that the victim was a female, though these days the earring could have come from a guy. And my forensics guy says, as long as I don't put it in my report, that he thinks the bones are ten to fifteen years old."

Nick looked at her. "I found the copy of the parking ticket," he said.

Her stomach twisted. "Nick—maybe I should have said something, but it's not like this was your case. And Beck wouldn't listen to me about anything, and no way was I—"

He put up his hand. "William Revere is your cousin, right?"

"Yes, but I'm not covering for him."

"Just tell me."

So she told him exactly what she knew—that the ticket had been in Kevin's apartment, she had questioned William, and he said he'd left before twelve thirty the night Lindy was killed. And he left her in the main house, alive.

"You know he could be lying."

"I know." The thought pained her.

"You can be logical about this? About your family?"

"What do you want me to say? I know William. I don't think he's a killer, but I could be wrong. Kevin lied to me, maybe William's lying."

"You don't think he is."

"I can't see William strangling Lindy, looking into her face and watching her die. I just—I can't see it. Maybe I'm blind."

"She was strangled from behind."

Max stared at him. "How do you know that?"

"While you were in the shower, I called a friend of mine at the coroner's office. She grumbled, but read me the report. There's some odd things, and she's sending me a copy. But I've got to tell you—I'm already getting shit from my boss about the calls I'm making."

"I'm sorry, I didn't mean—"

He waved off her apology. "I don't care. I told my boss there may be a connection between Jason Hoffman's murder and Lindy Ames's murder." He glanced over at her murder boards. "What's that drawing on the Ames board?"

Max got up and took off the sticky note. "This is Lindy's crime scene."

"You're not much of an artist, are you?"

"No." She pointed to the line. "This is the stone wall. This dotted line is the gate. This tree—"

"That's a tree?"

"Ha. That's the tree I climbed up the other night next to the old gym to see if I could see how close Lindy's clubhouse was from the pool."

"She was found in the school's pool."

"Yes. It's closer to her clubhouse than her own pool."

Nick got up and took the drawing off Jason Hoffman's board. "And this?"

"That's where the grave is, those are trees, and that's the wall."

"The same wall."

Max understood what he saw. "Yes."

"Where was Lindy found in relation to the grave?"

"A hundred, a hundred and twenty yards."

"Do you realize that Atherton has only had two murders within the town limits in the last twenty years?" Nick said.

"Three. Lindy, Jason, and the unidentified victim in this grave. All at Atherton Prep." She frowned. "It has to be a coincidence."

"You don't think so."

She stared at the boards. No, she didn't think this was a coincidence.

Nick said, "You put up a third board as soon as you found the grave, even before we confirmed there had been a body buried there."

"Because I think that Jason found the grave and that's why he was killed."

"So do I. That's why I've been on the phone for the last hour."

"But that doesn't mean there's a connection between Jason and Lindy. Thirteen years between murders. Jason didn't go to ACP. He's from San Carlos, ten miles north. Evergreen had no other business in Atherton, until the sports complex. Their families don't move in the same circles. Except—Jasper. He's the only connection between Jason and ACP. But he didn't even go to school with Lindy. He's several years older than us."

"But there is a connection between Jason and the grave, and the grave and Lindy."

"I don't understand. Because they were killed in the same area?" Max knew she was missing something.

"Your friend was killed thirteen years ago. The bones we found are between ten and fifteen years old. The lab will be able to pinpoint their age more accurately."

"You're saying Lindy and the grave are connected."

"I think it's something I need to follow up." Nick put out his hand. Max hesitated, then took it. "Go to bed," he told her.

"Bossy." But she was tired. "The hotel can call me every hour," she said. "You don't need to stay."

"It's fine."

"Why are you being so nice to me? You made it perfectly clear last night that you don't like me."

Nick stepped toward her. Now she recognized the expression on his face. Her breath caught in her throat and she felt like a teenager again, waiting for her first kiss.

He leaned over and put his lips on hers. A light kiss. A kiss that was longer than friendly, but shorter than passion.

It wasn't enough for Max. Not after that kiss in the restaurant, when she knew what they both wanted.

She took a step toward him, until her body was pressed against his, and she kissed him with the same intensity as he had the other night. He didn't hesitate, but held her behind her neck, holding her in place, returning the same.

This time, she stopped the kiss. She didn't want to. Her heart urgently beat a call to finish what they'd started. They were both experienced consenting adults who were attracted to each other. She wanted to take Nick to bed.

But not when she couldn't give herself the way she wanted.

She said, "If I was feeling one hundred percent, we'd be naked right now."

He tilted his head and gave her a quirky but sexy half smile. "Get well soon, Max."

Chapter Twenty-one

Nick had woken Max up at midnight, then again at three, to make sure she was coherent. Max woke up on her own at five in the morning feeling like she'd been hit by a truck. But her mind was running full steam, and she wanted to look at Kevin's files.

Nick had already gone through everything. He had it sorted, and Max quickly realized it was sorted into stacks of irrelevant, possibly relevant, and likely relevant. In the center were all the files on her and her family, which made her very uncomfortable.

She glanced over to where Nick was sleeping on the couch. He'd taken his pants off, they were on the chair, and he'd slept in the USMC shirt Max had borrowed from him Saturday. A blanket was tangled around his legs, but she could see his well-toned body. She admired and appreciated men who kept fit.

She didn't like that Nick now knew so much about her—Kevin had kept a lot of information, his personal notes about her and her family, as well as articles she'd written, reviews of her books and cable show, and her finances. A finance article was on top, about how her family had contested Genevieve Sterling's will because half her estate was supposed to be left to her charitable trust, and the other half split among her grand-children. Because Martha had disappeared and never been declared legally dead, the family objected to Max receiving Martha's share. Fortunately, Genie had left an explicit letter that the judge accepted stating that if Martha Revere didn't come before the court and identify herself within one year of Genie's death, that the inheritance—and the board seat that went with it—would be affirmed to Max.

That her family—led by her uncle Brooks— would try to convince the judge that Genie was senile had led to a rift that Max had never forgiven them for. While her other aunts and uncles hadn't been as emphatic as Brooks, they'd been complicit. Max still didn't know if their problem was because she had been a twenty-one-year-old college student who continued to cause problems for the family, or if they just wanted money, or if they didn't want her on the board of the trust. She didn't care. This was her slot, and her decision.

What pained her more than anything was that Eleanor hadn't stood up for her. Privately, she'd chastised the others for creating a public disagreement on a matter that should have been handled within the closed doors of the family. But Max refused to cave in to Eleanor's so-called compromise, and Eleanor refused to make any public statement on her behalf, nor would she go to the judge for Max. That she hadn't joined *with* Brooks and the others didn't matter to Max—this wasn't something she should have remained neutral on.

Max didn't like that Nick knew all this stuff about her. It's not something she talked about, and it's not something she wanted to share.

Then in the relevant pile she saw a drawing. It looked exactly like the northwest corner of Atherton Prep. There was the gym under construction, the line of trees, the old gym, the wall—also three small red x's where the three bodies had been found: Lindy, Jason, and the unknown victim.

He'd even put in distances.

"You weren't much of an artist," Nick said as he sat up.

"And you are," Max said, impressed. "You said there was a connection last night, but I don't know—there's no one missing from ACP or Atherton. I checked."

"I saw your notes. Honestly, I don't know what to think yet. I *do* believe that you're right in that Jason was killed because he caught the person removing the bones, or the person thought he'd been spotted, or that Jason had found something around the grave site and was going to contact the authorities. I don't see how that connects with your friend, Lindy Ames, but if the bones are as old as my forensics team says, it puts that death at about the same time as Lindy's. I can't discount the similarities."

"The gun that killed Jason—"

"Nine millimeter. Ballistics didn't show a match to any other crime. Nothing special about the bullets, either. No shell casings at the scene, so the killer policed his brass. The killer was less than ten feet away. Could have been a lousy shot and still hit him."

"And Jason was killed where he was found, here near the trailers."

Nick nodded, got up and stretched. Max stared. There wasn't an ounce of fat on the man. Nick gave her a half smile, grabbed his pants, and went into the bathroom.

Damn, he knew he was hot. A hot cop.

Danger, Will Robinson! Danger!

She almost laughed out loud. Yes, hot cops were her vice. She had to watch herself or she'd be flying west a whole lot more than she wanted to.

Her phone rang and she grabbed it.

"Max, what happened?"

It was her producer Ben, sounding hysterical.

"What happened with what? I haven't had my coffee yet."

"I got a call last night from the police, on my answering machine, about the rental car being totaled. Why didn't you call me? Are you okay?"

"I'm fine. It's nothing."

"Were you talking on your cell phone again?"

"No, *Dad,* I wasn't."

"Stop that, our insurance rates are through the roof. You're the definition of a distracted driver."

"I wasn't even driving," she snapped. "I was rear-ended."

"And the car was totaled?"

"I wouldn't say totaled. Undrivable?"

"Maxine Revere, tell me what happened."

She gave Ben the short version because she knew how stressed he got when she was working a dangerous case. "It was nothing. Really. I was reading something in my car—while it was legally parked—a van rear-ended me, stole some stuff, and left."

"What the fuck? You were robbed?"

"Don't raise your voice. It's not my fault!"

"I'm calling David. He'll tell me the truth."

"Go ahead, I already told him what happened."

"Dammit, Max, what are you working on? You were attacked? What have you been doing? It's Wednesday, you promised you would be in New

York by Friday. You're coming back Friday, right?"

Her head was hurting listening to Ben. "This is why I prefer e-mails," she mumbled.

"What?"

Nick had finished in the bathroom and was watching her from the doorway. His expression was both confused and bemused.

Max said, "I'll try to be back on Friday, but don't count on it. I can fly back with David Sunday." Or Monday. Or Tuesday. But she didn't say that to Ben.

"I have six interviews lined up for Friday. Your new assistant."

"Change them."

"I'll pick one."

"Don't you dare. Your track record sucks, Benji." He hated the nickname he'd had in college.

"God, I hate when you do that."

"You do the first interview. The three you like the least, set up a second interview with me and David next week."

"What?"

"Well, you've hired all my assistants because you only send me the people you think I'll like. That hasn't worked. Josh's incompetence still gives me nightmares. So send me people you think I'll hate or scare."

"That doesn't make sense."

"Good-bye."

"Don't hang up."

She didn't. She wanted to, but Ben had called David in the past when she didn't listen to him. "There's more?"

"The attack."

Damn, she thought she'd diverted his attention from that.

"I'm fine. Failed carjacking attempt." She was lying to Ben. God help her if he ever found out.

"That's not what the police said."

"The police? Who did you talk to? You said they left a message."

"Well, I called back and he'd given me his cell phone number and actually picked up this morning. An Officer Gavin or Graven. He said that you were attacked with a hammer and the person stole some notes? Yours?"

Max could bluff. She could use smoke and mirrors to change the direction of the conversation. She had a problem with outright lying. "Kevin left me some things," she said. "One of them, this journal, is apparently very valuable."

"This is the one time I'm going to tell you to let the police handle it." He paused. "Are you okay?"

"I'm fine."

"Max, David will come back for you. You know that."

"I do, which is why you can't call him. Ben, I'm *fine*."

Nick put his hand out. Max looked at him strangely, then handed him the phone. Nick mouthed to her, *"Who is it?"*

She whispered, "Ben Lawson, my producer."

Nick said into the phone, "Mr. Lawson? This is Detective Nick Santini. I'm working on the case involving Ms. Revere, and I'll make sure she's safe. There's no need to be alarmed, she's quite resilient." He listened to something, smiled at Max, then handed her the phone.

Max said to Ben, "Satisfied?"

"It's seven in the morning in California. Why is he in your hotel room? Are you sleeping with him?"

She smiled. It was clear that Nick had heard every word. "Not yet," she replied and hung up.

It wasn't until they were walking down for breakfast when Nick told her that he'd called a retired detective and invited him to meet them for a brainstorming session. Detective Carson Salter had been part of the initial investigation into Lindy's murder. Max didn't recognize the name, however, she recognized Detective Salter as soon as she saw him. He was short, lean, and black. She remembered that when she'd seen him, a couple times on campus during the week of interviews, his hair had also been black. Now it was almost completely white.

"Good to finally meet you, Santini," Salter said.

He firmly shook their hands, then sat at the table in the Menlo Grill.

Max said, "You two don't know each other?"

"Carson retired six months before I moved up here. I took his slot, but had to wait for a budgeting issue to be resolved."

Carson grunted. "They didn't want to bring him in until the new fiscal year."

"We've talked on the phone a few times because I inherited his desk and some of his cases."

"When you told me you were looking into the Lindy Ames case, I knew you'd face some problems."

Max was at a loss. "You're looking into Lindy's murder?" she asked Nick.

"Since last night when you were attacked for her journal."

Carson said, "Nick filled me in on what you've been up to, Ms. Revere."

"Call me Max."

He smiled. "My wife loves your show. It's grown on me, though I can't say I like it all the time."

"I'm not doing the show to make friends."

"Is that why you're here? Doing a show on Lindy's murder?"

"Do you see a camera crew?" Max realized she was on the defensive. She took a deep breath. "I'm sorry, Detective. I'm still upset about being robbed last night."

"Call me Carson."

The waiter came with coffee and juice and took their orders. When he left, Nick said, "When I called around last night about looking at the case files, I was given a red light by my boss. I need to know why."

Carson sighed. "It wasn't my case, but we all worked on it at some point, and we all were frustrated. But I was there initially with Harry Beck when Atherton finally called us. It was a mess. Her body was found in the pool at eight in the morning. Atherton trampled the entire scene, both at the school and at the Ames house. They didn't call us until six that evening. The body had already been removed by the coroner, the Atherton police had already contacted her parents who were in New York on a business trip. By the time we'd been called in, the parents had just rushed home and we had no answers, but they didn't know we had just gotten the case."

"Did Beck initially suspect Kevin O'Neal?"

"We didn't suspect anyone. We didn't know what had happened. We couldn't even say she'd been murdered—the Atherton police initially thought it was an accident. But after the autopsy, it was clear she was strangled. Then we interviewed her friends at the school trying to piece together what had happened on Saturday night."

"I remember," Max said. "We all knew she was dead."

"Word spread quickly. We had some issues with Atherton PD sharing information. On the surface they appeared to be helpful, but every time we asked for information about disturbance calls to the Ames house or the school, we met with a delay. O'Neal became a suspect because we learned during our interviews that he and the victim had had a nasty breakup two weeks before, and her friends said she was seeing someone else but no one admitted to knowing who."

Max tensed. She and Nick had talked briefly about William last night, but they hadn't resolved anything. She remained silent for now, figuring Nick would bring it up if he thought it was important for Carson to know.

But Nick didn't say anything.

Carson continued. "We interviewed O'Neal and he said he'd been home alone all night. Saturday night? Eighteen-year-old high school senior home alone? Beck didn't buy it. But there was no forensic evidence to tie O'Neal to the crime, and the coroner's report was very . . . vague."

"Vague?" Nick asked. "How so?"

"The coroner determined that the victim had sex the night she was killed, but sexual assault was inconclusive. It was combined with the other evidence—of manual strangulation—to come up with the theory that she was raped and strangled, possibly accidentally. After the anonymous tip that O'Neal's car had been spotted at the school the night of the murder, Beck went hard at him. He even posited the theory that O'Neal accidentally strangled her during sex games. Beck just wanted a confession. The DA even offered O'Neal a plea agreement of manslaughter, but O'Neal never waffled. He said he was home, and only that witness put him at the school. If that person had come forward and testified, the jury could have gone the other way, but O'Neal's lawyer was good. He showed enough reasonable doubt. The case was all built on circumstantial evidence and theories. All the people who testified were young, they testified to O'Neal having a history of fighting, breaking up, getting back together with the victim. One of the victim's close friends testified that the victim and the suspect had rough sex frequently. No one could confirm that he was, in fact, at home."

"Did you believe that Kevin was guilty?" Max asked.

Carson didn't say anything for a moment. "I didn't believe he was innocent, but I was never convinced of his guilt. It all fit—do you know how many cases I've worked where an ex-boyfriend goes after his ex-girlfriend? How many domestic violence situations came across my desk? I'm just glad I found my wife forty-two years ago, before I became old and jaded."

The waiter delivered their food and after he left,

Nick asked, "Were there any other suspects you looked at?"

Carson shook his head. "Not seriously. We wanted to find the guy who she allegedly was seeing after she split with O'Neal, but no one came forward, and we had no forensic evidence. Her clubhouse, where she spent a lot of time, had prints from a dozen or more people. All her friends who admitted being in the clubhouse the week before she was killed consented to being printed—we did it primarily to match them up, and if a print ended up somewhere it shouldn't have been, we'd have a suspect. There were no unaccounted for fingerprints in her clubhouse. We also printed her bedroom and all the doors of her house. One problem, though—"

"Atherton PD."

"I swear, I wanted to fire them all. Half of them searched without gloves. Half of them trampled the area between the Ames house and the school. There's a gate that passed through between the two properties. It was open, but we don't know if the killer opened it or if one of the police opened it. We don't know if the victim was killed in her clubhouse, the main house, and then brought to the pool, or if she was killed in the pool house. We had a theory, which we gave in court, but it was just a theory. A half-dozen other theories could have worked. The one we went with was that O'Neal found out that the victim was seeing someone else; he went to her clubhouse to confront her. She fled, through the gate to the pool house at the school, to hide from him. He tracked her down, attacked her, and when he realized he killed her, he pushed her into the pool and fled."

"And I always said," Max said, "that Kevin would never have done it."

"So you did. You were the only one, other than his mother. But juries don't listen to the parents of the accused." Carson assessed her.

"Kevin knew Lindy was cheating on him when he broke up with her."

"But," Carson countered, "according to statements, he didn't know who it was, and was obsessed with finding out."

"He wanted to know." She glanced at Nick. She saw in his expression that he was thinking about William—so was she.

Carson said, "You grew up the way I thought you would."

"I don't know if that's a compliment."

"It is. You were unusually self-confident when you were eighteen. Very self-aware. You didn't let the prosecutor under your skin."

"If I told you that Kevin lied about his alibi, and I could prove he was nowhere near Lindy's house or the school the night she died, what would you say?"

"I'd say either you fabricated evidence, or the killer called in the anonymous tip."

Max told him about Olivia Langstrom and what she'd said about the night Lindy died. "Kevin told me this the day the jury came back divided. I haven't spoken to him since then. I told Detective Beck, and he didn't believe me, but he questioned Olivia and she denied it."

Carson frowned "I never knew that."

"When I asked Olivia, she admitted to it. She lied because Beck questioned her in front of her abusive father."

"Why didn't she come forward?"

"She claimed she was scared of her father. Kevin said he was innocent and therefore didn't need Olivia's alibi. But the trial and the weight of the hung jury killed him. He left me a letter and confessed to his suicide. He also said he was dying. Proof should be in the autopsy report, which I don't have."

Nick said, "I'll get it."

Max continued. "Kevin contacted me four months ago saying he had information and thought I could use it to find out who killed Lindy. I had my assistant call him back and tell him I wasn't interested. He killed himself ten days ago and his sister asked me to come." She hesitated, then said, "I think he killed himself to force me to come here. He knew he was dying and he thought this was the only way to get me to look at Lindy's murder."

Carson shook his head. "That's disturbing."

Nick said, "He couldn't have known you would return. You said you haven't been home in two years."

"But he set up enough to entice me. Jodi called me because he sent her a message to call me the night he killed himself. Then he sent her a copy of Lindy's death certificate with a comment on the back—*Lindy drowned.*" She stared at Carson, assessing his reaction. "Did she?"

Carson was stunned. "I—I don't know how he got that information."

"You're not denying it."

"It was never in the coroner report." Carson let out a long sigh then sipped his coffee as if gathering his thoughts. "There were two coroner's reports, the preliminary and the official. In the preliminary report, which was never released and never part of the trial, it said there was water in her lungs. That was explained away in the final report as a reflex in a recently deceased victim. Meaning, as soon as the killer realized she was dead, he pushed her in the pool. Involuntary muscle contraction or something.

"But another theory is that she may have been unconscious when she was pushed into the pool, and that she did drown. It's something the head medical examiner felt would confuse the jury. This was *before* O'Neal was a suspect, so it wasn't a personal thing, but a judgment call based on experience."

"You have doubts?" Nick said.

"I don't know what happened that night. Usually, when it's my case, I have to know in my head and my heart that my theory of events is accurate. Then I will fight with my last breath to put the killer in prison. This time—it was like a puzzle piece that didn't quite fit."

Carson looked at Max. "Do you have a theory?"

She told him about the diary and then showed him Kevin's letter. He read it, taking his time, then said, "Well."

"Someone attacked Max last night and stole the diary," Nick said.

Carson slid over a file to Nick. "These were my notes on the case. As I said, I wasn't part of the investigation other than helping with the interviews. But if Kevin O'Neal is truly innocent, I'd start looking into that anonymous caller. We searched for him, but nothing. He used a pay phone and there were no security cameras. It was—damn, it's not there anymore. Over near where they built the new grocery on El Camino. There used to be a café."

"Drake's," Max said.

"Yeah, that's it."

"We used to walk there from campus. It was an open campus, and Drake would get us in and out fast so we weren't late. I remember when he shut down." Max hadn't been here. He'd been so good to them, and then development and business costs forced him out of business. When she was here for Genie's funeral, he was open; a few years later, by the time of Thea's wedding, he was closed.

"There was a pay phone in that strip mall. It's gone, too." Carson glanced at Nick. "Do you think Beck will give you the tape?"

"I don't need Beck. The tape was part of evidence. It's with the DA's office."

"He's going to find out."

"Let him." Nick glanced at Max. "Are you ready for a battle?"

"Hell, yes."

Two hours later, Max and Nick listened to the 911 tape. The voice, a male, was slightly distorted, almost a whisper, and it was very hard to understand exactly what the caller was saying.

> WITNESS: I saw a car at the school where that girl was killed.
> DISPATCHER: What is your name?
> WITNESS: I'd rather not say.
> DISPATCHER: You can remain anonymous, but if you can share your name and phone number it would help us verify your statement.
> WITNESS: Well, um, I saw this car. See, I wasn't supposed to be there, it was way

past my curfew. And I saw this car, it was a black Honda Civic. Kinda older.

DISPATCHER: Where exactly did you see the car?

WITNESS: Parked in the lot. Right under the weeping willow tree.

DISPATCHER: Do you remember seeing a person?

WITNESS: No, just the car. I really have to go. Oh—um, one thing. There was a sticker on the back. I don't know what it said.

DISPATCHER: Sir, if you can please give me your name so I can have a detective talk to you.

The call ended there.

Nick said, "And I assume Kevin had a black Honda Civic with a sticker on the back."

Max nodded. But she was thinking. Something about that call was very familiar.

Nick's phone rang. He answered, talked, then hung up. "The surveillance tapes came in. I'm going to go view them at the station. I think you should stay away from there. Beck knows I'm reviewing the Ames case."

"Promise," she said.

Nick eyed her as if he knew she was about to do something she shouldn't, even though she didn't even know, exactly, what she was planning on doing. "What are your plans?"

"I don't know. There are all these files to go through. I want to go back to the storage locker and get the rest of Kevin's things."

Nick frowned.

"What?" she said. "The guy's not going to come after me again."

"Detective Beck seized everything this morning. I've been avoiding him."

"Why didn't you tell me?"

"I don't want you to confront him."

"He has no right to those files. They were Kevin's, and Kevin gave me the key."

"He claims they're documents important to an unsolved homicide. He got a warrant."

She looked at her desk where the files she'd already taken were spread out. "These are my files, he can't touch them. I'll get those back—I'll petition the court. That bastard. You know he's not looking for another killer. He never believed Kevin was innocent."

"I'm not arguing with you, but right now it's touchy. Just stay away, *please*."

Max didn't want to agree—she wanted to get in Beck's face. But she had other things to do.

The weeping willow tree.

Only one person she knew would have called the large, old willow tree in the middle of the Atherton Prep parking lot the *weeping* willow tree.

"I'll stay away from him. For now."

Max convinced her grandmother to loan her the two-seater Jaguar Eleanor rarely drove. She took a taxi to the house and avoided a long conversation with her grandmother, before taking the Jag and driving to Andy Talbot's office. His secretary gave her the runaround, but eventually Max realized he wasn't there. She left and called him from the parking lot.

He didn't answer his cell phone.

"Dammit, Andy!"

She didn't want to believe that Andy had made that anonymous call, but she knew in her heart it was true. Nick and Carson believed that whoever made the call was Lindy's killer—which meant that Andy had killed her.

But why? There was no damn *reason!*

She slammed her fist on the steering wheel and called William.

"I need to see Andy; he's avoiding me."

"He's just angry with you, but he'll get over it. He always does."

"William, I'm serious."

"Why?"

She didn't say anything. She didn't know if she could trust her cousin.

William sighed. "Andy's on his way to the airport. He has a business trip."

"Going where?"

"China."

"Kind of sudden, don't you think?"

"I'm sure it's been planned for a while, he doesn't keep me apprised of all his business trips," he said with thinly veiled sarcasm. "What's going on, Maxine?"

She hung up and headed for San Francisco International Airport.

It was two in the afternoon, so rush hour hadn't started yet, but Max was still frustrated that it took thirty minutes to get to the international terminal. She'd used the time wisely, however, by conning Andy's secretary into giving her the flight information. It was scheduled to leave in just under an hour; he'd probably already gone through security.

Max bought a ticket to get through security check, then she detoured to Andy's gate.

He was sitting in an open bar, drinking Scotch, across from the boarding area. She stood in front of him and didn't say a word.

He looked up and stared. He raised his glass to his lips, sipped, and put it down, never breaking eye contact.

She stepped forward and said quietly, "Do you remember when we were freshmen and Duncan was a junior? He wasn't paying attention, arguing with his girlfriend or something, and backed his car into the willow tree? I said, now it's a weeping willow tree. And you called it the weeping willow tree from then on. Maxine, meet me at the weeping willow tree, you'd tell me. Or, Maxine, I'm parked next to the weeping willow tree. I always thought it was cute, but you were the only one who called it that, other than me. You kissed me for the first time, up against the weeping willow tree."

"Sit down and have a drink."

She took his Scotch from his hand and drained it, then put it down on the table. "Kevin didn't kill Lindy. His car was never parked next to the weeping willow tree the night she died. Why did you frame him?"

"You don't want to do this."

"Someone attacked me last night when I found Lindy's diary. I thought it was Lindy's killer, that her diary contained evidence against him. That means *you* attacked me."

"I didn't know you were attacked." He briefly glanced down. Lying? Guilt?

She pointed to the scrape on the side of her face and the bruise on her nose. "I'm good with makeup, but even you can see the bruises."

"I didn't kill Lindy." His voice was barely above a whisper.

"I don't believe you. You made the call."

"I had to."

"Someone held a gun to your head?"

"I was protecting someone."

She stared at him, her mouth open, feeling foolish for wanting to believe him. For wanting to believe she hadn't been so horribly wrong about Andy Talbot for all these years. She'd slept with him—not only that, he'd been her first. Her first for everything. For sex, for love, for betrayal.

But he was willing to send an innocent man, their *friend,* to prison to protect someone else. That meant only one thing: *family*.

"I've known you since I was ten years old. I loved you once. Tell me who you're protecting."

"No."

"Yes!"

She hadn't meant to raise her voice, but the patrons around her glanced at them. She took one step closer and was only inches from Andy's face. "If you don't think I won't call security and have you kept off that plane, you're wrong. I will use every contact I have, every amount of charm and wits to make sure you are arrested."

"You do that, you destroy your own family."

Mixed emotions flooded through her. But she stood firm. "Tell me the truth, Andrew."

His jaw was tight, trembling, and his eyes were glassy. Alcohol? Fear? Regret? Max didn't care. She needed the truth.

"That night, when Lindy died, William came to my house after midnight and said he and Lindy had gotten into a huge fight. He admitted they'd been bed buddies for a year—even while he was dating Caitlin and Lindy was with Kevin. He said he'd been vicious with her, accusing her of all sorts of shenanigans, when she broke up with him. Said she didn't want to go public, that she didn't trust him, that she wanted a clean break. He left my house at one, and I went over to her house, just to talk to her. If William was that upset, she must be, too. I found her in the clubhouse. She was dead. I was . . . in shock. I stared at her body. Then I knew William was going to go to jail. I thought of you because—"

"Don't. Don't put me in this!" She pounded her fist on the bar. This wasn't what she thought she'd hear. Why did she think that she would have accepted the truth better if Andy had killed Lindy?

Except, how could she even believe him? Maybe he was lying . . . again.

"William was like your brother. And I thought of me, because I've been his best friend our entire lives. I love him more than my own brothers, because he's always been there for me. *Always.* So I was there for him. I picked her up and was going to put her in her pool knowing that would mess with any evidence, at least enough for reasonable doubt. But the pool house at the school was closer, and there was a car in her driveway, I didn't know who might be home. And I thought the longer before she was found, the better chance that all the evidence would be gone."

"If I believe you, that makes you an accessory after the fact."

"I did it for you and William."

"What did William say when you told him?"

"We never talked about it."

"What?" She had to be hearing wrong. "You cleaned up after your best friend killed someone in anger and you never discussed it? Not even a wink, wink, nod, nod?"

Max shook her head. This just wasn't happening.

"I think *you* killed her," she said. Andy was capable of losing his temper. He was affable and charming most of the time, but as she'd seen the other night when he threatened her at the Menlo Grill, and then the attack on her to get the diary. William would never have wielded a hammer. It was laughable. And her attacker wasn't as tall as William.

Her attacker wasn't as tall as Andy either, she realized.

"I am telling you the truth." He looked over her shoulder. "My flight is boarding."

"No."

"You can't stop me, Max."

"Why are you fleeing the country if you're so innocent?"

"It's a business trip. I'll be back in ten days."

"You're not going. Do you realize Lindy might have been alive when you dropped her in the pool?"

"She was dead."

"The coroner reported that there was water in

her lungs. You'll never know if *you* really did kill her. You might have been able to save her life."

"You *fucking* bitch. That's not true!"

Behind her, she heard, "Andrew Talbot, you're under arrest."

She turned and was stunned to see Nick with two Homeland Security guards and two Menlo Park police officers. She stared at him, not quite making the connection.

"Why are you here?"

"To arrest Mr. Talbot."

She blinked, glanced from Nick to Andy. Andy looked as surprised as she felt. "How did you know?"

Nick tilted his head. "Know what?"

"Why are you arresting him?"

"We got the surveillance photos from outside your hotel. He was the person following you in the black sedan on Tuesday."

Max whipped around and faced Andy again. "You followed me? Did you attack me too?"

"I would never hurt you!"

But he wasn't looking at her. He was lying. She felt ill.

"He wouldn't," Nick said, "but he would hire someone. We found the guy, got his van on surveillance cameras outside the storage unit where you were attacked last night. He's in holding. He's already talked. He also admitted to breaking into

Kevin O'Neal's apartment when you were there last week."

Max turned to Andy and said, "Where's Lindy's diary?" When Andy didn't say anything, she said, "Where, dammit!"

Max reached back to hit him and Nick caught her wrist. "I would love to let you deck him. But I can't, at least not in front of all these witnesses and security cameras that could very easily get leaked."

She pulled away from Nick and walked down the terminal. She had to get away from Andy, from Nick, from everyone. She needed time to absorb the monumental screwup she was to have trusted people—again—that she should never have trusted.

William. She loved him like the brother she'd never had. She didn't see him as a killer. She couldn't.

But he'd lied. When she caught him in his lies, he could have easily made up another. Was she that easily fooled? Were her reporter instincts nonexistent when it came to her family?

Several minutes later, Nick caught up with her.

"Max, let's sit down."

"No." She paced. She didn't care that people were looking at them, or that she'd created a scene. "I wanted the truth," she said quietly.

Nick steered her to a bench of seats as far away from the others as he could find. Max didn't want

396

to sit, but let him push her into the seat. "What did he say to you?"

"He made the anonymous call to frame Kevin for Lindy's murder." As she said it she accepted it.

"He admitted it?"

Nick sounded surprised.

"I knew it was him when I heard the dispatch recording. After the first day when there was a ruckus in the courtroom, the judge banished everyone. I was there that day, and the day I testified, and that was it. I never heard the tape before."

"You recognized his voice?"

"No. It was something he said." She closed her eyes and put her head in her lap, her fists clenched behind her neck. She felt queasy and sick and so angry. With herself and with Andy and with William. With everyone. She took a couple of deep breaths, then felt Nick's hand on her back, rubbing in circles, slowly.

She sat up. "He said that William killed Lindy and he moved her body from her clubhouse to the school pool."

"He could be lying—again—to protect himself."

"No. He really believes that William killed Lindy."

"What do you think?"

"William swore to me he didn't. But maybe— maybe they've all been lying to me my entire life and I can't pick the truth from the lies."

"I'm going to have to talk to your cousin." He

almost sounded sorry about it. Or maybe that was just pity for her plight.

She nodded. "He's family, but if he's guilty, he needs to pay for his crime. Lindy—what about her? Why weren't they thinking about her? We were all friends, how could they throw her body into the pool—I just—" She stopped.

"Max?"

"Andy said something else—he said that there was a car in her driveway and someone was in the house. Or something like that—definitely he said he didn't know who was home, and that's why he didn't put her body in her own pool. He didn't want her discovered right away."

"What are you thinking? That there was someone else there?"

"Well, right now, based on what Andy said, either he or William killed Lindy, and Andy definitely screwed with all the evidence. But if there was someone else there, who was it? Andy didn't recognize the car. Her parents were in New York. So who?"

She looked at Nick, her eyes wet, but she didn't let any tears escape. She said, "Someone else was at Lindy's house the night she died. Someone other than Andy and William."

"Are you going to be able to accept the truth if Andy Talbot is right?"

"Right about what?"

"That your cousin killed your best friend."

"He didn't."

Nick caught Max's eye and she saw compassion as well as intelligence. He was looking at the case as an impartial investigator. He didn't know Andy, or William, or Kevin, or Lindy. He was looking at the facts and the statement of a witness.

"William didn't tell Andy he killed Lindy. Or even hurt her."

"But Andy believed he did."

"I know what you're thinking—"

"I have to look at the facts, Max. You do too. If William is guilty, are you going to be okay?"

"What other choice to I have? But I owe it to William to find that piece of the puzzle. To prove, beyond a doubt, that he's innocent."

Or prove that he's guilty. But Max couldn't say it out loud.

Chapter Twenty-two

The last people who Max wanted to see were the members of her family, but she had to tell her grandmother what Andy's accusations against William were. True or not, they were serious and were going to be investigated.

Eleanor wasn't surprised to see her.

"Chief Clarkson told me that Andrew Talbot was arrested for assaulting you. I see that it's true." She reached up and touched Max's face.

Her caress was almost gentle. "What happened?"

"He hired someone, Grandmother. He didn't do it himself."

"Is this all about that girl's murder?"

"Lindy. Her name is Lindy."

"*Lindy* has cut into our family, even in death."

"That's not fair." She hesitated. "May I come in?"

"Of course." Eleanor seemed surprised that she'd asked. "Maxine, this is your home."

She walked in and told her grandmother to sit. "I have something to tell you."

Eleanor didn't argue. She sat. "What's happening, Maxine?"

"Andy accused William of murdering Lindy. He claims he found Lindy dead in her clubhouse and put the body in the pool to get rid of any physical evidence that may have implicated William, to protect him."

Eleanor didn't speak. Like Max, she always had something to say; but like Max, this was throwing her.

"You don't believe that."

"I don't know."

"Maxine! This is your family."

"I don't *want* to believe, but William lied to everyone, including the police when they questioned him about the last time he saw Lindy. It's out of my hands."

"Is this—because of you and what you do?" The disdain in her voice was evident.

"Grandmother, I don't know where to begin. Andy has been acting suspicious from the minute I saw him. He's been following me, and then he was about to board a plane to China after he hired a thug to steal Lindy's diary. But that's not all. Detective Santini got a copy of the anonymous 911 call that implicated Kevin. It was Andy. He made the call."

"Nonsense. Someone would have recognized his voice."

"It was muffled, he deliberately disguised his voice. It's what he said, and I knew it was him. I asked him; he didn't deny it. He intentionally framed Kevin for Lindy's murder. Probably so the police wouldn't dig into Lindy's life, so they wouldn't look harder at who she was sleeping with."

"What? Who?"

"William! He admitted it to me when I confronted him about the ticket. It's a mess, Grandmother."

"Andy told you this, not the police."

"That's right."

"He won't accuse William."

She sounded so positive.

"Get William the best lawyer you can."

"Of course." She said it as if it didn't need to be said. "You shouldn't have come back, Maxine. It seems you make a point of hurting the people you love."

Max didn't want to be upset about what her grandmother said, but that hit her particularly hard. She straightened her spine and said, "I'm not sorry I did."

She didn't know if she meant that. This truth, about her family, was hard to swallow.

"Do you know what this is going to do to the family?"

"You always said that Reveres are survivors with class. Grandad Sterling had nothing when he built his company, which he lost, and then he built another one. And Grandma and Grandpa Revere were among the wealthiest families on the East Coast and then lost everything in the Great Depression and had to start over with nothing. And Grandfather's brother, Timothy?"

Eleanor tightened her lips. "We don't speak of him, God rest his soul."

"But we survived. And we survived my mother leaving me here when you certainly didn't need to raise another child."

"Maxine—I'm glad she did. The way she was living, it was no life for my granddaughter."

Maybe, but that wasn't a point she was going to argue. Not now. "Whatever happens with William, the one thing you taught me is that you stick by family. If what Andy says is true, William needs to be punished—but not disowned. I love him, you know that."

"I know," she said quietly. "Which makes this

all the more difficult to understand why you would do this."

"Do what? Find answers? Give Mr. and Mrs. Ames peace of mind?"

"Will they have peace? Lindy will still be dead."

Maybe she'd never get through to her grandmother. How Eleanor thought this way, Max didn't understand. Max understood loyalty, but not to the point of letting a killer walk free.

There was a pounding on the door that made Eleanor jump. Max said, "I'll get it." She walked across the foyer and looked through the side window.

Detective Harry Beck, with two uniformed officers.

She opened the door. "Detective."

"I thought you might be here, running to your well-to-do family."

"I don't run," she said.

Eleanor rose from her seat and walked over. "Grandmother," she said, "this is Detective Beck with the Menlo Park Police Department. Detective, my grandmother, Eleanor Sterling Revere."

"Ma'am," Beck said with a nod, then told Max, "Maxine Revere, you're under arrest for obstruction of justice, and a few other things I'll think of once we have a chat."

"Absolutely not," Eleanor said, stepping forward. "You're not putting my granddaughter in jail."

"Yes, ma'am, I am."

"I'll post your bail immediately, Maxine."

"Not until her arraignment tomorrow morning," Beck said. "It's after five. She'll be spending the night in lockup. Should be fun, with the drunks and whores."

Eleanor paled.

Maxine stared at the detective. "That's my grandmother you're speaking to."

Eleanor put her hand on Max's arm. "I've heard worse, dear. I'll call a lawyer. I can't bear the thought of you being in prison."

Eleanor was sincerely worried about Max. Her grandmother was never one to show affection. A light kiss on the cheek in greeting, but no hugs, no spontaneous laughter or affection. But in this one moment, Max saw everything that Eleanor was. A matriarch. A grandmother. A survivor. Fear, love, and honor shone in her eyes.

Max kissed her grandmother on the cheek and put her hands on her shoulders. "Thank you." An odd response, perhaps, but Eleanor understood. She nodded and closed her eyes. Took a deep breath. And when she opened them again, the fighting Eleanor was back. "Call my producer Ben," Max said. "He'll contact my lawyer."

No matter what happened, they would survive.

Max returned to her cell after her phone call with Gia Barone, her attorney. Gia specialized in working with reporters and had gotten Max out of jail in the past.

"The case is nothing," Gia had said, "but the timing sucks. Arresting you after five. That's just fucked. I've got a lawyer to come in for your arraignment if you need it, but I'll get the charges dropped before then. I know a guy who plays golf with the DA and he's telling him the case is fucked."

She loved Gia, the plain speaker.

"So," Max said, "what you're really telling me is that I'm spending the night in jail."

"In a word, yes. But I'll make their life hell."

"I appreciate that."

Max laid down on the cot. She wasn't in a group cell, she was alone. She assumed Gia had arranged that. Max could hold her own with the "drunks and whores" as Beck had said, but it would make for a long night. At least now she might be able to sleep. If this cot wasn't so damn uncomfortable.

She sat up and her back cracked. She was too tall for the bed, but she was too tired to pace. She had no phone, no computer, no book, not even paper and a pen.

She didn't know what was going on with Andy, or William, or her grandmother. She hadn't spoken to Nick since the airport. Was Andy already out on bail?

She had a long night to think about her life. Her career, her family, her judgment.

She must have dozed off at some point because she heard her name and she slowly struggled to sit up. She rubbed her eyes and smiled when she saw Nick.

"You shouldn't be here," he said.

"I've been in worse." She glanced around. "And better."

"Contempt of court?"

She sat up and stretched. "A couple of times. Once in Mexico. That was definitely worse than this."

"And you got out."

"It was a long time ago. Long before I had the show. I was a lot more reckless back then."

"*More* reckless?"

She smiled but didn't say anything. That week had been hell, and she never wanted to repeat it.

"Your producer is a pit bull."

"I can handle Ben."

"He knows you're in jail."

"I'm sure my attorney called him, since Gia is retained by the show and not me personally."

"She's good. You'll be out in the morning."

"Gia's the best. Do not tell me that Ben is on his way here."

"No, but I realized when he called me multiple times that he doesn't know what you're doing."

"I told him it's personal."

"Well, maybe you should retain Gia personally,

because she works for him and everything she knows, he knows."

"Shit." She should have seen this coming. Maybe that bump on the head was more serious than she thought.

"However, I smoothed it over. But not before this guy David called me. He says he's your personal assistant, but he doesn't sound like an assistant to anyone."

"He's more than an assistant."

"Boyfriend?"

She laughed. "No."

Nick raised an eyebrow. "Well, he's former Special Forces and didn't pull any punches about what he thinks of you spending the night in jail. He's definitely concerned about you, over and above being staff."

"David was originally hired to be my bodyguard during a trial I was covering in Chicago. There were threats, I didn't take them seriously, but Ben did. And it wasn't even connected to the trial, it was about the last book I wrote. I'm not an easy person to work for." She ignored the humor that crossed Nick's face. "David is extremely organized and has a knack for getting information. And he tolerates my eccentricities."

"Sounds like a match made in heaven."

"Nick, I'm not a saint, and I'm not a prude, but I don't hit on a man when I'm involved with someone else." She walked over to the edge of the cell. She didn't touch him, she didn't kiss him, but she wanted to. He saw it in her eyes, and she smiled.

He said, "I wish I could get you out now, but we're waiting for a judge. Beck lied to get his warrant, and I have to go to the issuing judge. He'll be more receptive if I don't wake him up."

"What's happening with Andy?"

"He has a lawyer, he's not talking." Nick hesitated, then said, "He made a statement to you. Are you using him as a source?"

The way he said it told Max they still had some big issues with Nick's animosity toward reporters. "Meaning, will I testify against him?"

"I didn't mean—"

"Yes, you did. I understand. And I will testify. Tell him that. And, if you think it'll help, I recorded our conversation. It's saved to my cell phone."

"Well, that's a call for the lawyers. I have no idea if they'll allow it."

"I'm more concerned about William," she admitted.

"We haven't arrested him, we haven't even interviewed him yet. We have an agreement with his lawyer that he'll come in for questions at our request. We have no evidence, only hearsay— basically what you said Andy told you. His attorney is one of the best criminal defense lawyers in California. Until we have physical proof, I don't think I can arrest him. And based on what Talbot told you—he didn't see your cousin kill Lindy."

He added, "For what it's worth, I'm sorry."

"I'll be fine. Get some sleep. It seems we're both going to have a busy day tomorrow."

He lightly took her hands in his, then frowned as he inspected her fingers. She looked down and realized she'd not only scraped off all her nail polish, but she'd also broken off the tips of all her nails.

"Do you think I could get a manicure while I'm here?" She forced her voice to be light, but the pit in her stomach became heavier.

"I'll see what I can do," he joked. He squeezed her hands, then let her go.

Max watched Nick leave. She laid back down on the cot, but didn't sleep again that night.

Chapter Twenty-three

Max wrote in a small notepad she'd procured from the night guard. Writing kept her focused and not stressed about being in jail for the night. By the time Nick walked into the holding cell, just after seven that morning, she had drafted an article for the "Maximum Exposure" Web site about Jason Hoffman's murder and investigation. There were still holes in the case, and they hadn't caught the killer. And, if Andy or William really killed Lindy thirteen years ago, that meant their theory was wrong that whoever killed Lindy had also buried the unidentified body at ACP and killed Jason Hoffman. It didn't make sense anyway—other than location, there was no connection between Lindy and Jason. Max still believed that Jason had been killed by whoever buried the girl among the trees. Two completely different cases connected only because of location.

Nick handed Max coffee from Starbucks as soon as the guard unlocked her cell.

"It's what you ordered on Saturday, but full caffeine this time."

She was surprised and pleased at his thoughtfulness. "And here I didn't think to get you anything."

He grinned and shook his head. "I'm surprised you're in such good humor."

"You caught me at the right time then. And I had pen and paper." She smiled at the guard. "Thank you for that."

"Thank the detective," the guard said.

Now Max didn't know what to say. How did he know she needed an outlet to keep her from going stir-crazy?

Nick leaned over and whispered, "You can thank me later."

Nick didn't look like he'd gotten much more sleep than she did. He walked her through the release process, and drove her back to the hotel through a thick morning fog. "Beck was pulled from the Ames case; I'm working it. I sure didn't make any friends in the process."

"I appreciate it. Fresh eyes—you'll solve it."

"Thanks for your vote of confidence, but knowing who killed her and proving it are completely different things."

"Boy, do I know that."

He glanced at her. "What does that mean?"

"My college roommate, Karen—I know who killed her, the FBI knows who killed her, but there was no evidence, nothing but circumstantial evidence at best. And no body. They wouldn't take it to trial. He's walking free today, the bastard." She took a deep breath. "I don't want that to happen here. If my cousin is guilty, he needs to be charged."

"I can't talk to you about this case, not anymore."

"I understand." She understood on an intellectual level, but emotionally she had a hundred questions that she knew Nick wouldn't answer.

Nick pulled into the Stanford Park parking lot and turned off the ignition. "I'm meeting with William first thing this morning, I agreed to go to his office."

"That's more than he deserves, if he's a killer."

"He's cooperating. Andrew Talbot isn't. I have your statement about what Talbot said—are you okay with this?"

"Yes. And I'm sure a half-dozen other people heard our conversation at the airport."

"Family can be complicated—"

"Just prove it, okay? No doubts. William is a kind person. He's also weak. He's never stood up to anyone, not when they pushed back. I can't reconcile what I know about him with someone who can strangle his girlfriend to death. He'd known Lindy his entire life. She was my friend." Max unconsciously rubbed the tattoo on her lower stomach, a tangible memory of one of the best weeks of her life.

"If he doesn't talk, unless we find physical evidence—highly doubtful this long after the murder—there's not going to be anything to charge him with."

"That's not good enough."

"I'm not going to fabricate evidence."

"That's not what I mean!" She turned in her seat and took his hand. Squeezed it, to show she was serious. "Kevin O'Neal's life was ruined because nearly everyone in this town thought he was a killer. I don't want that for William. Andy already believes William is guilty."

"Unless he's the one who killed Lindy and is trying to confuse us."

"But it will be hanging over William and his family for the rest of his life. He has two young boys. You know how kids are—they'll be teased and talked about and grow up hearing all these things about their father. I don't want that. Either William is guilty, and you need to prove it, or he's innocent, and you need to prove it!"

"You may be asking for the impossible."

"I'm not leaving until the truth comes out."

"And what if it never does?"

"I can't accept that."

"You should know that Beck searched your hotel room and took the boxes from the storage unit and your boards."

He reached back into the rear seat and pulled up her laptop. She stared at it. "He went through my laptop?"

"No—the lab had it. He tried, but couldn't crack your password." Nick was trying to make light of the situation, but Max was livid.

"Those were *my* personal boards. He had no right."

"They're in my office, and I will return them tonight. I would have done it this morning, but I got sidetracked—"

"It's okay," she snapped. She tried not to be angry with Nick. It wasn't his fault Beck got the warrant—illegally—and went through her things.

"I understand how you feel."

"I don't like anyone going through my notes. My ideas. That's my *life*."

Nick's phone rang and he said, "Damn, I have to take this, stay—we're not done with this conversation."

He got out of the car and paced. Max watched. He was angry. His face was hard, his body all angles and rigid lines. When he was done with the call he stood outside in the fog, not seeming to care that it was cold and damp.

She used the time to control her anger at the violation she felt. She had to separate Nick from his job, from Harry Beck.

He finally got back into the car. "I have to go. I'll tell you what I can, but don't expect all the answers."

"Was that about the case? Bad news?"

"It was personal." He added, "It's not about the case."

Max made no move to get out of the car. She was intrigued by Nick Santini, and she wanted to know what made him both lose his temper and look like he'd lost his best friend.

"My ex-wife," he finally said. He wasn't looking at Max, and his eyes were damp. He took a deep breath. "She's moving again. Says she's getting married." He slammed his hand on the steering wheel.

"You still love her?"

"Hell no. I couldn't care less about her remarriage. But she's taking my son. Again."

He took a deep breath. "I moved here three years ago because she wanted to raise Logan closer to her parents. I get that, even though my family is in L.A. We were divorced, she wanted to be with her mom and sister. I didn't like it, but I made it work. I knew unless I moved close to her, I'd never see my son except a couple of times a year. I couldn't fly or drive up every other weekend, not with my crazy schedule. Now I have to do it all over again. After I finally get settled here, I'm going to have to try to get into Denver. It's not that easy to transfer, especially out of state."

"When is she leaving?"

"Right after school's out. Six weeks."

"I'm really sorry."

"Yeah. Well, I shouldn't have dumped all that on you."

Max saw a side of Nick that she hadn't before— or that she'd only caught glimpses of. That he would change jobs, forsake promotions and seniority, to be with his son showed his true character. She said, "Denver's nice. Do you ski?"

"Not for years."

"When you get settled, maybe I can come for a visit and reteach you. I'm a wicked good cross-country skier." She smiled, though it felt forced.

"I'll hold you to that." But he was looking at his phone again. "Max, this is the lab."

"I'm gone." She got out of the Bronco and went into the hotel. She glanced back over her shoulder and Nick was writing something frantically in his notebook, his cell phone propped up by his shoulder.

He had news.

Max itched to know what it was, but she understood that her personal connection to the suspect kept her out of the loop.

When Max stepped in her hotel room, the anger returned. Housekeeping had straightened the mess, but dammit, it wasn't fair, having her privacy violated by that jackass Beck.

She closed her eyes. "Grow up," she told herself. Life certainly wasn't fair, and she had to trust that Nick would bring back her notes. She plugged her laptop into its charger, relieved that at least her primary work was protected.

She showered, then changed into clean clothes. The bed looked inviting, but she had work to do. She typed up the notes she'd written last night for the article she wanted to write about Jason Hoffman and his senseless murder. She talked to Ben, then her attorney, then David. She repeated everything three times, and wished she'd just put them all on a conference call. She was fine. She was out of the loop because her cousin was a suspect, she was safe. Ben pushed her about doing a show on the Lindy Ames case, and she refused, but told him about the article she was writing about Jason Hoffman. That marginally satisfied him. David was boarding a plane in Hawaii and offered to cancel the Giants game that night; Max said that wasn't necessary and to call her tomorrow.

The only thing she didn't tell anyone was that

she wasn't leaving until she had answers. If it took a year, it would take a year.

And they would all just have to live with it.

By the time she was done with the shower and calls, it was nearly noon. She called William's cell phone; he didn't answer. She called his office; his secretary said he was gone for the day. Max didn't know whether to believe her, but she was inclined to—if Nick had interviewed William, it would throw her cousin off enough where he wouldn't be able to concentrate. She'd check his house.

She really didn't want to confront him with Caitlin hovering around being the worried, protective, passive-aggressive wife, but she didn't have much of a choice, especially if he wasn't answering his phone.

Max still had her grandmother's Jag. Driving in it reminded Max how much she loved sporty cars, and missed having her own. But in New York City, she didn't need a car, and she didn't want the headache of storing one. When she traveled, she rented. When she was on a long-term assignment, she leased.

The attack that totaled her rental, however much it wasn't her fault, was going to make leasing future cars far more expensive.

William and Caitlin lived in a grand house around the corner from Eleanor's estate. The estate was definitely more Caitlin, with luxurious everything—though William made a six-figure salary at his law firm, plus ample bonuses, he couldn't afford to buy or maintain the house. The house had been a wedding present from Caitlin's family, and William's trust fund ran the place. It bordered on ostentatious, unlike the quiet money of her grandmother's home.

Max walked up to the front door and knocked.

Caitlin opened it and slapped her.

Max would have stopped the blow had she been expecting it, but even she was surprised at Caitlin's sudden move.

"Touch me again, and I will put you on the ground," Max said.

"Get out of here. You're not welcome."

Max walked in. "Where's William?"

"He doesn't want to talk to you." Caitlin tried to push Max back out the door, but Max grabbed her wrist and held tight.

"Caitlin, Maxine, please stop." William stepped into the entry and stared at Max. His eyes were bloodshot and he had a Scotch and ice—mostly Scotch—in his glass. It was twelve thirty.

"She's destroying our family!"

Max ignored her and stared at William. She really, really looked at him.

For years, she'd trusted her instincts about people. Perhaps, fighting her inclination to distrust people, she relied on her gut feelings.

But family was different. Family members weren't strangers, they had history and baggage and secrets. With all their shared history, the dreams they'd discussed, the times they snuck out of their houses and met up to swim in the lake under the moonlight, long before they were truly aware of who they were, their similarities and differences, could Max stand here and look at William as a killer?

"We need to talk," she said.

William nodded and turned toward his study. Caitlin tried to follow, but Max stopped her. "This is between William and me," she said.

Caitlin ignored her, until William nodded. His wife looked pained and betrayed. Then she stomped down the hall, angry. A moment later a door slammed somewhere in the house.

William closed the double doors, refilled his half-empty glass, and sat down heavily on the couch. His normally impeccable suit was rumpled, his tie misaligned. This was her *GQ* cousin, who never had a hair out of place, looking like a worn salesman.

Max didn't know what to say.

"Andy thinks I killed Lindy," William said bluntly. "Did you?"

He shook his head and looked like he was going to cry. William had always been sensitive, even when being a cad. He teared up at movies. He didn't like violence. He told Max two years ago, when she visited for Thea's wedding, that the best thing about having two boys was that he could be here for them like his father wasn't there for William. Except for college, William had never lived more than two miles from his father, yet Brooks Revere might as well have lived on another continent for all the attention he paid to his son.

Except William was falling into the same patterns as Brooks. Infidelity being the number one similarity. Did William not see that he was becoming his dad?

"I told you before, and I'll tell you now, and I'll tell anyone who asks, I didn't kill Lindy. I'm stunned and hurt that Andy thinks I did. That he thinks I'm capable of, of *strangling* her. You know me, Max. At least, I thought you did. I always thought you could read my mind when we were younger, that you knew what I was thinking even if I said something different."

"So did I."

"You did. Really. I don't like my sister. Nora's rigid and judgmental and mean. You were always more of a sister to me than she ever was."

"Nora used to rat us out for breaking the rules. Like when we snuck out and took Brooks's car to San Francisco for the day."

"Neither of us had our license."

"We had a blast."

"I was grounded for a month."

"A month? I was grounded for two."

"They like me more." He gave her a wistful smile.

"Tell me what you and Lindy were fighting about the night she died."

"I told you—I wanted to go public with our relationship."

"Weren't you dating Caitlin?"

"Not then—we'd broken up after prom, remember?"

"Why'd you and Caitlin break up?"

He didn't say anything.

"William, you know, this will all come out eventually. If you can't tell me, you're only going to make everything worse. Let me help you."

"Caitlin was clingy—I wanted to end it before college. So I told Caitlin we needed time apart. She was cool with it, and then she started dating what's his name, um—"

"Peter something."

"Right. He was at Stanford."

"She wanted to make you jealous."

William dismissed that. "I told Lindy that I was going to break up with Caitlin, and when she and Kevin broke up I thought she was ready to be with me. Because Lindy and I knew when we left for college, that would be it. But, she was mad about this other girl I dated for a while. It wasn't serious, I swear, and it was over, but she wouldn't let it go." He rubbed his eyes. "I wasn't always faithful."

"You still aren't," she said. He looked stricken, but Max knew that finally, now was the time that William needed to turn his life around. "I love you, William. I always have. You're going to get through this, and you need to make some changes. Like firing Minnie."

"This has nothing to do with that."

She didn't know what to say to make him understand, maybe he never would.

He stared at her, his eyes pleading with her. "Do you believe me, Max? Do you have the faith in me that you had in Kevin O'Neal?"

What was she supposed to say? *No? Yes? I don't know?* She wanted desperately to believe William. But she didn't understand him. She didn't understand why he cheated on Caitlin, why he had slept with Lindy when she was dating Kevin, and all the other girls he'd been with in high school and presumably in college. She didn't understand why he was sleeping with his secretary, and why he didn't see that he was becoming just like Brooks.

But she knew him, and he was gentle. Could he strangle Lindy with his hands? Never showing regret? Never questioning where Lindy's body had been found? Not say anything when another man was tried for her murder?

The William she knew might have—*might have*—killed Lindy if he snapped in anger, but it would have been an accident. The perpetual silence would have eaten him up. He was a mess now, knowing what his best friend had done, what his best friend believed about him. That

Andy had destroyed evidence because he thought he was protecting William. If he had killed Lindy, he would have been a far worse mess thirteen years ago.

There was another car, an unfamiliar car, in the driveway.

"I believe you, William," she said before her brain decided to say it.

Then he started crying and Max didn't know what to do. She walked over to him, wrapped her arms around his neck, and hugged him.

Max drove by Kepler's and found Jodi working. "Do you have a minute?" Max asked her.

"You have news." Jodi looked hopeful.

"Yes, I have some information. Let's get coffee."

They walked next door, but because of the chill in the air, they sat inside the coffee shop. After ordering coffee and a muffin, Max said, "The police know that Kevin didn't kill Lindy."

Jodi looked at her skeptically. "I don't understand."

"They don't know who killed Lindy, but they found the anonymous caller who placed Kevin at the school the night she died, and he lied. Detective Beck has been removed from the investigation. I don't have all the answers, but his name will be cleared."

Tears were streaming down her face. "I—I don't know what to say."

"You don't need to say anything." Max sipped her coffee because this second part was going to be harder.

"Who did kill her?" Jodi asked.

Max considered telling her, but that would simply start even more rumors. She didn't know what would be in the press tomorrow, if anything, about Nick's investigation into William and Andy, but that was something she would deal with tomorrow.

"The police are questioning several people, and when I know for certain, I will tell you. But I don't want to spread a rumor that might not be true."

"I—I guess I understand."

"Did you know that Kevin was dying?"

"Dying? What do you mean?"

"I found the storage unit with all his files that were missing from his apartment. Inside, he'd written me a letter and said to tell you he's sorry, but it's better this way because he'd have been dead by the end of the year."

"No." She closed her eyes, her bottom lip trembling.

"Jodi?"

"He was sick, but everyone gets sick."

"Was he seeing a doctor?"

"A couple of times, because he was losing weight." Jodi stared at Max with damp eyes.

"I don't have his autopsy report, only the preliminary was in his file. As family, you have a right to the report. It'll tell you if he had any underlying medical conditions."

"My mom—she told me Kevin's obsession was killing him, that he was losing weight—what if he was really sick? Like really, *really* sick?"

"He believed he was. I think—I think he killed himself to spare you and your mother from watching him die." That was partly true. At least, Max believed that was one of the reasons running through Kevin's head. She didn't need to tell Jodi that the other reason was to pull Max into this investigation. Max had been fighting the guilt of not listening to him four months ago when he attempted to contact her. She didn't know if that would have changed anything, but it might have.

"Thank you, Max."

"Don't." Max didn't want kudos. Kevin had still killed himself. Lindy was still dead. And her cousin was now under suspicion for murder.

Her grandmother's comment the other night—*nothing good can come from this*—ran through Max's head.

It wasn't completely true. Kevin had been exonerated. Wasn't that enough?

Deep down, Max knew that it wasn't.

Chapter Twenty-four

It was nearly three, and since Max was so close to Atherton Prep, she swung over to the construction site. She found Brian Robeaux talking to the foreman, Roger Lawrence. Brian approached her as soon as he recognized her.

"Ms. Revere, can I help you?"

"I was hoping to take a few pictures for an article I'm writing about Jason's murder."

"Absolutely. Anything you need."

She must have looked surprised—usually, she had an uphill battle getting access to crime scenes, even from the family. They sometimes didn't know how she was going to present the information or show their loved one.

"Thank you."

"Anything, really. Detective Santini came by this morning to talk to my sister and Michael. He said they've moved Jason's case back up to a priority. He explained that Jason was most likely killed because of that grave you found."

"Santini's a smart cop."

"But if you hadn't pushed, I wouldn't have remembered about Jason's concern about the digging, it just wasn't something I connected."

"Sometimes, Mr. Robeaux, a case needs a fresh

set of eyes. That's what I gave, but Santini's going to be the one to solve it."

"He told us that whoever killed and buried the woman thought her body might be found during construction. Even though those trees are outside of the construction plan, the killer may not have known that, or he might have thought we'd be laying pipes or cables."

Max nodded. "That makes sense. And after all these years, he didn't remember where he'd buried the body, that's why Jason found the small, deep holes."

"Detective Santini thinks when they identify the remains, they'll find a suspect."

Max held up her camera. "I won't be long. And you can tell Jason's parents that I'm writing about his life and what he accomplished. His murder is not going to be sensationalized."

"No one is worried about that. We just appreciate everything you've done. Again, anything you need, you let me know. Be careful over there—the police released the area yesterday, but it's been dug up and picked through. I wouldn't want you twisting your ankle like Mr. Pierce."

"I'll be careful. Thank you."

She took her Canon digital camera and snapped a few pictures of the beginning of construction, of the trees, of the old gymnasium that attached to the pool house where Lindy's body had been found. Nick's theory that the victim in the grave may have something to do with Lindy's death had been on Max's mind. If Jason had been killed because he'd caught someone removing the body, maybe Lindy had been killed because she saw someone burying the body in the first place.

Could it really be that simple?

Simple, perhaps, as to the killer's motive, but until they identified the remains from the grave, nearly impossible to use to identify the killer.

Max could see the top of Lindy's clubhouse about seventy yards down the stone wall, on the other side. Could Lindy have been watching from the top floor? Maybe saw a flashlight and investigated? Why investigate and not just call the police?

Because nothing bad ever happened in Atherton. They'd all felt exceptionally safe growing up, and it was Lindy—the girl who lived for secrets. If Lindy thought anyone was hanging around, she'd assume they were up to something and would want to know who and what.

Except, if someone was digging a grave, why wouldn't they have put Lindy's body in it?

That was easy—Lindy would have been reported missing. Which suggested that if this theory was accurate, the victim was someone who wouldn't be missed.

And why hadn't the police searched the area and found the grave? If it was fresh when Lindy had been killed, wouldn't they have found it? Or was it far enough away from the pool that no one looked?

Maybe Lindy's death had nothing to do with the grave at all. Just because the bones might have been buried roughly the same time as Lindy's murder didn't mean that the victim had been buried the very same night.

Max finished with the pictures, then walked among the trees again, toward the old gate in the wall. Until Carson Salter explained how screwed up the crime scene was, she hadn't realized that the gate might have been used by the killer. If it was, the killer must have known Lindy, at least as an acquaintance. Anyone from the school might have known Lindy used the gate, and of course her friends. But what about a stranger?

None of this was helping William, Max thought as she walked back to the construction trailers.

Nick's Bronco was parked next to her grandmother's Jag, but she didn't see Nick anywhere.

Her curiosity was definitely aroused. Forensics had released the crime scene, so there didn't seem to be any reason to be here, unless Nick had more questions. If he had more questions for Brian and his staff, then maybe he had new information.

Max glanced around. She didn't see Nick, or hear his voice. Or anyone else. She walked over to Nick's Bronco and noted it was unlocked. On the front seat, just like the other day, were his case files.

Before she could talk herself out of it, she opened the passenger door and flipped open the top file, which was a preliminary lab report from the grave site. She skimmed the information—some of it Nick had already told her. But there was new information—confirmation that the victim was female, between the ages of sixteen and twenty-one. Testing of the dirt showed that the body had decomposed at the site and had been buried approximately four feet below the surface.

She turned the page and saw a lab photo of the bones, plus the earring Nick had mentioned, as well as part of a broken bracelet with a silver butterfly attached. Max pulled out her phone and took a picture of the charm. It looked familiar, but she didn't know why.

The trailer door opened and Max closed the file, but stayed next to the Bronco. Nick was going to be suspicious, but why give him more reason to be?

He caught her eye, his expression unreadable. He shook Brian's hand, then walked over to her. "Why are you in my car?"

"Waiting for you."

He frowned and looked at the files on his seat. "Max—"

"I just looked at the lab report. I swear."

He sighed. "I have your boards in the back, if you want to take them. I was going to drop them off later tonight, but I have plans I can't break."

"Thanks."

He retrieved the three trifolds from the back of the Bronco and put them in the small trunk of her Jag. "Nice car."

"My grandma's."

He smiled. "I think I'd like her."

Max tried hard not to laugh. Nick raised his eyebrows and took a step closer. For a moment, Max thought he was going to kiss her. Instead, he grabbed her camera from around her neck, pulled her close, and turned the camera around so he could scroll through her pictures.

She wanted to slap him, she wanted to kiss him, but mostly she was relieved that she'd already pocketed her cell phone that she'd used to snap the picture of the broken bracelet.

"For your article?" he said.

"Yes. Not that it's your business."

He stood, only the camera's width between them. "Oh? Didn't you promise you wouldn't write an article without talking to me first?"

"I haven't written the article yet."

"Are you?"

"Can't you trust me on this?"

He stared at her. "I don't know."

"At least you're honest."

Why that bothered her, she didn't know. Did she want him to lie and say he trusted her when he didn't? And with good reason, too. She was a reporter, he was a cop. They might have the same goal, but their means were vastly different. Maybe irreconcilably different.

"Stay away from the case."

"Which one?"

"All of them."

"You know I can't."

"I don't want to put you in jail."

She heated up. "Are you really threatening me?"

"No, I just need you to understand this is highly sensitive, and your involvement is pissing off a lot of people."

She stepped away from him, and he let her.

"I don't care who I piss off. I'm not going to screw up your case."

"That's not what I meant. But, dammit, there's a killer out there, and if he thinks you're a threat to him, he'll go after you."

"What do you want me to do? Hide in my hotel room until you, big, bad, brave cop Nick Santini solves the crime?"

"Why are you so damn defensive?"

"Because I'm not stupid. I'm not going to confront a killer."

"I've been reading about you, Max. You're not stupid, but you're far too reckless."

"This is getting us nowhere," she said. She didn't like the way he was looking at her, as if he was trying to protect her. How much information had Kevin gathered about her? What had Nick read? Why did he look like he wanted to lock her in Rapunzel's tower? She didn't like it, but at the same time she felt that lustful pit in her gut, her inner girl craving him.

Traitor.

She said, "I'm going."

He watched her leave. Max breathed easier when she was out of sight.

Max settled into her room and called Dru Parker at the hospital. The young woman sounded better, and told Max that the doctors would probably release her on Sunday. Max gave her the name and number of an attorney in the area. Dru had made some really stupid decisions, but she didn't deserve to spend years in prison for them.

Max hung up and retrieved the picture on her cell phone of the broken bracelet and butterfly charm. She'd seen this before. Recently. It probably didn't mean anything, except that few women she knew wore actual charm bracelets. The chain that the butterfly was attached to had the larger links that could hold multiple charms. Her grandmother had always thought they were tacky, but Max thought they were sweet, a lifelong memento of a favorite vacation, sport, or pet.

She reclined on her lounge chair and considered going down to the hot tub and ponder the bracelet. She closed her eyes and mentally went through her week from the minute she landed at the San Francisco airport. She pictured the women she'd met, who she'd spoken to. Jodi, Dru, Mrs. Hoffman, Dru's roommates, Kimberly Ames—

Max jumped up. "Faith Voss."

Faith wore a charm bracelet when she took notes for the headmaster. Max had noticed it because the multitude of charms clinked and she'd thought how much that would annoy her on a daily basis.

It may not mean anything. Just because Faith Voss had a charm bracelet didn't mean that she had anything to do with the missing body from campus. It was just . . . odd.

Sweet, kind Faith Voss didn't seem capable of murder, and she didn't appear to have the strength to dig up a grave. Looks were often deceiving. Except, as the director of admissions, she'd be privy to the sports complex plans and know that the structure would be nowhere near the grave. So if she *had* killed someone and buried the body on campus, she wouldn't have moved it.

Max rubbed her temples. Sometimes her thoughts turned macabre, as she pictured petite Faith Voss digging up a grave, then shooting Jason Hoffman in cold blood.

But there was no question that it was suspicious that part of a charm bracelet was found in the grave, and Faith Voss wore a similar charm bracelet. Maybe Faith would recognize the charm. Or maybe she'd lost it. Or given it to someone . . . someone who ended up dead and buried on the edge of campus?

It could mean absolutely nothing, or it could be a lead. Max had followed far weaker clues and ended up with valuable information. It was worth checking out.

She was about to leave to track down Faith Voss when her cell phone rang. It was David.

"We just landed," he said. "Catch me up."

She glanced at her watch. It was after six in the evening. "Don't you have a baseball game to get to?"

"It doesn't start for ninety minutes. Tell me what's going on, or I'll be in your room in less than an hour."

"There's no need for drastic measures," she said. She filled him in on the basics, and then said, "Until the victim from the grave is identified, we're spinning our wheels."

"How are you doing?"

"I'm fine."

David sighed loud enough that Max could hear. "Max, how are you doing with the idea that William could be Lindy's killer?"

"David, I believed that Kevin was innocent, and I was right. I can't envision any scenario where William could have killed Lindy." She sat back in her chair and closed her eyes. "If I'm wrong, I'll deal with it."

David said, "I'll be there tomorrow afternoon before two."

"I already have a room reserved for you."

"How was jail?"

David tried to sound light, but he was the only one who knew what she'd been through in Mexico.

"Best I've been in. By the way, I know you talked to Santini. I assume because you didn't change your flight that you were comfortable with his credentials."

"I checked him out. He's fine."

Max laughed heartily. In fact, she hadn't laughed enough this week and David was the one constant in her life; she knew he'd have her back and remind her that sometimes, she could count on people. Sometimes, they didn't fail or disappoint you.

"That he is," she said. "David, enjoy the baseball game. I wish I could be there."

"It's sold out, but I'm sure you could get tickets if you lifted your little finger."

"I'm sure I could. I have some research to do."

"I know that tone."

"I have this niggling feeling that I'm missing something." She described the bracelet. "But Faith is this small woman, sweet, sincere. Now, her sister was a wild child—"

Carrie.

"Max?"

"Her sister. . . . I didn't even think about it, but she moved to Europe thirteen years ago."

"The same time Lindy was murdered?"

Why would Carrie kill Lindy and another girl? Why bury one body and not the other? Except Carrie definitely had a wild streak and a temper. She was taller and stronger than her sister.

Why would she return to dig up the grave if she was eight thousand miles away overseas? If the victim could be connected to her, the authorities would have to track her down.

"How can I find out the last place someone used their passport?" she asked.

"I think I missed part of the conversation."

"I had it in my head," she said.

"That's tricky. You need someone in the state department to find out if someone even has a passport issued—it's not public information. But to find out where it was used? The information is out there, but again, it's confidential. Marco could get it, but even an FBI agent would have to justify needing the information."

Max typed rapidly on her computer. Carrie Voss . . . there weren't hundreds, but too many to sort through in just a few minutes. She narrowed the search a variety of ways, but no one popped up that matched Carrie's description. She searched for Faith and instantly found her social media pages. Flipping through them, she couldn't find Carrie listed as a friend, follower, fan, any-thing.

Were they that estranged?

Maybe Faith had killed her sister. Lost a charm

in the process? But the bracelet found in the grave had been broken. Perhaps, Faith had help.

But why? They hadn't been a wealthy family, there was no trust fund or inheritance. But with family, nearly anything could be a motive.

"Max, just tell me if you need me."

"David, I need you *tomorrow*. I've got this covered." She checked another database. "Seriously. Like you said, Santini's a good guy and I'm in my room and all is well."

He grunted.

"Give my love to Emma." She hung up.

It seemed that Carrie Voss had disappeared from the face of the earth.

Or had been buried four feet under.

Max grabbed her purse and left.

Faith Voss lived in a quaint, older English Tudor on a quiet street off Whipple Avenue in nearby Redwood City.

Max was thrilled that she was home.

"Maxine Revere?" Faith said in surprise when she opened the door. "I—well. Come in."

Although it was just seven in the evening, Faith was already in her pajamas and had a bowl of popcorn and a Diet Coke situated in front of the television. Books—mostly romances with a few thrillers and classics intermixed—bulged from the bookshelves to such a degree that they spread over to the end tables. Faith might have more

438

books than Max—and that was saying something.

She looked self-conscious, and Max wanted to put her at ease. "Hey, if I'd known it was a pajama party I would have brought mine."

"This is a surprise," Faith said. "A good surprise," she added quickly. "I just didn't expect to see you here." She glanced around the house and frowned.

Max glanced down at her wrist when she heard the *clink*. She still wore the charm bracelet.

"I love your charms," she said.

Faith smiled. "Thanks. My mom gave me the chain when I turned thirteen, and a new charm every year for my birthday. Some I bought myself." Her voice trailed off.

"It's a nice tradition."

Max walked halfway across the living room and saw a James Bond movie on the coffee table. "I've seen every Bond movie at least twice," Max said. "I love Daniel Craig as the new Bond, but Connery will always have my heart."

Faith smiled. "Craig is definitely at the top of my list. Do you want something to drink? Eat?"

"No—I should have called first."

"It's fine, really. It's been a long week, I usually don't—"

Max said, "Faith, this is your home, don't apologize. I came to talk to you about your sister."

Faith blinked. "Carrie?"

"Yes."

Faith frowned and sat down. "Why?"

Max sat in the chair across from her. She didn't want to lie to Faith, but at the same time she couldn't very well say she thought that Carrie might have been dead for the last thirteen years. Yet . . . if the body in the grave was Carrie, Faith most certainly would have had to have been involved. Otherwise, why would she create a farce that Carrie was in Europe? And why did no one call her on it?

Their parents were gone, could they truly have not had any other friends and family who would notice that Carrie was missing all this time?

"When was the last time you heard from Carrie?" Max asked.

"Um, six years ago?" She nodded. "Yes. Six years. Carrie—I try not to think about her too much. She didn't even come home for Mom's funeral, just sent a postcard months later saying she didn't have the money to fly home. I thought that was her way of telling me she needed money to come home." She played with her hair. "Except, she never called or gave me an address."

Faith sounded more sad than bitter. "Why the questions about Carrie? You and her were never close friends."

This was going to get tricky. If Carrie was alive six years ago, maybe she had returned home and Faith was the only one who knew. That meant she might be a danger to Max—except she was so petite and frail-looking Max could knock her over with a feather.

Of course, she could have a gun.

"I started looking for her online. You'd be amazed at what is available on the Internet. It's very hard to completely unplug. Yet, there's nothing on your sister anywhere."

"She's been living in Europe."

But her voice caught, and she didn't look Max in the eye.

"Faith, when was the last time you actually saw Carrie?"

"Why are you asking all these questions?" Her voice rose and cracked. Max had spoken to enough survivors to know that Faith was in deep denial about something.

"Faith—"

"Look, after our mom died, I did everything I could to find Carrie. And then I get this postcard out of the blue, months later, from France, saying she didn't have the money to come home for the funeral and she was sorry. I just—washed my hands of her. When she didn't answer my e-mails, I said no more. So why do you care? You weren't friends with her."

"Do you know for a fact that she went to Europe?"

Faith stared at her like she was an idiot. "I told you—she sent me postcards. I'll show you."

Faith left the room. If she was guilty, now was the time she'd get a gun and try to kill Max.

INVESTIGATIVE REPORTER SHOT DEAD IN HOME OF CHILDHOOD FRIEND

Or, INVESTIGATIVE REPORTER CONFRONTS KILLER IN HOME; MURDERED

Headlines weren't her strength. She left titles and teasers to her producer, Ben. He had the gift.

Still, she kept her eye on the hall. A few minutes later Faith returned with a shoe box and handed it to Max. "These are all the postcards Carrie sent me. *From Europe.*"

Max opened the box. There were maybe a dozen inside. "May I?"

"Go ahead." Faith sat back down. Her hand was shaking. "Do you think something happened to her? Is that why you're here? Because this is what you do, right? Investigate cold cases? Do you have friends in France? Did someone find a body and you think it's Carrie?" Her voice cracked on the word *body.*

"Faith, I'm here because I don't know if Carrie ever went to Europe."

"Of course she did!" Faith pointed to the box.

Max started going through the postcards. France. Italy. Australia. "I don't see any pictures of Carrie."

"She didn't send any."

"I have a hard time believing a girl who went to

442

live in Europe didn't take pictures of herself and send them. She didn't have a cell phone?"

"No, she said it was too expensive . . ."

Max laid the postcards in chronological order on the table.

Faith pointed to the first one. "See? That was dated six months after she left. From England."

"You took her to the airport?"

"No—Carrie had a bad breakup. I thought, maybe, it had been one of her professors. Carrie wasn't bad, but she made some really bad choices about men, and she came home crying one night, saying she was dropping out of school, she needed to get her life together. I told her to sleep on it, that she shouldn't drop out of school, but maybe just take some time off. Mom and her got in a huge fight about it—asked her if she'd gotten herself pregnant. Carrie said no, but Mom wouldn't let it go and they just—well, they were oil and water. She left the next day, said she was going to get her life together and she'd call when she had answers. Then six months later we got the postcard from England."

"You saw her leave?"

"Well, no, but that isn't important. She left a note on the table. You don't know what it was like trying to mediate between Carrie and my mom."

"I have an idea."

"Tell me—right now—what you're thinking. Because you're scaring me."

Max didn't know how to sugarcoat it. And she might be wrong. But if she was wrong, she'd spend a small fortune tracking Carrie Voss down and hauling her ass back to her sister.

"Did Carrie have a charm bracelet like yours?"

Faith frowned and stared at her wrist. "Yes, why?"

She pulled out her phone and showed Faith the photo from the crime lab.

"What's that?" Faith asked.

"Is this your sister's?"

"I—I don't know." But her voice rose and Max knew she was lying.

"It is, isn't it?"

Faith's lower lip quivered. "It looks like it. She—I—I got her a butterfly like that when she graduated from high school. But there's lots of butterfly charms. Where did you find it?"

Max said quietly, "The police found it."

"No." She shook her head. Max didn't say anything for a long minute, and Faith put it together. "No—not at the campus. The bones they found? No. Not Carrie. It *can't* be Carrie. Bascomb said the bones were more than a decade old. Carrie sent me a postcard *six years ago!*" She covered her mouth and ran down the hall.

Max didn't have anything she could say that would make Faith feel any better, not right now, so she focused on the postcards.

Faith said she received the first postcard six

months after Carrie left. It was postmarked in December. That meant Carrie had left the previous June.

The same month that Lindy was killed. One week before high school graduation.

Max made a list with all the postmarks—day and location. New York. France. England. Australia. England again. Germany. Nearly every European country. There were sixteen postcards total over a seven-year period, but several were clumped together—the last three were all sent a week apart. From France, Italy, and Ireland.

Max had a hunch that Carrie never sent these cards, but there was one easy way to prove she didn't. Only, she wouldn't be able to get the information. Only law enforcement could find out whether Carrie Voss had a passport and if she'd used it.

The chances were, she died the night she wrote the note to her mom and sister, and was buried on the Atherton Prep campus.

Max looked carefully at each postcard. The picture from Australia looked familiar. She turned it over and read the inscription.

I'm in beautiful Australia! It's summer here, totally the opposite of the U.S., ha, ha. I could live here forever. Maybe I will. Carrie

All the other messages were just as generic. Nothing personal. Nothing asking about Faith or giving an address where Faith could write back.

Someone else sent these cards so Faith wouldn't report her sister missing. Max was certain of it.

She looked at the last card sent. Six years ago next month.

Six years ago. France. Italy. Ireland.

William had been on his honeymoon then. He'd been married in the middle of April, then went on a honeymoon for three weeks, to France, Italy, and Ireland.

Nausea washed over Max and she put her head down for a minute. She had to have remembered wrong. She did the math again; it was right. But William—if Carrie Voss was dead, if she'd never gone to Europe, *someone* had to have sent these cards. And William was in Europe when the last three were sent.

What about the others?

Max took pictures of each card, front and back, then went upstairs to where she heard Faith softly crying. She knocked on the door.

Faith opened it a moment later. "I—I think I always knew she was dead."

"I don't want to leave you alone."

"Are you positive?"

"No. Not one hundred percent."

"But you think that—the remains—that it's Carrie."

Max nodded. Faith stifled another cry, but controlled herself. "I know how you can find out," Max said.

"How? They only found a couple bones."

"I'll call Detective Santini and tell him what we've figured out and they can compare your DNA with hers."

"I should have called the police," Faith said quietly.

"Why? Did you doubt Carrie wrote these? Was it her handwriting?"

"Because—I don't know. I thought it was her writing. I didn't think anything of her leaving. She did it all the time. She wasn't even living here full time—she'd just come back from college, and was already looking to live with a friend because she and Mom fought so much. And we weren't all that close, but—I should have realized she wouldn't have just gone off to Europe without saying good-bye. In person."

"You had a reason to think it."

"She always wanted to go. *Always.* She had posters in her bedroom, she wanted to study abroad—yeah, it was believable, but just like that?"

"Faith, this isn't your fault. We don't know what happened." Max asked the hard question. "You said she was having trouble with a boyfriend."

Faith slumped against the door. "She was seeing someone at college. She never told me his name or anything, Mom said she was probably sleeping with one of her professors."

"And your mom thought she was pregnant."

"My mom was paranoid about Carrie getting pregnant. Mom got pregnant in college. Got married, had Carrie and me, got divorced because they fought all the time. My mom was very bitter about it. She dropped out of college to raise us, she didn't want the same thing to happen to us."

"Why did she think that? Did Carrie say something?"

"Carrie denied it. But, deep down, I thought she might have left because she got an abortion, and she didn't want us to know. The way Carrie thought—she might have thought our mom would hold it over her forever. It wasn't a good year for any of us."

New tears rolled down Faith's face. "I love my sister, but after she left, there was no more drama."

"Do you have any idea who Carrie had been seeing that spring?"

"No. But I have a box of everything she left. It's in the guest-room closet. I'll get it."

Max knew she should tell her no, to give it to the police. But she didn't. She wanted to see the box.

They went back downstairs and Max called Nick while Faith hunted for the box. His cell phone went to voice mail, and she remembered he said he'd had plans.

"Nick, it's Max Revere. I'm pretty certain I know who was buried at Atherton Prep. I'm at her sister's house now, and she's willing to give her DNA to compare. Faith Voss. Her sister Carrie hasn't been seen in thirteen years. There's more, but we should talk in person. Call me." She hung up.

Faith put a shoe box on the table. "I got rid of most of Carrie's things—clothes and junk. These are papers and stuff my mom boxed up after we got the first postcard."

Max went through everything quickly. There was nothing important here, at least at first glance. School papers, report cards, photos, lots of sticky notes.

One sticky note stuck out at her because of the date: Greenwald, Thurs. 5/31 at 10.

Two days before Lindy's murder.

She looked up Greenwald on her phone. Amelia Greenwald, OB/GYN, in practice in Redwood City for the past twenty-two years.

Carrie had been pregnant.

"What's that?" Faith asked.

"I don't know," Max said. She wasn't going to share her theory with Faith, not yet.

Max flipped quickly through the pictures. They were all from high school, which made sense even though Carrie had been a first-year college student. You leave your high school memories at home, make new ones in college.

"Where did Carrie leave her stuff from college?"

"I don't know," Faith said. "I thought she brought it all here. She might have taken it with her to—" She cut herself off.

The sticky notes were Carrie's calendar. Max spread them out by date if there was a date. She'd been home for two weeks. The sticky notes showed appointments, plans, her last days written in abbreviation.

LUNCH WITH LINDY.

No date. But sometime during the two weeks Carrie had been home from college, she'd had planned a lunch with Lindy Ames.

And they both were dead.

Max resisted the urge to box everything up and take it with her. But this was a police investigation. She said to Faith, "The police are going to want all of this." She kept an old school paper to compare Carrie's handwriting.

"What happened?" Faith asked. It was hypothetical, but she still looked at Max for answers.

Max didn't respond. Instead she said, "If you think of anything else that happened the week Carrie was supposed to leave for Europe, call me."

Chapter Twenty-five

Max left Faith's house and went straight to Eleanor's. She was ready to steamroll over any of her grandmother's objections to what she was going to do, but the house was empty, even though it was nine at night. Not unusual, since Eleanor was involved in many charitable groups and had many friends she dined with. Since Max's grandfather died, Eleanor spent more time out with friends, as if being alone in this big house without James saddened her.

For all of Eleanor's faults, her grandmother had loved her husband dearly. It was their unity, their mutual admiration and respect, and the love Max had seen in their eyes that told Max that for some people, marriage worked.

People who didn't lie or commit adultery.

Max went straight to Eleanor's office and turned on the lights. She'd always been a bit in awe and intimidated by the stately, Queen Anne–style room, with real antiques and delicate touches. It was also immaculate, and Eleanor would be certain to know that Max had been in here.

Eleanor had kept old-fashioned date books most of her life. One page per day, with plenty of room for appointments, notes, and a daily diary. They went back to the year she was engaged.

Fifty-nine years. She had the next two years already purchased. The current year was on her desk.

For a moment, Max was in awe of her grandmother's diligence. Unlike Lindy's secretive, gossipy diary, Eleanor had marked days of importance. On days of historical significance, like 9/11, the Kennedy assassination, royal weddings, peace treaties, she wrote what her initial thoughts were, and often referenced the major event through the months and years ahead, from a different perspective. But she also noted smaller things.

Like the day William and Max graduated from high school. Like the day her mother left Max to live in this house to be raised by a family she didn't know.

Max had never gone through Eleanor's date books before, other than with express permission, and it made her uncomfortable, like she was peeking in her underwear drawer or worse. And while she didn't want to believe that Eleanor would destroy fifty-nine years of history, she knew that for her family, she would.

Max wanted to pull out the archives and read what Eleanor really thought when Martha left Max behind. But right now she needed to prove she was wrong. Prove that William hadn't been to all those places abroad at the same time Carrie Voss allegedly sent Faith the postcards.

She pulled out the book from thirteen years ago. It opened in the middle, on Max and William's high school graduation.

After Lindy's murder, but before Kevin had been arrested.

Eleanor had written:

> Pride fills my soul at my grandchildren today. James said, "Ellie, we are lucky." I don't believe in luck, but today, I feel greatly blessed.
>
> William—he is intelligent, considerate, and has a heart with far more compassion than his father. Today, he looks more a man than I've ever seen him.
>
> Maxine—More my daughter than my granddaughter. I never understood Martha, but Maxine—she says what I wish I could say. I admire her passion for life. Her love of friends and family, her firm commitment to her values, the depth of her self-awareness. I will miss her greatly.

Max had to reread the comment because she'd never heard her grandmother say anything like this to her.

I will miss her greatly.

Max had walked away from home, gone to college, rarely come home because she never thought she would be missed. The friction her presence caused the family had always upset her grandmother. Yet, she admired her?

Max had to put it aside because she wasn't here to read about June. And that what she was about to do would tear apart the family from its very foundation made her want to leave for New York on the next flight and forget everything she'd seen or heard.

Except, of course she'd never do that. The truth had to come out. Gerald and Kimberly Ames deserved to know what happened to their daughter. The Hoffmans deserved to know what happened to Jason. Faith deserved to know what happened to her sister.

And why.

In December after graduation, during his winter break, Eleanor took William to England as his graduation present. They didn't go over the summer because of Lindy's murder.

December tenth through the twenty-second.

The postcard from Carrie was postmarked December eleventh.

She didn't want to believe it. How could she? How could she not only believe that her cousin was a killer, but that he'd been so calculating? That he'd lied to her, and she'd believed him, because she had believed Kevin O'Neal and had been right about him?

William has a heart with far more compassion than his father.

Could kind, considerate, polite, compassionate William have brutally murdered *three people?* Lindy? Carrie? Jason?

William's explanation of their fight didn't make any sense. Lindy was mad about another girl he dated—why would she be? She'd been cheating on Kevin with William, William had been cheating on Caitlin with Lindy, it was one big cluster-fuck and Max had been totally in the dark.

Had she been? Had she truly been that clueless about her friends?

Maybe. She had Andy then, they'd been together all the time. She'd been planning for college, playing volleyball in the fall, skiing in the winter, swimming in the spring, she'd always kept busy, and her senior year was particularly hectic because of the added stress of college applications. Had she been so wrapped up in her own life that she'd forgotten to pay attention to the world around her?

Or maybe, subconsciously, she knew everyone had secrets, and she was willfully ignorant of them. Because she didn't want to think about people she loved lying to her. Intentionally blind.

If William killed Lindy and Carrie, why? If he killed them, that meant he'd also killed Jason Hoffman because Jason had seen him removing Carrie Voss's remains. Then William had taken her bones and . . . what? Reburied them? Burned them? Scattered them in the woods?

Max felt physically sick as she looked at the next date, the following winter—when it was summer in the land of Oz. Genie, her great-grandmother, had been ill. She had never been to Australia and said that before she died, she wanted to visit. It had been a difficult trip for the woman, but Max had never seen her happier. She'd died nine months later, but at peace.

While Genie and Eleanor had stayed for six weeks in a house they rented in Sydney, Max had joined them for a week. William was there. The Talbots had all visited at different times.

The dates William was in Sydney matched up with the postmark.

Max almost didn't keep looking, but one thing being a reporter taught her was that she had to have all her facts. She had to make a solid case. If she was going to convince William to confess, she had to give him incontrovertible proof that he had no option. That there was enough evidence to put him in prison. She took pictures of each page in the date books, in case her grandmother destroyed them. She hoped not, because as she read notes in her grandmother's impeccable, formal script, she saw a history unfold that she wanted to read more about. A history she wanted to write about.

She knew if she did this, if she used these date books to put William in prison for murder, her family would disown her. She'd still be part of the trust, she'd still have her money, but she would never be able to come home again. No matter what Eleanor had written about her in the books, some things would be unforgivable.

It was perhaps ironic that she never wanted to come home . . . until the idea that she couldn't terrified her.

The money had never been important to Max, yet that would be all she had left of her family and her heritage.

But what choice did she have? She'd promised herself long ago that exposing the truth was the only way she could live in balance. That harboring secrets would only give her heartache and failure. Her mother's lies and deception, Lindy's secret diary, Karen's disappearance and murder . . . the truth wasn't pretty, but it was real, and Max had to hold on to that.

Eleanor kept a copy of everyone's travel schedule because she wanted to know where they were in case she needed to reach them. She also said once, over dinner, that knowing where her family was gave her a continuity in her life, so she would remember to ask about their trips, to view their pictures, to remember what it was like to be young and active. Eleanor was the most active seventy-nine-year-old Max had ever known, taking after Eleanor's mother, Genie. Strong, active, smart women. Even with all the secrets and the battle of duty and family over truth, Max greatly admired the women in her life.

The women who stayed.

As Max compared the postcards to the date books, she realized that something was off. There were several dates that didn't match up with postmarks. The postcard from New York City—that was sent nine years ago. William was supposed to fly to New York to stay with Max for a month after he'd graduated from college, but he canceled it because Max was still in Miami looking for clues in Karen's disappearance.

Then, a year later, Brooks Revere had just divorced his wife and taken his girlfriend to France. William refused to go. Brooks went with the Talbots. There weren't details on who in the Talbot family had gone. Andy? Andy and William often traveled together, especially when they were younger, before William married. Max didn't know why, but she'd much rather have her ex-boyfriend be the villain in this picture than her cousin. Somehow, it made the situation more tolerable. How bad did that make her?

The last postcard was sent six years ago from Ireland. William was definitely in Ireland at the time—he and Caitlin were both there, on their honeymoon.

It was the only time period where Carrie allegedly sent three postcards closer than several months apart. France. Italy. Ireland.

There were seventeen postcards total. William had been to half the locations where the cards were sent from. But Caitlin had also been to many of them . . . and could easily have sent them. Caitlin had been in Australia the same week as William and Andy and Max. The only one that didn't make any sense was the first postcard, from England.

Did Andy use Caitlin? Or could Caitlin have planned all this? Was she so twisted and methodical that she forged postcards from Carrie and sent them to her family? So her mother and sister would think she was alive and living it up in Europe? How could she be so calculating?

Except . . . Max had known Caitlin as long as she'd known anyone in Atherton. Caitlin had been the competitive girl. She'd been the angry one, always finding a way to embarrass Max or Lindy or any of the other girls they hung out with. And she'd always been infatuated with William.

The more Max thought about Caitlin Talbot Revere, the more she knew she was guilty. All the years Max studied crime and criminals, all the books she'd devoured and psychologists she'd interviewed trying to understand the psychopathic mind—and her cousin was married to one. Why hadn't she seen it before?

Maybe she had—in the small ways. She hadn't completely been joking when she commented to William that Caitlin would put hemlock in her salad. Caitlin had that manner, that aura that she wanted to hurt Max, and would if she could get away with it. Max had always dismissed it as jealousy—Caitlin was jealous of Max's independence, of her relationship with William, of everything others had that Caitlin didn't. Money couldn't buy real friends, and it couldn't buy class.

Proving Caitlin was a killer was going to be difficult. Not everyone kept records as meticulous as Max's grandmother. There might not be travel records going back more than a decade. And then there was the question of the first postcard, when Max knew that William and her grandmother had gone to England together.

Did Caitlin simply fly to Europe herself? Or maybe she'd given the card to William to mail. Why wouldn't he have questioned it?

Because, as Eleanor noted in her date books, William was intellectually smart, but had little to no common sense. He believed what people told him.

There was no proof that William killed Carrie Voss. Nick didn't have access to these date books, and even if he did—even if Max did her responsibility and told him about them—there were holes. The stigma of being a murderer would be held over William's head for the rest of his life.

There was no proof that Andy had killed Carrie Voss. But that made more sense—he'd admitted to being at Lindy's house, to moving her body to the pool. How could he have been there and not seen the murderer?

Maybe he'd moved Lindy's body and Carrie had seen him. He killed her to cover it up. Based on the notes in Carrie's house, she and Lindy had been in contact during the weeks prior to their deaths.

But Andy was smart—very smart. He would have thought to check the blueprints of the sports complex before deciding whether he needed to move the remains. Wouldn't he? That had been over Thanksgiving—where was he that weekend?

The door opened and Eleanor walked in wearing a shimmery silver-blue cocktail dress with a matching wrap. She stopped and stared at Max. "What are you doing?"

"Trying to prove that William didn't kill Lindy."

"You're a little late."

That's when she saw how pale her grandmother was. How red her eyes were.

Max went to her side. "Grandmother—"

Eleanor walked around to her desk slowly. "He was just arrested. The police searched his car—with his permission because he said he had nothing to hide—and found evidence."

"What evidence?"

"Dirt. I don't know what that means. I thought we had the best defense attorney—Maxine, William will not survive in prison."

Max put the date book she was reading back on

the shelf and took out the book for last year. She opened it up to the day Jason Hoffman died. William was in town. Dammit. She put it back.

"Does William own a gun?"

"I don't think so. He doesn't like guns."

That didn't mean anything. People who didn't like guns used them all the time.

"I need to know something, Grandmother, because I'm going to take a huge leap and hope it works."

Eleanor looked very old in that moment.

"What, Maxine?" she said quietly.

"Do you believe William killed Lindy? Do you think he's capable of killing a woman in a rage, then methodically burying her body and keeping the secret for the last thirteen years? Do you think that he's capable of shooting an innocent man in cold blood because he was caught removing the bones of the woman he killed thirteen years ago?"

"I don't think anyone is capable of all that."

"People are. Of that, and worse. So you're saying, you don't know."

"No, I'm not. This is William! He's weak, he's just like his father, but he's not cruel."

"No, he's not." Max had to act fast to clear William's name. "Grandmother, this is extremely important. Find out from William's attorney exactly what the police found in his car. I need to go to his house before the police get there with a search warrant."

"No one's there—Caitlin took the boys to her parents' house."

"Good. No one should be there. And call me or send me a text message when you find out. The faster, the better."

"Are you going to destroy evidence?"

Max looked at her, stunned. "No, of course not."

"But if William did what they say, we need to take care of it."

Max didn't know if she was talking to the same woman. "You just said you didn't believe William did all these things. I don't, either."

"I don't want to believe, but there is evidence. And if not William, who?"

"That's what I'm going to find out."

"Maxine, you could make it worse."

"Worse? It can't get worse, Grandmother."

Max let herself into William's house using the security code her grandmother gave her.

She didn't know how long she'd have before the police showed up to search the house. If they had the warrant to search the car, they probably did it after the interview that morning. Once they found evidence of a crime, they could go back to the judge and ask for a broader warrant. She might have a few hours because it was late Friday night, but most likely the clock was ticking down fast.

She didn't know exactly what she was looking for, but she slipped on leather gloves and started

463

in William and Caitlin's bedroom. Drawers, the desk, cabinets, boxes—nothing was obvious.

"Think," she said to herself. If she were hiding something she knew she should get rid of, but was compelled to keep it, where would she hide it?

She wouldn't. If she killed someone, she would get rid of the evidence as fast as possible.

Unless she was framing someone. Then she'd put it exactly where the police would be most likely to find it.

She went to William's office and searched the room.

She found a 9 mm. gun in a box on the top shelf, behind WW II history books.

She left it there and went to Caitlin's study.

Caitlin was almost as meticulous as Eleanor. She had a date book, like Eleanor's (and probably copied her in other ways, too) but she wasn't as detailed in her notations, or as neat. Max took a picture of the date book and sent that, along with a photo of one of Faith's postcards, to a friend of hers who was a handwriting expert. Were these written by the same person?

On the Saturday after Thanksgiving, Caitlin had the day blocked off as time at her parents' house. But there was no notation as to when she had returned.

Caitlin drove a Range Rover. William drove a BMW. If she took William's car, it was deliberate.

In fact, if Max was right—if Caitlin orchestrated

this entire thing—she'd wanted William to be found guilty if the investigation got this far.

William had a fight with Lindy the night she was murdered, and had Andy not messed with the evidence, physical evidence of his affair would have been on her body. The police would have looked at him—seriously looked at him.

The postcards from Carrie to Faith almost completely matched up with trips William took to Europe with Caitlin. The gun in William's office, his car being used to transport Carrie's remains, all of it—Caitlin had planned, that if the police got close, they would stop at William.

Just like they'd stopped at Kevin when they thought they could make a case.

Motive. Motive was the one thing Maxine couldn't figure out. Caitlin had always been half in love with William. She told everyone in high school that they'd get married one day. Max never believed it, just the dreams of a teenager; she always thought William would go to college and find someone. Instead, he slept around and never settled down, until after college and he came home and Caitlin was here.

Max pulled Kevin's letter from her pocket, the letter he'd left with the diary. He talked about Lindy's last entry. *Hester has returned.* Max thought that meant the teacher who'd been having an affair with the headmaster. Except . . . what if it meant Carrie? William had never been faithful to any of his girlfriends, but it was usually the girl who got the bad reputation. William didn't kiss and tell, it was more just by reputation that everyone knew he fooled around. And he always went back to Caitlin.

Carrie was only a year older than William, he could easily have had a fling with her. But how would Lindy have known? Was that why she and William fought?

She squeezed her eyes shut. That gave William another motive to kill Lindy.

Except. Why would he? He'd been eighteen, he wasn't married, why would he kill Lindy to keep his relationship with Carrie a secret?

Carrie and Lindy had lunch prior to their murders. What if Carrie told Lindy about being pregnant? What if William was the father? Lindy would have been furious—at Carrie, at William, at the whole situation. Calling Carrie *Hester* was a bit harsh, but it fit with Lindy's character and her obsession with keeping her secret diary in code to prevent it from getting out like it had when they were freshmen.

Olivia had said that Caitlin had been the one to show Lindy's first diary to Mrs. Frauke, which got Lindy suspended. It had been the impetus for Lindy to write in code and be more secretive.

Competitive Caitlin, who'd been obsessed with William from an early age. And William had repeatedly cheated on her. Broken up with her.

Lied to her. Because he was weak and couldn't just stay away from her for good.

Obsessed. In hindsight, Max saw the obsession of Caitlin. It wasn't something she would have recognized back in high school. She hoped she saw it and wasn't just wishing for it to be true. But what woman would repeatedly take a man back who had strayed? Someone who was obsessed with him, who could lie to herself about a perfect life, who helped perpetuate the myth that all was well. It was the same mentality that abused wives had, that if they only did this or that other thing, their husbands wouldn't hit them anymore. Did Caitlin lie to herself that each mistress was the last? That it would never happen again? Or did she keep her blinders on and refuse to see that William was sleeping with his secretary? Max was pretty certain that Minnie was only the latest in a long line of bed buddies.

She desperately wanted to talk to William, but since he'd been arrested late Friday night, there was no way she'd get to him until tomorrow. He might be in jail until Monday.

She hoped not. Jail wasn't a fun place to spend the weekend.

Max finished searching Caitlin's office, but it wasn't until the second time through that she saw something just a little off about her wedding portrait.

She took it off the wall. Behind the portrait was

a slight lump, like a second picture was behind it. She carefully removed it.

It was an ultrasound picture, faded by time. Dated thirteen years ago.

And the name on the photo was C. Voss.

Max stared at the image that was unmistakably a tiny baby. Carrie had been pregnant when she was killed.

Could William have done this? Killed Carrie because she was pregnant? Is that the secret Lindy had found out? That William had gotten Carrie pregnant . . . Max counted backwards. It would have happened during spring break. While William was not only dating Caitlin, but sleeping with Lindy.

"Oh, William," Max whispered.

But if William had done it, would he have kept the ultrasound behind his *wedding* portrait? Hardly. Would Caitlin?

What kind of sick psychological reason would Caitlin have for keeping the ultrasound? As some sort of proof of William's infidelity? Could Caitlin justify her actions by looking at this?

Caitlin was just as privileged as William. Carrie wasn't. Had Carrie threatened William with a paternity suit?

But William wouldn't have cared. He'd have gotten a good lawyer and fought it or paid whatever the court said. It wasn't like he didn't have the money, and he'd never been so obsessed with his money that he'd have thought twice about paying child support.

But someone like Caitlin would have hated the idea that William had gotten another girl pregnant. It would have been proof, in her twisted head, that William didn't love her best. Her competitiveness, her obsession with William—it all now made sense.

Max might never know why she kept the ultrasound, unless she could get Caitlin to talk about it. Could she even prove that Caitlin was the killer? The gun in William's den would point to William as Jason's killer. There would be no way of proving he killed Lindy, but enough circumstantial evidence might convict him.

Less had nearly convicted Kevin.

If she laid it out to Nick, he would call Caitlin in to interview, she would get a nine-hundred-dollar-an-hour criminal defense lawyer and he'd shoot holes in Max's theory. Worse, Caitlin had a way to frame William. It's why the gun was in his office. Why the victims were his ex-lovers. He had no alibi for Lindy's murder because he'd been there that night. And he lied, by omission. But if Kevin could find evidence of the parking ticket, someone else knew about it as well. Caitlin? And then there was Andy—the icing on the cake, unwittingly both saving and condemning William.

But one thing was clear. Carrie Voss was already

dead and buried when *someone* copied her handwriting and sent those postcards to her sister Faith.

Max had to get Caitlin to confess. William might try to save her, because he'd always felt guilty for cheating on her.

Max thought back to his secretary. Not guilty enough to stop.

She called Nick again; again his cell phone went to voice mail. She said, "Nick, it's Max again. You said I don't know how to ask for help, but you're wrong. I'm asking. I'm also asking you to trust me. I have a plan to prove who killed Lindy." At least, she hoped to have a plan by the time Nick called her back. "Call me."

Her phone vibrated and she hoped it was her grandmother with word from William's lawyer, or Nick returning her call.

It wasn't. It was the handwriting expert with a text message.

> I would need to see both originals to make an official determination, but I will give you a qualified yes. Both samples came from the same person. Don't quote me on it, until I examine the originals.

Max was right.

Caitlin Talbot Revere was a killer. How could she prove it?

Chapter Twenty-six

Max sat in the great room, drinking a mimosa, the French doors open, bringing in a cool, fresh spring breeze. It was just after eight in the morning, and if Max had set this up right, Caitlin Revere would be walking through the door any minute.

She only had one chance. If she messed this up, it would be next to impossible for the police to prove Caitlin killed three people. According to William's lawyer, the police now had their warrant to search the house. The search team would be here soon.

Max had asked her grandmother to call Caitlin and tell her about the warrant. She told Eleanor that Caitlin was a murderer, and if she didn't want her great-grandsons to grow up in a house with a cold-blooded killer while their father rotted in jail, she had to trust Max.

Eleanor said she'd do it. But now, Max feared her grandmother had cold feet. Because it was eight ten and Caitlin hadn't come home.

Just as Max was about to call her grandmother and make sure she'd talked to Caitlin, the front door opened and Caitlin rushed into the house. She stopped midstride and stared at Max.

"What are you doing here?" she demanded. Her eyes darted down the hall. Toward her study?

Toward William's study? What would she do first? Make sure the gun was where she'd left it to frame him, or destroy the ultrasound picture she had stolen from a dead woman thirteen years ago?

Max figured she was here to destroy the picture. In fact, she was betting her life—and William's—on it.

"You're a lot smarter than I ever gave you credit for."

"I'm calling the police. You're harassing me and my family!"

"It's *my* family," Max said. "And please, call the police. I'm not letting you out of my sight until they arrive."

Caitlin glanced back down the hall, but she obviously wanted to know what Max knew. "What are you talking about?"

"I know you killed Carrie Voss. I know you killed Jason Hoffman. Lindy? I'm not certain about. I haven't figured out the logistics of how you killed Lindy and Carrie on the same night."

"You're insane."

"I've been called worse." Max sipped her mimosa. She'd only put a dollop of champagne in the glass, needing her full wits about her, but she wanted Caitlin to feel like she had the upper hand. That Max was sitting here drinking as she often did, casually. Chitchat. The Taser was accessible, but that was only if absolutely necessary. She needed Caitlin to confess. She wanted to believe in the system, that there wasn't enough evidence to convict William, but sometimes the system failed. And sometimes the system hiccupped. And there were some people, like Kevin, who would die in limbo, neither guilty nor innocent.

Max didn't want William to live in limbo. She had to settle this now.

"You broke into my house, you're drinking my champagne, and you're making awful accusations."

Max tilted the flute in Caitlin's direction. "Thank you for your hospitality. As for the accusations, they are truly awful. Awful crimes committed by an awful person."

Tears welled in Caitlin's eyes. "How can you say that about William?"

William? What the hell was she thinking? Max began to see that Caitlin had not only been rewriting history for the past thirteen years, she was rewriting the history of the last thirteen minutes, as if Max hadn't already accused her of murder.

Caitlin said, "Do you know how many times he's told me you're like a sister to him? How often he's defended you to the family when you go off and do embarrassing things?"

"William is flawed, like most of us, but he's not a killer."

"Get out of my house!"

Max didn't budge. She took another sip, to

steady her nerves. She hadn't realized how difficult this was going to be. If she blew it, she wouldn't blame Nick Santini for being angry with her for destroying his case. She'd never forgive herself, either.

"I have a theory about what happened the night Lindy was killed. I'm a little sketchy on the details, but it's the only thing that makes sense. You followed William over to Lindy's. Or you saw him leave. Whatever reason, you were so mad because you didn't know that your best friend was sleeping with your boyfriend. At the time, your ex-boyfriend, but you and I both know you'd been obsessed with William for years. And honestly, I don't blame you for being mad. William couldn't keep it in his pants. He was rich, he was good-looking, he was charming. And a horny eighteen-year-old boy. And it's not like he had a good role model. We all knew Brooks was cheating on Aunt Joanne long before I exposed him. Or, maybe, like you, she knew, but chose to look the other way."

"William has always been faithful to me."

"No." Max stretched and put down the champagne flute. She rested her arms casually in her lap. "So you went over to confront Lindy. You could easily walk from your house. I don't know what she said to you that set you off, or maybe it was nothing, because she was strangled from behind. Maybe you planned it all, heard William and Lindy fighting, and intentionally killed her hoping William would go to jail for it.

"Then, this is where I'm not sure, but the time line works. Carrie had lunch with Lindy earlier in the week. I'm thinking it was after Carrie's appointment with the baby doctor. Carrie told Lindy she was pregnant and William was the father. She asked her for advice, why Lindy I don't know except they'd been on the swim team together, so maybe they were sort of friends. Carrie didn't know Lindy and William were screwing around behind your back.

"At some point, Carrie went home and fought with her mother, then said she was leaving for Europe. That bugged me because why would she say that if she didn't have any money? Either she thought William would pay her off, or maybe Lindy said she'd give her money to leave. Because Lindy, for all her flaws and all her secrets, cared about you, she cared about me, she cared about William. And she knew William would marry Carrie because it would be the right thing to do. If not marry her, then he would support the baby. I know that in my heart because that is the person William is."

Caitlin laughed. "God, you should write fiction, you're so good at it. Or maybe you're projecting on William what you wish your own father would have done. Oh, wait, you don't even know who your father is."

Max let it go. This wasn't about her.

"For some reason—maybe for money or just a place to stay—Carrie goes to Lindy's house. And she sees you standing over Lindy's body. She runs and you kill her too. Maybe it's an accident, maybe she hits her head, I don't know because the police only found parts of her body."

"What? What body?"

The fear was palpable in the room. Good. Caitlin was getting scared.

"You left Lindy because chances were, the police would think William killed her and you could have your revenge on the man who betrayed you. At least ruin his life—the same way that Kevin's ended up ruined.

"You didn't count on Andy listening to William pour his guts out about the fight, deciding to go over to the house to console a distraught Lindy. Except, she was dead. Based on the time line, Andy was there ninety minutes after William left. He moved her body, put it in the pool to destroy any evidence, and then two days later, called in an anonymous tip to the police identifying Kevin's car as being at the school that night. Brilliantly stupid on his part."

Caitlin gave out a dramatic sigh and half collapsed on the couch. "They did it together, I knew it, I can't believe it—I'm sure it was an accident, William shouldn't go to jail over an accident, should he?"

"You were never in the drama club, were you? Now I know why." Max crossed her legs, as if she were having a chat with a friend. "See, Lindy kept a diary. A secret diary, in code. She wrote in her last entry that Hester had returned."

"Lindy didn't keep a diary after her mother burned it when we were freshmen."

"You're wrong," Max said bluntly. "Andy hired someone to steal it from me when I found it, because he thought it implicated William. It's only a matter of time before the police find it. Hopefully when Andy starts talking. He's stubborn that way, but he'll talk if it keeps him out of jail. You know," she added conversationally, her eyes never leaving Caitlin's, "sometimes I wondered if they're the ones having an affair because what Andy is willing to do for his best friend is over and beyond what most of us would do. William never told him he killed Lindy. Andy simply made the assumption. But it was you. You did it."

"Get out!" Caitlin jumped up.

Max stayed her ground. "Carrie was Hester, sleeping with another girl's boyfriend. Lindy was furious at first, but I think because Carrie was pregnant, she wanted to help her. And that's why she picked the fight with William.

"He told me yesterday, before he was arrested, that Lindy was angry about a girl he'd dated over spring break. I checked with Carrie's sister— she'd come home from college for spring break.

Ten weeks later, she's back and pregnant. Easy for me to put two and two together; easy for Lindy."

"Lindy's one to talk," Caitlin said.

"She had an ultrasound taken when she was ten weeks pregnant, a little peanut of a baby, but obvious, dated May thirty-first." As Max spoke, Caitlin's eyes looked toward the left—the direction of her study.

Caitlin was too stunned to talk, so Max kept going. "What I don't know is if you knew Carrie was pregnant when you killed her. I don't think so. I think you killed her because she saw you kill Lindy, and when you were cleaning up your mess, you went through her car and found the ultra-sound picture. Maybe you didn't even know it was William's baby."

"She was a slut. If she was pregnant, it could have been *anyone's* baby."

"When Andy arrived at Lindy's, he saw a car he didn't recognize. That's why he moved Lindy's body to the pool house and not her own pool. But when the police arrived the next day, the car was gone. It was Carrie's car. And you moved it. I called Faith and asked her about the car. She said it had been left at the train station, and they got a call from the police a few days later about an abandoned vehicle. They weren't worried initially that she was missing because she'd told them she was leaving town. You killed her, left her car at the train station, and waited."

478

"I didn't kill anyone."

Her eyes, again, darted toward her study.

"Then, when the sports complex was approved, you panicked. What if someone found the bones? What if they were traced back to you? Which made me think you killed her with something you owned and buried it with her in her grave. So you went back to find it. And Jason Hoffman wondered what all those holes were, because you couldn't remember exactly where you'd buried her. He surprised you that Saturday night, you shot him, and used William's car to move Carrie's remains."

"No."

"Do you know how long I've been here this morning? Nearly an hour. That's a long time. Do you think the police will find the gun that killed Jason in William's study . . . or in yours?"

Her eyes widened. "You bitch! You planted evidence! You moved the gun! You—" Then she realized what she'd said. Caitlin forced herself to calm down. "Nice theory, but William is going to pay for his crimes."

"His crime of cheating on you?"

"All his crimes."

"The thing is, I can prove he didn't kill Jason Hoffman."

"No, you can't."

"I called his secretary, Minnie—nice girl, very pretty, very smart, but no common sense, a lot like

William—and asked about his car. She said that your Range Rover had been in the shop after a fender bender the day before Thanksgiving, so you were driving William's BMW for the week. Why? Because he flew to New York Sunday for a business trip."

"That's the day after that man was killed."

"His name was Jason," Max snapped. "Jason Hoffman. He was twenty-three and had a great life and a family who loved him." She paused, got herself back on track. "Minnie also had a hotel receipt for Saturday night because William was flying out early Sunday morning and stayed near the airport. Why? Because he wanted one last night with Minnie before he left."

"You're lying."

"It's ironic, isn't it, that William's mistress is going to be his alibi."

She was watching Caitlin closely. Because Max had made all that up. Not the business trip—that was true—but the hotel. According to Minnie, William had taken the 6:00 A.M. flight out of SFO, which meant he likely left his house at four in the morning.

Max was counting on Caitlin not having seen William that morning and there was a chance he *could* have left earlier than he needed to.

"Then she's lying," Caitlin said. "Now, I'm calling the police."

She strode down the hall toward her study.

Max grabbed her purse and followed.

Caitlin burst into her study and went right for her wedding picture. Instead she stared at a blank wall.

She turned around and shouted, "Where is it? Where's my picture?"

"Why?"

"You bitch! You don't know anything!"

Caitlin lunged for her, but Max sidestepped away.

"What don't I know?" Max said. "Did I get something wrong?"

"Do you know what it's like loving someone who doesn't love you? I've done everything for William. Everything. I love him so much and he hurts me again and again. Why am I not enough for him?"

Max wanted to say something cutting, but she needed Caitlin to go on. Because Max knew she had a lot of holes in her theory, and hoped Caitlin would fill them in. She needed Caitlin to confess. Right now it was all circumstantial.

"Lindy called me Saturday morning and told me that William got that slut Carrie Voss pregnant. She said to forget William, Carrie was going to tell him about the baby and William was going to be paying for the rest of his life. Lindy said I could do better. I didn't want better! I wanted William! And then—I saw William's car parked down the street and saw them. Saw them making out. She wanted William all to herself. I didn't even believe then that Carrie was pregnant, it was all Lindy's lies to get me to walk away. While *she* got him. That wasn't right! It wasn't fair! I walked and walked and came back and he was gone. Lindy wasn't in her house, so I went to the clubhouse and . . . and I saw her there, dead. He killed her. And that's what I'm going to tell the police."

"Whose fingerprints are on the ultrasound picture? Yours? Or William's?"

Rage and fear twisted Caitlin's face until Max was certain she saw the ugly, broken soul underneath the surface.

She has no soul.

"Give it to me."

The front door slammed closed and Max frowned. She hadn't gotten a confession yet. No one should be here.

"Mommy? We're hungry."

Not Tyler. Not the boys.

"In here, baby!" Caitlin called.

"Tyler!" Max shouted. "Go back to the car!"

He came into the doorway, a confused look on his face. "Auntie Max?"

"Come to me," Max said, crossing the room toward the four-year-old.

Caitlin got to him first and ran out of the room.

"Nick!" Max called.

Nick and his team were upstairs recording everything, listening for the confession Max had promised she could get. She had failed, and now Tyler was in danger.

Nick was already running down the stairs.

Max met him in the hall. "She went out through the side door. She has the boys."

Nick ran out the front and Max ran out the side. Caitlin was already in her Range Rover. Max didn't have time to get to the Jag, which was parked at a neighbor's house.

Caitlin turned the ignition and Max ran to the driver's side of the car. The door was locked. Max jumped onto the narrow running board, wishing she had smaller feet but glad she'd worn her sneakers.

The boys were crying in the backseat, and she could see that Tyler wasn't buckled into his booster seat. Talbot was still in his car seat.

All Max could think about was that Caitlin had nothing to lose. That she would kill herself and the boys to hurt William the only way she could still hurt him—by taking away the two things he loved more than life itself, his kids.

As the SUV gained speed down the street, Max started to lose her grip. She grabbed the luggage rack on top and pulled herself up onto the roof. She faced backwards, holding on with both hands. She had no plan, her brain told her this was the stupidest thing she'd ever done, but she could not let Caitlin drive off with the boys.

Caitlin wove through the wide streets of

Atherton at thirty miles an hour. In two minutes, she'd be on a main street and it would be easy to force Max off by slamming on the brakes. She'd go flying.

Nick was following them in his Bronco. Great, make Caitlin drive even faster. But he was gaining on them.

Nick's head came out the driver's side window. He was holding his gun.

What the *hell* did he think he was doing? There were two little boys in the car!

Caitlin slowed for a stop sign, but didn't stop. Nick used that opportunity to shoot out both rear tires. Because Caitlin was slowing, the SUV rocked but didn't flip over. She tried to keep moving forward, but the rear wheels were rolling on the rims, and the car slowed down.

Max jumped off the roof and ran along the slowing car. "Tyler! Unlock the door!"

Caitlin was crying, trying to steer, putting on the gas but not going fast enough.

Nick had jumped out of his Bronco and was running to catch up with them.

As soon as Tyler unlocked the car, Max opened the back door and climbed in. Her breath was coming in gasps. Talbot was crying hysterically. Tyler looked terrified. Max hugged him tight.

"No, no, no!" Caitlin cried as the car jerked forward, then came to a stop.

Max unbuckled Talbot and took the two boys

out of the car. She sat on the side of the road holding them close and watched as Nick put handcuffs on Caitlin. He walked her over to his Bronco and put her in the back, then came back to where Max was still sitting, trying to console the terrified children.

Nick squatted next to her. "That was really stupid, Maxine."

She nodded. She couldn't talk. She kissed each boy on the head, breathing in their little boy smells.

And then Nick grabbed her face and kissed her.

Chapter Twenty-seven

Max sat in her grandmother's library drinking Scotch. She shouldn't imbibe alcohol right now, but her nerves were still raw and she thought of all the things that could have gone wrong. What had gone right? She hadn't gotten a full confession out of Caitlin, William's boys had been scared to death, and she'd pretty much torn her entire family apart with very little effort. They'd been coming through all day, looking at her as if she were a wild, exotic animal, then leaving without saying a word.

The boys were in the playroom with Eleanor's dogs, hopefully sleeping.

But Max knew the truth. And she would prove

it, somehow. Nick had the partial confession, he had the gun from William's office, and the ultrasound that Max was certain would have Caitlin's prints on it. If she had been right in that bluff, then maybe Caitlin would spill everything. Max could only hope.

David walked in to the library. He took one look at her and said, "I should throttle you."

"You look tan."

"I just got off the phone with Santini. He told me what you did."

"I don't want to talk about it."

"But you're okay."

She nodded. But she couldn't muster up a smile. What would Tyler and Talbot remember about today? What would they know about their mother? How would they grow up, knowing what their mother had done?

She couldn't protect them from the truth, but they still had their father. And they had Eleanor. Max had to believe they would survive and be stronger for it. They were Reveres, after all.

Eleanor came in a moment later. "Hello, Mr. Kane. Good to finally meet you."

"Mrs. Revere." He took her hand.

She smiled at his manners, and that made Max feel like maybe things would go back to normal. "Maxine, come, join us for an early dinner. William's attorney is bringing him home. Just wrapping up the paperwork."

She shook her head. "I can't. I just want to explain to William."

"He might not understand now, but he will, later." She looked at David. "Would you please give us a moment?"

"Of course." He said to Max, "I'll take you to the hotel when you're ready."

He left, and Max asked Eleanor, "What did the attorney say?"

"The dirt in William's car was from the grave site where Carrie Voss's body had been buried. That's why they arrested him yesterday. But the police said there's enough evidence against Caitlin that they're releasing William, thank God."

"A good lawyer might get her off. The police have one solid piece of evidence against her. She had a copy of Carrie Voss's ultrasound. Framed, behind her wedding picture, in her office."

"How did they find that?"

"Grandmother, I set it all up. I called Nick last night and arranged for him to be in the house listening. They already had the search warrant, so they had every right to be there. I told you to tell Caitlin about it because I wanted her to come and try to remove the evidence."

"I don't understand."

"I used you."

Eleanor didn't say anything for a long minute. "Why didn't you simply tell me the truth?"

"I didn't know if you would agree to set up Caitlin for the police."

The door burst open and William stood there. He looked . . . defeated.

"How could you?" he said to Max.

"I couldn't let you go to jail for Lindy's murder."

"You destroyed my family!"

"Caitlin killed three people and planned to frame you."

"She wouldn't. It's—it's just not right."

"You're not thinking straight."

"What am I going to tell my boys?"

Max went to William, put her hands on his shoulders. "You are going to man up and be a great father. Tyler and Talbot have Grandmother, they have you, they have a solid family who loves them."

He shook his head and brushed off her hands. "Maxine, I don't know what to do." Tears coated his eyes. "My boys—they're motherless. Wasn't there another way?"

"Caitlin made her choice a long time ago. You can't condone what she did then, what she did only a few months ago."

"No. No, I can't. But—there had to be a better way than yours."

Eleanor went to William and said, "You are strong. You will survive this. The boys are in the playroom. Go see them."

He nodded and left.

Max wanted to go after him, to try and explain herself, but she knew it would be fruitless. At least for now.

Her grandmother said, "You've chosen a very difficult path."

"Maybe I didn't choose it," Max said quietly.

"I don't believe that. We all make choices and must live with them."

"I couldn't let Caitlin get away with murder. She destroyed so many lives. She impacted everyone. Andy isn't getting out of this unscathed. I doubt he'll do jail time, but he should. He has his reputation, and that is damaged. His friendship with William—he thought William was a killer. Had he not intervened, there may have been evidence pointing at Caitlin."

"And I wouldn't have two precious grand-sons."

"You cannot believe that she should walk away from this!"

Her grandmother sat down wearily. "No. She shouldn't. She is ill."

"She's not insane."

"She might as well be."

Max knew exactly what her grandmother was going to do. "You're going to have her committed. It's not easy to get the court to accept an insanity plea."

"Do you doubt me?"

Max thought about the disappearance of William's ticket. About all the things Eleanor had done through the years to protect the family.

"No, Grandmother, I do not doubt you."

"It is best for everyone—for William, for the boys, for the family—that Caitlin is in a sanitarium for the rest of her life."

"Grandmother, I need you to believe me. I didn't do any of this to hurt you or the family."

"Some secrets are necessary. It's better that the past stays in the past."

Max asked the question she'd been wondering since she realized that the postcards Faith received had been forged. She couldn't help but think about the birthday cards from her mother that stopped on her sixteenth birthday. What if something happened to her mother the day she left town, like what happened to Carrie?

"Do you know where my mother is?"

"No."

"Would you tell me if you did?"

Eleanor didn't answer that question. Instead, she said, "Martha was always wild. James called her a free spirit and doted on her. I saw her—I see everyone—for who they are. I assess how I can protect them from themselves and protect the family from their actions. Martha was selfish. She wanted what she wanted when she wanted it. She was irresponsible with her wealth, irresponsible with her body, and irresponsible with her relationships. I don't know where she is, and I never looked for her. I didn't want to know."

"Why? I've been looking for her for years!"

"I know."

"Have you been working to stop me? To thwart me?"

"Of course not."

"I don't know that I can believe you."

"Believe this: I don't approve of everything you do, but you are my granddaughter." "You are my granddaughter" was Eleanor's way of saying "I love you." "You were wild, but in a different way than your mother. You're much smarter than she ever was. You have common sense. You're responsible with your wealth and generous with your philanthropic duty. I respect you in ways I can't say I do of William and the others. But you will never be happy if you think the truth is the key to peace. On the contrary, the truth is dangerous. Whatever truth you're looking for, you will be hurt. And it pains me that I can't protect you from the damage, I can't protect William from his coming trials, or from his weakness for women. Your chosen path has filled you with an emptiness that grows with each day. I'm just relieved that my James isn't here to watch our family suffer."

Max went back to her hotel with a heavy heart. David, thankfully, understood that she needed to be alone, and he went to his room.

She didn't regret exposing Caitlin; justice had to be served.

It didn't make it fun or satisfying. She kept thinking of her cousins, and it left her feeling empty inside.

All she wanted was to go home. To her apartment in New York City. To the trials and cold cases she didn't have a personal stake in. Where the truth didn't hurt her heart.

She had a completely new perspective on the people she helped. She didn't regret anything that she'd done, but she looked on the families, the victims, the survivors with an empathy she hadn't had before. She didn't know if this insight would make her a better investigative reporter, or if her emotions would cloud her judgment. Or worse, make her hurt like she did right now.

She unlocked her door and was stunned to see Nick Santini sitting on her couch.

"Breaking and entering?" she said.

He held up a key. "You gave it to me when I stayed the other night. To make sure you didn't lapse into a coma." He smiled. As he watched her, he lost his humor. "What happened?"

"Family." She shook her head. She really didn't want to talk about it, but she added, "I came here and set off a bomb, but I'm not staying around for the cleanup."

"It's pretty messy out there," he said.

She didn't know why, but she thought she might

get a little more sympathy from him. She put her things down on her desk, averting her eyes. She was so tired and weary. "I need to go home."

He stood behind her and placed his hands on her shoulders. "Max, I wasn't laying blame. It's messy for your family, it's messy for law enforcement, and I'm pretty certain the district attorney is sitting in a fallout shelter just waiting to wade in. But it couldn't be avoided."

"I keep thinking about my cousins."

"You were really stupid," he said.

"You said that already."

"And brave. When I saw you swing up to the roof of the SUV, all I could think was that Wonder Woman's real name is Maxine Revere."

She laughed. The first chuckle in days. "I wasn't thinking. I just acted."

"I would have done the same thing."

"If you didn't have a gun to shoot out the tires . . ." She hesitated, then said, "Off the record—"

He turned her around and smiled. "Shouldn't I be saying that to you?"

She conceded the point with a tilt of her head. "Caitlin is going to push for an insanity plea. And my grandmother can make it happen. Don't doubt that."

"We'll see."

He didn't believe Eleanor Sterling Revere could do it, but Max did. This was family. Eleanor would pay anyone and call in any favor to make it happen so Tyler and Talbot didn't grow up with a mother in prison. Better to be insane than calculating.

"William isn't going to forgive me."

"Give him time. He can't possibly have absorbed everything yet. He'll work through it. Especially when he learns that you saved his sons."

"Surprisingly, my grandmother didn't disown me. Instead, she told me, in her own way, that she loves me. And that I have an empty life which will lead me to suffer greatly, and it's a bed of my own choosing."

"You don't believe that."

"She's partly right."

"Your life is not empty. After I turned Caitlin over to the jail, I went to tell the Hoffman family that we have Jason's killer in custody. They have peace knowing what happened. Yes, it would be better if he were alive, but I wouldn't be a cop if I didn't think that bringing criminals to justice wasn't a worthy goal. If I can't stop them, I'm sure as hell going to punish them."

She sighed. Spoken like a true cop. She just wished there was something more she could do, something to make it right.

Nick said, "We're not going to agree all the time, but you earned my respect, Max." He stepped closer to her. "When do you have to be back in New York?"

"If Ben has his way, I'd be on a plane tonight."

"I have tonight and Sunday off."

Max smiled. "I can leave Monday morning."

"Are you feeling a hundred percent yourself?" A half grin brightened his handsome face.

"Better than one hundred percent," she said and kissed him. In his ear she whispered, "Did you bring your handcuffs?"

He pulled them from his back pocket with a lopsided grin. "Never leave home without them."

Center Point Large Print
600 Brooks Road / PO Box 1
Thorndike ME 04986-0001 USA

(207) 568-3717

US & Canada:
1 800 929-9108
www.centerpointlargeprint.com